# The Crystal Warrior

# The Crystal Warrior

## Book One of The Crystal Warriors Series

Maree Anderson

ISBN-13: 978-0-9922498-5-4
ISBN-10: 0-9922498-5-6

THE CRYSTAL WARRIOR
Copyright © 2011 by Maree Anderson
First print edition, 2014

Publisher: Maree Anderson

Cover Design: Rob Anderson

# PROLOGUE

PIETER OBSERVED THE approaching warriors in the fist-sized hunk of polished beryl that served as his scrying ball. The raiders called themselves *Styrians*, Storm Riders. Pieter's countrymen had named them the Stone Warriors—men hard and cold and unforgiving as the crystals for which each was named. They ranged far and wide, raiding village after village with swift and deadly precision. Comely women of childbearing age, they enslaved. Children and those females too young or too elderly for their purposes, they abandoned to fend for themselves. Not a hint of mercy shadowed their piercing, sapphire-hued eyes. Truly, they were men of stone.

The inhabitants of the defenseless small villages scattered around the countryside quailed before these fearsome warriors. None had dared make more than a token stand. Until now. Magic had brought them here, just as Pieter had foreseen, and 'twas magic would vanquish them. He had read the portents and spent years preparing himself for this day, searching far and wide for the necessary crystals, be-spelling them to the best of his ability. He was ready.... He hoped. And prayed in his heart of hearts that he would prove himself worthy of the gifts his goddess had bestowed upon him.

He shuffled to the hearth. Using a wadded cloth, he took his battered old kettle from the fire and poured the pain-killing tea into the silver cup that was his most prized possession. As he sipped the tea, Pieter ran gnarled fingers over the patterns engraved on the cup and muttered the incantation beneath his breath. He must remain strong and focused. His intent must not falter, not even for an instant.

He drained the cup and set it carefully aside before snatching up the precious bundle of crystals. He cradled it to his chest as he hurried from his hut. 'Twas time to meet his destiny.

The thundering of hooves heralded their arrival. Pieter had to shield his eyes against the glare of the noon-day sun before he spied them, silhouetted against the hillside. They rode with no accompanying hue or cry. Each man was silent as the grave.

The same could not be said of the villagers. Shrieks of terror split the air. Most ran to their huts and cowered within. Bah. As if mere wood and thatch would save them.

A few brave men arrayed themselves at the muddy path that was the village entrance, clutching whatever weapons they could find. Amidst those waving pitchforks and shovels, one man brandished a pitted, rust-splotched sword. Fools. Pieter shook his head at their folly as he hobbled past.

"Go back inside, Pieter," one of the men called, his voice thick with fear. "Ye be getting yerself killed!"

"Have ye taken leave of yer senses, old man?" another cried. "What d'ye think ye be doing?"

"Saving you all." Thanks to the tea he'd brewed, Pieter's joints did not bite and protest when he knelt. Goddess grant this spell would be just as potent. He untied the linen and spread it out on the ground. He placed the eleven large gemstones in a circle, with himself at the center point. He was the focus, a man named after a crystal, a man who'd dedicated his life to learning how to harness the power of such stones. He struggled to his feet to await his fate.

The warrior called Wulf spotted Pieter barring his way. He reined in his battle mount and raised a hand to halt his men. He quirked one brow at Pieter, then barked a scornful laugh.

"A graybeard who should be a-bed, nursing his aching joints. This is the best defense you offer."

A small figure hurtled toward Pieter, momentarily distracting him. Amie. His great-granddaughter had torn herself away from her mother's arms. Her actions did not surprise him. She was a fiery little creature with the heart of a warrior. Goddess. Please let him save her from these men.

"Amie, no!" Her mother lunged as if to go after her, but was forcibly restrained by the other women.

The little girl skidded to a halt beside Pieter. Hands on hips in a perfect imitation of her mother, she faced down the fearsome warrior. "Don't speak to me grandda' like that, ye big bully! Go 'way and leave us be!"

One of the mounted warriors, the flaxen-haired one they called Kyan, snickered.

"Silence!" Wulf snarled. His assessing gaze raked Amie's body from head to toe. "The girl-child is comely. Too, she shows no fear. When she comes of age, I will honor her courage by bidding for her on the Choosing Block. You show courage also, old man, so to appease this child of your blood I will spare your life."

"My life is already forfeit. But not to you Lord Keeper Wulfenite."

Wulf's eyes widened momentarily before he shuttered them with an emotionless stare.

But it was too late. Pieter had noted the telltale signs of his disquiet. *Yes, Styrian, I know your true name. And, Goddess willing, my knowledge will help me to defeat you.*

The huge warrior kneed his mount forward but the beast shied, forcing him to haul back on the reins. His men shifted restlessly behind him. "Much good knowing my true name will do you, old man," he said. "If you insist on resisting us then so be it. The earth will drink your foolish old blood as readily as it does that of younger men."

Pieter merely smiled. He bent and whispered to Amie,

praising her for her courage and instructing her to return to her mother. Then he raised his hands to the skies and began to chant. "Verily the crystal for which thee be named/ Shalt form the prison in which thee be bound/ To atone the sins for which thee be blamed/ 'Til thee be blessed and thy true love be found."

Wulf threw back his head and laughed. "Blessed? What nonsense is this, old man? Mayhap you are addle-brained, yes? Warriors such as we have no need of blessings. And as for true love? Bah. 'Tis naught but a woman's fantasy."

The crystals surrounding Pieter began to glow. Black clouds scudded across a rapidly darkening sky. An ominous crackle of lightning haloed beams of light—each a different, unearthly hue—shooting up from the gems.

"What sorcery is this?" Malach, Wulf's second in command, demanded.

Pieter raised his arms to the sky. "Kyanite, Malachite, Shattuckite, Okenite, Danburite," he intoned. "The stone thee be named for shall bind thee. I, Pietersite, bind thee."

The heavens answered with a rumble. The five Styrians Pieter had named vanished. In the precious moments it took Wulf to comprehend the peril and react, Pieter had named his five remaining warriors and bound them, too, to his stones.

Wulf pivoted his battle mount, already unsheathing his sword. He charged, screaming his defiance, his sword raised for the killing strike.

"Wulfenite. The stone thee be named for shall bind thee." Pieter did not flinch as the blade descended. "I, *Pietersite*, bind thee!"

The Styrian warrior vanished. His sword clattered to the ground.

WULFENITE, LORD KEEPER of the Shifting Sands fief, veteran of countless battles, awoke to unceasing blackness, a vast emptiness devoid of sensation. It was not the afterlife warriors of his ilk fondly imagined, not this godsforsaken place. It was *Halja*. Hell.

Centuries passed. Time enough for fury to turn to despair, for despair to turn to acceptance, and finally, for Wulf to mourn what might have been.

He harbored no hope of redemption… until the guardian of the crystals spoke her name. *Chalcedony*.

# CHAPTER ONE

C HALCEY LAUREANO GLANCED at her Mickey Mouse watch. Fifteen minutes early. Fat chance the finance guru might already be here, waiting for her to arrive. He'd made it very clear his time was precious. She straightened her shoulders, plastered what she hoped resembled a confident smile on her face, and strode into the café....

And pivoted on her heel to walk straight back out the exit again. Her breath whooshed out in a ragged little whimper. She couldn't do it. Couldn't sit alone in that soulless, too-trendy café, pretending to be professional and calm and totally in control of her emotions. Couldn't stomach any more angsting over operating statements and income projections. Reducing her dream of owning a successful dance studio, her *passion*, to mere numbers on a page? It sucked.

Right now, she'd rather be crawling 'round on her hands and knees, plugging holes in her studio's floorboards. But she couldn't blow off this meeting. She needed this loan.

For the gazillionth time she rifled through her handbag to reassure herself that she'd brought along all the required forms.

Yep.

Another glance at Mickey. Still thirteen minutes left. More than enough time to work herself into a tizzy. Why, oh why couldn't she swallow her stupid pride and take Sam's offer of an interest-free loan? Sam was a trust-fund baby. That girl had more money than she could spend in a lifetime and—

A blaze of sunlight refracting off the neighboring store's window display washed Chalcey's face. Wavering and flickering with a rainbow of colors, like some heat-induced mirage it beckoned—

And the next thing she knew, she'd spilled through the store's open doorway, arms wheeling and heels screeching as she fought for balance on a gleaming polished floor.

Her eyes watered, dazzled by fiery, multi-colored brilliance. WTF? She blotted her face with her sleeve and blinked rapidly until she could focus. Okay, Chalcey. Calm down. Just a store selling rough-hewn gems, rocks, and crystals, and all the usual paraphernalia that went with them.

"And here you are at last," said the weather-beaten elderly man perched on a chair behind the counter. At least, that's what she thought he said.

He caught her gaze as he took a sip from a rather elaborate silver mug etched with complex designs. Her crazy heartbeat slowed and steadied as he abandoned the mug on the counter.

"How may I help you?" he asked, shuffling toward her and smiling with his entire face. Poor deluded soul probably figured she had money to spend.

"Thanks. But I'm, uh—" *Trying to figure out how the heck I got here.* Chalcey pulled her shit together and assumed the businesslike tone she'd been practicing in front of the mirror. "I'm just window shopping."

His head bobbed on his scrawny neck. "As jackdaws are drawn to a shiny trinket, many curious visitors are drawn to my crystals. Unfortunately, few are willing to loosen their purse-strings enough to make a purchase."

Uh oh. Busted. A flush burned her cheeks. She managed a tight smile and turned smartly on her heel. Sooo out of here.

His hand snaked out to grab her arm with a speed that belied his age. "Do not be so hasty, child. Please forgive an old man his ill-humor." His bright blue eyes twinkled and his deeply seamed face cracked another broad grin. "You need not feel obliged to make a purchase. Please, browse and enjoy the fruits of my labors."

Chalcey glanced first at his arthritic fingers clutching her arm, then at the clock on the wall. She still had a few minutes to kill. Where was the harm? She allowed him to usher her over to the window display.

"These crystals are no mere baubles to delight the eye," he said. "Each should be approached with respect. They have been formed by the very birth of Earth itself and thus, each crystal is indelibly marked by the power of the force which created it."

She couldn't place his accent. It seemed strangely formal, out of place in the modern world. He droned on about his crystals, projecting such reassurance that she didn't protest when he placed his hand under her wrist to wave her outstretched palm over some hunks of gemstone. "Feel the energy of the crystals, Chalcedony."

Hang on. He knew her full name. How—?

"*Choose*, Chalcedony."

The frisson of alarm skittering down her spine was smothered in gentle, soothing waves of benevolence. It seemed completely natural—right—for her to do as he instructed. The last remaining tension drained from her body and as she relaxed, he released her, leaving her hand hovering over the gemstones.

A ripple of energy surged from one of the crystals, agitating the air beneath her palm. A sensation of knowing, of *connection*, smacked her. Warmth, like the afterglow of an expensive brandy, pooled in her belly. Emotions roiled around her, raw and intense and profoundly disturbing. She sensed despair, remorse, and such immeasurable hopelessness that her mind instinctively reached out. And then she was united with the crystal, empathizing with its pain, soothing it.

The dark emotions ebbed, replaced with curiosity, burgeoning hope and a sense of longing so powerful that she retreated, alarmed. But the crystal refused to relinquish its link to her. Its power licked through her mind and Chalcey couldn't suppress her response. She wanted more—yearned for more—and the alien energy rejoiced. Its essence caressed her with gentle phantom fingers, the intimacy causing her to gasp. There was a moment's respite before it exploded through her in an electrifying rush.

"Wulfenite!" A woman's voice. Her own. Why was she screaming? She didn't know, couldn't think, couldn't do anything at all except succumb.

"Chalcedony!" A man's voice this time, hoarse and raw.

Blackness ate her.

CHALCEY PEELED OPEN her gluey eyelids and shook her head to clear hangover-style grogginess from her mind. The polished stainless steel decor of a café needled her cringing gaze. She bit back a squeal, rearing back from the table with enough force that she rocked her chair. Shit! How the hell had she ended up *here*?

The man she'd arranged to meet observed her antics with a frown and thin, tightly compressed lips.

Sickly dismay roiled in her stomach. Her heart plummeted to her toes. "M-Mr. Chapel! I, uh— I'm sorry, did you say something?"

"You dropped this on the table, Ms Laureano." His nostrils flared as he brandished a palm-sized chunk of dirty-brown stone.

She took it from him, turning it over in her hands, frowning as she struggled to recall how she'd gotten the darned thing. She sure as heck didn't remember paying actual money for it. Ohhh crap. *Please, please don't tell me I lifted it from the store next door.*

"This? Um, I think it's a crystal." The child-caught-in-the-act squeak she heard in her voice made her wince. A missing chunk of memory and the possibility she had a new hobby: Shoplifting. Way to start off this meeting on a positive note. It'd been a hellishly stressful few months but…. Sheesh. Way to appear eminently worthy of a nice, fat, low-interest loan.

She stuffed the offending item in her handbag and when she glanced up, caught Mr. Chapel doing the nostril-flare again as he wiped his fingers thoroughly on a napkin.

Time for damage control. "I arrived a bit early for our appointment, you see, and I—"

"Quite. Well, that concludes our meeting."

His tone was clipped and sharp and so very disapproving that Chalcey bit her lip. And then the full meaning of his words smacked her. "Huh? I mean, it does?"

He indicated the briefcase sitting on the spare chair at their table. "I have your income projections and all the required documentation. You've told me everything I could possibly need to know about your circumstances, Ms Laureano."

"I have?" Oh, no. *That* couldn't be good.

"I'll call you in a few days regarding the lender's final decision," Mr. Chapel said. "Good day." He cracked a semblance of a smile as he rose from his chair and held out his hand.

She stared at his manicured fingernails.

His eyebrows shot upward, forming little pinnacles of displeasure.

Heat bloomed on her face. She struggled gracelessly from her chair to shake his outstretched hand. "Right. Yes. Yes, of course. Thank you, Mr. Chapel. I look forward to hearing from you."

He threw her another of those soullessly professional smiles as he adjusted his tie and tweaked the hem of his jacket over his bony ass. He snatched his briefcase, and with a glance at his fancy wristwatch, hurried out the door.

Obviously a very busy man was Mr. Chapel.

What were the chances that she'd made a really fantastic impression on him?

Probably nonexistent, considering she couldn't recall a single thing she'd said to the man. Who, despite sounding very encouraging over the phone, in person made even Chalcey's asshole of a bank manager seem sympathetic. She could only hope she was reading far too much into the abrupt way he'd ended the meeting. Perhaps he used that tone with all his potential clients. After all, she was in effect begging him for money.

She flopped back into her chair, grimacing as the stylishly uncomfortable metal frame grated her spine. As she toyed with her water glass, her gaze skittered across the tabletop and lit on the crisp bills placed so very precisely across the café docket. Mr. Chapel had already settled up his bill—not that she could remember him eating or drinking anything. The last thing she remembered was being in that funny little store, waving her hand over bunch of crystals like some freaking New Age hippy. Weird. The stress of the past few months had obviously come back to bite her on the ass at the worst possible moment.

She delved into her bag to check the contents of her wallet. Just enough cash for coffee and a muffin, plus the credit card she kept for emergencies. No new receipts. Hmmm. She drummed her fingernails on the tabletop, nervy and unsettled. Something weird had happened to her in that crystal store. Something profound. And if she'd believed in woo-woo stuff, she might have concluded she'd been hypnotized. The pragmatic side of her snickered at that fanciful thought.

The waitress swooped in to collect the cash and clear the table. Chalcey pulled her fractured thoughts together and asked for her check. She copped a sideways look and raised eyebrows—the kind people gave someone who was losing it. "You didn't order anything, ma'am. There's nothing more to settle up."

"Oh. Okay. Thanks."

Now what? Uncharacteristically, the last thing she felt like right now was coffee. Not when her stomach was swooping with nervy unease. First thing on the agenda, have a chat with the old guy and find what the deal was with the damned crystal. And, if she really lucked out, perhaps he could shed some light on whatever the heck was up with her.

She exited the café. It was an effort to walk rather than give into the growing panic that threatened, and run flat out. She hung a hard right at the door, all the while rehearsing her defense in the event she had actually stolen the crystal from the poor old guy.

She needn't have bothered. There was no sign of the store. Or its owner.

A cold worm of dread slimed her skin. She wrapped her arms about her middle, shivering, struggling to process the truth of what she was seeing. Namely, a fancy designer boutique immediately to the right of the café, and an even fancier antique store to the left.

Oh God. She really was losing it.

She shook off the numbness of disbelief and forced herself to move. The store had to be somewhere nearby. She couldn't have imagined it.

She wandered the entire block in vain. She even stooped to questioning snooty store assistants, enduring one sneering put-down after another. Doubtless they all thought she was certifiable but she kept at it, until even her particular brand of stubbornness was reduced to a whine of protest. No one recalled the crystal store she described. It was as though the store, and its mysterious owner, had been conjured up by her fertile imagination.

Defeated, she slumped against a storefront window to catch her breath. Was it too much to hope this had all been a dream, and it was early morning, and she'd wake in her bedroom out back of the studio? She pinched her arm. Hard. But her bizarre reality didn't magically change for the better.

As a last resort, she opened her bag to check that the hunk of crystal she'd somehow *acquired* really did exist.

There it was, right at the bottom, vying for space with her brush, a packet of tissues, and a tube of lip gloss—rock-solid evidence that *something* weird had gone down. Her head reeled as she sought valid explanations for something so out there, she couldn't even imagine trying to explain it to anyone. But there was no logical explanation for the time she'd lost. Wasn't like the old guy had had the opportunity to slip her a roofie. And even if he had, why? What was his motive?

Reality check. The meeting with Mr. Chapel was already done and dusted. Nothing she could do about it now so there was little point in fretting. Plus, there was a heap of work to do at the studio. It was time to head home, put this whole experience behind her, and hope that after a decent night's sleep it'd all make sense.

She wiggled her cramped toes in the low heeled pumps she'd bought to go with the cheap suit. Should have gone with a pair of old dance shoes. Sure, the pavement would have ruined the soles but at least they would have been more comfortable than these cheap crappy things. She shouldered her bag, and started walking.

When she rounded the final street corner she paused to gaze up at the *Laureano's Dance Studio* sign. The space was perfect. She'd known it the instant she laid eyes on it. And, after months of backbreaking physical work, the basic refurbishment was nearly complete. Her opening-night party advertisement had run in the local papers and everything was good to go.

Tears stung her eyes. She was so damn close to achieving her dream she could taste the syrupy sweetness of success on her tongue. She could almost hear her dad's voice launching into his favorite pep talk about how Chalcey could do anything she set her mind to. He'd given her the Mickey Mouse watch as a gift after her first dance recital at the tender age of six. He would have been so proud of her.

The sweetness faded, leaving behind the bitter aftertaste of anxiety. The lease and renovation costs, and even her own meager living expenses, had eaten through the small legacy her dad had left her. And now that she'd finally convinced her dance partner, Jai, to ditch his straitlaced ballroom studio and come teach with her, she had an employee to worry about, too. If class numbers didn't reach her expectations….

But she wasn't going to think about worst case scenarios right now. Mr. Chapel's cronies would come through with the loan she needed to ease her temporary cash flow woes. Why wouldn't they? Her stomach rebelled with a lazy somersault. Why wouldn't they, indeed.

"WHY THE HECK aren't you ready?" Sam's outraged screech careened through the studio and made Chalcey jump like a startled cat. She glanced up to see Sam approaching, and sucked in a sharp breath in preparation for some screeching of her own. "Stop right there!" She reared on her knees, menacing Sam with her pallet knife. "Lose the shoes or I'll do you bodily harm!"

"Huh?" Sam froze, deer-in-headlights startled.

"Your fuck-me-big-boy spike heels—" she waved the knife at Sam to better emphasize her words "—are gouging holes in my floorboards. How many times do I have to tell you about heel protectors?"

Sam kicked off her shoes and surveyed Chalcey, hands on curvy hips, Botoxed brow doing its darnedest to wrinkle. "You've forgotten."

"Forgotten what?"

"It's Friday."

"Oh, yeah. Well, now you're here in person, Happy Birthday, hon. Muwah!" Chalcey blew her a kiss. "See? I didn't forget."

Sam waved a dismissive hand. "We're going clubbing. Tonight. To celebrate."

"Clubbing? No dice, girlfriend. Got too much to do."

Chalcey crawled over to plug one of the holes Sam's heels had made with a smear of wood-filler, smoothing it carefully with the pallet knife before moving on to the next one. Thank goodness Sam had only taken a few steps before losing the shoes. Chalcey had nearly finished filling all the holes, and she ached in places she didn't know could ache. The thought of going back over what she'd already done was just about more than she could bear.

"God, Chalce, you're freaking hopeless. You *promised*."

Chalcey sat back on her heels and worried her lower lip with her teeth. "When?"

"A couple of weeks back. DVD night?"

"Ah. Right." Damn. It was all coming back to her now. And in her defense, after downing a couple of Sam's designer cocktails, a girl would promise the soul of her firstborn. "I'm really sorry, hon, but I don't feel up to partying tonight. I've, uh, had some bad news."

Chalcey ducked her head, concentrating on the floor in the hopes Sam wouldn't notice how close she was to bawling. A scoop of filler, a swipe of her knife over the gouge in the old, battered wood, press firmly, and smooth before scraping off the excess. Automaton-like, she shuffled from hole to hole, performing the mundane task with single-minded concentration. Which was way the hell better than dwelling on that horrible phone call from Mr. Chapel.

Silence. Then the *swish* of Sam's skirt as she crouched. Her hideously expensive floral scent tickled Chalcey's nose.

"You got turned down for the loan, huh?"

Chalcey peered at her friend through bird's-nest hair. "You psychic or something?"

Sam squeezed her shoulder. "Hell. That really sucks. Anything I can do?"

She hadn't offered Chalcey the money she needed, thank God. Sam didn't make the same mistake twice. She knew Chalcey needed to do this all herself, without anyone's help.

Prove to her mother and her mother's know-it-all husband once and for all that she could turn this "silly dream" into a viable business.

She blotted her brimming eyes with the back of a dusty hand. "I'll get through this," she said, more for her own benefit than Sam's. Maybe if she said it often enough, it'd be true. "It's no biggie—I'll still make the first lease payment. It just means I'll have to forget about finding an apartment any time soon. And if I pull some additional advertising I'd planned, and don't take Paulo and Leah on board until next year—"

Her shoulders sagged at the thought of breaking the news to the enthusiastic couple. They were superb dancers, and had the potential to be excellent teachers. "They'll be gutted but they'll understand. Means I'll have to work heaps longer hours than I expected but— Yeah. Anyway, I'll manage. Though I'm kinda wishing I hadn't spent up large on those fancy shower units."

Sam snorted. "If I was all hot and sweaty after a dance class, I'd sure as heck want to shower and change before I headed out for the night. You've got a fitness club kind of setup, now. It's classy—a huge draw-card for students. Which is why you did it. And please don't tell me you're cancelling the opening night party on Monday. You *have* to go ahead with that. It's too good an opportunity to sign up people for classes."

Chalcey summoned a weary smile. "You're right."

"Good." Having straightened Chalcey out to her satisfaction, Sam bounced to her feet and smoothed her skirt down her thighs. "Hurry up and get ready. You need to get plastered. Have a good time and forget all about this for just one night. Besides, I'm pretty sure I mentioned that you promised."

A moan escaped Chalcey's lips. "Do I have to?"

"Yeah, you do."

"You know I don't *do* clubbing."

"You think you got problems? I'm a whole year older. Hell,

I think I found a gray hair this morning. You're my best friend and I'm relying on you to help me commiserate. C'mon. It'll be fun. A heap more fun than the fancy birthday dinner my mother has planned for me Wednesday week at Adagio."

Adagio was the hottest new restaurant in town. Chalcey would never in a million years be able to afford to eat there. "But your birthday's today," she said.

"Mom couldn't get in any earlier—and that didn't go down well at all, I'm telling you. Would have loved to have been a fly on the wall for that conversation." Sam snickered. "I'm told it's my birthday gift, and it's gonna be just me and Mommy Dearest. Won't that be fun. Not."

Chalcey appreciated Sam's attempts to cheer her up—really she did. But as of right now she was time-poor *and* cash-poor. "Since we're being painfully honest, bottom line? I can't afford to go out on the town."

"My treat."

Chalcey tried another tack. "I've got people coming in to wax the floor tomorrow lunchtime. And I had to pay extra for them to work Saturday. The filler from there, back—" she waved a hand to indicate half the studio "—has hardened enough for me to sand, and if I get it done tonight, it'll leave me less to do in the morning."

"I'll help you with the sanding tomorrow morning."

"You? Up before noon on a Saturday?" Chalcey's gaze lingered on Sam's purple-lacquered nails. "And sanding floors with those talons? Riiight."

"I will, I promise." Sam clutched both hands before her chest, prayer-like. "Pleeease!"

"All right, all right." Chalcey threw up her hands. "I give in. But only because I've finished plugging holes, and only because you're a pain in the ass when you don't get your way. And you have to promise to get me home by one at the latest. Deal?"

"Deal."

"Give me a half-hour to shower and change, and I'll be right with you."

Sam treated her to a Samantha Greenwood once over, and wrinkled her nose. "Take as long as you need, okay?"

Apparently her dust-smudged clothes and filthy hands were not particularly reassuring. "Thirty minutes is all I need," Chalcey said. "It's your birthday. Doesn't matter what *I* look like."

Sam waggled her perfectly plucked eyebrows and made a show of leering at Chalcey's chest. "With that rack, you'd show me up even if you wore a sack and— Hmmm." A pregnant pause if ever Chalcey had heard one. "I've just thought of the perfect present you can give me."

Chalcey climbed to her feet, and stood massaging the small of her back. "Free Salsa lessons?"

Sam cocked her head to one side, pursing her lips and considering the offer. "If you can promise me a hot dance-partner—one who looks as hot as Jai, but *isn't* gay—then I might just consider signing on. But I insist on paying." She waggled her finger like a teacher lecturing a student. "If you keep offering your friends free classes you'll never get this place in the black. No, I was thinking."

Uh oh. Wait for it—

"Why don't you let me choose your outfit for tonight?"

Chalcey closed her eyes and prayed for salvation, all too aware that her dreams of wearing something comfortable were about to go up in smoke. "What's wrong with what I usually wear?"

"Skanky old jeans and a t-shirt?"

Ouch. Just as well they were best friends. She'd hate to think what Sam might have said otherwise. She opened her eyes and speared Sam with a you-have-no-freaking-idea look. "I have to dress up and look the part for every single frickin' class I teach. Is it any wonder I can't be bothered tarting myself up in my downtime?"

"How 'bout a dress to show off your killer legs?" Sam wheedled. "Guys'll take one look and be all over us."

"They'll be all over *you* more like."

She pouted. "For me? Pretty please?"

Sam was a five-foot-two package of man-eating gorgeousness. Tonight she'd paired the hooker-worthy heels with a deep purple dress that had a tight bodice and sinfully short flirty skirt. She looked spectacular. She always looked spectacular—it was coded in her DNA.

Of course Chalcey caved under the relentless pressure of that cutesy damn but-it's-my-birthday pout. She jerked her chin toward the pokey storerooms she'd converted to a barely adequate bedroom, only slightly more adequate office-cum-lounge, and a pocket-handkerchief-sized kitchenette. "Fine. Whatever. Have at it. At least I won't have to listen to you harping on about my dress sense all evening. But the rack with my dancewear is off-limits, okay?"

Sam's green eyes glinted. "Deal."

Should have known Sam would win this one, Chalcey thought ruefully as she slid into a booth at the Cabana Club. She'd been conned into wearing a *costume*. Specifically, a costume intended for a dance competition. Sam—damn her beady little eyes!—had found the thing stuffed away in the bottom of a drawer, all but forgotten.

Almost worse than the dratted dress was the lack of what Chalcey considered appropriate, non-breezy underwear. And that was a whole 'nother sad story featuring laddered hose, and starring her not having done her laundry in far too long.

She glanced down at her sparkly self and grimaced. Again. Her ex dance partner had bought the costume for her a few years ago. Talk about scandalous masquerading as a dress. What had he been thinking?

Okay. She had half a brain so she knew exactly what he'd been thinking. But like she'd have lowered her standards and worn this piece of trashy flash for a competition. Or slept with him just because he'd bought her a hideously expensive dress—and made sure she'd known exactly how much it'd cost by leaving price tag attached. Way to be classy. He'd been a total jerk-wad about her not putting out, too. Boy, had she ever misjudged him. Dumping his ass only a month before a competition had been a singular delight.

She focused her glare on her perilously-close-to-being-ex best friend. Sam gyrated with uninhibited abandon to the horrendous booming that passed for music in this club. Sam didn't need Chalcey to lure men to her, they took one look and came running. Panting with tongues lolling, even. As she pranced off the dance floor with her two latest victims in tow, she caught Chalcey's gaze. And smiled. With "look what I've found for us!" delight shining in her eyes.

Chalcey scooted across the leather booth-style seating, intent on making a dash for the Ladies, and knocked her battered old handbag—the only handbag she owned—to the floor.

Aw, heck! She dove under the table, scrabbling for the contents that had spilled all over the place.

"Nice ass," a male voice said.

The owner of the voice was a good-looking blond sporting a not-so-good-looking leer. Great. Just freaking great. Seemed today was her day for making excellent first impressions.

Chalcey scooped her wallet, the crystal, and a tube of lip gloss into her bag, and crawled out from under the table. She didn't need to glimpse herself in a mirrored wall panel to know that her face was fire-engine red as she tugged the short skirt down over her butt, and resumed her seat with as much dignity as she could muster. Which wasn't much.

Sam's eyes sparkled with mirth as she squeezed in next to Chalcey and grabbed her cocktail. "Ducking for cover, huh?"

"Of course not."

"Mmmm." By the time Sam had gone down on the cherry decorating her cocktail and finally popped it into her mouth, the blond was slack-jawed and practically salivating.

"Chalcey's a really great dancer, Ray," Sam told him. "She owns her own dance studio. Isn't that, like, so cool? Hey," she prompted with such transparent obviousness that Chalcey cringed. "Why don't you ask her to dance so she can show you some of her moves?"

To Chalcey's surprise, the blond—Ray—didn't appear too disappointed to be fobbed off with the booby prize. "Let's go show 'em how it's done, eh, babe?"

Chalcey glared at Sam, shooting imaginary daggers out of her eyes, but her attempt at malevolence was blitzed by Sam's pleading puppy-dog gaze. Sam wanted alone time with the other guy she'd hooked. And Sam was the birthday-girl, after all.

She blew out a defeated sigh. "Okay."

Ray dragged her toward the dance floor. "Babe!" he said, as he copped the full effect of Chalcey's dress and all its low-cut glitzy glory. "*Some* outfit."

"Gee. Thanks." She favored him with a saccharine smile and fought the impulse to turn tail and flee for home. Boy-next-door good looks aside, the heavy-lidded way he kept looking her over made her skin crawl. Pity Sam hadn't pushed the dark-haired, brooding type with the Van Dyke beard her way instead. He gave the impression he was capable of holding a real conversation. Maybe it was a sign Sam's taste in men was improving. One could always hope.

She began to shuffle from foot to foot in time to the music. "I'm Chalcedony, by the way." She had to lean in to him to be heard over the noise.

"Huh?" He was so busy ogling her barely covered cleavage that he didn't hear her.

Gee. A breast man. Lucky her. "Just call me Chalcey," she yelled, thankful at least he wasn't the touchy feely— "Eep!"

Ray cupped her butt in his hands and ground his groin against her. Probably imagined that he was doing the

Lambada. God save her from amateurs.

When he wasn't grinding, he squeezed her butt in perfect time to the beat of the music. Gosh, was that supposed to win him points? Enough already. She wasn't big on scenes, but nor was she going to put up with some guy she'd just met pawing her. She ground the lethally pointed heel of her sandal into his instep and pushed him away, making it quite clear her actions had been deliberate.

He staggered, glaring at her through watering eyes. "Bitch! What's your fucking problem, Chel-sea? Thought you were gagging for it."

Wonder where he'd gotten that idea? Stupid dress. She silently cursed her ex dance partner for his slutty taste in costumes. And herself, too, because if she hadn't been feeling so tired and depressed about the loan being declined, she would have put up more of a fight.

The pair of dancers closest to Chalcey took one look at her expression and gave her some space. She sucked in what was supposed to be a deep, calming breath. And got even more riled when Ray couldn't tear his gaze from her chest. Just because she hadn't seen any action in a couple of years, didn't mean she would jump any half-decent-looking guy who showed an interest. A girl had to have standards and Chalcey's were pretty high. She was hanging out for the perfect man… if such an animal truly existed. And Ray wasn't anywhere near a close contender. He was shaping up to be an ass-hat of monumental proportions.

"Even if I *was* gagging for it, I don't appreciate being treated like a piece of meat."

He sneered, his upper lip doing an impressive curl. "Cock-teasers like you really piss me off."

"*Excuse* me?"

"Whaddya expect? Don't put it out there if you're not offering. Yanno what I'm saying?"

"Gee, you sure know how to compliment a girl." Chalcey

bared her teeth in what was probably a truly hideous parody of a smile. Unfortunately, Ray didn't take the hint and run screaming into the night.

To hell with him. She turned her back on him and marched straight back to her seat. It was so time to make tracks.

"You two seem to be getting on all right." Sam dragged her attention from Ray's hopefully less sleazy friend to wink at Chalcey. "Ray's a babe, right, Chalce?"

Chalcey gave Ray-the-babe another once-over as he slunk back to his seat. Around six-foot. Hair a shade of blond most women would open a vein to possess. Blue eyes. Great physique. Shame about the toxic personality. "I don't think we're exactly compatible. Listen, I'm gonna head home. Got an early start tomorrow, remember?"

"But it's just gone eleven-thirty," Sam said. "Another hour?"

Chalcey shook her head. Sam wasn't going to railroad her a second time. "It's been a rough day."

Sam held her gaze and gracefully conceded. She knew Chalcey well enough to know when she was fighting a losing battle. "See you tomorrow, then, huh? Bright and early? And promise me you'll take a taxi home." She flicked open her evening bag.

Chalcey flushed. She didn't do well with charity. "Thanks, *Mom*, but I don't need cab money. I'm a big girl and I—"

"You sure are." Ray sniggered and nudged the other man. "Tits on a stick, eh, Marcus?"

"I can take care of myself." God. Sam could sure pick 'em.

"Quit being an asshole," Marcus said to Ray, winning some major kudos for coming to Chalcey's defense. He seemed like a pretty decent guy. If Sam went home with anyone tonight, Chalcey sure hoped it would be him.

Ray made some smart comeback and Chalcey made her getaway, leaving Sam to soothe both men's egos with her usual flair. They wouldn't realize what had hit them.

She ignored speculative glances from a group of guys hanging 'round out front of the club. Damned dress had a lot to answer for. Mind you, given her chest measurement, so did her gene-pool. She rummaged through her bag, half-hoping for a miracle in the form of a previously unnoticed wad of cash. No such luck. The inner depths revealed one worse than useless hunk of crystal, the usual assorted junk, and the wallet containing a pathetically small amount of cash plus her emergency credit card.

She could strangle her stupid pride, head back inside and accept the cab fare from Sam— Nah. Damned if she'd put up with a certain foulmouthed sleazoid again. An emergency this definitely wasn't, so a brisk stroll home it would have to be.

Once she'd left the main street behind, Chalcey regretted her decision. Big-time. The shadows thrown by the empty warehouses, so innocuous during daylight hours, morphed into spooky watchers eyeing her as prey. She quickened her pace.

*Those aren't footsteps behind you, okay? Don't look back. Don't look back—*

She dared a quick glance over her shoulder. Shit. There was someone behind her. A man. So shrouded by shadows she could barely make him out. Wait. He was turning down an alley, headed toward a group of warehouses. Just some guy going about his business—like she was. He wasn't following her. He had no reason to be interested in someone like her.

Panic over. She slumped against a chain-link fence to catch her breath. Okay, okay, to scold her fertile imagination and wildly thudding heart into submission.

Chalcey was confident she could hold her own against most people. She wouldn't have walked home alone, otherwise. She was no too-stupid-to-live character in a horror movie—no way. She was taller than average, and years of dancing had given her a few more muscles than the average girl, too. Plus all the dancing meant she was ultra-fit, so she could run pretty damn fast if required. As a last resort, she always carried 'round so much junk in her handbag, one solid wallop with it would knock anyone's brains for six. But walking home alone in the dark, imagining big bad maniacs with all manner of nasty intentions, wasn't for her. She wouldn't be doing this again in a hurry.

Lesson learned. If you're too damned proud to accept the fare from your best friend, then do the smart thing and always keep aside enough cash for a taxi. *Hah. Guess I'm not that much of a badass after all.*

The grumble of a car engine snagged her attention. Headlights lit up the sparkly material of her dress like some flashy Christmas tree ornament. The vehicle slowed as it approached and the driver leaned out the open window. "Hey, babe. Need a lift?"

Great. A different kind of nasty. "No thanks, Ray. I'm nearly home."

"Awww, c'mon. You're not still pissed about our little misunderstanding are you?"

"Haven't given you a second thought."

He frowned, probably mulling over whether he'd just been insulted. "It's what I said about your tits, huh? Sheesh. Cut a guy a break. It was meant as a compliment. Let me drive you home—show you what a real nice guy I am."

"Gee, let me think. No thanks." She continued walking. Sam had obviously made her choice and it wasn't Ray. Hence him out trolling for someone else to play with. How many other girls had he come on to at the club before he got desperate enough to come looking for her? The mind boggled.

His car purred along beside her, matching her pace. He obviously wasn't the type to give up in a hurry. Time for some plain talking. "Look, Ray. I'm just not interested, okay? You're so not my type."

"Pity, 'coz with those tits, you *so* are mine." He giggled, a high-pitched, incongruous sound coming from such a buff guy.

Chalcey didn't respond. She focused straight ahead, keeping her pace not too slow, not too fast, projecting a confidence she hoped she could maintain.

The car slowed and fell behind. She risked a glance behind her and saw it pulling over to the curb. Ray got out and leaned on the door, striking a pose. "Think you're too good for the likes of me, huh?" he called.

"Go home, Ray."

He sauntered toward her. "Don't be like that. You and me, babe. How 'bout I show you a real good time?"

"I don't think so." She increased her pace to a full-out march and, just her damned luck, caught the heel of her shoe in a crack in the pavement. The heel snapped right off, throwing her forward onto hands and knees. "Owww!" To add insult to injury, her handbag went flying.

Ray reached her before she could scramble back to her feet. He grabbed her arms and hauled her up on tiptoes so that her body was plastered against his. "Aw, you hurt yourself, huh? Let Ray kiss it better."

His face loomed closer. Chalcey jerked her chin aside. Yeah, he was strong but she could take him. Not to mention insure that he thought twice about forcing his attentions on any other woman. She'd had a gutful of men who assumed a girl was begging to be pawed just because she had a larger than average cup size and wore something a bit revealing. Well, okay, a lot revealing. But it didn't matter what she happened to be wearing, he was way out of line. She'd show him. And while she was at it, she wouldn't feel the slightest bit guilty about taking all her frustrations about the male of the species out on him, either.

She could easily have broken his grip. There were three simple and very effective maneuvers she'd learned in self-defense classes a couple of years back that she could use in this situation. Instead, she pretended to give in, melting into his arms, tempting him to relax and let down his guard so she could hit him where it hurt and deal to him in a way he wouldn't forget in a hurry. She didn't have quite enough leverage to knee him in the balls—yet. And she'd only have one chance at making that maneuver count. If it didn't work, it was no biggie. She'd simply resort to some of the other dirty stuff she'd been taught, stuff that would leave a guy in a moaning sniveling heap on the ground.

He mashed his lips onto hers.

Ick.

His tongue probed her mouth.

Double ick! There sooo was a bottle of mouthwash with her name on it when she got home.

His grip eased up… so he could grope her breasts. Huh. Why did that particular move not surprise her?

While he was occupied, she toed off her useless damn sandals. She'd found her balance and was preparing to carry out Plan A to devastating effect, when an ear-splitting roar sounded behind her.

She froze.

A shadow loomed. It ripped Ray away from her.

"Aaargh!" Ray flew through the air and landed in a sprawling heap on the pavement. He groaned and lay still.

Chalcey sucked in a shaky breath and confronted the shadow's chest. She gazed up. And up some more. Until she locked eyes with an incredibly large, incredibly furious man, who threw back his head and bellowed so forcefully that the tendons in his neck distended.

# CHAPTER TWO

**W**HOA. CHALCEY MENTALLY fanned herself so she didn't do something stupid. Like hyperventilate, and get all dizzy and fall on her ass. He'd been poured into those scarred leather pants. And as for the chest-hugging leather vest and shit-kicker boots…. Lord have mercy. He looked like a warrior king of old. He could have stepped right out of one of her private nighttime fantasies.

He turned his back on her and stalked toward Ray. The stiffness of his spine, and the rhythmic clenching and un-clenching of his fists, screamed deadly intent and purpose.

Oh no. This could get out of hand real quick. She wasn't the sort who'd stand helplessly by, wringing her hands in dismay, while a guy got pulped—not even if he did deserve it.

"Hey!" She darted forward and clutched her rescuer's arm, hauling him around to face her.

His gaze latched onto hers again, ensnaring her. She couldn't look away. Her heart raced, its beat echoing manically in her ears. Her bare skin prickled as though he'd run cool, caressing fingers down her flesh. She flushed with heat as parts lower down clenched and throbbed with lust. Her body re-sponded to him, cried out for him, even though she'd never met him before in her life.

"Who—?" Her question died when he grabbed her and planted a kiss on her lips that stole her breath.

He speared his fingers through her hair to cup the back of

her skull with one big hand. He held her immobile and lowered his mouth to hers again. This time his kiss was hungry, demanding, brutally intense. She was so stunned that she didn't even try to struggle. He took her mouth as though he would brand her as his own. And she would have let him mark her. Hell, she would stoop to begging!

When her legs wobbled, he clasped her so tightly against his body that she was forced up on tiptoes. She stared into his eyes. So intensely blue… like the sky viewed from a mountaintop on a crystal-clear day.

His mouth hardened on hers, forcing her lips apart so that he could thrust his tongue inside her mouth. Still she didn't protest. Her head spun. Her eyelids drifted shut. She became a creature of pure sensation. There was only him and her. His lips on hers, her body pressed against his. Her yearning for him to fill a gaping hole in her soul that she'd not realized existed before now. His needs and wants and desires, all of them focused upon her, all of them centered around her. The rest of the world dissolved beneath his sensual assault. Nothing else mattered. Nothing but him.

"Hey!" somebody—Ray—shouted. "Who the fuck d'ya think you are?"

Chalcey blinked. The hulking great hunky stranger, the one who had dealt to the sleaze-bag mauling her, was now… well… *mauling* her. Did she have "Grope Me" tattooed on her forehead, or something? What was with this guy? He was just as bad as Ray.

So she did what any self-respecting girl who's had enough of men would do—even if the man *was* an incredibly hot one who kissed like there was no tomorrow. She totally overreacted. She grabbed a handful of his hair and yanked his head back. And kept on yanking until he quit kissing her and released her enough that she slid down his body. The instant that she had her balance, she drew back her arm and punched him in the face. Hard. Putting all her strength and the power of her body behind it.

He grunted and backed off.

"I don't know you from a bar of soap. Where the hell do you get off thinking you can manhandle me?" She flexed her fingers, shaking out the pain as she squinted at him, trying to spot where she'd hit him. She'd been aiming for his nose but he'd angled his head at the last second and she'd missed her target. The cheek, perhaps? A reddened patch of skin was the only evidence.

His gaze suggested that he was more shocked that she'd dared hit him than hurt. Huh. Obviously she hadn't punched him as hard as she'd thought. And she didn't quite know whether to be relieved she hadn't done him serious harm, or majorly pissed that she hadn't defended herself more effectively.

"Nice move, babe." Ray peeled himself off the pavement. He limped toward *The Warrior*, as Chalcey had christened her would-be rescuer-turned-victim in a fit of inappropriate whimsy. All semblance of boy-next-door good looks had fled, leaving Ray's features twisted and ugly.

In one hand he clutched a wicked looking knife.

The unholy glee lurking in his eyes sickened her. She lost it. She saw red—literally, for her vision became washed in a blood-red haze. "Stuff your ego back in your pants and fuck off, Ray!" Her shout hung in the air, unnaturally loud and menacing in the stillness. "And while you're at it, how about you stuff that stupid knife where the sun don't shine, too."

Ray sized her up as though testing her resolve. She straightened her spine and socked him with the "I'm totally serious so don't piss with me!" evils.

He resorted to what passed for charm for a guy like him. "Just wanted to give you a lift home. Was worried about ya, babe. 'Specially with assholes like *him* looking for some hot tail to tap."

"For fuck's sake, spare me the 'I'm such a gentleman' routine, Ray. You and I both know it's a crock. Piss off."

Ray's gaze cut to the man behind Chalcey, as if sizing up his opponent. Then he had the nerve to turn his full attention back to her and leer at her chest. "Shoulda told me you liked it rough, babe. I can do rough."

"Be gone, scum," a voice rumbled from directly behind her. "The woman is mine."

"Ex*cuse* me?" Chalcey glanced over her shoulder at The Warrior, and before she could so much as squeak, he grabbed her and thrust her behind him.

Ray lunged at him. A scream ripped from Chalcey's throat. The Warrior slapped the knife from Ray's hand, sending it skidding across the pavement. Then he grabbed Ray by the scruff of the neck and tossed him aside like he weighed nothing. Again.

Ray scrabbled about on all fours, shaking his head like a confused dog. The Warrior stood legs planted wide, arms akimbo, lips curled in a derisive sneer. "Do you wish to try that again, scum? I do not believe that you will provide much of a fight but I find myself in the mood for some light entertainment."

Huh. The Warrior was goading Ray.

Men! Testosterone-fueled dickwads.

Well, she refused to provide these two with an audience while they beat on each other. She made a beeline for the knife and crouched to pick it up between thumb and forefinger. A full-body shudder racked her. Nasty. It was so going in the Dumpster. She stood on tiptoe and tossed it in. The foul stench of the garbage made her gag but it was all good. Ray wouldn't be keen on jumping in to retrieve it any time soon.

Next on the agenda was her handbag. She peered around until she spotted it, stalked over and bent to snatch it from the ground, then kept on walking. There. Just like that she'd wiped her hands of Ray and The Warrior.

It was a pretty good plan except, fool that she was, she

couldn't resist glancing back.

The Warrior had twisted Ray's arm behind his back. His piercing blue gaze caught hers and, as he forced Ray to his knees, they shared a moment. A really intense "you're gonna be mine, all mine!" moment.

Commonsense finally crawled out from whatever hole it'd been cowering in, and Chalcey took off at a flat-out run. Jerk-off Ray she could handle, but *this* guy? Not so much.

All the way home thoughts of him haunted her. His eyes, that expression on his face as she'd turned away—she'd never seen a man look so bereft. And as she searched for her keys to unlock the street door to her studio, she was forced to admit another truth. Never in all her twenty-five years, had she experienced such instant, gut-wrenching wanting for a man.

WULF EYED THE pathetic excuse for a male cowering before him. He speared his fingers through the man's hair and dragged him upright. The stench of the man's piss stung his nostrils. Weak-minded coward. For all his foulmouthed bravado, the man was soft as a cushion. Even a cosseted priest could have given Wulf a better fight. Or a woman.

One woman in particular. The woman he'd just kissed. She slammed into his mind, rocking him back on his heels as she pervaded his senses and sank deep into his soul.

Wulf did not hesitate to toss the man he had been about to punish aside. Nor did he attempt to prevent him from slinking off like a cowardly dog. A vision such as this was a gods-sent portent, ignored at one's peril. Wulf would not risk inflaming the ire of those omnipotent beings who might, on a whim, choose to pluck him from this alien world and return him to his homeland. He closed his eyes and acceded to their wishes, allowing the vision to sweep him away.

She was tall for a woman, slim but strong, with breasts that would overflow even his large hands. Riotous curls framed a strong, elegantly boned face. Bones could not lie. She would be a beauty even in her dotage. Her syrup-dark eyes had spat ire at him, before clouding with wanton desire as his mouth possessed her full, soft lips. She'd worn a short, clinging gown. It appeared to have been spun from spider's silk kissed with starlight, allowing tantalizing glimpses of the pale skin beneath. She was a prize, indeed. A woman worthy of a Lord Keeper, worthy of him.

An emotion he was loath to name clawed his gut. It was a twin to the despair that had smote him when she fled the scene.

He'd let her go, telling himself all the while that chasing after a mere female was far less pressing an engagement than dispatching an opponent. In truth, he'd let her go because his reaction to her had troubled him to the very depths of his warrior's soul. One kiss had hauled him to the brink of losing himself in her to the exclusion of all else, unworthy opponents and lurking enemies alike. For a warrior of Wulf's caliber, allowing himself to be so thoroughly distracted when all about him was unfamiliar and potentially deadly was unforgiveable.

He dared open his eyes, blinking until she faded from his mind and his surroundings resolved into light and shadow, and reality—such as it was—again held sway. He swept his gaze about the alien surrounds and spotted his opponent climbing into a strange conveyance the likes of which Wulf had never before seen. Its exterior glinted like the hard carapace of a beetle.

The thing roared, and lamps that shone like miniature suns pierced the darkness ahead. The wheels of its undercarriage spun. Wulf's jaw dropped as it rumbled past him. He glimpsed the hunched form of the man inside, one of his hands clenching a circular device, the other manipulating something in the interior. He appeared to be directing the apparatus.

Gods above and below. What would the priests make of such an infernal thing? Wulf had listened to the tales of many an old warrior dispatched to alien worlds, but never had such a thing been described.

His awe was a fleeting thing, soon supplanted by disgust. If it had been he who had escaped a superior opponent and could command such a device, he would not have hesitated to run his opponent down. One should never leave an enemy at one's back. The man was not only craven, but a fool.

He made a concerted effort to cease flexing his sword hand, aware that he sorely felt the lack of the weapon that had become so much a part of him. If the conveyance the man had climbed into was commonplace in this world, Wulf would have to learn more about it, and quickly. He did not relish the task. He much preferred dealing with living beings that he could bend to his implacable will. Horses, for example, were simple creatures. Train them to the bit and bridle, feed and water them regularly, pet them and praise them when their behavior merited, and they were yours to command. Much like a woman....

*Hah.* He snorted. The woman he'd kissed, the woman who'd drowned his senses and haunted his gods-sent vision, would doubtless protest such simplistic treatment. She would chafe at the bit, challenge him. He would enjoy taming a fiery one such as her.

He didn't realize he'd moved until he found himself standing at a crossroads of sorts. For the first time in his life, Wulf was unsure, undecided which path to take. A tug of insistence pulled him to the left. Stubbornness made him head right. He managed half a dozen strides before pain knifed his belly. A half dozen more, and pain spiked through his skull. He forced himself to keep walking, and with each step, the throbbing in his skull increased twofold.

So be it. Wulf was a stubborn man, but not foolish, never that. He would not ignore such obvious portents. The pain dimmed to a dull throb as he backtracked and took the left-hand path. He would allow himself to be led by the nose. For now. And, gods willing, he would find her again. The woman who'd set his loins aflame with her kiss, and then shown her displeasure at being manhandled without her permission by punching him in the face.

He prodded the bruise forming on his cheek. His lips curved ever-so-slightly upward. This world's females were not fragile creatures, easily cowed and overwhelmed by a man's superior strength. And, despite its unnaturally constructed dwellings, and a myriad other aberrant sights that made his hackles rise and his sword hand ache with the need for a weapon, this world promised a thousand-fold improvement over the unending black-on-black void of his former prison. At least here he could feel—even if what he felt was a desire so intense he burned with it. Even if his warrior's soul yearned for something he could not yet name.

So far as tortures went, lusting after a woman and suffering the indignity of an unsuccored cockstand, was an exquisite agony. Still worse would be to go haring after her, and then, just as he reached her, pressed his lips to hers, filled his hands with her, to be snatched up and condemned to the crystal once more.

To be imprisoned again, eternally enduring memories of the woman he had been so close to possessing. That would be hell, indeed. But Wulf had never been one to back away from a challenge.

CHALCEY SHUDDERED AT the memory of Ray's handsome face twisted by something dark and loathsome. It could have been worse—so much worse. An unarmed man, no matter how skilled, was no match for a man armed with a knife and the desire to use it.

God only knows what she'd have done if Ray had stabbed The Warrior.

All the perfectly logical reasons why she'd never bothered to spend her hard-earned money on a cell phone seemed ridiculous now that she'd been a hair's breadth away from being forced to watch a man bleed. And she had no doubt that Ray, goaded into drawing that knife in the first place, would have then turned his attentions on her.

Dragging herself up the two flights of stairs to her studio seemed to take a lifetime. She flicked on one set of lights, leaned against the wall and... slid slowly down it, weak-kneed and shaking, her pulse beating a rapid tattoo. Whoa. Between money worries, Ray's unwelcome attentions, and The Warrior's far too welcome ones, she was about ready to break out her last bottle of tequila. But she had an early start and a helluva lot of work to put in before lunchtime tomorrow. She crawled to her feet and wobbled through to her bedroom. Drowning her sorrows would have to wait.

Not one, but two pieces of crystal spilled out when she tossed her handbag on the bed. The crystal must have cracked and broken when her bag hit the pavement. Shame, but hey, wasn't like she'd had to pay for it or anything. She placed the pieces atop the crate that served as a bedside table, figuring she'd give them to Francesca when her mother next decided to inflict her with a visit. Francesca had been heavily into crystals and all that New Age baloney, hence naming her daughter after the crystal chalcedony. It was supposed to be a nurturing stone, or crystal or what-the freak-ever, that absorbed negative energy, removed hostility and promoted feelings of benevolence and generosity.

Yeah, riiight.

She peeled off the cursed star-spangled dress, smooshed it into a ball, and hurled it at the wall. It didn't make a gratifyingly satisfying splat that might have appeased her somewhat. It merely unraveled enough to slither gracefully to the ground. Damn thing. She was never wearing it again. Ever.

She stalked through the studio to the women's bathroom to tend to her scrapes and bruises. Turned out none of them were bad enough that they'd bother her during classes. Ditto her feet, thank goodness. Limping 'round during classes because she'd been stupid enough to run through the streets barefoot, wouldn't give that good of an impression to new students. At least she'd had the presence of mind to curl her fingers into a proper fist so she hadn't damaged her hand when she'd landed one on the big guy's face.

Dammit. She'd forgotten the makeup remover. She trudged back to her bedroom, promising herself that one day she'd earn enough to rent a really nice apartment. The novelty of living in her studio and sharing the bathroom designated for female students was wearing off real quick.

While she creamed off her barely-there makeup, she wondered how Sam was making out with that other guy. Marcus. He seemed halfway decent. And he wasn't lacking in the looks department, either. Definitely more Chalcey's type than Ray. Mind you, after getting to know him better, *any* guy was more her type than Ray. What a creep. A scary, sinister, horror-movie-worthy creep. If he ended up haunting her nightmares, so help her, she'd track him down and finish him off herself.

But the last thing she saw before she crashed into sleep was a pair of intense blue eyes in a darkly tanned face. She relived The Warrior's hunger when he'd kissed her. And the profound despair that she'd witnessed on his face as she fled from him pierced her heart.

An insistent pounding echo yanked her from the bliss of sleep. She rubbed her eyes and rolled onto her back. It took her a few moments to realize that someone was banging the bejesus out of the street door downstairs. It'd be Sam, of course. Funny that she hadn't rung, like she usually did when she visited, but whatever. Or perhaps Chalcey had been too deeply asleep to hear the phone.

She flung herself out of bed, yawning as she made her way through to the main studio. For such a small woman, Sam was sure making a hell of a racket. But at least she was dropping in to help out as she'd promised—and doubtless to burn Chalcey's ears with all the icky details about her latest sexual exploits, despite knowing very well it grossed Chalcey out.

Honestly? Considering Chalcey hadn't had a date in like, forever, it was plain depressing hearing about guys with magic tongues who gave multiple orgasms—especially when she'd never *had* a multiple orgasm.

She flicked on the studio lights and padded across the cold floorboards. And she resolved not to squirm and make "eeeew!" noises if Sam got too personal with her descriptions. It would only encourage Sam to elaborate. Instead, she would—

The clock on the studio wall slammed into focus.

Three-thirty in the freaking morning? She would wring Sam's darned neck, that's what she'd do.

She stomped down the stairs. Various weird and wonderful torture methods caroused through her sleep-deprived mind. She rarely bothered with the security chain on the street door, so the instant she disengaged the lock, the door flung inward, nearly rearranging her nose. "Jeez, Sam! Watch it, will you?"

Except it wasn't Sam. A large hand grabbed her and spun her around. Before she could utter a word, another hand covered her mouth. A big body crowded her forward into the small stairwell entranceway. The door slammed shut and the sound resounded loudly in her head like a knell of doom, shutting her away with the consequences of her stupidity.

Instincts zoomed into overdrive. She wasn't going down without a fight. She managed to pry open her jaws just enough to sink her teeth into the hand covering her mouth.

The intruder released her and as she whirled to confront him, the shadows resolved into a really large man dressed like an advertisement for "We Love Leather".

*He* was back.

The Warrior. The man who'd kissed her. The man she'd run from because he scared her—not because of his physical strength and the way he'd dealt to Ray, but because of what she'd felt the second she'd laid eyes on him. Instant lust. Instant wanting. A need so powerful that her heart ached, and her body demanded things she'd never before wanted from a man.

He was dangerous. She didn't want to admit it but it was the stark truth. And this time, she might not have the strength to resist him.

# CHAPTER THREE

THE WARRIOR GRABBED her by the elbows and lifted her until they were both eye-to-eye. Boy, was he pissed. Chalcey could tell from the barely restrained fury seething in those baby-blues. Drumming her bare toes against his legs didn't provoke so much as a flinch. Crap. She was really in trouble this time.

"Unless we are about to indulge in a romp amongst the cushions, do not bite me again, woman."

"*Excuse* me?"

"You bit my sword hand."

"Yippee for me!" Hang on just a sec, his *sword* hand? Fabulous. Trapped in the stairwell with a reeeally large, really *delusional* man.

Chalcey tensed her muscles, intending to kick him right where it hurt, but he must have read her intentions in her eyes. Being an exceptionally tall man, when he dropped her it was from a great height. She hit the concrete floor in an ungainly sprawl, landing hard on her butt. Really hard.

"Owww owww owww!" Her bruised butt hurt like… like… forty bastards, as her dad used to say. She blew the hair out of her eyes before scowling up at The Warrior. It was her best "you so don't want to be anywhere near me right now if you know what's good for you!" expression, the one Sam assured her was guaranteed to send guys running for cover.

It was completely wasted on him.

"Now we are even," he said, tone laced with an irritating degree of smug male satisfaction.

She peered up at him in the dim light afforded by the street lights outside. Had that chiseled, square-jawed face of his actually cracked a smile? Stop the presses.

He reached down to grasp her wrist and yank her to her feet.

"Okay," she said, opting for sarcasm to cover her dismay. "Now you've stroked your male ego and we're *even*, get the hell out!"

"I cannot."

"It's really simple, bud. Just turn around and stroll on out the door. Oh, and don't come back or I'll call the cops."

"I do not wish to leave. And my name is not Bud."

Chalcey digested this first piece of information with growing confusion and had another thought. "Uh, how exactly did you find me?" He sure hadn't followed her home. She'd checked as she fled hell for leather. Numerous times.

He hesitated, as though unsure exactly how to explain. "I followed your… call. I sensed your… your *presence* calling me in my mind, and I followed it. You became clearer the closer I came to you. Thus I tracked you to this abode."

She inhaled a deep breath, held it, and puffed it out sharply through her nose. He had some sort of a crush on her, poor guy. It was kinda sweet. And kinda hot, too. And… kinda disturbing.

He still had hold of her wrist so she punched her arm straight up in the air to shake off his manacle-like grip. Epic fail. Damn. It'd worked just fine in self-defense classes. "Okay. You look like a decent enough guy—" an absolute babe, in fact, even if he wasn't the brightest star in the galaxy "—and I'm incredibly flattered. Not to mention grateful for you helping me out with jerk-off Ray, and all. But flattery and gratitude only gets you so far. Hence the reason I punched you in the face in the first place. You need to leave now."

His attention flicked to the light filtering down from the studio above. He gazed up the stairwell. "Your abode is up there? This world contains wonders beyond imagination! Come. You will succor this bite before it festers and then we will discuss our situation."

He pulled her toward the stairs. She dug in her heels and leaned her weight backward. Another wasted effort, for he merely yanked her off her feet and into his arms.

"Woman, you are a most stubborn creature."

His breath tickled her temple. His arms caged her, holding her tightly. Her body told her exactly how much she liked being in his arms. She bit her lip to keep from moaning.

"I have found there is only one way to deal with stubborn creatures." He heaved her up and over his shoulder, and then proceeded to climb the stairs as though she weighed no more than a small child.

The indignity of hanging head down over someone's shoulder helped Chalcey shake off the haze of sensuality he'd wrapped her in when he'd hauled her close and she'd been plastered against his big hard body. Manhandling her? Again? This was so gonna have to stop. She kicked and thrashed her arms, all the while hollering like a banshee. He patted her rump but otherwise ignored her.

Chalcey had been many things in her life but because of her height and in-your-face cleavage, ignored by men had never been one of them. And she wasn't at all convinced this was a good time for it to start, either. She screamed louder, putting her heart and soul into it.

She generally considered herself of above-average intelligence, too—aside from opening the door without checking who was on the other side first, which was obviously just plain stupid—so when he got halfway up the stairs, she quit struggling. But only because she didn't want him to lose his balance and for them both to take a nasty tumble down the stairs. And by the time he reached the top of the stairwell, she'd concluded that screaming her lungs out wasn't going to do her any good at all, either. Her studio was located in a semi-commercial area, it was excruciatingly early on a Saturday morning, and the chances of anyone hearing her and coming to investigate were practically zilch.

Maybe it was lack of sleep screwing with her judgment, but she decided that despite his superior height and obvious strength, he was relatively harmless. If he'd really wanted to harm her, it made sense he would have done so before going to all the trouble of hauling her kicking and screaming up a steep flight of stairs. Besides, her throat hurt from all the useless screaming.

He shouldered open the door to the studio and halted. She turned her head to one side to watch his reflection in the wall of mirrors. He stood blinking in the bright lights, mouth agape. He turned full circle, slowly, before striding over to examine the mirrors more closely. From the curiosity wrinkling his brow, she would have bet her last dollar that he'd never seen one before.

"Heyyy," she said. "How about I fix up your hand, so you can go back to wherever you came from? How does that sound to you?"

Again she was thoroughly ignored while he reached out to tap the mirror with a fingertip. He turned his attention to the UV lights striping the ceiling. "Mayhap you are a priestess of magic?"

A priestess of *what*? "They're just lights."

"Lights?"

"Yes, lights. See that switch, there? By the doorway?" She waved a hand in the general direction of the wall-mounted switch. "Press the top button-thingy down and see what happens. Go on, I dare you."

He reached out a tentative hand. Huh. This should be interesting....

He thumbed the light switch, blanketing half the room in

darkness. He reared back, his arm tightening about her legs so he didn't drop her. Considerate of him. "That is powerful magic, indeed," he said.

Sheesh. Compared with her recent encounter with Ray-the-Knife, her current situation struck her as way more comical than scary. The laugh bubbling from her lips morphed into an unladylike snort. "I wish I was one of those priestesses of yours. Then I could just turn you into a tadpole, flush you, and crawl back to my comfortable bed. It's a light switch, okay? Nothing special. Every house has one. Just turn it back on."

"I can do this?"

"Of course you can do this. Jeez! Anyone would think you're straight off the plane from Timbuktu or somewhere, and that you've never seen electricity in action before. Actually— You're not, are you? From like, Timbuktu?" That might explain a few things.

"Nay. My land is called Styria." He hesitated, as though fearful of the consequences should he actually dare touch the switch again.

She rolled her eyes. "Oh. My. God. I give up. Turn the thing on, already."

He did so and surprise, surprise, more light flooded the room. He amused himself by playing with the light switches. Off, on. Off, on. Off, on. She stifled a sigh. *Me and my big mouth.*

Off, on. Off, on. Okay. Enough was enough. "Who's a clever boy," she cooed. Or at least, tried to. It took a lot of effort to summon a convincing coo when you were slung over someone's shoulder. "All right. You've had your fun. Put me down so I can sort out your hand and send you on your way." *And go back to bed, and dream about you doing terribly naughty things to my terribly willing body.*

"Where do you store your herbs and medicinals?"

"If you mean my first-aid kit, then it's thataway." She pointed toward her private rooms off the main studio. "And last time I looked, I had two legs and knew how to use them. You'll do yourself a real injury if you insist on being all macho and don't put me down. And that, I won't be able to fix."

He ignored her—of course—and strode toward the partially open sliding door… only to hesitate before it.

She craned her neck around to see what the problem was. "It's a door. Open it fully and we'll both fit through just fine."

More hesitation. "I do not see how."

"You could put me down. Then I could—"

"I think not."

"God! What the hell have I done to deserve this? It's a sliding door. See that indentation in the metal handle there? Just put your fingers in and slide it—no! Not that way. To the right."

He followed her instructions… with such brute force that the unfortunate door sailed right off its runners. It teetered for a second or two, then tipped over, smashing down on the newly filled floor. Chalcey moaned and covered her eyes with her hands. "I so do not need this crap at this ungodly hour of the morning. Will you just put me down? Please?"

To her immense surprise, this time he didn't ignore her and actually did as she'd asked.

Hot-faced and disheveled, she tossed her hair out of her eyes, hitched up her drawstring pants, and ladled her breasts properly back into the crop top she'd worn to bed. When everything was at last back in its correct position, she glanced up to find him staring at her.

He had hungry written all over his face.

Ulp. She turned her back before her own appetites got the better of her and gave him the wrong idea. She led the way through to the kitchenette, smacking the light switch on as she entered. Her butt chose that moment to remind her it was bruised. She rubbed the offending portion of her anatomy as she bent to fish the first-aid kit from the cupboard.

He was still staring at her, head cocked to one side, when

she turned back, clutching disinfectant and cotton swabs. No man had ever looked at her with such single-minded concentration before, as though he was trying to see inside her, to know and understand every little thing about her. Warmth bloomed on her face, in the pit of her stomach. Lower down. He mesmerized her. It took all the will she possessed to break his spell and rip her gaze from his.

What was she supposed to be doing again? Oh, yeah. Playing nurse. Despite herself, her gaze flicked to his face. Her eyes rounded when she spotted the bruise blooming on his cheekbone. "Uh— Did I do that? To your cheek?"

"Indeed you did."

"I'm, ah, sorry. I didn't mean—" Liar. She really had meant it. And from the amused quirk of his eyebrow, he knew it, too.

"If it hurts, I can get you an icepack," she said.

"I, too, am sorry."

"Huh?"

"For dropping you on your rump. I did not wish to hurt you." A pause and a gaze that glinted with amusement. "Too much."

She opened her mouth and shut it again with a decided snap. He declined to comment. Smart man. "Sit there at the table and give me your hand," she said.

Again, he did as he was told.

Nice! Chalcey resolved to practice that tone in front of the mirror. A girl never knew when instant obedience from the opposite sex might come in handy again. Pity she hadn't made use of the same technique earlier. But then she wouldn't have ended up with the best kiss of her life. Her face heated at that particular memory, and the blush crawled down her neckline. She ducked her head and concentrated on the task at hand.

Her teeth marks marred the tanned, callused skin of his hand. She tried not to feel too guilty for mauling him while she swabbed his palm with disinfectant. "Uh, bandage or band-aid?"

He quirked a puzzled eyebrow then shrugged. "You are the Healer, not I."

"Riiight. Whatever." She opted for a band-aid because she'd never been that good with bandages. Whenever she had to do the Florence Nightingale thing her victim ended up looking like something from *The Mummy*. Without thinking, she kissed his palm before releasing it. "There, all better."

"Is it your custom to bestow a kiss upon those you heal?" His voice was deep and husky. His odd accent rolled even commonplace words liquidly off his tongue, making them sound incredibly exotic.

Her face flamed again. Something about this guy really had the power to turn her insides all marshmallow-soft and gooey. "It's, ah, something mothers do for small children when they're hurt."

"And you are likening me to a small child?" His blue eyes darkened and he eyed her in a purely masculine, let's-get-naked-so-I-can-lick-you-all-over-and-prove-you-oh-so-wrong sort of way.

"Um…. No?" No way. Definitely not. Nyuh uh.

"Allow me to return the favor and banish your own hurts." He took her hands in his, turned them both palm up and kissed the grazed skin on her left palm. Then the right.

Whoa. Instant gut reaction the instant his lips touched her skin. What would those lips feel like on her scraped knees? Or other sadly neglected body parts?

His blue-blue eyes were made even more startling by his deeply tanned skin. He might have been carved from a slab of stone, all hard muscular planes and angles. There was nothing muted or gentle about him, from his broad forehead, knife-blade cheekbones, and square chin, to his practically bare chest—complete with abs most men of Chalcey's acquaintance would sell their souls for. Not to mention his heavily muscled thighs straining the worn and faded leather of his pants.

She moistened suddenly dry lips with her tongue. Time to

quit ogling before she melted into a little puddle on the floor. She repossessed her hands and busied herself with cleaning up the detritus of her latest first-aid attempt.

When she'd regained her composure, she fixed him with a stern, schoolmarmish gaze. "Right. Time for you to go." Before she threw herself at him and begged him to do some of those exciting x-rated things she was planning on dreaming about.

"I cannot leave you," he said. "It causes me pain to venture far from your side."

"Awww, you say the sweetest things. But seriously, you have to go."

He stood, flexing his "sword" hand and Chalcey could well imagine he'd look right at home with one.

"I tell the truth, woman. It causes me physical pain when I am parted from you. I know not why. 'Tis obvious this is a land where magic abounds, and that I am somehow bound to you. I like it not at all, but until the gods decide I have atoned for my sins, I will endure my punishment. And mayhap—" he gave her *that* look again "—some pleasure might be had from it."

She backed away and scooted from the kitchenette, out into the main studio. Where it was not so confined. And safer.

He followed her.

Or not. "Ah, there'll be no binding, okay? So not into that stuff. And there'll be no pleasuring either. Look, I'm exhausted and I can hardly think straight. You need to leave. Now."

He crossed his arms over his fabulous chest.

Sigh.... Focus, Chalcey, focus!

"I will not leave."

She glared at him through slitted eyes. His jaw was set and she'd swear his teeth were clenched. He had that expression on his face guys get when they're determined to have their way, and absolutely nothing is going to stop them from getting what they want.

"Get out." She stamped her foot and pointed to the exit.

"Now."

"I will not leave."

"I'll call the cops."

He stared down his nose at her and smirked. "If these *cops* be as weak and ineffectual as the male I encountered earlier, then by all means call them." He cracked his knuckles. "I look forward to sparring with them. And sending them on their way."

All-too-vivid Technicolor visions ran through Chalcey's mind. She pictured her beautiful studio, completely wrecked after this total badass had waded through a couple of unfortunate cops and tossed them around the place a few times. She shuddered and banished the thought. Nope. Not gonna happen. She couldn't afford for it to happen.

And speaking of unfortunates— A frightening thought smacked her, raising goose bumps on her arms. "Uh, how's the jerk-off you thought you had to save me from, by the way? Still breathing, I trust."

"Do you truly care about such scum?"

"No, but—"

"Good."

She was getting that sinking feeling again. Surely he wouldn't have—? "Shit! If you've done something really dumb, like, accidentally beaten him to death or something, I really will have to call the cops. He might be a first-degree asshole, but he didn't deserve *that*!"

His hard expression softened just a little in the face of her obvious distress. "The only serious wound he suffered was to his pride when he pissed himself. And he should not be bothering you again—provided that he has brains enough to comprehend what is good for him."

Whew. She wasn't dealing with a murderer, at least. Merely a stubborn, extremely determined man, who had the hots for her so bad he'd followed her home. Sam would be lapping this right up. But Chalcey wasn't Sam.

"Right. Well, thanks for helping me out. Not that I needed your help but— Thanks. And now you need to go. Don't you have anyplace better to be? A harem of panting women waiting for you at home?"

"No."

"No harem, or no home?"

"No harem. I do not believe in such things."

She didn't want to think too hard about why his answer gave her warm fuzzies. Now wasn't the time for warm fuzzies. Now was the time for being a hardass. "Fine. Good for you. So how about I just kick you in the balls and toss you out on your butt?" *Your extremely tight, deliciously sculpted butt.*

He grinned and she just about swooned. Ohhh. Yum!

"Now that I am fully apprised of your fighting capabilities," he said, "I will be more cautious. I do not think you will best me in combat. However, you are most welcome to try."

She believed him. Just like she believed he'd be delighted by the opportunity to wrestle with her. And take advantage of her. Again. Hand on hip, she pointed firmly to the exit. "Fine. The door's thataway."

"I will not leave."

"I will not leave," she mimicked. "What *is* your problem?"

"I have no problem."

Aaargh! This conversation was fast becoming mega-frustrating, and it wasn't helped any by the fatigue spots dancing before her eyes. "Why me?" she lamented. "How come you couldn't find some other girl to bother?"

He surveyed her with a puzzled frown. Then his face cleared and his features set into that familiar stubborn male resolve. "I believe the gods have chosen you."

Oookay then. They were at an impasse. And, if she were honest, maybe this entire situation was her fault. He could have gotten completely the wrong impression about that kiss. And the fact that she'd tried to protect him from Ray-The-Knife.

Ray, she wouldn't trust as far as she could throw him. But this guy? He didn't seem like the type who'd attack a defenseless woman in her sleep.

He *did* seem like the type who'd wake a sleeping woman and fuck her to within an inch of her life, *and* insure she enjoyed every minute of it. But frankly, if having sex with a limp, exhausted woman was his scene, he could be her guest.

She raked her hands through her hair and pushed it back from her face. Which she thought was pretty restrained, considering. "Okay, have it your way. Sleep on the floor of the studio for all I care. I'm going to bed. And if you come anywhere near me during what remains of the night, you'll get a face-full of mace that'll make you cry like a girl for the next week." She didn't have any mace, but he didn't have to know that. "*And* if you're still here tomorrow when I wake up, I'll have the workmen I've hired toss you out on your ass. So there!" She stalked off, muttering imprecations about her sheer unmitigated stupidity for letting him in.

"My name is Wulf," he called after her. "By what name do *you* travel?"

Curiosity got the better of her. She halted in her tracks and slowly swiveled to face him. "Wulf, huh? That sounds German, or maybe Scandinavian, but you sure don't look like you hail from 'round there."

He was silent for a moment, as though considering how much to reveal. Obviously the trusting sort.

"Fine. Whatever. Don't tell me then. I'm going to bed."

"'Tis short for the crystal I was named for. My true name is Wulfenite."

Where had she heard that name before? Incomplete pieces of a tantalizing memory swirled in her mind, drifting just beyond reach. Brilliant lights dazzling her eyes. A silver cup. A voice in her head, murmuring a name…. "Wulfenite."

A deafening click echoed in her mind. Her brain exploded like a firecracker and went supernova.

# CHAPTER FOUR

**W**ULF LUNGED FOR her as she crumpled, and managed to scoop her up before her head hit the floor.
His heart beat a rapid tattoo. Every muscle was
tensed and battle-ready. A skirmish or an ambush he would
have handled without a moment's indecision. He would have
thrown back his head and roared his battle cry, waded into the
fray trusting that his own strength and skill and determination
would prevail.

This? He hadn't the faintest idea how to banish this fear
churning in his belly, this upwelling of heart-wrenching worry
over a mere woman. He was peripherally aware that he'd
cradled her in his arms like she was some precious object as he
turned full-circle, his gaze darting about a bare room that was
still so alien, in any other circumstances it would have con-
founded his senses. But numerous things he'd witnessed since
escaping his crystalline prison—the vast majority in fact—
were alien to him. The woman's abode, the cleverness of its
construction and the materials used, were just one more mind-
boggling strangeness to add to all the rest.

Reflected in the shiny surfaces running the length of the
room, a wild-eyed, stricken man stared back at him. A man
who projected an air of indecisiveness, and worse, fear. A man
who was no longer worthy to be named Lord Keeper, a leader
of men. He tore his gaze from the disturbing sight, and fixed
his attention on the woman's face. What was it about her that

had ensnared him so thoroughly?

A notion struck him like a well-placed blow from the flat of an opponent's sword. He staggered, and sank to his knees with the woman's body draped across his lap. Could she have been struck down by the sleeping sickness that had taken so many of his people when Wulf had been but a small boy? It was a cruel affliction, caused by a spell gone awry. The weak had died quickly. The strong had lingered, wasting away to skeletal caricatures of themselves, until finally, mercifully, their hearts failed.

He clenched his jaw against his overwhelming desire to berate this world's gods for their cruelty and forced himself to calm, logical thought. She'd been hale and full of fight when he'd confronted her at the entrance to her abode. And before, when he'd kissed her, her breath had been sweet.

He transferred her limp form to the crook of one arm so that he could brush the unruly curls back from her face. Her breathing was even and unlabored. He laid the back of his hand on her forehead. Her skin did not feel overly warm or clammy. His panic eased. He told himself she'd merely become overwrought because he would not obey her by leaving at once, as she'd demanded. He would not dwell on the possibility that she might never awaken.

Wulf was not a man of unbridled passions. He valued clearheaded weighing up of the options, considering the risks and acceptable losses before fully committing himself or his men. It was a trait that made him not only a leader, but a man other leaders were wary of crossing. And yet, he had lusted after this woman, yearned to sink his cock into her feminine flesh the instant he set eyes on her. And then there was the strange connection urging him onward, leading him to her abode and punishing him when he strayed.

She'd been placed in his path to beguile him.

But to what end?

Regardless of the implications, it was an unparalleled relief to blame forces beyond his ken for his weakness. The alternative, that his unholy obsession for this woman had driven him to his knees like some lovelorn young stripling, was not one he was prepared to countenance.

Enough. Females were for seducing and bedding, bearing children and rearing them. Outside of that, he had little need of them.

He should not care about her. It would be the height of foolishness to feel anything at all for her. Such a weakness would distract him and get him killed. So, he would keep watch over her until she recovered her senses. If—*when*—she awoke, he would treat her as he would any other comely woman. If she balked, he would do what he always did. Convince her to fall in with his wishes. Seduce her, and when he tired of her, move on.

He stood with her cuddled against his chest. He did not sling her over his shoulder as he'd done previously. She'd stood up to him, refused to back down. She'd earned a measure of his respect.

He strode toward the sleeping area, carefully angling his burden through the doorway so that he didn't bruise her body against the frame. He bent to strip back the bed-covers before laying her on the mattress. Unease gripped his belly as he stared down at her too-still, pale face. It could be that he was fooling himself and that she needed the services of a Healer. He would never forgive himself if she sickened and died because he'd done nothing.

Doubtless she would deem it an unforgiveable liberty for him to touch her while she lay unconscious and defenseless, but it needed to be done. He pressed two fingers to the pulse at her neck. Her heart beat strong and steady. Carefully lifting her lids, he peered into her eyes. The dilation of her pupils appeared normal. As he did with any prime horseflesh he intended to acquire, he ran his hands over her skull, torso and limbs, probing for hidden injuries. And, given his limited knowledge of human anatomy gained from treating wounds taken during a skirmish or battle, she seemed in excellent physical health.

He would not risk leaving her alone and defenseless at night while he sought a Healer, however. The man she'd encountered—the one called Ray—might seek her out to do her harm. A feral grin stretched Wulf's lips. Let him come. He would rue the day he tried to lay hands on Lord Keeper Wulf-enite's woman.

His woman.

His. If she recovered. If he could woo her to his bed. If she wanted him. So many ifs.

*If* she'd not regained consciousness by morning, he would seek outside help. He tucked the covers around her. But try as he might, he could not slip into that relaxed, watchful doze that seasoned warriors used to their advantage.

His gaze fixed on the jagged hunks of stone sitting atop one of the upended crates either side of her bed. Crystals. Wulfen-ite crystals, if he wasn't mistaken.

He left the woman's side to examine them more closely.

He wasn't mistaken. This woman had two pieces of his namesake crystal sitting beside her bed. Coincidence? Or something more sinister.

He reached out, his hand hovering above them, hesitating. He barked a laugh, berating himself for his nameless fears. He picked up first one crystal and then the other, weighing them in his hands. And then he saw it. A frisson raised the hairs on the back of his neck. His hands trembled as he fitted the broken pieces together. Not two crystals, but one.

He replaced them and paced the room, trying to comprehend what it all meant.

At last, restless and frustrated and none the wiser, he sought diversion. The gaping doorway beckoned him. She'd been uncommonly distraught when he broke the door whilst trying to open it as per her instructions. Perhaps fixing it would appease her somewhat.

It took him far longer than he liked to puzzle out how to re-hang the cursed thing, and despite his efforts, he could not coax it to slide smoothly on the cleverly designed metal runners. He fell to brooding over the unconscious woman in the next room. And he didn't recall abandoning the door, and striding into her room to stretch out atop the mattress. But here he was.

He could not prevent himself touching her, winding a lock of her hair about his finger, stroking her cheek, curling his fingers about her wrist when he checked her pulse. She stirred both his protective instincts and his passions. And, when being so tantalizingly close to her became a torture he could no longer bear, he shed his clothes and gave in to the inevitable. He climbed beneath the covers, settled her against his chest, and closed his eyes.

She felt good in his arms, right in a way that no other woman had felt. Sleep pounced, clawing him under. It was a welcome relief from the turmoil of his inner thoughts, and he did not fight it.

CHALCEY AWOKE TO the wonderfully masculine scent of a healthy male in his prime. In fact, Wulf's skin smelled slightly spicy. Mmmm. If she could bottle that scent and sell it to all the lonely women out there, she'd make a fortune. She sucked in a deep, appreciative breath—

Huh? *Wulf's* skin?

She lay on her side, cuddled up to him, her cheek resting on his chest and one leg flung possessively across his thighs. He'd ditched the pants and vest, and found a much more comfortable place to spend the night than the studio floor. Uh oh.

She started to edge away but his arms caged her.

She froze, wanting more, and terrified of that wanting and what it meant. He was a stranger—of dubious mental state.

She shouldn't be lusting after him, craving him, wishing he'd sink that hardness she'd felt nudging her leg into her lamentably willing body. "What happened? H-how did I get here?"

"You swooned." His lips tickled her ear as he spoke, and darned if she didn't just about pass out again. "This seemed the logical place for you until such time as you awoke. How do you feel?"

"Fine! P-Peachy." God. She sounded like a flustered teenage girl who'd wandered into the wrong locker room and copped an eyeful of hot guy.

Being a typical man, he didn't take her at her word. He rolled her on her back, levered himself up on his elbows, and loomed over her so that he could brush back the tangles from her face and examine her through narrowed, thoughtful eyes. The sprinkling of coarse hair on his legs stroked her skin. Oh boy.

"Happy now?" She took refuge in snark—better to go on the offensive straight off rather than face up to how much he was getting to her. Or be tempted to give in and reveal how much she wanted him to take this, ah, *situation* to its natural conclusion. One bed. One gorgeous guy and one horny, turned on woman. It wasn't hard to do the math.

"I'm fine," she said. A straight-out lie. But he couldn't know that. "Now please would you get off me, or so help me, I'm gonna kick your sorry ass!"

He quirked a tiny smile. "Please, do try."

Stubborn to the last, she tried her very best. And after a humiliatingly brief struggle she was still lying on her back. Only now, his lower body pinned her to the mattress. So much for girl-power.

She stifled a gasp when he shifted and it became very obvious that he was very pleased to be on top. Her stupid mind chose that moment to run a few possible scenarios. All involving a variety of x-rated positions that required two naked bodies. His and hers.

She squeezed her eyelids shut and tried to picture Dirty Dave, a guy with breath like a sewer and no comprehension of personal hygiene. Dave would regularly inflict his smelly self upon the other dance students before the girls banded together and refused to partner him unless he cleaned up his act. But the recollection of Dave's disgusting odors had absolutely no effect on Chalcey's inappropriate lust. Her heart raced. Her skin flushed with heat. Muscles in certain private places quivered. She was a goner.

"I will make, as you say, a *deal*," Wulf said. "Tell me by what name you are known and I will remove myself from your bed before you are forced to kick my sorry ass."

She opened one eye and squinted up at him. "You promise?"

He nodded. "I am a man of my word."

That rang true. She allowed herself to relax. "Okay. I can live with that. My name is Chalcey."

"Chalcey." He tried it out a few times, frowning and screwing up his face as though he didn't like the sound of it. Then his expression cleared. "That cannot be your true name. Tell me your true name."

She blinked. "My given name is Chalcedony."

"Chalcedony." He stiffened like he'd been stabbed in the back. He managed one loud groan before he collapsed…. Leaving her pinned beneath a really large naked man, whose dead-weight was impossible to budge.

His chest rose and fell, rose and fell. Still breathing, thank God. Chalcey heaved and pushed, trying again and again to shift him before fatigue forced her to give up. She lay there, feeling somewhat squashed, wondering what the fuck to do next.

The phone out in the studio rang, its strident tones echoed by the softer ones of the kitchenette phone. After the requisite number of rings, the answering machine picked up.

Dammit. Why hadn't she gotten a bedside extension? She

would just have to hope Wulf woke up before the workmen arrived and discovered her embarrassing predicament.

The workmen. Her floorboards. Crap!

She was girding her loins—so to speak—for another go at rolling Wulf off her, when she heard someone calling out.

Sam. Thank you, God.

"Help!" she screamed. She heard Sam's footsteps pounding across the studio floor and sagged with relief—so much relief that she didn't even care if Sam was wearing heels again and making more holes in her floorboards.

"Chalcey, when the hell are you gonna get a cell phone? That was me ringing, by the way, so you'd come down and let me in. And then I realized you'd left the street door unlocked. How many times do I have to— Jeez! What the hell's up with this door? Chalcey?" Sam shoved the sliding door aside and burst through the doorway like a pocket-sized avenging angel. "Hey. What's wr—? Ohhh!"

"Don't ohhh me. Just get him off me, will you? Before I'm completely smothered. Pleeease?"

Sam didn't hesitate, thank goodness. She braced herself on the mattress and grabbed Wulf's hip. She heaved, while Chalcey pushed, until finally, she managed to wriggle out from under him. She collapsed on her back atop the mattress, exhausted all over again. "Samantha Greenwood, you're a lifesaver."

Sam tore her gaze away from Wulf's gorgeously sculpted ass to give Chalcey owl-eyes. "Way to go, Chalce," she said. "I never knew you had it in you."

"I didn't— We didn't... uh... you know."

"You brought him home with you and didn't let him screw you senseless?" Sam raised her gaze ceiling-ward and clucked in a despairing fashion. "God, why the hell not? Look at him." She slapped his ass for emphasis.

"Don't do that!"

"Sorry. Not. He's totally out to it, huh?"

"Uh. Yeah. Sure seems that way. He—"

"What *did* you do, then? Chat? And then invite him to get naked and use you as a mattress? You chickened out at the last minute, didn't you? Jeez, Chalce." Her gaze slid back to Wulf's butt and lingered, leaving Chalcey in no doubt that Sam would have had her wicked way with Wulf. And then some.

Mickey's gloved hands informed Chalcey it was just gone six. No point in trying to get any more sleep. She massaged her temples with trembling fingers. "I need a caffeine fix."

"If you didn't wear Sleeping Beauty out by jumping his bones, what's up with him?" Sam asked. "Don't tell me you tried some weird-ass martial arts thing on him and stopped the blood-flow to his brain. I told you those self-defense classes were dangerous to your health."

If only. Weird-ass martial arts things sure would've come in handy with Ray. Chalcey crawled off the bed and was forced to lock her knees against wobbly legs. "Damned if I know what happened to him. One minute we were having, uh, a conversation. The next? K-O. No warning." Panic squirmed down her spine. "Shit. What if it's like, a brain aneurism or something? Do you think I should call for help?"

Sam leaned in close to observe the steady rise and fall of Wulf's chest. "Nah. If it was an aneurism, he'd be dead and he looks healthy enough to me. Probably party drugs. Or maybe someone slipped him something. He's a big boy. Give him a couple of hours to sleep it off and he should be sweet."

Chalcey mentally bowed to Sam's superior knowledge. She was way more experienced with the club scene.

"Where did you pick him up, Chalce? I thought you went straight home."

"I did. He sort of… um… followed me here."

But Sam was no longer paying attention. She'd gone back to raking her hot gaze down Wulf's body.

Could have been worse, Chalcey supposed. He could have been lying on his back with all his considerable masculine glory on display. Not that she'd seen his masculine glory, but she'd felt it. And it'd felt pretty darned considerable. But right now, *she* felt increasingly discomfited by this situation. They were treating Wulf like a himbo whose sole role in life was to titillate women. She grabbed a spare sheet from a shelf and flung it over him. When he woke up, he could wear it, too.

"Spoilsport," Sam said.

Chalcey ignored her to play Florence Nightingale again, and check to make sure Wulf's pulse was strong and steady. It seemed to be—not that she knew much about pulse-rates. She figured Sam was right. He'd wake up in a few hours and then—

Then she could give him his marching orders.

If she wanted to.

She mentally slapped herself upside the head. Of course she wanted to get rid of him. Didn't she? Gahhh! "I'm making coffee. You want one? Or are you going to try bouncing on him to see if he wakes up?"

"Mmmm. Tempting."

Chalcey grabbed Sam's arm and towed her from the bedroom. "I was kidding. Leave him alone. When he wakes up, then you can have him."

Now why the heck had she said that? The thought of Sam and Wulf together made her want to gnash her teeth. And slap Wulf. Not to mention pull Sam's hair.

"Really?"

"If you want," Chalcey let her hair fall across her face to hide her expression from Sam's speculative narrow-eyed gaze.

"Don't you want him?"

"Me? I don't think so!" Her laughter sounded forced, brittle. She cringed, waiting for Sam to call her bluff.

To her relief, Sam didn't appear to notice anything amiss. "You sure?"

"He's hardly my type. And it's not like we've slept together or anything, is it? He's all yours if you want him." *Sheesh! Just give me a wall to bang my stupid head against.* Chalcey bit back a groan. Why couldn't she keep her big mouth shut?

Sam chewed her lower lip in a childlike gesture completely at odds with the, ah, subject matter being discussed. "Maybe an hour or two with— What's his name, Chalce?"

"Wulf."

"Right. *Wulf* could be just the thing I need right now."

Chalcey pinched the bridge of her nose to dismiss the unwelcome visual of Sam and Wulf rolling around on her bed. Naked. "I sooo need coffee."

"Yeah. Me, too."

Chalcey blinked at her friend's tone and peered at her more closely. "Don't take this the wrong way, hon, but you look like crap."

Sam wrapped her arms about her middle. Actual tears glittered in her eyes.

Sam, crying? Sam never cried. Whatever had happened, it had to be pretty bad.

Chalcey put an arm around Sam's shoulders and guided her to a chair in the kitchenette. "Just let me put on the coffeemaker." She broke all speed records with coffee filters and such, and then flopped into a chair opposite. "Now, tell me what happened."

"M-Marcus happened."

Chalcey fumed. First the scumbag tried it on with her, then he had a go at Sam? He better pray she didn't come face-to-face with him again or she would—

Hang on, halt the rave. *Marcus*? "Um, Marcus? The dark-haired guy from the club, right? The one who seemed like a halfway decent human being?"

Sam gave her "Well, duh!" eyes. "Yes. Marcus. The guy who told Ray to get off his ass and offer you a lift home. Ray jumped at the idea 'coz he figured you might, you know, be grateful?"

"I would have to be a whole lot more than just grateful to

sleep with Ray."

"But he's sooo hot-looking."

"Hot or not, he's an asshole. Period."

Her curt tone provoked a startled frown from Sam. "Did he try something on?" she asked. "I thought his story sounded a bit off."

"Huh?" Chalcey rubbed the bridge of her nose and prayed the coffee would be ready sooner rather than later. "I'm not following you. What story?"

Sam sniffed and blotted her eyes with the heels of her hands. But instead of meeting Chalcey's gaze, she pleated the skirt of her dress with her fingers. "When Ray came back to the club, he told me he *had* caught up with you, but you acted like a total bitch. He said you tripped and fell, and when he tried to help, you went bat-shit—decked him one and ripped his shirt, and told him to piss off. He claimed he had to go home and change because of you."

"Huh. Asshole sure knows how to spin it."

Sam's chin jerked up, revealing big worried eyes and quivering lips. "What happened?"

"Nothing."

Those worried eyes turned "Don't fuck with me" hard. "Tell me."

Chalcey heaved a sigh. "Yes, Ray tried something. No, I wasn't keen. But *I* didn't deck him. I didn't get the chance. The guy who's currently in my bed dealt to him for me. And he had to go home to change because when Wulf confronted him, he pissed his pants."

Sam's eyes did the whole owl-thing again. "Ohhh!" She clapped a hand over her mouth and giggled. "Serves him right."

Chalcey's weary hand-rolling motion encouraged Sam to elaborate. "Ray got really POed at how well me and Marcus hit it off," she said. "He tried it on with me but Marcus told him to get lost." Sam sighed, her face going all soft and dreamy. "It was sooo hot watching Marcus stand up to him. And after we left the club, we went back to his place."

So Marcus had slept with Sam on a first date. Typical. Ah, who was she kidding? They were talking men, here. Of course Marcus had slept with Sam. Not that Chalcey could take the moral high ground. She'd spent the past half-hour or so with a naked man she'd only just met draped all over her. "And?" she prompted.

Sam's eyes filled with tears again and she blinked them back. "A-And what?"

"What did Marcus do to get you so upset?"

"I still can't believe he did it."

Sam's face had dissolved into an expression so woebegone that Chalcey suspected Marcus must have committed the most heinous act in the history of Sam's illustrious dating career. Her mind boggled, envisioning handcuffs and whips and chains and the like. "Did *what*?"

"Made it *really* clear he'd really like to see me again."

Huh. "That's *it*?"

"Not quite. It was the expression on his face when he said it. He was, you know, deadly serious. Like, wanting a *relationship* serious."

Chalcey gaped at her. "And that's heinous? I would think you'd be, well, you know, thrilled to bits."

Sam managed to stop sniffling enough to enlighten her. "God, Chalcey. You are so freaking clueless. I've spent my entire life trying *not* to be the sort of girl a guy wants to settle down with. I work my ass off to keep myself in shape. I make it clear upfront I prefer no strings attached sex and—"

"Gee, Sam, we've been friends forever and I did not know that about you."

Sam ignored her. There was a lot of that going around lately.

"For Marcus to see me as potential girlfriend material—" Sam uttered the G-word like it was the worst epithet in the

English language "—means I'm slipping. I'm putting out the wrong vibes. Potential wife vibes instead of party-girl vibes. I don't want to be a carbon copy of my mother, getting sucked in by the romance of it all and leaving behind a string of ex-husbands. I don't want to settle down with one man. Not now, maybe not ever."

Chalcey suspected she was going to regret it but she just had to ask. "What's so wrong with wanting to settle down?"

"What? And end up like you?"

Chalcey jerked back like Sam had reared up from the chair and tried to bitch-slap her. Although she did her utmost not to feel offended by Sam's comment, it hurt. She silently counted to five. Slowly. "And what's wrong with ending up like me?"

"I didn't mean— Oh, you know what I mean!"

"No, I don't." Chalcey rose to grab the coffee mugs so she had something to do with her hands. It was either that or ruin their friendship by shaking Sam 'til her teeth rattled. "Why don't you explain it to me? In simple terms somebody *like me* can understand."

Sam paid no heed to the sarcasm and launched into another tirade. "Well, look at you! Even when you were teaching at a proper dance academy, you barely earned enough to make ends meet. You live in your dance studio because you can't afford an apartment. You don't have a boyfriend. So far as I know, that vibrator I bought you for your last birthday is the only action you get. Then this incredibly hot guy follows you home, ends up in your bed, and you don't even jump him. And why? Because he's not the perfect man. Because he's not potential *marriage* material. Well, I've got news for you, Chalce, and it's all bad. There's no such thing as the perfect man. So you've got to stop living like a hermit and get out there and have some fun. If you don't use it, you'll lose it."

By "fun" Chalcey guessed Sam meant letting random guys feel her up and drool all over her cleavage. Been there, done that. Sure wasn't her idea of fun. Still, it was hard to stay pissed at Sam when she'd had such a "traumatic" experience. And Chalcey suspected that all the not wanting to settle down palaver was BS, because Sam had protested a wee bit too much. All this wasn't about Chalcey's search for the right man, and her love life—or lack of it. This was about Sam. Specifically, Sam freaking out over a guy.

She poured Sam a coffee. "Here. Get this down you. You're obviously caffeine-deprived 'coz you're making no damn sense whatsoever."

"Thanks." Sam took a sip, sagged back against her chair, and heaved a shaky sigh.

Chalcey leaned her hip against the counter and swigged a good third of her coffee to bolster her courage. "It's like this, hon. Just because I'm not into screwing men on a regular basis, doesn't mean I'm not happy the way I am. Sure, I'd love a fabulous man to shack up with but I have standards. Quite high standards. And I'm more than happy to wait for someone who meets them to happen by. So don't feel sorry for me, okay?" She pinned Sam with her best flinty-eyed glare. "And don't use me as an excuse, either."

Sam eyed her over the rim of her cup, all big-eyed confusion. "Don't know what you mean," she said.

Hah. What a crock. "I think the reason you're so spooked is you like Marcus. As in reeeally like."

That got a really fine snort of derision. "Ray's definitely more my type. Bet I wouldn't have got any of that relationship shit from him."

"Yeah. Bet you would have got something else, instead. Like a nasty STD." Chalcey tried her best not to shudder. "And did you know he carries a knife? He pulled it on Wulf."

But rather than being duly horrified, Sam didn't seem at all fazed. "Can't say I blame him. That guy in your bed is quite capable of pulverizing even a buff guy like Ray with one arm tied behind his back."

"It was a freaking knife, Sam."

"So?" Sam shrugged. "My mother carries a gun. People need to be able to defend themselves. There are far too many weirdoes out there."

"People don't carry knives to defend themselves, Sam. They carry a knife to threaten people with. What if he'd pulled it on me when I didn't want to play? Would you have blamed him, then?"

"Get real, Chalce. Guys like Ray don't need to pull a knife to get some girl on guy action. It's just an affectation. Goes with the whole bad-boy image, you know?"

Sam was worldly-wise in many ways. In others, she was so damn naïve it freaked Chalcey out. Part of it was her upbringing. The obscenely rich, born to a life of privilege, never imagined that bad shit would happen to them. They drifted through life oblivious, believing themselves charmed. Sam was no exception.

Unwilling to discuss Ray further, Chalcey focused on delivering the rest of her mini-lecture. "Whatever. I think when it comes to Marcus and his maybe-being-keen-for-more-than-a-one-night-stand, the teeny tiny part of you that's a normal girl is doing the happy dance. Go on, admit it."

"Maybe."

Sam wasn't going to budge. She was such a hardass. Chalcey would have to work on her a bit to make her see sense and give Marcus another chance.

Her stomach growled, reminding her she hadn't had time to eat last night and it was practically breakfast time. She popped a couple of slices of bread into the toaster. "So what did you do after Marcus made this heinous confession? Render him unconscious by some underhanded means, then leap out of bed and holler for a taxi?"

"Not exactly." Sam had the grace to appear embarrassed. "We, um, cuddled until he fell asleep. And then I snuck out of bed and caught a cab straight to your place."

"You stuck around in his bed after sex? With him?"

Sam blushed—a moment that should have been preserved for posterity and hailed as one of the wonders of the known universe. "Yes."

"Sweet Jesus!" Chalcey grabbed at the countertop before she fell over from the shock. "You could really be into this guy. Like, he could be The One."

"Far too soon to tell. The potential's there, sure." Sam's eyes had gone all wide and shocky, like she hadn't admitted that to herself before now, and saying it aloud made it true.

"Whoa. What are you going to do if he calls you?"

Sam sighed. "He won't. I didn't give him my number."

"And you're unlisted." Chalcey's head was spinning from trying to follow Sam's dodgy reasoning. Meeting a guy who could be The One. Having fabulous sex. Exchanging phone numbers. Dating on a regular basis. Next stop, giving happy ever after a really good shot. It wasn't rocket science. "Never mind," she finally said. "It's not as if you can't call him."

"I won't." Sam's lips compressed into a thin, bloodless line.

"Why the heck not?"

"Because I'm so not interested in hooking up with a potential The One right now. As I said before, I'm having far too much fun being single. Why would I want to tie myself to one man?" Her lower lip quivered, belying her whole single and loving it stance.

"Oh. Right." Boy, Marcus had really gotten under Sam's skin. She was running scared.

The toast popped up. Chalcey buttered it and handed Sam a piece. Poor Sam. Oh how the mighty had fallen.

She yawned and glanced at Mickey. She blinked, and peered at her watch again. "That's the time already? Crap! I'm going to be invaded by workmen in a few hours and I've still got to sand the rest of the filler and clean up before they get here." She licked the last buttery crumbs from her fingers as she dived for the door.

"I'll wash these up then come help you," Sam called after

her.

Chalcey stuck her head back through the doorway to eye-ball the alien who had replaced her best friend. "You sure?"

"I promised I'd help, so I'll help." Sam glanced down at her dress. Which had probably cost more than all the dresses Chalcey owned put together. "Can I borrow some old clothes?"

"Sure. Help yourself to a t-shirt and shorts—which of course will be like, halfway down to your knees. But I'm sure the fashion police will forgive you this once. Just try to keep your hands off Sleeping Beauty, okay?"

Sam gave her some excellent snarky face. "I'll consider it. So long as you tell me what he was doing lying naked on top of you if you're not interested in him."

She didn't want to tell Sam what had gone down. It was too intense, too private. Too weird. "No more questions, Sam. I absolutely have to get all this sanding done before the work-men arrive."

"Hang on, I know I said I'd help but haven't you already sanded the floor?"

"I de-waxed it, scoured it, and then sanded it," Chalcey corrected. And a shitful, thankless job it'd been, too.

"Then why are we sanding it again if you've already done that?"

"We're sanding the filler."

Chalcey rolled her eyes at Sam's doubtful expression. Samantha Greenwood definitely wasn't DIYer material.

"Take it from me, it's yet another step that has to be done before waxing. Which I'd have also done myself, except that I'm running short of time and professionals can do it much more quickly than I ever could. And did I mention that I had to pay extra for them to come in on a Saturday? No more chitchat. Move it!"

They managed the deadline with a few minutes to spare.

While Sam showered, Chalcey vacuumed up the dust. Only

then did it cross her mind to wonder who'd re-hung the sliding door into her bedroom.

Duh. Wulf, obviously.

Chalcey hid a grin. He hadn't done a very good job of it, but at least he'd tried to make amends.

And speaking of Wulf, her unexpected guest was still dead to the world. There went her fond hope that the workmen could hustle him off the premises. In all conscience, she could hardly ask them to lug an unconscious man down a couple of flights of stairs and toss him out on the street. And it was pretty cowardly of her to want backup when she asked Wulf to leave, but there it was. She had moments where she felt as though she could take on the world. Now wasn't one of them.

God. She sooo didn't need this crap right now.

A grizzled old guy and his younger offsider poked their heads into the studio.

The workmen. Right on time.

Chalcey figured she must have looked a real sight, all covered in yellowy dust. That and the fact she was still wearing her pajamas and hadn't gotten around to brushing her hair. Too late now. She fixed a welcoming smile on her face, prayed they both had strong constitutions, and ushered them inside.

Before they got down to work, she coaxed them into taking a look at the sliding door. The two of them had it sliding smoothly back and forth on its runners in no time.

"Hey, thanks. You guys are the best!"

"No problem, ma'am," the old guy said. "Easy when you know how."

Sam picked that moment to sashay from the women's bathroom wrapped in a towel. "Why, thank you, gentlemen," she cooed, making eyes at both men. "We girls do appreciate our privacy." And with that, she zipped into the bedroom and slid the door shut.

Chalcey hid a smile as the two workmen picked their jaws up off the floor. "Sorry about the peepshow."

The older man recovered his aplomb first. "Nothing to apologize for, ma'am."

*Yeah. I'll bet.* Aloud, she said, "Where do you want to start?"

He grinned at her. "How 'bout down the far end, so you can shower off the grime without us getting in your way."

She choked down a laugh. "That bad, huh?"

He shook his head and mimed zipping his lip. "C'mon, bo-yo. Quit drooling over the pretty girls and let's get to work." He cuffed the younger man about the head and prodded him toward the stairs. "We'll go grab our gear from the van."

Chalcey waved them off and leaned against the door to survey her studio. This was the last big thing that needed to be done. She was on the home stretch. All she needed was enough cash to take on Paulo and Leah, buy some decent office equipment and maybe a laptop that didn't take ten minutes to boot up, invest in some more advertising, oh, and find herself an apartment, and everything would be sweet. She would have everything she'd ever wanted.

Voices from inside the bedroom snatched her from dreams of packed classes and financial security. Sam must have woken Wulf. Excellent. She could always rely on that girl to—

"What do you think you're doing, woman?"

"I would have thought that was pretty obvious, sweetie."

Chalcey backed away. She didn't want to hear any more. The thought of Sam seducing Wulf, using him to take her mind off her own issues, was more than Chalcey could bear.

It'd sounded great in theory. Sic Sam on Wulf, and free herself from the insidious attraction the man held for her.

How could she have been so stupid?

How could she be hurting so damn much over a guy she'd just met?

Why did she feel so damned betrayed when it'd been her idea to throw Sam at him in the first place?

Putting on a stoic face, and trying to ignore the anguish in her heart, Chalcey made her way downstairs to help the workmen unload their gear.

# CHAPTER FIVE

WULF SNAKED OUT a hand and grabbed the woman's wrist. He squinted up at her.

"You're hurting me," she said through lips thinned to a tight white line.

He took her measure. She was a pretty little thing. Her hair was the color of flames—a burnished red-gold. Her baggy, short-sleeved garment and short pants displayed skin like fresh milk, and hinted at luscious feminine curves. She would have provoked a fierce bidding war on the Choosing Block.

In another place, in another time, he would have lain there and allowed her to rouse him before taking his pleasure with her. Now, in this room, lying in Chalcedony's bed, breathing in the scent of the woman who haunted his dreams and wishing it were *she* who had run her hand down his naked chest, *her* hot, wanton gaze licking his body, indulging in sexual congress merely because the opportunity presented itself seemed a travesty. Evidently his limp phallus supported that notion. Despite this young woman's obvious charms, he felt nothing. And he wondered, sourly, whether some capricious god had cursed his male parts to insure Wulf would only find release with a certain female. A certain female who, as the fates would have it, was also named for a crystal. And whose true name had had the power to smite him unconscious. Gods. He should be running for the hills. Instead, he only wanted her more.

He released the redhead's wrist. "My apologies."

She perched on the side of the bed, shoulders hunching as she rubbed her wrist and flexed her fingers. "I should be apologizing to you. I shouldn't have groped you without asking. And Chalce is my best friend. So I shouldn't be groping you at all. No matter what she said."

He yanked the sheet over his privates.

She grinned at him, shedding her sullen demeanor so abruptly that it brought to mind Kyan, his kinsman. Kyan, too, tended toward mercurial changes of temperament.

"Worried I'll be tempted to jump you, huh? Chill, sweetie. You're not that hot. I can control myself."

He schooled his features to remain neutral, to reveal nothing of his innermost thoughts.

Her grin turned into a peal of laughter. "Oooh," she said. "You're good."

"What did Chalcedony say, exactly?"

"Uh uh. That would be telling." She stuck out her hand. "Samantha Greenwood."

He clasped her hand because that was what she seemed to expect of him. And hid his surprise when she returned his firm grip, and shook his hand up and down. This must be how people of this world greeted one another, and evidently, it was nothing remarkable for a woman to instigate such a greeting. "You may call me Wulf."

"Okay, Wulf. So what are we gonna do about Chalcey?"

He hid his surprise. "Why do we need to do anything about Chalcedony?"

Samantha blinked at him. "You're kidding me, right? You beat on a guy who was trying to get into her panties. You followed her home. You're here, now, in her bed. Don't try'n tell me you don't want to get laid because I don't believe you."

"Laid?"

She puffed out a breath that smacked of disbelief. "You're really not from around here, are you? How can I say this without sounding totally crass. Look. Chalcey likes you. A lot. And I'm pretty sure you wouldn't have followed her home unless you wanted to scr— Ah, I mean, if you'd not found her *attractive*, right?" She glanced at him, waiting for confirmation.

"You are correct," he said, wondering where this strange conversation was leading. "I find Chalcedony attractive. Most attractive, indeed."

Samantha's answering grin could only be described as wicked. "And I assure you, the feeling is entirely mutual. But she's so not ready to admit that she wants you in the worst way. Which is why she backed off and said I could have you if I wanted you."

Now it was Wulf's turn to blink. Women owned men in this world? The irony of his situation was not lost on him. Too, it galled him to think Chalcedony might find him so lacking that she would toss him aside before he could prove his worth to her. But if it transpired that she would not give him a chance, and he must stand on the Choosing Block, he would do so with all the pride that he could muster. He would fetch an excellent price if the pathetic specimen of manhood called Ray was any indication of the men this world's females had to choose from. Nor would he fret like a woman over things that could not be changed. He would endure, as he'd always done. "When will the Choosing take place?"

Her brows pleated and she chewed her lower lip. "Choosing? What choosing? What're you going on about?"

She'd never heard of the term? Interesting. He waved away her confusion. "'Tis of no matter. Continue, please."

"It's complete BS, of course. No matter what Chalce says, she'd be gutted if I slept with you. And I wouldn't do that to her. I wouldn't! She's my best friend."

Wulf noted the sheen of tears in her eyes. Compassion sparked in his belly, and his voice was uncharacteristically gentle when he said, "If you care about Chalcedony's feelings

as much as you say, then why did you touch me so intimately?"

The tears that had been threatening spiked her lashes. She
pressed the heels of her hands to her eyes and the words tumbled out in a hurried stream that made his head spin. "Because
I met someone last night. A-and how I feel about him after
only one night scares the panties off me. I thought that maybe
if I slept with you, I might be able to forget about him and go
back to how I was before. Because... because I'm a stupid
bitch. I wouldn't have gone through with it, you know. I would
have teased you some, had a bit of fun with you, and then cut
you loose. But you'd better believe I'd have told Chalcey if
you'd been keen to try it on with me. A harmless fling with a
hot guy is one thing, but no way would I set her up with a two-
timing scumbag who'd screw anything that puts out. She's not
built to cope with that sort of shit." She scowled at him so
fiercely that he was reminded of a desert fox protecting its
pups.

"I see." The crux of what she'd confessed and her intent
were crystal clear, even if the finer details escaped him because
of her colloquialism-ridden speech. Samantha had met a man
and the depths of her feelings for this man scared her. Chalcedony, too, was scared—so scared of her desire for him that
she'd pushed her friend Samantha into seducing him. And in
turn, Samantha had been provoked into testing the strength of
his feelings for Chalcedony. It was a twisted chain of events,
but one that seemed logical—so far as females were capable of
logic when it came to matters of the heart. Her forward manner aside, Wulf decided that Chalcedony possessed a worthy
friend in Samantha Greenwood.

"So. Did I pass your test, Samantha?"

The scowl smoothed into a rueful grin. She waved her wrist
beneath his nose. "Only with flying colors. I'll have a good-size
bruise there by tomorrow."

"I find myself wanting to apologize for hurting you, but

unable to be truly repentant, given the circumstances."

"Apology—such as it was—accepted. Now listen up. I have a plan to get Chalcey to realize how much she wants you. If this works, she's gonna think it was all her idea to jump your bones. You game?"

His cock stirred. To have Chalcedony come to him willingly would be a gift beyond price. He was not foolish enough to believe that earning her favor would be as simple as Samantha claimed. Still, he would not hesitate to take advantage of whatever opportunities arose. "I am indeed game."

Samantha clapped her hands like a gleeful child. "Goodie. So here's how it's gonna work. Ooh, just one more thing. I hope you're not the shy type? Because this is going to work a whole heap better if you lose the sheet."

He decided it prudent not to answer until he'd listened to her plan.

A BELLOW SOUNDED from the bedroom. Chalcey's head jerked up and her startled gaze clashed with that of the younger workman. "What the—?" She dumped the carton of gear she'd been carrying for him on the floor and headed for the bedroom.

The sliding door flew open before she could reach it. She skidded to a halt, arms wheeling, floored by the sight of Wulf, stark naked, and moving like he was being chased by ravenous hellhounds.

He stopped dead when he spotted her. Just as well. If he'd smacked into her, he'd have sent her flying. "Wulf, what's wrong? Are you feeling sick?"

"That female. She— When I awoke, she was taking liberties with me!" His tone quivered with what she guessed to be outrage. So did his impressive male parts.

She tore her gaze from those, er, parts. But oh, it was hard! Uh, to not look, that is. Yikes. She gave herself a mental slap upside the head and instructed her brain to engage. "Saaaam!"

she called. "Get your butt out here, right now."

The perpetrator of the crime sidled through the door, cute-as-a-button in a clean pair of borrowed shorts and Chalcey's favorite "FCUK It" t-shirt. "I'm sorry, Chalce. He was laid out like some delicious feast and I couldn't help myself. I—"

"Enough!" Chalcey flung up a hand to ward off what was sure to be a graphic description of exactly what Sam had gotten up to. She didn't want to know. Worse, she was uncomfortably aware that they were providing free entertainment for the workmen, who were hanging on to Sam's every word. "Apologize to him right now."

"How was I supposed to know he—?"

"Say sorry, Sam."

"Do I have to?"

"Sam."

Sam thrust out her lower lip into a cutesy sexpot pout, and turned to Wulf. "I'm very sorry for, er, feeling you up." She fluttered her eyelashes at him. "But if you ever change your mind, I—"

"Samantha Greenwood!" Chalcey winced as her screech echoed through the studio. Jeez. She sounded like Sam's mother. A shudder rippled down her torso. Scary thought.

Sam heaved a sigh. "I promise I'll behave," she said. And, catching Chalcey's obvious disbelief, stuck out her tongue before flouncing off into the kitchenette. "Coffee anyone?" she yelled over her shoulder, as if nothing untoward had happened.

Chalcey abruptly realized she'd gotten a little too close to her naked houseguest for comfort, and skittered back a couple of steps. She heard a muffled imprecation and spotted the younger of the two workmen standing stock-still, his jaw agape in a classic pole-axed expression.

The old guy sniggered. "What's up, boyo? Ain't never seen a schlong that big afore? Puts yours to shame, I'll bet. Never mind lad." He cuffed the young guy on the shoulder. "You're only a greenhorn, so maybe you've still got some growing to do. Time to get to work. Lady's not paying us to stand 'round and gawk."

The "lady" in question shot a quick glance at Wulf to see how he was taking it.

He was taking it well, standing there in all his glory, apparently quite gratified by all the attention being paid to his "schlong".

Men.

"Uh, so here's the floor," she said to the workmen. She had a habit of stating the obvious when she was horribly embarrassed. Like now. "If you feel like getting started, now's good." She grabbed Wulf's arm and dragged him back into the bedroom, shutting out the knowing smirks by the simple expedient of sliding the door shut behind her.

"Where are your clothes?" she said. "Find them and put them on, for God's sake!"

"The other woman, the short one with hair the color of flames, tells me she is your friend."

"Sam? Yes, she's my best friend. Why?"

"You may wish to reiterate to her that I am not interested in her that way," he said, frowning fiercely.

"Jeez. She had a rough night, and—" *Shut up, Chalcey. Sam sure as heck won't appreciate you going there.* "Look, I apologize again for Sam's behavior, okay? But most guys I know would happily lie back and let her have her wicked way with them."

To her private satisfaction, Wulf did not appear at all impressed by this claim. "If I wanted to bed her, I would take her and be done with it. But she holds no sway over me."

Chalcey didn't know quite what to make of that statement, distracted as she was by his impressive nakedness. So very, very, distracted that she clapped a hand over her eyes. "Will you please find your clothes and put them on? Pleeease?"

He gently pulled her hand away from her eyes. "What is it

about my body that disturbs you so, Chalcedony? Does something about me displease you?"

"Er.... No. Not at all. It's a very nice body." She cleared her throat, forced herself to stare him straight in the eyes, and endeavored to speak without squeaking. "Very nice. Now would you put some clothes on?"

He released her hand to stretch the cricks from his shoulders and back. And render her speechless with an astounding display of rippling muscles and simply delectable pectorals. Ye God, he was gorgeous. Mesmerizing. She'd really like to—

She bit her lip. And when that didn't work, pinched her arm really hard. That didn't work, either. Her brain was still mush. "Huh? Sorry, did you say something?"

"You are filthy, Chalcedony."

Rats. Busted. Was what she'd been thinking *that* obvious?

"Do you have a particular liking for this state of dishevelment?" He swiped a smudge from her cheek with the pad of his thumb and held it up for inspection.

Oh. He meant filthy physical state. She shook herself and mentally kicked her brain up a gear. "No, of course I don't *like* being covered in dust and crap. I was going to take a shower but I got a bit, um, distracted."

His eyes lit up. "A shower? Is it raining outside? That would be a miraculous sight to behold. In my homeland, it has rained but once in my lifetime."

"Desert-dweller, huh? Sorry to disappoint you but I was talking about taking a shower, like, in the bathroom."

A wistful expression crossed his face, softening his features. "I would like very much to bathe. And to eat. I have not broken my fast since arriving in this place."

"And when was that exactly?"

"Yester-eve, when first I encountered you." He gazed off into the distance. "But truly, I cannot recall my last meal."

OMG. The really buff bodybuilder-type she'd once dated "had" to eat every couple of hours. Little wonder poor Wulf had passed out. Poor guy had to be starving. "And where were you, uh, before?"

"I existed in a place of endless darkness where no time passes."

"Oh. Oookay." Nothing like obvious insanity to poor cold water on the heat of lust. And as much as she wanted a shower, she decided to hold off until she had the studio to herself again. Face and hands would have to suffice. "Okay, Wulf, here's the deal. You're going to take a shower while I fix you something to eat. Then, after you've eaten, you're going to leave."

He slanted her an enigmatic "you think?" type of look, and picked up his clothes.

Mmm. Nice ass. But…. She shook her head at her own gullibility, then snagged a towel from her hamper and tossed it at him. "Cover yourself with that so you don't tempt Sam any further." She turned away rather than watch him wrap the towel about his hips and embarrass herself further with uncontrolled drooling. "C'mon. I'll show you how the showers work. I'd hate you to burn your, ah, self."

She ushered him into the men's bathroom and left him contemplating the shower mixer in one of the cubicles while she ducked her head through the doorway to answer a yelled query from Sam. "There's more sugar in the top cupboard, okay? And don't eat all the leftover mac 'n' cheese. I'm saving that for dinner."

She turned back to discover Wulf already wallowing under a jet of water. Without having pulled the shower curtain closed.

Whoa. Nice. Nice *everything*, really.

"Do you have something to wash with?" he asked.

"Do I have something—? Oh. Yes. Of course. Sorry. Won't be a tick." She dragged her gaze away from the incredibly hot naked man in her shower, and whizzed back to her bedroom to retrieve soap, shampoo and conditioner.

It took more than a couple of deep, bracing breaths before she felt up to entering the men's bathroom again. And all that carefully won surface composure was wasted because, gosh darnit! he still hadn't bothered to shut the curtain. Apparently her brain turned to jello and leaked out her ears whenever she got too near him. It took far too much effort not to stare. Sheesh. Sam was right. She *so* needed to get laid. Sighing like a teenage girl over a crush, she gave in, and stared.

Realizing that he was watching her watch him, and his lips were quirked in an altogether smug masculine grin, was enough to snap her out of it. She averted her eyes, and held out the soap and bottles. And while she was congratulating herself for her strength of character at not sneaking another peek, he grabbed her wrist... and hauled her into the shower cubicle with him.

"Gaaaaaahhh! The water's fricking freezing!" She fumbled with shower mixer, adjusting the water to a more desirable temperature. "What the hell did you do that for?"

"You are covered in dust from head to toe, Chalcedony. When you have wonders such as this at your fingertips—" he cast a hand about the shower cubicle "—why would you not desire to take advantage of them?"

"Well, thanks for the offer but I prefer to shower in private. So I'll be getting out now."

"I think not." He crowded her into a corner of the cubicle. "At least, not until you are clean."

"I'm fully capable of washing myself, thank you very much."

"Of that I am certain. However, is it not more fun to have assistance?" He brandished the soap in an insinuating sort of a way.

"Oh, yes. I mean, no!" She wasn't doing this. No way. "Let me out or I'll scream. A-and those guys will come and rescue me. I mean it, Wulf. Let me out right—"

His mouth swooped down and captured hers, an oh-so effective way to smother her protests. All thought of escape fled as his lips worked their magic and his tongue thrust deep into her mouth, licking and exploring. His hands cupped her breasts, squeezing and rolling the pebbled nipples through the soaking wet, stretch-cotton fabric of her top.

She squirmed and his mouth left hers to lick and nibble her neck—one of her major erogenous zones, dammit.

One big hand left her breast to pin her hips against the tiles of the shower cubicle. His lips traveled lower, fastening around her breast, sucking, biting gently, teasing with his teeth.

He pushed up her top and her breasts sprang free. He cupped them.

She sucked in a deep shocked breath. "Wulf… I'm not… I don't… I don't do this sort of—" He drew her left nipple into his mouth, suckling strongly, sending tiny shockwaves of pleasure directly to her groin. "Ahhhh!"

Her IQ was reduced to absolute zero as he squeezed and massaged her other breast with fingers that were so skilled and clever, they should have been illegal. He pulled the top over her head, slowly, laving each inch of newly bared skin with his tongue. She shuddered, her skin becoming almost unbearably sensitized beneath his touch.

He knelt, lipping his way down her stomach, tongue flicking her belly button, lapping water from her skin. She felt his hands on her waist, fingers insinuating themselves beneath the waistband of her pajama pants, dragging the sopping wet material down over her hips.

She reached down to grab his hands, a last ditch attempt to prevent what she knew was going to happen next. "Wulf, I—"

His gaze sought hers, blue eyes dark with desire and raw need. "Chalcedony."

The tenderness with which he uttered her name was her undoing.

"I desire you above all others," he said, and at that moment she believed him with every fiber of her being. "Do you want me to stop, Chalcedony?"

"No."

"I want there to be no misunderstanding about what I intend to do to you. Say you want me to continue. Say yes, Chalcedony."

"Yes," she whispered, her voice shaking.

He tugged and her pants pooled at her ankles. He spread her with gentle fingers and licked her once, just once, before resting his forehead against her stomach. Waiting. And, oh God, she couldn't help it. She thrust her pelvis forward, giving in to her body's demands, surrendering. And there could be no lies because her body couldn't lie. She wanted him as much as he wanted her. And they both knew it.

He licked her again, suckled her clit until she wanted to scream—would have screamed except that what he was doing to her with his mouth and his tongue and his fingers had stolen her breath and all she could summon was a hoarse gasp.

He tantalized and teased until heat spiraled through her belly and her vision washed with a golden haze and the muscles in her legs gave way. But she didn't fall. He wouldn't let her fall. He surged upward, and lifted her so that she was cradled in his arms with her legs wrapped around his waist. Eye to eye with him. No secrets. No pretense.

Stainless steel pressed against her spine, the chill shock of it threatening to yank her back into reality and gift her with reason. But the heat of him, his craving for her—and hers for him—was too powerful. The stream of water pounded his back. He rolled his shoulders, luxuriating in the heat, and the play of muscles in his upper body sent tingles of anticipation down her body. She was at his mercy. Utterly. Right now, he could demand anything of her and she would give it to him. And right here, right now, with this man, she wouldn't have it any other way.

He rubbed himself against her until all she knew was the sensation of his skin against hers and his hard cock pressing against her stomach. And all she could think about was how it would feel when he was inside her.

He shifted his grip, reaching down to stroke her clit with his thumb while he worked a finger deep inside her. Then two. In and out, stroking her, teasing, until her inner muscles clenched against his fingers. From deep in his throat came a rumble of pure masculine satisfaction. And then he expelled his breath in a harsh, needy gasp that made her revel in her femininity. She was doing that to him. Her body. Her.

He cupped his hands around her butt and positioned her over the head of his cock, nudging himself against her core until she ground her hips down, craving all of him. Answering her unspoken demand, he lowered her onto his thick hard shaft, stretching her, impaling her so achingly slowly that she wanted to scream with the need to have all of him inside her. Every incredible inch. She writhed and moaned with the need.

"Am I hurting you?"

"Wulf! For God's sake. Please. Don't stop. Don't you dare stop!"

He stared deep into her eyes, into her soul. And then he drove himself all the way in and began to fuck her in long thrusting strokes that had her whimpering with pleasure.

Vaguely, through the fog of sexual sensation, she heard someone enter the bathroom. And she didn't care. "Go 'way. Be with you… later."

"Much later." Wulf growled, driving into her with such hard, forceful strokes that she buried her face in his shoulder and bit her lips so that she didn't scream aloud.

"You all right, Chalcey?" Sam's voice, uncertain.

And she didn't give a damn. "Yes. Yes!"

Sam left, closing the door behind her, shutting Chalcey away from the real world.

There was only Wulf. His body and hers. His powerful cock pumping deep inside her. Her inner muscles milking him. His hands stroking her body.

The pressure inside her rose, intensified, continued building until—

She tensed, gasped for air. Her orgasm rippled through her, stripping away the final shreds of self-awareness. She shrieked his name and didn't care who heard her. "Wulfenite!"

He drove into her and stilled, pulsing hot, quivering. And then he buried his face in her neck and whispered her name. "Chalcedony."

The catch in his voice was so heartbreakingly poignant that her soul sang. She couldn't even bring herself to care that she'd just had unprotected sex—the most incredible sex of her life—with a virtual stranger.

# CHAPTER SIX

C HALCEY REGISTERED THE swoosh of the bathroom door as Wulf slid it shut behind him. And then she was on her own, with all the privacy she could possibly desire. Whoopee.

She slumped to the floor of the cubicle and covered her face with her hands, unwilling to face reality let alone crawl out of the shower. The hot water pounded over her. Pity the drumming of high-pressure water on stainless steel couldn't drown out her thoughts.

She was still taking the pill, thank God. But what she had just done was so completely out of character that it was darn near incomprehensible. Visions of brain tumors danced in her head. One of Sam's stepfathers—the second, or maybe the third—had been diagnosed with one, giving his wife a brilliant excuse for any personality trait of his that she'd particularly disliked. She'd been in heaven. Until he finished treatments, recovered, and his personality didn't change one bit. Mrs. Greenwood was a real piece of work.

Maybe—

Oh, wise up, girl! There were no excuses. She'd allowed hormones and the rather prolonged sex-free spell in her life to get the upper hand. Honestly, who could blame her for taking full advantage of the gorgeous guy who'd been more than willing to screw her 'til she was reduced to a quivering mass of orgasmic nerve-endings? It was something modern women did all the time. And as Sam frequently insisted, it was just sex. Really, really, incredibly great, mind-blowing sex, but just sex all the same. Nothing to wig out over.

So why had her heart been shredded into teeny tiny pieces when Wulf had untangled himself from her and stepped from the shower without a backward glance? Why did she feel so bereft at the sneaking suspicion that now she'd given him what he wanted, he would disappear back to wherever the hell he came from?

The door to the bathroom opened and Chalcey reached out to tweak the shower curtain closed. That was her, modest and all. Nothing like closing the stable door after the Wulf had bolted.

"You in there, Chalce?" Sam asked.

"Yep. Won't be a moment. Just—" she fumbled for an excuse "—washing my hair." Silence reigned. Figuring that she might as well authenticate her lie she grabbed the shampoo, crawled to her feet and slopped goop onto her hair.

"Wulf sent me in to see if you were okay. He mentioned you might need a towel."

"Oh, he's still here?" He hadn't used her for sex and taken off. She hugged the knowledge tightly to her heart. Not that it made the slightest bit of difference, she told herself sternly. She was still kicking him out on his sculpted backside as soon as she'd fed him.

"Of course he's still here," Sam said. "Why wouldn't he be?"

"I, uh, thought he would have— Oh, never mind."

A muffled sigh was the only warning before Sam yanked back the curtain. She pinned Chalcey with cat-like green eyes that examined every little nuance of her expression. All-seeing. All-knowing.

Chalcey did a full-body blush and cringed. "Jeez. Quit with the x-ray vision, will you? You're making me feel like I'm the latest viewing attraction at the zoo." She adjusted the water temperature, making it cooler to counteract the heat of her humiliation.

"So. You and Wulf got it on. You go, girl!" Now Sam had a huge smirk on her face—the kind proud moms got when their kids had done something extra special. Anyone would think she'd planned this whole encounter.

Chalcey decided her best chance of retaining a smidgeon of dignity was to brazen it out. "I would have thought that was patently obvious when you came in before. And I'm sure you're thrilled that my sexual drought is over. In fact—" her voice wobbled only the teensiest bit "—now I know what I'm missing, I think I'll fuck strange men more often." Warming to her I-just-fucked-a-hot-guy-so-what? theme, she muttered, "Can't believe I've spent so many years wedded to vibrators when I could have been screwing the real thing."

Sam smacked her forehead with her palm, apparently not buying Chalcey's pathetic declaration of sexual emancipation. "God, I'm so stupid. I should have known. Sex isn't merely sex for you. It's *making love*. It's relationships and togetherness, white picket fences and a brood of ankle-biters kinda stuff."

Chalcey rinsed conditioner from her hair. "Don't be ridiculous. I had sex with a guy I just met. We had fun. End of story. I don't expect it to go anywhere. I don't expect anything at all. And neither does he."

"That's what you think," Sam muttered.

"What makes you say that?"

"Be careful, is all. Wulf's not a man to trifle with and I don't want you getting hurt."

"You were happy enough when you thought I'd screwed his brains out last night. What's changed?" Chalcey shut off the water, grabbed her sopping wet clothes and wrung them out before hanging them over the shower rail.

"It's funny. He's got exactly the same look on his face as you do right now. Like he's experienced something so damn profound, he's not sure how to cope with it. The two of you are made for each other." Sam handed her a couple of towels. "I'll go find you some clothes so you don't have to walk past those workmen in a towel. I reckon they've had enough entertainment already, don't you?"

"Yeah," Chalcey said. "Probably." But her stunning rejoinder fell on deaf ears. Sam had already marched from the bathroom.

DRESSED, AND HOPEFULLY able to face the world without bursting into idiotic tears, Chalcey ventured into the kitchenette. Sam had managed to find something more appetizing than leftover mac 'n' cheese from a packet. She and Wulf were tucking into a huge feed of bacon, sausages and eggs.

Despite wallowing in a huge bout of woe-is-me, Chalcey's mouth watered. "Where did you find all this food? Is there some magical hidden compartment in my fridge I didn't know about, or something?"

"I zipped to the deli while you and Wulf were, ah, washing up," Sam said. "Figured you'd both be hungry. Afterward."

"Thanks." Chalcey cooled her burning face by searching in the fridge for juice.

"Oh, by the way, the phone rang," Sam said. "Wulf took the call."

Chalcey glanced toward him, expectant, but the man in question merely applied himself diligently to his food. "So, who was it?" she asked. "A wannabe student, with any luck. Did you get their number so I can call them back?"

Crimson flares painted his cheekbones. "When I picked up the device, a voice came from it. But when I spoke into it, all I heard was a click and a loud, monotonous tone. I must have used it incorrectly."

Sam patted his arm. "Not your fault—it was a hang-up. Chill. If it's important they'll ring back."

"So, Wulf." Chalcey threw herself into a chair at the table, toyed with her drink, and hoped like hell her faked air of unconcern was convincing. If he sensed the slightest hesitation in her, he'd walk right over her and stick around. Worse, she'd probably let him. "Now that you've been fed and watered, it's time for you to make tracks. I'm sure you have places to be, people to meet, yadda yadda."

"Jeez, Chalce," Sam said. "Let the poor man at least finish his food before you boot him out on the street, huh?"

She choked on her mouthful of juice. Sam was siding with her one-shower stand? Some best friend.

Wulf leaned over and pounded her back. And before she could catch her breath to protest, began to gently rub the now painful place between her shoulder blades. The touch of his big hand against her skin, doubtless meant to soothe, only served to remind her what else those hands had recently been doing. To her.

She shrugged him off, slapping away his hands. Humiliation made her waspish. "Haven't you got anything else to wear? You look like a walking porn star in all that leather. He's all yours, Sam. And maybe the first thing you should do with him is take him shopping for suitable clothes."

Wulf arched his eyebrows. "What is wrong with my attire? 'Tis made of sand-lizard leather and eminently suitable for the climate of my homeland. Regardless, I have no choice in the matter, for I have no other clothes."

"Great. And I suppose you have no cash, either?" He threw her a blank look, and she hastened to elaborate. "Money. To purchase clothes and other stuff you need."

"Alas, that is true." He caught and held her gaze in a way that was so very intimate, Chalcey felt her face—and other more intimate parts—tingle with warmth. Again. "I have no currency. I am completely at your mercy."

Her mind filled with an explicit visual of Wulf spread-eagled on her bed. Naked. And aroused. Yikes. "S-so you're some sort of a refugee? No clothes, no money, nowhere to stay?"

"Indeed. I have nothing in this world but you, Chalcedony. But *you* are riches indeed."

Sam heaved a dramatically gusty sigh.

Thank God Sam was there to distract Chalcey from this man who was so mesmerizing, so compelling, that she felt like a deer caught in headlights. She tore her gaze from Wulf's face. "What?" she said to Sam. "You're buying that line?"

Oh yeah. Sam totally was. Her face was all soft and dewy-eyed.

"Oh, c'mon. Snap out of it. You're scaring me. I rely on you to tromp all my romantic notions into the ground before delivering me a lecture on the real world."

Sam forked up more bacon and contemplated Chalcey in a half smug, half wistful sort of fashion as she chewed. "You've got it real bad, haven't you? Listen up, Chalce. Wulf and I had a little talk while you were trying to wash away all your sins. And—"

"Excuse me?" Sam and Wulf having heart-to-hearts? This was bad. Really bad. It sucked that Sam wasn't backing her up. Like she always backed *Sam* up. Unconditionally. "And you thought what, exactly? That since I'm all on my lonesome with only a battery-operated fake penis to keep me happy, you could just pair me up with little orphan Arnie, here, and we'd live happy ever after? No way. As soon as he finishes eating he's outta here."

Sam continued speaking as if Chalcey hadn't just launched into an emotional tirade. "I think you need some space to get your head around things. I've got plenty of room, so I offered Wulf my guestroom. Just until he gets himself sorted."

A green worm of jealousy burrowed into Chalcey's soul and curled there. She surged to her feet, glaring at the man who'd turned up out of the blue, and turned her world upside down. "You bastard. You barge into my home, fuck me sense-less, then sweet-talk your way into my best friend's apartment? Get out. Get out now."

He rose to his feet slowly, deliberately, leashed fury in every muscle.

Chalcey backed up. And kept backing up until she was plastered against the wall. He placed his hands on the wall either side of her head, and leaned into her.

There was no escaping him. She tried to duck beneath his arms but he held an arm across her waist and trapped her there, against the wall, helpless. "Let me go," she spat, wanting nothing more than to rake her nails down his face. And then repeat the shower episode. With interest.

"It's not what you're thinking, Chalce," Sam said. "I'm offering him a place to sleep. Nothing more."

"Right. Like he's going to resist you when you next get the urge to take your mind off your own problems and decide to screw him senseless."

Hurt flashed in Sam's eyes and Chalcey felt a pang of guilt for throwing Sam's words back in her face.

"I wouldn't make a play for any guy I thought you were interested in, Chalce. At the very least you should trust me on that."

Crap. Some friend she was. Chalcey peered at Sam beneath Wulf's shoulder. "I'm sorry. I do trust you." With any guy but this one….

Sam's emerald gaze had turned a distressing shade of poison-green that shouted "you really went too far this time, girlfriend". Uh oh. "You've made it quite clear you're not interested in Wulf," Sam said, "and you absolutely don't want him around. So why would anything *I* do with him matter so much to you, anyway?"

"I, too, would like an answer to that question," Wulf said.

Chalcey glowered at him, glad for an excuse to pull her gaze from Sam's wounded, angry eyes. "*You*, stay out of this. Like, you're such a—" His mouth swooped down, cutting off what she'd planned to be a really pithy insult midstream. His lips—oh lord, he was such a fabulous kisser. Her brain shut down again, squeezing out reality, narrowing it until her only focus was him.

When he finally moved away, she could only stare up at him, mesmerized. Again. And shiver while he nuzzled her neck, his lips bestowing little soft butterfly caresses that made her knees tremble.

His lips hovered close to her ear. "Delightful as she is, I do not want your friend Samantha," he whispered. "I only want you, Chalcedony."

The phone rang, jolting Chalcey back to the here and now. And a clear view of her best friend's hurt-filled face. "I-I... I should get that," she said. But she couldn't move.

Sam grabbed the phone. "Hello? Hello?" She slammed the receiver down. "Huh. I hate hang-ups. Rude prick could have at least apologized for dialing a wrong number."

Sam dumped her plate in the sink and grabbed the plastic bag containing the clothes she'd worn last night. The high-heeled strappy sandals she'd worn clubbing should have looked ridiculous paired with oversized shorts and a t-shirt, but Chalcey knew that once Sam had slipped them on, some-how they would work.

"Be seeing you, Chalcey. Call me when your brain's work-ing again and you can be reasonable. Coming, Wulf?" And with that, Sam stalked out, barefoot, thank goodness. Not that Chalcey would have dared call her on it.

Wulf sauntered out the door after her. Leaving Chalcey alone with a major case of confusion, a heap of dirty dishes, and a couple of tradesmen who probably figured she was an evil-tempered bitch who couldn't make up her mind what she wanted. And that was if they'd overheard only part of what had gone down.

She'd never let a guy get between her and Sam before. She'd never been this screwed up over a guy before, either. It was doing her head in. *He* was doing her head in. Oh boy. Not good. Sooo not good.

"ARE YOU CERTAIN this is the right course of action?" Wulf asked as he dutifully trailed down the steep staircase after Samantha. Being dutiful was an unfamiliar concept to him, but Samantha was the mastermind of this plan, and if it aided him to win the prize he sought, then dutiful he would be. "Chalcedony strikes me as a stubborn woman. I cannot imagine her being so easily manipulated."

Samantha gave a snort worthy of Wulf's battle-mount when the beast hadn't bitten anyone in a while and was sorely irritated. "I know Chalcey. She'll drive herself bat-shit crazy up the wall wondering whether I've seduced you. Or you've seduced me. You'll see. I give her two days, tops, before she can't stand it any longer and comes looking for you. Then all you have to do is make like you're the kind of man she's been searching for her entire life. Easy, right?"

"I suspect not," he muttered.

"Me, neither," Sam said. "But all you can do is try. At least this way you've got a fighting chance." She paused at the bottom of the stairs and stared up at him through narrowed eyes. "You do want a fighting chance with her, right?"

"I do."

"Good," Sam said. "She'd only just met you and she had sex with you. That's a monumentally freaking huge step for her. She obviously likes you. A lot. If you play your cards right, the two of you might even make a go of it."

The thought of entering into something other than a fleeting relationship based on sex did not bother Wulf as much as it should have. Not if it were with Chalcedony. She would not allow him to rule the roost. He could not imagine finding such a complex, stubborn, frustrating, and wholly desirable woman, boring.

Hah. He would be foolish to believe that that his unexpected respite from his crystal prison would be anything but temporary. Foolish to believe that he had any chance to make a life for himself. The old crystal sorcerer had been powerful enough that he must surely have commanded the ear of a god or two. If he yet lived, doubtless he was biding his time, plotting how to punish Wulf anew.

It was obvious as a raincloud in the desert sky to Wulf that Chalcedony had been marked as a pawn in some great game. And she made an excellent pawn, indeed. She'd taken him into her body, given herself to him in such an abandoned, whole-hearted way that she had thoroughly seduced him into baring his soul. She'd forced him to care for her…. Only to then accuse him of using her, and moving on to another woman.

He shouldn't have cared. He should have been able to dismiss her as a lost cause, inconsequential. He should have been more than willing to sacrifice her to gain the upper hand, as was so often necessary in battle. But he would not have Chalcedony suffer the anguish of believing herself used and abandoned.

He would not have her suffer at all. And so he resolved to protect her—as much as he was able. Gods willing, Samantha's plan would convince Chalcedony to let him back into her life. If not, so be it. He would take whatever drastic measures he deemed necessary.

Samantha's harsh laughter slapped at him. In the dull light of the stairwell, her green eyes glittered like soulless gems. "Boy, you are *so* a goner. Just like her. I'd go so far as to be envious if I wasn't pissed to the max I've fallen head over heels for Marc—"

She bit off the name. Her eyes rounded and her parted lips trembled with sudden realization that smacked of profound shock. "Shit. Must be something in the damned water." She abruptly turned on her heel and shoved through the doorway, out into the street.

Wulf followed her. He had nowhere else to go. Under other circumstances he would not have hesitated to stride away and fend for himself. But this world was so unfamiliar, so beyond his experience, that all his instincts shouted at him to accept Samantha's offer and learn what he could. Too much was at stake. And knowledge was power. Knowledge would keep him alive, help him remain one step ahead of vengeful crystal sorcerers and capricious gods. At least until he had worked his unholy desire for Chalcedony from his system.

The hollow feeling in his belly made him uneasy given he'd recently eaten a hearty meal. And as he slid into the conveyance—the *taxi*—that Samantha had summoned, the hollowness dissolved into a pain so sharp and unexpected, that he might have been sliced by a sublimely honed blade. A blade so deadly that he hadn't felt it parting his skin, and his brain was only now registering the injury. He ignored it. He was a warrior, accustomed to pain, and this was but a trifling niggle, unworthy of notice.

The farther they travelled from Chalcedony's abode, the more the pain bit at him. Until, by the time the taxi halted outside a building that was so high it scraped the clouds, his belly was alight with a fierce burning.

Wulf grit his teeth and stoically bore the pain, refusing to reveal his weakness to the woman he'd chosen to follow. He knew what it meant. He'd left Chalcedony behind, let her push him away on the flimsiest of excuses. He should have insisted on staying, overwhelmed her objections, thrown her over his shoulder and fucked her until she lost the capacity for rational thought. It was the best way to tame an overly obstinate woman. It had always worked for him previously. No woman could remain angry when she'd been thoroughly pleasured.

The pain he was now forced to endure was a fitting punishment for his stupidity.

# CHAPTER SEVEN

WULF HAD NEVER in his life been beholden to anyone, let alone a woman. It did not sit well with him that he must rely on Samantha, despite her insistence that it mattered not, and she was glad of his company.

He didn't like to admit it, but he'd been glad of her company, also. In the two days since she had taken him into her home, he had endured a series of most discomfiting situations. From the instant he'd been freed from the crystal, he had stubbornly refused to be overwhelmed by this world's many wonders. Magic, he had no control over. To his way of thinking, there was little point concerning himself with it—what would be, would be.

Anything non-magical was a different matter. From the age of five, as soon as he was strong enough to lift a sword, Wulf had spent his life proving that little could prevail against wily tactics, consummate skill with weaponry, and, if all else failed, brute force. He had been confident he would cope with anything non-magical this world tossed in his path. Mere hours with Samantha had proven him a fool many times over for that deeply held belief.

The metallic box—the *elevator*—that had flown them to the top floor of the building had been but the first of many rude shocks. He'd not been at all appreciative of Samantha's pealing laughter when, as the elevator had begun to move, he'd plastered himself against one side and held on for dear life. He cared not what she swore in that bantering tone of hers. He had absolutely not turned "chalk-white" and been on the brink of "tossing his cookies". He had merely been… surprised by the novelty of such an apparatus. As he'd continued to be "surprised" by televisions, sound systems, laptops, and all manner of other seemingly magical electronic appliances.

His prowess with a sword, and ability to lead men through strength of will alone, had ill prepared him for coping with such contraptions. But at least the effort of coping with the constant barrage of alien-ness freed his mind from dwelling upon the physical agony of being parted from the woman who haunted him, mind, body and soul.

Compared with Chalcedony's cramped living space, Samantha's *penthouse apartment*, as she'd informed him the abode was called, seemed a veritable palace. And careful questioning of Samantha revealed that while she lived a life of luxury, her every whim catered for, it was not so for every inhabitant of this world. And very much not so for Chalcedony, who was struggling to build a life for herself. Moreover, that she was far too stubborn to accept assistance was a source of much frustration for Samantha.

Wulf admired that about Chalcedony. Especially as it was abundantly clear to him that Samantha—generous to a fault, and possessing more wealth than she could hope to spend in a lifetime—would have showered Chalcedony with gifts had Chalcedony permitted it.

Samantha loved Chalcedony like a sister, and their disagreement pained her heart. Wulf knew nothing of love. But he knew whatever *he* felt for Chalcedony wasn't at all sisterly.

He'd come to believe that she had been placed in his path as a test. And, as with all tests, doubtless it was one with a scorpion's sting hidden in its tail. Perhaps the secret to passing this test was to not fall into the trap of treating Chalcedony as he would any other desirable female. Rather than wooing her to his bed, perhaps his role was to assist her to attain her dream of self-sufficiency. But how? He understood now that he would be hard-pressed to make his own way in this world where "cash" and material possessions were valued over physical prowess. He had much to learn before he himself would be self-sufficient, let alone capable of supporting a woman.

Furthermore, like Chalcedony, he was far too proud to allow Samantha to do anything more than feed him, and provide him with clothing more suited to this clime. And speaking of clothing, the vast market Samantha had taken him to had almost overwhelmed him with its raucous music and eye-searingly bright lights and noisy crowds. He'd watched carefully as Samantha handed over a shiny silver card to pay for her purchases, signed a slip of paper, and took possession of the card again. He could not fathom how such an exchange benefited the sellers, but from their fawning deference, he guessed that Samantha had impressed them. And Samantha had seemed bound and determined to impress *him*, by providing him with more sets of clothing than he could ever need.

He'd been forced to put his boot down. She was a generous woman, Samantha. Too generous. It would be easy to take advantage of her largesse.

Just as it would be easy to become inured to the luxury of lounging in the back of a taxi rather than walking, or spending countless hours in the saddle.

From Samantha's lack of pointed comments, he believed that he'd successfully hidden his disquiet when she had bundled him into the conveyance to take him "shopping". Unlike his first journey in a taxi, when he'd been too caught up in the maelstrom of his own thoughts to truly register the experience, his second journey had been unnerving in the extreme. It had not been easy for Wulf to put his life in the hands of an elderly driver he wouldn't have trusted to hold the reins of his mount. But Samantha had shown so little concern that Wulf felt compelled to trust her judgment. He'd bitten his tongue and not questioned the man's ability to operate such a complex apparatus. And, as the taxi careened around a corner, closed his eyes and wished fervently for a horse. Now, he sprawled in the back seat and barely batted an eyelid as the world careened past in a blur.

A sharp elbow nudged him in the ribs, thrusting him into the here and now. He turned to Samantha, his eyebrows raised. "What is it?"

"We're nearly there. Want me to walk you up?" She nibbled her lower lip, gazing at him like a mother concerned for her child. "Chalce isn't gonna make it easy for you. She's probably been torturing herself, imagining you and me screwing each other senseless."

Samantha's tone was sharp, leading Wulf to conclude that when the two next confronted each other, it would be Samantha who wouldn't be "making it easy" for Chalcedony. He hid a smile at the thought of the two women bickering. An entertaining spectacle, indeed.

He patted Samantha's hand. "I thank you for your concern, but in case it has escaped your notice, I am a man grown."

Samantha puffed out a breath and rolled her eyes most comically. "Yeah, I'd kind of noticed you were all grown up."

He grinned at her. "So long as all you do is notice, there is no harm in it. And I will make Chalcedony understand that we have not broken her trust, and that she owes you an apology for her unkind words."

"Yeah. Good luck with that, Champ. I thought she'd have caved by now."

The taxi pulled over to the curb outside the studio, and Wulf opened the door. Before he got out, he turned to Samantha. "I do not like the idea of you being out alone at night, unescorted. You should attend Chalcedony's celebration with me. I would see you both on speaking terms again for your sake, as much as hers."

Samantha only waggled her eyebrows in an insinuating

fashion. "I don't plan on being alone for long."

He scowled at her, believing her carefree attitude foolish. Women might hold the power in this world, but there were still predators about. Scum such as Ray, who'd tried to impose himself on Chalcedony against her will. "Be cautious with your choice of bed-partners, then. I do not believe you would appreciate me teaching whomever you choose a lesson he will never forget."

"Aw, it's so sweet that you care, Wulf. Muwah." She pressed her lips to his cheek, and then rubbed at the sticky mark her lip-rouge had left with her thumb. "You look hot, by the way. She won't be able to resist you. And I have impeccable taste in clothing. Not that you need to thank me again or anything. I'm just sayin'."

He rolled his eyes in what he hoped was a fair imitation of her most favored gesture. "Thank you."

"Now get your fine ass up there and show Chalcey Laureano who's boss, okay?"

He stood at the curb, and lifted a hand in farewell as the taxi sped off. The booming of loud music provoked him to glance up at Chalcedony's studio and to envision the woman herself. She'd drifted through his dreams and his every waking moment since he'd left her. His yearning to lay eyes on her again had become so strong, so compelling, that he'd awoken in the dead of night with his palms pushing on the locked door as if to escape Samantha's apartment, and no recollection of leaving his bed.

He pressed a fist to the dull throb pulsing in his belly. Unsurprisingly, the pain had eased the nearer he drew to Chalcedony's studio. This magical link he had to her was a cleverly designed torment, indeed, but the constant physical pain of being parted from her had been nothing compared to the mental torment he'd endured. It had taken all his considerable will not to go to her. But when it came to dealing with what Samantha termed a modern-day woman, he deferred to

Samantha's opinion. Chalcedony was as at least as strong-willed and stubborn as Wulf knew himself to be. It would not have helped his cause to present himself at her studio merely hours after he'd departed, and thus concede her the upper hand.

Samantha had convinced him that this celebration was the perfect opportunity to go to Chalcedony with the expectation that she would, gods willing, be distracted by the other guests and prepared to be reasonable. He intended to spirit her away somewhere private to discuss what the future might hold for them both. And this time, he would restrain his urges—provided that he did not lay his hands upon her and lose himself in her scent, and her body. Her.

He pictured her yearning for him, wondering about him, dreaming of him… as he yearned and wondered and dreamt of her. Gods almighty. He had set himself a difficult task.

The street door was propped open to admit guests. He could delay no longer. The lure of her was too forceful to deny. Wulf strode inside and took the stairs three at a time.


A REMIXED VERSION of Kaoma's *Lambada* echoed throughout the room. The opening night party was in full swing and Chalcey's studio was packed. Even better, her scheduled classes for the weeks ahead were already filling fast. Jai, her dance partner and fellow teacher, was thrilled to itty bitty pieces. He was already rubbing his well-manicured hands with glee, mentally calculating his share of the class fees, and, if Chalcey knew him as well as she thought she did, planning an expedition to the mall.

She should have been dancing with joy. Instead, she felt completely gutted, like a huge part of her was missing. She'd not heard a peep from her so-called best friend for two whole days. And as for her so-called best friend's new houseguest….

It was because of *him* that she'd hardly slept. Her nights had been spent lying awake, chewing over every conversation she'd had with Wulf, examining it for every little nuance. And every time she closed her eyes she relived the best sex she'd had in her life. Her appetite had run for cover, too. Pathetic really. Anyone would think she was pining for a lover instead of a one-shower stand.

If all that wasn't bad enough, she'd been hounded by random phone calls all hours of the day and night. Whenever she picked up there was silence. She knew someone was there—she could hear them breathing. But he or she never spoke and the caller ID was blocked, so Chalcey finally resorted to turning down the phone's ringer and letting the answering machine pick up. She knew she'd have to do something about the harassment at some stage, but right now, prank calls were the least of her worries.

"What's up with you, doll?" Jai insinuated his knee between her thighs and arched her backward in a deep, slow-motion arc that swept her hair across the floor.

Once he'd pulled her up 'til they were groin to groin, nose to nose again, she said, "I'm fine."

He curled his lip. "Yeah, babe, you're completely fine. You've barely got your mind on this demo and that's not like you at all. What gives? You look like you're fretting over a man. Either that or you've lost your best friend."

She pondered his prophetic words as she wiggled atop his thigh and pretended to gaze lustfully into his worried brown eyes. "I fucked a guy on Friday night, Jai. A complete stranger who followed me home from a nightclub." His eyes widened in shock but before he could respond further, she shimmied off to do the split part of the routine.

Jai came up behind her and grabbed her hips, grinding himself into her nether regions, and sliding his hands down the sides of her breasts. Lambada is a blatantly sexy dance, especially when performed while wearing a short, flirty, ass-skimming skirt and a midriff-baring top. There was nothing personal between her and Jai. Sensuality is key when performing a couples demo that will draw in an audience, and Chalcey and Jai always liked to give it their all.

"Go, Chalce!" Jai murmured into her ear. "Was he good?"

"Mmmhmm. Very good."

"Are you going to see him again?" He twirled her a few times before they settled into the groin-grind again.

"I don't know. He's staying with Sam at the moment."

"Oh noes!" He rolled his eyes before burying his face in her neck and pretending to nuzzle her. "You can kiss his sweet ass goodbye, then. If he's got a cock and can get it up, he's history. She won't be able to keep her hands off him. Ready for another dip?"

"Always."

"How about the Nutcracker?" That was Jai's pet name for a move that ended with Chalcey clasping both legs around his waist, and arching backward with her arms outstretched.

"It's hardly a Lambada move."

"So? It'll really get the crowd going."

"You're the lead."

He twirled her out until their arms were fully extended, and as he tugged her back toward him, she launched herself into the air. The idea was that she ended up with her hands on Jai's shoulders, with him grasping her waist, holding her high in the air. Then he would let her slide down his body until she was positioned right, and she would wrap her legs around his hips and lean backward. They'd christened the move the Nutcracker because the first few times they'd tried it, Chalcey kept kneeing Jai in the crotch. He swore blind that she'd bruised his family jewels so bad they'd never been the same.

Jai's previous dance partner had been a diminutive little thing who was easy to sling around, so it took a while for him to adjust to Chalcey's height and much bigger boobs. Chalcey knew from experience that it was seriously off-putting for a guy to cop a face full of breasts when he was seriously trying to dance. Thankfully, the Nutcracker went off without living up to its name and Jai's 'nads remained intact for another night. Plus, she didn't smother him with her cleavage. All in all, a raging success.

As she arched backward, she opened her eyes and glimpsed Wulf watching her. He was dressed in unfamiliar clothes— jeans and a light silky sweater—but even upside down, she'd have recognized him anywhere. Or to be accurate, her body recognized and responded to him. Some unseen link that'd been forged between them snapped into place and surged with such yearning, such desire, that Chalcey thrummed with the need to lift his sweater and run her hands across his bare skin. She wanted to throw herself at him, cling to him and beg him to fuck her senseless.

Her world tilted again but all she could see was Wulf. She didn't even register Jai bringing her back up to a standing position. She didn't even notice him spinning her out, and then winding her in to his side to perform the closing move of the demo.

The crowd clapped and whistled.

Blinking like a myopic owl, she snapped from her trance and glanced up. Her arm was fully extended upward, hand angled, fingers elegantly spread, exactly the same as when she'd practiced this final move with Jai. She didn't remember performing the actions. Complete autopilot. Just went to show what lots and lots of practice could achieve.

Her gaze sought Wulf's again.

Smart man that he was, Jai took mere seconds to conclude that she was too distracted to get her shit together. He announced that the next demo would be in a half-hour, and encouraged everyone to get up and dance.

"Chalcey, doll, what—?" He absorbed the expression on her face, and then followed the direction of her gaze. "Wahoo, baby! That hunky dude eyeing you with blind lust is your casual fuck-buddy? Somehow don't think he's too interested in what the lovely Samantha has on offer. Poor chicky. She must be losing her touch. And I gotta give you full marks for your choice of man, Chalcey. I'd go for him myself if I thought he'd be interested. Pity he's so... so... obviously hetero."

Jai sauntered toward Wulf.

Chalcey fought free of the shroud of raw sensuality that had mantled her and hurried after him. For some reason it was vitally important to her that Wulf understood Jai was her dance partner. That they were employer and employee. Friends, yes, but nothing more. And it was even more imperative that she confirmed whether or not Wulf had succumbed to Sam's wiles. She had to look him right in the eye to know for sure.

Some best friend she was. Chalcey loved Sam to bits and beyond, and she knew damn well the feeling was mutual. She trusted Sam implicitly... didn't she?

Yes! Huh. Usually. Maybe not in this case. Heck, Sam was only human. How could she resist a guy like Wulf? Plus, Chalcey had insisted she wasn't interested in him, even tried to fob him off onto Sam. So if they *had* gotten together, Chalcey only had herself to blame.

If they had gotten together, she would back off, pretend she didn't care. She'd even go so far as to congratulate Sam. With any luck she would be totally convincing, too. Only trouble with that stellar plan was the nearer she got to Wulf, the more uncertainty gripped her. All her staunch resolve twittered around the room and flitted out the metaphorical window. There was a reason people claimed that ignorance was bliss. Did she really want to—?

Shit! Chalcey launched herself at Wulf and hung on to his arm to prevent him from landing a punch in Jai's face.

"Whoa, big boy!" Displaying an excellent sense of self-preservation, Jai had scuttled backward, out of reach. "Hey, cool it, man. I'm her dance partner, nothing more. I don't *like* women that way! They're just too—" He waved an ineffectual hand. "Well, suffice it to say, gimme your big hard body over her soft girly bits any day, *capiche*?" He cut his gaze to Chalcey. "Sorry, doll, didn't mean to be insulting."

"No probs, Jai. I'm sure Wulf understands. Don't you, Wulf?" Chalcey could feel the tension thrumming in his arm, his muscles tensed and poised to inflict a great deal of pain. "Wulf, meet Jai. My *dance* partner."

Jai stuck out his hand then snatched it back when Wulf growled at him—really growled, like a... a... hungry wolf.

Uh oh. This was so not going well. "Jai likes men," she blurted. "Not women. He'd much prefer to take *you* to bed than me."

Wulf relaxed minutely. And then, as her words sank in, he tensed again, staring at Jai. "You desire to *bed* me?"

Jai struck a pose, head cocked to one side and finger tapping his nose. His eyes raked Wulf from head to toe, lingering on the considerable bulge in the crotch of Wulf's jeans.

Chalcey stifled a giggle at Wulf's shocked expression.

"I do not—" Wulf composed his features, smoothing all dismay from his face. And when he spoke, his tone was careful. "I am unfamiliar with your customs, and I can only tender my apologies for any misunderstanding. I am not a lover of men."

Jai chortled. "Chill, Wulf-man, you're too much testosterone for poor little ole me. I'm off to find a partner who don't mind *me* being the man." He sashayed off, blowing Wulf a cheeky kiss over his shoulder.

Jai was hardly little *or* old. Six-foot-even, he could only be described as one gorgeous male specimen. He had a physique to drool over and he was strong too—otherwise he would never have coped with being Chalcey's dance partner. And being gay didn't prevent every red-blooded girl he met from trying to get into his pants. Even the thought of Wulf and Jai as a couple made Chalcey grin. Women all over the world would weep buckets and gnash their teeth in dismay.

Wulf caught her by the shoulders, and with the touch of his

hands, all thoughts of Jai fled. There was only Wulf. No one else mattered.

"I have missed you these past two days, Chalcedony. Samantha told me of this celebration and I waited eagerly for the day to arrive so that I could see you again."

"Oh."

"That is all you have to say to me? I have suffered the pain of being parted from you and you say only, 'Oh'?" He gave her a little shake and her body thrilled.

She blinked up at him. It took a huge effort of will to prod her brain to logical thought. "Where's Sam?"

"Samantha is seeking other entertainments, tonight. She thought it best if she stayed away until you and I had resolved our differences."

"She couldn't face me, huh?"

Wulf shook his head. "That is not the impression I received when she brought me here. She is a complicated woman, Samantha."

"You and Sam. Did you—? Um, you didn't, like, you know—"

Her fears and doubts and the dread that overshadowed everything must have been etched on her features. Or perhaps it was the ever-so-slight tremor in her voice that she hadn't been able to prevent, because he hugged her to his chest, tucking her head beneath his chin. "I did not bed her, Chalcedony. She is not the woman for me."

"Oh." She sighed, inhaling his unique scent, letting it curl through her. "Good. I'm glad."

He nuzzled her hairline. "Why are you glad?"

"Because... because.... Just *because*, all right?" She pushed away from him, suddenly uneasy with the potency of her feelings for a man she barely knew. And unwilling to blurt any premature declarations that might reveal her as even more vulnerable than she already felt.

"Chalcedony—"

"Don't push me, Wulf. This is—" She speared her fingers through her hair, tugging viciously on the ends, willing the small pain to lend her the words she needed. "I don't know what this is. And there're too many other things going on in my life right now—important things. I don't know what to do about you. Just give me some time, okay?"

His face hardened. "'Tis ironic that even though I have been waiting an eternity, I now must grant you more *time*. Will you risk losing this bond we share because what you feel for me scares you? Are you that cowardly?"

"And what exactly *do* I feel for you, Wulf? Tell me please, 'coz I'd really like someone to explain it to me."

"You want to bed me as much as I want to bed you, Chalcedony. You want me inside of you. You know that is what you want."

"That's not fair. I hardly know you, Wulf. You just waltz into my life and take what you want, then expect me to fall panting at your feet? I can't deny I'm attracted to you. But I don't do casual sex."

"What we have is in no way casual, Chalcedony." And damned if he didn't scoop her up and kiss her again. His lips had no need to punish and demand, not when hers softened and sighed open and gave him permission to plunder. He rewarded her with tenderness, with hands that cradled her nape and cupped her face like she was a precious jewel, and lips that claimed hers with the gentlest of butterfly brushes. It was not enough. She wanted more. She pressed herself against him, entwined her hands in his hair and held his head immobile while she took his mouth, thrusting with her tongue, drinking him down, until he responded in kind.

When she came up for air, she bunched her fists in his silky sweater and struggled to catch her breath. "I wish we hadn't done that."

"Why?" His blue eyes twinkled at her, smugly pleased. He knew very well why.

"Because I can't think straight when you kiss me, that's why."

"Why?"

"How the fuck should I know?" she said.

"You can't think straight because you're mesmerized, Chalcedony," said a clipped, I-know-it-all-and-you-need-to-shut-up-and-listen voice.

The fine hairs on the back of Chalcey's neck rose. Her stomach plummeted to the floor. Oh no. Not her. Not now. What the heck had she done to deserve this?

She tried to twist around, only succeeding when Wulf finally permitted her to turn in his arms. And there Chalcey's nemesis stood in all her Ice-Queen glory. Elegantly dressed, perfectly coiffed, unnaturally composed.

Crap. Chalcey squeezed her eyelids shut and leaned back against Wulf's chest, grateful for his protective arms, thinking that he might just be the lesser of the two evils.

# CHAPTER EIGHT

A SURPRISE VISIT from her mother. Just what Chalcey needed. Not.

They had issues. Long-standing ones that dated back to when her dad had died... and that had never been resolved.

Beryl Francesca Laureano-Owens—she went by her middle name of Francesca—was Chalcey's antithesis. Blue-eyed and svelte. No in-your-face boobs for Francesca. She was a woman who could have her pick of men, a dead ringer for those blonde Germanic beauties so often featured in glossy European magazines. Which, to Chalcey's mind, had always made it even more surprising that she'd fallen head over heels for a stocky, nice looking but nothing special, Puerto Rican bricklayer.

Benigno had loved Frannie—as he called her—with a passion. And when their daughter was born, he had more than enough love for them both. Chalcey had adored her father. He had been the glue that held his family together. And when he died, everything fell apart.

Chalcey had only been ten. At first she didn't understand why her mother could barely even look at her without flinching, why Francesca had spent more and more time hanging out in the little store she managed with her New Age friends. It was only when one of those friends had mentioned Chalcey not resembling her mother at all, and getting all her looks from her father, that she'd understood. It didn't hurt any less, but at least she understood.

And she would have forgiven her mother, too, if Francesca hadn't remarried barely a year after losing her husband. Worse, it was to Edgar Owens, a man who was all about appearances, a man who was as polished and brittle and fake as Francesca had become.

As a child, Chalcey had hated this man who smiled at her with her mouth, but not his eyes, and pretended to be interested in her. She would have traded all the expensive gifts he showered on her in a heartbeat for one of her dad's hugs. But all her childish prayers for Edgar to vanish from their lives had remained unanswered. The marriage worked—unlike Edgar's relationship with his stepdaughter. Edgar's fussy, pedantic ways drove Chalcey up the wall and she'd left home as soon as she could stand on her own two feet. She didn't have a clue how her mother put up with him. Evidently, if a man was rich enough, he'd always find someone willing to stick around and put up with him. Unfortunately for Chalcey, that someone had been her mother.

"Hello Francesca," she said. Her tone sounded as flat and colorless as she felt inside. She couldn't help it. Her mother always made her feel inferior. "So nice of you to drop by."

"Chalcedony." Francesca's gaze skimmed her and flicked to Wulf. She eyed him with her own particular brand of speculative eyes—think drills boring through a person until they graunch on bone.

"Darling." The endearment was directed at Chalcey, but her mother's gaze remained firmly fixed on Wulf. "Are you going to introduce me to your handsome lover?"

"Why, no, Francesca. I don't think I am." Chalcey felt Wulf shift restlessly behind her, doubtless disconcerted by her rudeness. She didn't gave a rat's ass about how rude she sounded. He didn't know her dear, darling, not-so-adorable mother. Francesca could make Sam's mom seem like Mary Poppins.

"I am Wulf," he said.

"I'm sure you are, dear," Francesca said. "But I'd like to know your *true* name." At complete odds with her saccharine-sweet tone, her gaze was fiercely intent.

Chalcey wondered at Wulf's unnatural stillness—not to mention Francesca's bizarre phrasing and emphasis on the word "true".

"'Tis Wulfenite."

Chalcey had switched her attention to her mother, so although Francesca quickly blanked her expression it was too late. Chalcey had already noted her strong reaction to learning Wulf's full name.

Fear? Loathing? Dismay? Whatever, it sure as hell piqued Chalcey's curiosity.

"And I'm Francesca," her mother said. "I'm delighted to meet you… Wulf."

Delighted, my ass, Chalcey thought. Beneath the excruciating politeness there were some major undercurrents swirling.

"Do you mind if I whisk Chalcedony away for a minute, Wulf?" Francesca asked. "I need to speak with her."

Nyuh uh. No way was she dealing with her mother's dramas right now. Chalcey had enough dramas of her very own to deal with.

"I'm sure you do, Francesca," she said. "Unfortunately, I have another demo scheduled. Because yanno, surprising as it may seem, my priority right now is promoting my new studio so I can make a decent living. I'm off to find Jai." She shoved Wulf's protective arms away and stalked off, hugely grateful for a valid excuse to escape her mother's clutches.

There was an art to pulling off a really good stalk when her skirt barely covered her butt—the same butt Chalcey knew was swaying a heap more provocatively than she intended because of her four-inch heels. But she managed it. And she was even more proud that she didn't glance back to see whether Wulf was noticing the aforementioned swaying butt. She'd bet anything that he was noticing, though. And, if there was a God, suffering.

Her pride was short-lived. Her shoulders had tensed up and she was hunching in on herself, as always happened around her mother. Francesca had a habit of arriving at the most inconvenient times. It was just like her to turn up now, right when life had become reeeally complicated.

Chalcey made straight for the drinks table in search of something to bolster her courage and help her loosen up a bit. And damned if she didn't bump into another complication.

"Marcus? Uh, hi! What are you doing here?" Chalcey fixed what she hoped was a welcoming smile on her face and prayed that her expression didn't send him gibbering with terror out into the night.

"Hey, Chalcey." He took her hands and leaned in to kiss her cheek. "Sam mentioned your new studio was about to open, so I tracked it down."

"If you're looking for Sam—"

"I'm not." A muscle worked in his jaw.

"Oh?" She allowed him the lie. "Come to check out potential *dance* partners or potential partners?"

"Maybe both." He relaxed enough to grin, at least until his gaze focused over her shoulder. His jaw dropped and his eyes widened. "Phwoar. How many classes do I have to take before I can dance like *that*?"

Chalcey swiveled on her heel to see Jai bumping and grinding with a pretty little blonde perched astride his thigh. Her tight black skirt had worked its way so far up her thighs that anyone who cared to look could see her panties. Plenty cared to look, so Chalcey could only be grateful the girl was wearing some.

She watched Marcus watching Jai. Or rather, the girl. Some of her own tension eased. *This* she could handle. Sam had skipped out on Marcus. Made sense that he was on the prowl. And given that Marcus had never been interested in Chalcey, she wouldn't have to worry about Wulf going all alpha and whupping Marcus's ass. Things were looking up.

"Dance *like* that, or *with* that?" she said, her tone deliberately teasing.

"Depends," Marcus said, turning his full attention back to her.

"On what?" Too late she caught the gleam in his eyes.

He swooped in, cupped her chin in his hands, and planted one right on her lips.

She froze. Usually she'd have been thrilled to itty bitty pieces to have a guy like Marcus make a play for her. But he'd recently slept with her best friend. And Sam was confused about her feelings for him. So until Sam sorted out those feelings, Marcus was off-limits.

There was one other thing. A really big, quite unexpected thing. Marcus was a pretty damn fine kisser, and his kiss would normally have curled Chalcey's toes. But she couldn't help comparing him to Wulf. And there was no comparison.

Drat the man. He'd better not have ruined her for any other male.

As though magically summoned, the man of her thoughts appeared. He towered over her and his growl stroked delicious shivers up and down her bare arms. He plucked Marcus from her and tossed him aside.

Scenting trouble, people gathered around them. The air of gleeful anticipation was palpable. Shit. The absolute last thing that Chalcey needed was for her studio to have a rep as a place where men brawled over women.

Dance studios were the last bastion of socially acceptable sensuality between strangers. Her students could get up close and personal with people of the opposite sex—within the strictures of the particular dance, of course—and not have their actions taken the wrong way. Partner dancing provided an opportunity to flirt and be a little bit naughty, without all the inevitable strings attached. No freaking way was she going to have everything she'd worked for ruined by some testosterone-driven display of pathetic male jealousy.

She rounded on Wulf, pissed to the max by his inappropriate public display of possessiveness. "Cut it out, Wulf. You don't own me. If I want to kiss another man, I'll kiss another man. Back off. This OTT behavior is unacceptable and I will not tolerate it in my studio. Is that clear?"

Marcus had picked himself up off the floor. He strode over to stand beside Chalcey, providing a united front. Ironic, much? Hell yeah, considering that he was part of the problem. She didn't dare take her gaze from Wulf but from what she could see out of the corner of her eye, it appeared that Marcus was fairly bristling with indignation.

Great. Just freaking great.

"Who's this guy think he is, Chalcey? He your boyfriend?"

"No! He's not my boyfriend. He's a… a… an *acquaintance* who, uh, turned up at the studio needing a place to stay." Chalcey's gaze slid from Wulf's, unwilling to witness the impact of her words.

But focusing on Marcus was worse. He was eyeing her like he'd decided she was some dimwitted bimbo who hadn't the faintest idea how to look after herself. "Is that a good idea?" he asked. "If you don't know him that well—"

"Quit worrying. Sam's looking after him and—"

Marcus paled and jerked back like he'd been sucker punched. "He's *Sam's* boyfriend?"

"I am Wulf. Samantha is under my protection. State your claim, or be gone."

"Not helping, Wulf!" Chalcey closed her eyes and rubbed the tension spot between her brows. Crap. This was so not going well. Why couldn't she keep her mouth shut? She'd just made everything a thousand times worse.

When she dared open her eyes again, it was to see Wulf staring at Marcus with a semi-bored expression, like Marcus was a particularly insignificant bug, unworthy of his notice.

"Is that right?" Marcus threw back his shoulders, puffing himself up to appear larger. The gesture was so intrinsically male, Chalcey would have laughed if she hadn't been frantically trying to figure out how best to smooth things over and clue Marcus in without betraying Sam's confidences.

"That is indeed right," Wulf said, in a fair imitation of Marcus. "In all fairness, I must warn you that in my experience Samantha requires a man who will challenge her. Not a sullen boy who seeks solace with another man's woman."

Marcus's jaw worked and his eyes slitted with rage. He lunged at Wulf.

Chalcey darted forward in a misguided attempt to prevent an all-out brawl just as Marcus swung a punch.

Bad move—real bad. Because Marcus had an impressive right hook and even though he did his utmost to pull his punch at the last instant, when his fist connected with her chin it still laid her out flat.

The room spun. She couldn't move except to blink. And try to breathe. She shut her eyes against the sparkly stars cavorting through her headspace.

Wulf—she'd know his scent and the feel of him anywhere—plucked her from the floor. Vaguely, as though from a great distance, she heard Jai diverting the enthralled crowd by announcing a free Salsa class and enlisting Paulo and Leah to teach it. Thank God for Jai. The swell of the music, the murmurs of the crowd and Paulo's yelled instructions were abruptly quelled as the bedroom door slid shut.

Wulf sat on the edge of the bed with Chalcey cradled in his arms. Her jaw chose that moment to begin to throb and when she moved it experimentally, the pain swelled.

The door swooshed open and then closed again. She heard her mother's voice issuing instructions and Jai's murmured assent. Wulf's body tensed, and the arms that held her tightened to steely bands.

And then Marcus said, "Chalcey, I'm so sorry. I just lost it.

I didn't mean to hit you."

"'S all right, Marcus," she slurred, peeling open her eyelids to focus on his stricken face. "I know it was an accident. 'S one of those stupid things that happens, huh? 'Sides, I shouldn't have gotten in the way."

"Yeah, that was pretty dumb."

"Indeed," Wulf said.

"You two agree on something?" she joked weakly. "Oh, be still my beating heart!"

"Hush, Chalcedony," Francesca said. "This is hardly a laughing matter."

"The highlight of my opening night party's gonna be a brawl instead of dance demos. Yeah, it's not funny at all." The tears she'd been holding inside spilled out and she buried her face in Wulf's chest.

He stroked soothing circles on her back with his palm. "What is wrong, Chalcedony? Do you suffer pain?"

"Do I suffer pain?" She giggled through her tears. "Oh, I suffer pain all right. I'm suffering from a couple of really big ones, in fact." She mopped at her face with her palms until Francesca pressed a lace handkerchief into her hand.

"I think she means you," Marcus informed Wulf, his tone insufferably triumphant.

Chalcey sniffled, and struggled to sit up a bit straighter in Wulf's arms. "I meant you, too, Marcus. You've put me in a really awkward spot here." She pulled herself together. Time to quit sniveling because no matter how shitty she felt, it was time to go in to bat for her best friend. "Aren't you interested in Sam anymore? I thought you were like, *really* interested."

He stared at her, eyes darkened with what Chalcey thought might be a combination of anger and hope. "Sam told you."

"Duh. Of course Sam told me. Well?"

"I— Fuck. Maybe. Depends on Sam. I haven't been able to track her down since she cut out on me. And now there's *this* guy." He indicated Wulf with a gesture that managed to convey disgust and a heap of dislike.

"I am not interested in bedding Samantha." Wulf's flatly implacable tone brooked no argument.

"Sam really likes you, Marcus." Chalcey blew her nose on her mother's pathetic little excuse for a hanky.

"If this is interested, she's sure playing hard to get," he muttered.

"Mmmm. She's not the only one."

He had the grace to appear abashed, which would have gratified the heck out of Chalcey if her jaw wasn't throbbing. "Sorry," he said.

"Sorry for what? For sleeping with my best friend after she picked you up in a club, and when she leaves you high and dry, hitting on me to try and make her jealous?" She knew she'd hit a raw spot when Marcus winced.

"Sam made it pretty clear she was only interested in keeping it casual, so I knew exactly what I was getting in to. I suppose I thought she'd changed her mind when we—" He scrubbed his face with his hands. "And when she took off without leaving her number— Shit. Anyway, you can't blame a guy for trying."

"'S okay, Marcus. Sam's pretty hard to resist when she wants someone. Better men than you have tried and failed."

"Thanks a lot."

"Marcus, please. Don't write her off completely. She's scared about what she feels for you, is all."

"Really."

"Yes. Really. Look, deep down she's looking for the same thing we all are, the—"

"Right man!" Jai crowed, as he rejoined the crowd in Chalcey's small bedroom. "Gotta agree with that sentiment."

"Do you want Sam's number or not?" Chalcey asked, determined to see this through to the end. She'd already betrayed Sam's confidence. Might as well make it really count.

Marcus stood there, all "no woman's gonna make a fool

outta me" staunch, and just when Chalcey was about to give him up for a lost cause, he nodded.

She recited Sam's number for him and waited for him to program it into his cell.

"Good decision, dude," Jai said, clapping Marcus on the back. "Everybody out. Right now. Chalcey needs quiet, an icepack and some painkillers. Take your manly crap elsewhere, you two." He fixed Wulf and Marcus with the evil eye à la Jai. "And don't even think of taking it back into the studio or I'll call the cops and have you both booted out on your fine asses. Heck, I'll even sell tickets to the grand event."

Marcus eyed Jai, and then backed out of the room without a murmur.

The same couldn't be said for Wulf. Huh. Why did that not surprise her?

It was tempting to snuggle into the warmth of his body, let him block out the world and help her forget about her problems. In other words, beg him to repeat the shower incident. In the bed, this time. And maybe afterward they could adjourn to the shower.

She wished she could channel Sam right now. Sam wouldn't have any problems with bundling everyone out of her bedroom and asking a guy to stick around. But she wasn't Sam. She didn't have that kind of "the future can go shoot for the moon because I'm getting laid by a hot guy" attitude. Besides, Wulf was part of Chalcey's problem. A big part. If she were completely honest, she was so damned gone on him that he'd become The Problem, almost to the exclusion of everything else in her life. And Chalcey had worked too hard, come too far, to toss her dreams aside for a man she'd just met. Even if that man was Wulf.

CHALCEDONY STIRRED, PRODDING Wulf to fight free of the haze of lust and longing that she'd enveloped him in. The tiny jerking of her muscles, the tension in her spine, told him she was conflicted. Part of her seemed content to stay right where she was, in his arms. Another part of her wanted very much to move away, most likely to distance herself from him so that she could think.

He couldn't blame her. The vanilla-sweetness of the shampoo she used on her hair, the berry flavored salve she'd painted on her lips, the heady scent of whatever she'd sprayed on her body, were honeyed traps that enticed him to hold her closer, to taste her, to press his lips to the skittish pulse in her throat and soothe her concerns… despite the knowing stare of the man she'd danced so provocatively with, and the antagonistic eyes of the woman, Francesca. Instead, he eased Chalcedony from his lap, onto the mattress, and stood staring down at her.

"You, too, Wulf-man," her dance partner—Jai—said. "Give her some space."

Wulf wasn't inclined to allow any man to dictate to him where Chalcedony was concerned. "Do you wish for me to go, Chalcedony?"

"It's not about what she wants," Francesca said, her tone sharp enough to cut. "It's about what's best for her. And you're not it."

Wulf fixed his gaze on her. She flinched, but held her ground. He wondered what he'd done to earn her instant dislike, and why she was so protective of Chalcedony.

"Quit mothering me," Chalcey said, sounding tired and distant, lacking her usual spark of stubborn defiance. "I've been pretty much looking after myself since Dad died."

Francesca's face blanked of all expression but Wulf had spent many years observing potential opponents. With her words alone, Chalcedony had delivered a painful blow to the other woman. Ah yes. He could see it now—the similarities in the bone structure of their faces, the set of their mouths, the graceful way they held themselves. Mother and daughter. With a lifetime of shared hurts to overcome.

Still, it was not his concern whether Chalcedony's mother

approved or disapproved of him. The only one whose opinion mattered was the woman huddled on the bed, knees drawn up to her chin, unwilling to meet his gaze. "Do you wish me to leave you be, Chalcedony?" he asked.

"Yes. I do. Please."

She lied. He knew it in his gut, in his soul, in the telltale slump of her shoulders, and the tears trickling down her cheeks that she didn't attempt to hide. He didn't argue with her, even knowing that it would have been so very easy to bend her to his will. One kiss and she would have been his. But tempting as it was to use that knowledge to his advantage, Wulf held back. If he used such underhanded wiles, she would only repeat her previous actions. She would use him to assuage her physical needs and afterward, be so racked with guilt and self-loathing that she would push him away.

No. He would not make the same mistake again. This time, she would have to come to him, knowing full well what she sought, and what the inevitable outcome would be. "You know where to find me," he said, and left her to her watchful guardians.

Walking away from her, again, was the hardest thing he'd ever done. Especially when he was well aware from Francesca's carefully worded phrasing that she somehow understood the significance a true name held for Styrians of the warrior caste.

How had Chalcedony's mother come to possess that sort of knowledge?

If he'd correctly interpreted the protective determination in Francesca's gaze, Chalcedony would soon become privy to whatever Francesca knew. Or thought she knew. And *he* knew in his bones that a woman like Francesca, a woman who looked at him with such fear and loathing in her eyes, would not hesitate to twist the facts and try to turn Chalcedony against him.

# CHAPTER NINE

J AI DEMONSTRATED ONCE again that he was Mr. Efficiency
in a crisis. Chalcey was tucked beneath the comforter, and
given painkillers and an icepack for her bruised jaw before
she could form a coherent thought. Unfortunately, even Jai
was fallible. The quiet he'd promised was not going to happen,
because when he left, he didn't take Francesca with him. She
so wasn't looking forward to Francesca's inevitable lecture.

She waited. And waited. And waited some more.

Finally, hoping her mother had sneaked out of the room,
she pried open her eyes.

"Chalcedony."

Drat. "Yes?"

"Are you in love with Wulf?"

"In love? Puhlease. I hardly know him. I'm certainly not in
love with him." In lust maybe, but not in love.

Francesca sighed. Theatrically. She'd always been a master
at highlighting Chalcey's supposed inability to grasp what was
really important. "Unfortunately, Wulf loves *you*—in his way.
As much as a man like him is able to love."

*Broadside your daughter with a change of subject, why don't
you?* "Yeah, riiight. Like you can tell after having met him for
what, five whole minutes?"

"I know what I know."

Argh. She hated it to bits and beyond when Francesca
pulled that crap. How was anyone supposed to muster a co-

herent response to a cryptic statement like that?

"And I have no doubt that *this* has something to do with the way you are feeling." Francesca thrust something so close to Chalcey's face that her eyes crossed and she saw double. She heaved herself upward from her prone position and scooted up the mattress to lean against the wall... and  discovered that she wasn't seeing double at all because Francesca happened to be brandishing the two halves of broken crystal Chalcey had stuck on the crate beside her bed.

"That? Gee whiz, Francesca, they're broken hunks of stone. Are they by any chance supposed to be a brilliantly accurate metaphor representing my hypothetically soon to be broken heart?"

"Where did you get this crystal from, Chalcedony?"

"So far as I can figure out, some weird old guy gave it to me after I wandered into his store. It's obviously some cheap crappy stone because it broke shortly afterward. Do you want it? You can add it—them—to your collection if you like."

Her mother's gaze sharpened. "Can you take me to this store?"

Unease twisted Chalcey's stomach. She tried for light and airy, hoping that she could play down the incident. "Probably not. I looked for it again after—" She bit her lip before she could blurt all about the café and the episode of lost time. Francesca would have a field day and Chalcey would never get rid of her. Less was definitely more.

"I searched for the store but I couldn't find it again. Now don't start booking me in for psychiatric evaluation or anything, okay? I was distracted and probably got the wrong street. You know how it is in the city—the entire area is a planning disaster of monumental proportions."

"This old man, can you describe him to me?"

Chalcey sagged with relief. Thank God her mother didn't seem interested in her inability to locate the store. She'd dodged that bullet.

"Focus, Chalcedony. Can you describe the old man?"

"Other than him being old? No. Not really. Why?"

"One more question. Now think very carefully. Did anything strange happen when the crystal broke?"

"Jeez, Francesca, since I'm not sure exactly *when* it broke, I couldn't tell you. Why the second Spanish Inquisition, huh? You heard Jai, I need rest and quiet—*quiet* being the operative word here."

Her mother dished some superlative evil eyes but Chalcey hung tough and refused to volunteer any further information. "Very well," Francesca finally said. "I'll leave you alone to rest for a while. But before I go, would you like to know the name of this crystal you value so little?"

"You mean the useless damn crystal I got for *free*?"

"It's wulfenite." Dropping the pieces into Chalcey's lap, she swept from the bedroom. She always did know how to make an impressive exit.

Chalcey fingered the broken pieces of wulfenite crystal and tried very hard to think happy thoughts. Because if she dwelled on the possible implications of that stunning coincidence, she was likely to go nuts.

She flopped back down on the bed and closed her eyes... and ended up reviewing the moments immediately before her encounter with Wulf. She'd tripped and fallen when the heel snapped off her sandal. Her bag had gone flying. Was that when the crystal had broken?

Maybe. Probably.

And then.... And then Wulf had appeared on the scene to rescue her from Ray.

Shit. Could Wulf have emerged from the crystal when it broke?

Nah.

But then she recalled the crystals she'd seen in the store, and the old man who had chatted about them and been so eager to show them to her. She stewed over the time she'd lost, obsessed over the overwhelming suspicion that she'd somehow been irrevocably changed since that encounter. And darnitall, she was forced to conclude that it appeared all too possible Wulf *had* come from the crystal. If she believed in that kind of stuff, of course.

Which she didn't.

But what other explanation was there?

Sleep dragged her under and the explanation become crystal clear in her dreams. She saw a man she recognized. Wulf. Strangely, or perhaps it wasn't so strange because this was a dream, she knew his innermost thoughts.

He reined in his mount. He slid from the saddle, stepping back the instant before its yellowed teeth would have torn a chunk from his shoulder. He clouted the beast's nose with his fist. The stallion snorted its displeasure but bothered him no further with its tricks. It was a fine battle-mount but it had an evil temper. And Wulf saw no reason to tame it. He and the horse had an understanding. Wulf was master absolute and in turn, he allowed his mount to indulge itself with any other unfortunate who strayed too close to its teeth or hooves. He knew, though, that if he allowed the beast to better him even once, he would end up flat on his back with a broken neck when he least expected it. And, by the gods, if that ever came to pass he would deserve his fate.

He gazed at the cluster of dwellings nestled in the hollow of the gently undulating, fertile valley far below. A sneer curled his lip. A land of plenty. A soft land, overflowing with bounty and ripe for plucking. Easily conquered—much like its people.

A fine rain misted his exposed skin, its unaccustomed coolness raising tiny bumps on his arms. His clothing, a vest of supple sand-lizard leather, matching trousers and sturdy boots, was well-suited to battling with the other tribes back in his homeland of endless sands and relentless heat. But not so comfortable in this realm.

Whispers of some unnamed power carried on the breeze,

taunting him. The inexorable greenness of the vista before him made his eyes ache, and he found himself yearning for Sol's warmth.

Damn this land to *Halja* for eternity! If he stayed here much longer he would be in danger of becoming as weak and pliant as the females he and his men had captured.

He left his mount to graze, knowing the horse would not stray from such excellent fodder, and strode down from the hillock, calling for his tehun-Leader. "Malach, have we filled our quota of females yet?"

The older man shook his head. "Not quite, Lord Keeper. This last village ought to be doing it."

Wulf grunted. "Good. Then let us make haste so that we may depart this benighted land."

"If I might make a suggestion, Lord Keeper?"

"Speak."

"It has been noticed that Kyan is eyeing up one of captives."

"What do my men say of this, Malach?"

"They *say* nothing. They merely bide their time to see whether or not Kyan will be permitted to take his pick."

Wulf's lip curled. "Like the priests, my kinsman has become overly concerned with his own comforts. Doubtless he bemoans the chill, and rather than riding into battle, he desires a female to warm his privates. If he does not take due care he will become a pathetic and sniveling coward—as are the men of this land." He flexed the shoulder of his sword-arm, working a strained muscle.

Malach remained silent and Wulf allowed himself a moment of pride at the fearsome reputation he had so carefully cultivated amongst his peers. Men learned quickly to hold their tongues around the Lord Keeper of the Shifting Sands fief. One careless word would find a man on the wrong end of Wulf's fist and leave him with his teeth rattling about in his skull—if he were fortunate.

"The females do not yet comprehend the truth of their situation and I would not have it said my men take advantage of their ignorance," he said. "If Kyan harbors a fondness for one of them, then he will offer for her on the Choosing Block as is our way. He rides with us. See to it."

"It shall be done, Lord Keeper." Malach strode off to deliver his Lord's orders.

Wulf watched his tehun-Leader give the blond man the dressing down he deserved. Kyan's hand drifted to his sword but Malach placed a cautionary hand on his arm.

Wulf met his kinsman's gaze, unblinking. A silent battle of wills ensued until Kyan dropped his eyes. Then the man shrugged and grinned, appearing to shed his bad humor as easily as a sand-viper shed its skin. Pounding his fist over his heart, he gestured obeisance to his Lord Keeper.

Confident that he'd asserted absolute authority once more, Wulf turned his back and climbed the hill to his horse. The beast must have sensed his ill-humor and it stood peaceably, waiting for its master to mount up.

From his lofty position, Wulf observed the flurry of activity within his makeshift camp. As the women were herded into a large tent, five men assumed sentry positions about the tent and five more melted into the surrounding countryside to keep vigil. The priests kept to their private quarters and did not deign to make an appearance. Doubtless too busy with their cursed magic rituals to wish their warriors good hunting.

Wulf's second tehun—a troop of ten men—mounted their horses and assumed formation to file out of the camp.

"We ride!" Wulf punched the air with a clenched fist, signaling his men to fall in behind him.

Chalcey's dream took on an eerie familiarity.

An old man named Pieter observed the warriors—the Styrians—in his scrying bowl. He drank his tea, muttered the incantation, sent a fervent prayer to his goddess that he would not fail. He hurried from his hut, his bundle of crystals cradled to his chest.

While the warriors amassed on the hillside, he placed eleven large gemstones in a semicircle on the ground before him. And when Wulf challenged him, Pieter raised his hands to the skies and chanted the incantation.

"Verily the crystal for which thee be named/ Shalt form the prison in which thee be bound/ To atone the sins for which thee be blamed/ 'Til thee be blessed and thy true love be found."

One by one, as Pieter named each of Wulf's men, they were bound to their namesake crystals.

Too late, Wulf charged, screaming defiance. Pieter did not flinch as the blade descended. "Wulfenite, the stone thee be named for shall bind thee. I, *Pietersite*, bind thee!"

Lord Keeper Wulfenite was not spared the fate of his men. He vanished, condemned to a void, imprisoned in the unceasing blackness of a chunk of wulfenite crystal. Until the Crystal Guardian uttered a name. *Chalcedony….*

CHALCEY CLAWED HER way back to consciousness and awoke sweat-glossed, her hand throbbing. Only when she flexed her fingers did she realize she was clutching the broken pieces of crystal. Foreboding slimed her skin, making her shiver. She thrust the pieces under her pillow, out of sight….

Unfortunately not out of mind. The old man from her dream, the one who'd cast the spell. He was so very familiar—

The jolt of recognition that smacked her was so strong she bolted upright, clutching the sheet and gasping for breath. She *did* know him.

Memories crashed in on her, and she flopped back against her pillows, limp as a dishrag as she fought to process them. Oh. My. God. The old man who'd defied the Stone Warriors was the same old man from the store. But…. But he had to be centuries old. That was impossible, wasn't it?

Apparently not.

And this same old man, Pieter, had held her hand over his crystals and one had responded—

No. It hadn't been the *crystal* that had responded, it had been the man entrapped in the crystal. He'd reached out to her and she'd answered. Wulf. The leader of the men Pieter had trapped in the crystals, and the same man who'd turned her world upside down with a mere kiss.

Unbelievable as it all seemed, she knew in her soul it was true. And although she fully understood Pieter's desire to protect his people from alien raiders, she could only be appalled that he would condemn living breathing beings to such a fate. For centuries, Wulf had been imprisoned in a black hole where he could neither see, hear, nor feel. It was a wonder he wasn't stark raving insane.

Dammit! Why hadn't Wulf told her the truth? Her brain churned with so many unanswered questions that she didn't know where to start. She needed to track Wulf down. Confront him. Insist that he tell her what the eff was going on. Like, right now.

She stripped off her dress, threw on jeans and a t-shirt, and armored herself with determination. She was not going to let her unholy lust for Wulf's delectable pectorals and fabulous abs get in the way of answers. She would have to be strong, and not allow herself to be distracted by his masculine charms.

The instant she stumbled from her bedroom, Jai hailed her with the news that their classes were now all bulging at the seams. Witnessing the studio's owner embroiled in an altercation between two men seemed to have done wonders for class enrolments.

Huh. Whatever worked. Even if it involved getting clipped on the chin by a very confused wannabe boyfriend who had a thing for her best friend. Though next time she needed to boost student numbers, she'd volunteer someone else as the punching bag.

Francesca's voice was so unexpected that Chalcey jumped

like a startled cat. "If you're looking for Wulf, he's gone back to wherever he's staying for the moment."

Her mother's brow was creased. Fine lines bracketed her mouth. Francesca worried about Wulf? Surely not.

"I presume he's chosen a place nearby," she said. "He'll be hurting if he hasn't."

"He's staying with Sam," Chalcey finally admitted when she couldn't put up with her mother's expectant gaze any longer.

"The little redheaded man-eater? Excellent." Francesca blew out a sigh and relaxed somewhat.

What the eff? Chalcey frowned as her overloaded brain finally caught up with her mother's earlier statement. "Hang on, what do you mean 'he'll be hurting'? And why are you so damn pleased he's staying with Sam? You know something about Wulf. Tell me. Right now."

Francesca's gaze slid to Jai, who was chatting with some of the departing partygoers and handing them class timetables "Later, Chalcedony. Please don't make a scene."

"Fine. Whatever." Wulf's issues would have to wait until she'd sorted whatever her mother was hinting about. "But don't even think about disappearing and leaving me hanging or I'll hunt you down."

Francesca dimpled at her—which in itself was plain worrisome. "Chalcedony, darling, you have no idea how nice it is to hear I'm wanted. And you should rub some arnica cream on your chin before the bruise starts to form."

Inwardly seething, Chalcey trotted off to do as she was told. Francesca had a knack for making her feel like a clumsy little girl again. Why did her mother always have to have the last word?

As she rummaged in her first-aid cabinet for the arnica, she toyed with the idea of really pissing off Francesca by calling her *Beryl*. Francesca had always hated her real first name, labeling it old-fashioned, plain, and boring—all things, she would announce to anyone who cared to listen, that she most definitely was not. Being insatiably curious, Chalcey had once looked up the name and discovered that *beryl* was a crystal, too, just like chalcedony. But at least Beryl was a *proper* name, one that people had actually heard of, unlike the one her mother had stuck her daughter with. Chalcey would have embraced the name Beryl.

By the time she'd rubbed stinky arnica all over her chin, Jai had shooed the last stragglers out the door. Chalcey heaved a sigh and got stuck into the clean-up. If she could have put it off until tomorrow, she'd have done so with a huge amount of delight, but the place needed to be tidy for her teachers' meeting.

Speaking of the meeting— "Jai, are Leah and Paulo still on for tomorrow? Even though I can't take them on for a few months, I still want to include them so they'll know I'm dead serious about them joining us soon as I'm solvent."

He nodded. "Yep. All confirmed. And they get it, okay? So you can quit stressing, doll. With me at your side, and Paulo and Leah champing at the bit to join us, how can you fail?"

Chalcey couldn't help but grin at his positive attitude. If Jai's rampant enthusiasm were all it took to run a successful dance studio, she'd be sweet. But life was rarely that simple. She'd never had employees of her own before, but she'd been a senior teacher at someone else's dance studio, and witnessed plenty of behind-the-scenes bitching. It was a truth universally acknowledged that if your teachers weren't happy, neither were your students. And everything could go full-speed downhill from there. Her worst nightmare.

Or maybe not her worst. Being imprisoned for centuries in a freaking *crystal* was waaay the heck up there with the other scary-ass stuff now. God. The horror Wulf had endured, the devastating awareness that it was useless to struggle, pointless to scream. He'd been a warrior, a fighter. He would have fought regardless, because to do otherwise would be giving in and giving up. How he must have despaired when he'd finally weakened so much that he'd not been able to fight anymore. Chalcey doubted she would survive complete sensory depriva- tion for more than a week without losing her mind. For someone so strong, so completely confident and sure of him- self and his chosen path as the Wulf in her dreams…. It truly must have been a living hell.

He hadn't deserved such a dire punishment for his crimes.

Human beings invariably cling to life and to hope, however fruitless the situation might seem. But Chalcey had known the instant Wulf forged a link with her while he was still trapped in the crystal, that he'd given up all hope of redemption.

She shivered, rubbing her arms. A sense of his hopelessness still lingered, staining her soul. She had to help him. But to do that, she needed to know the truth.

"You right, doll?" Jai asked, gliding toward her. He placed his hands firmly on her shoulders to peer into her eyes. "Want me to get you more painkillers?"

She shook my head. "Nah. I'm right. Just tired."

"You've had a rough night, what with two men fighting over you. Why don't you hit the hay and leave me to finish up here?"

She summoned a hopefully convincing smile and gave him a quick hug. "Thanks, but I'll be okay. Really. And how can I possibly sleep imagining you out here, slaving your handsome butt off?"

He rolled his eyes at her pathetic attempt at humor, and sauntered off to grab another garbage bag.

Jai had made peace with who he was, and what he wanted out of life and love—even if it meant flitting from lover to lover and keeping it casual. So why couldn't she?

Maybe real love would eventually find her if she stopped wanting it so bad it hurt. Bumble along and the universe would provide when it deemed her ready…. Whenever *that* might be. Before her boobs started heading too far south, she hoped.

And before her mother's subtle suggestions that she find a decent man and settle down drove her insane. Chalcey thought her mother could be more understanding of her plight, given Francesca had indulged in messy, scream-out-loud, never-know-what's-gonna-happen-next, *real* love with Benigno Laureano, before settling for predictable, comfortable, mutual *like* with Edgar Owens. Still, at least Francesca had experienced the joy of the real thing. Which was more than Chalcey could claim.

She observed Francesca from of the corner of her eye. And she experienced an epiphany of sorts, right then and there, amongst soggy remains of chips soused in stale puddles of beer and wine and soda. Maybe, deep down, Francesca believed you only got one shot at real love, and she'd had hers. Which is why she'd settled for Edgar.

Huh. One of these days, Chalcey might even pluck up the courage to ask her.

Yeah, right. Like when cows turned purple and mooed their way to Jupiter.

"That's it, Chalce." Jai wrung out the mop and stowed it in the broom closet. "They did a great job finishing the floorboards. They've come up like new."

Chalcey tossed the last plastic cup in the trash and surveyed the studio, discovering to her surprise that everything was indeed cleaned up. "Thanks Jai. You're the best. You off now?"

"Yep. Gotta get my beauty sleep, 'coz I know you're gonna work us all hard tomorrow. Bye, doll."

"Bye, Jai. See you tomorrow." She walked him downstairs and even remembered to throw the door's security chain after he left.

As she hauled herself back up the stairs, she glanced at Mickey. It was nearly one a.m. Amazing how quickly time flies when you're having fun. Even more amazing, her mother emerged from the kitchenette cradling two mugs of hot chocolate decorated with the marshmallows Chalcey vaguely recalled hiding away somewhere so she wouldn't be tempted by them. Hmmm. Wait for it….

"I'd like to stay for a few days, Chalcedony."

"You and Edgar having problems or something?" Not that she wanted to know the details.

"No. We're fine. It's you I'm worried about, darling. I've been sensing something not quite right with your aura. The last time I spoke with you, you seemed so tired."

"Me? I'm fine, Francesca. I sounded tired when you phoned because, as you always do, you got the time zones mucked up and woke me up in the wee small hours. But if you were so worried, why didn't you save yourself the airfare and just phone me?"

Her mother made a prissy little moue. "I loathe trying to discuss important matters over the phone. It's so… impersonal. And it's impossible to know how you really are unless I see you face-to-face."

"And?" Chalcey held her arms out from her sides and turned full circle. She meant it as a joke, but of course her mother didn't take it that way.

"I was right to be worried about you."

Chalcey sighed. "For goodness sake. If you're so worried about my health then just recommend one of those nasty herbal tonics you give Edgar. Hang on, I've got an even better idea. I'll sleep with those broken pieces of wulfenite permanently under my pillow. Hell, maybe they'll shrink my boobs and all my troubles will be over."

Francesca ignored her jibes. "It's not your physical health that I'm concerned about. It's your state of mind."

Chalcey ground her jaw, and counted to ten in effort to keep her sarcasm in check. Sheesh. Her mother could be so relentlessly kooky at times. "Oookay then. And that would be because—?"

"Because of Wulf. *You* and Wulf to be precise. There are some things you need to know about him, Chalcedony, before you get in too deep and your chance to choose is taken away from you."

"I suppose you've checked his aura and seen deep into his soul, so you know he's no good for me, huh? God, can't you cut the crap and be straight up with me for once?" Chalcey turned away from Francesca and headed for the kitchenette, before she said something she was really going to regret. She plunked down on a chair, made herself comfortable, and took a gulp of the melting pink and white marshmallow goop atop her drink. It was so hot she burned her tongue and the roof of her mouth. Typical.

Francesca chose the chair opposite and sat, looking far too put together for someone who'd just spent an hour cleaning up partially eaten snacks and spilled drinks. "Have you slept with Wulf yet?" she asked.

Chalcey's jaw sagged. "Francesca!"

"This is important, Chalcey."

Yikes. Her mother *never* called her "Chalcey", even though she'd been told a million times Chalcey preferred the diminutive. It was always Chalcedony this, and Chalcedony that.

"Have you?" she asked again.

Chalcey's incredulous expression provoked yet another surprise.

"Please, Chalcey. I wouldn't ask if this wasn't a serious situation."

Double yikes. Now her mother was saying "please". Chalcey caved. "All right. Yes. I have slept with him."

"And you had sex? Proper sex?"

Jeez this was sooo cringingly embarrassing. Like being a teenager again and getting the birds and the bees lecture. "Yes, Francesca. We had real sex. Complete with anatomically correct body parts, full penetration, and even orgasms. Happy now?"

Francesca was anything but happy. She'd gone sheet-pale and her eyes had turned huge with worry. She reached out as if to touch Chalcey, then quickly pulled back her hand and cupped it about her mug. "I'd hoped that since he's staying with Samantha, she might have been the one."

Chalcey and her mother shared an awkward moment—the kind where wishes that things could have been different hung poised in the air. Until reality intruded and the moment passed.

"Why is me having sex with Wulf so terrible?" Chalcey blurted. "I've had sex with plenty of men before. Well, not plenty, but—ah crap, you know what I mean. I'm no virgin and I know you know that. Why is this time, with *this* man, such an issue? What is it about Wulf and me that's such a big freaking deal for you?"

"Darling, you haven't a clue what you've gotten yourself into. You see, Wulf's a Crystal Warrior. And he comes from another world."

# CHAPTER TEN

C HALCEY JUST MISSED spraying Francesca with her mouthful of hot chocolate. Whoa. Sure hadn't seen that one coming. She wiped her mouth with the back of her hand, and gulped another mouthful. A sugar-rush was definitely required to handle this situation with any sort of aplomb.

Francesca blotted up the mess with another lace hanky. "Centuries ago, Wulf was cursed and imprisoned in a piece of wulfenite crystal by the Crystal Guardian."

Hel-lo. Déjà freaking vu. Had her mother somehow invaded her mind and shared her dreams?

Francesca interpreted Chalcey's reaction as disbelief. She compressed her lips and puffed out a delicate sigh. "It's true," she said, smoothing her dress down her thighs.

"Sure it is." Chalcey imbued her tone with a large dollop of skepticism. Not because she was being confrontational, but because right now, she just needed someone—anyone—to clue her in on what the fuck was going on, and needling her mother was sure to do the trick.

"I don't suppose you'd just take my advice and stay away from him?"

Chalcey shook her head. "Nope."

"I suppose you want to know everything so you can make an informed decision."

"You got it. Now spill."

Was that an eye-roll? Nah. Chalcey must have been imagining it. Francesca didn't do eye-rolls.

"Before I explain, I need to ask you another personal question. How many times have you had intercourse with Wulf?" She stared at Chalcey with über-intentness, as though her daughter's entire fate teetered precariously upon the answer.

Apprehension burrowed into the pit of Chalcey's stomach and hatched into great big butterflies. "That's pretty personal, even for you," she managed to say in a very normal voice, even though her mouth had gone dry. "I don't make a habit of discussing my sex life."

*And especially not with my mother.*

Francesca had the grace to look abashed by the probing question—so abashed and flushed with embarrassment that Chalcey felt sorry for her and relented. "Sheesh! Once, okay? We've had sex once."

Her mother exhaled long and loud, sagging back in her chair, so obviously relieved by the answer that worry bit at Chalcey's mind. "Why do you seem so darn thrilled to hear that?"

"Because there's a chance you're not irrevocably bound to Wulf yet." Francesca sipped her chocolate. She didn't seem in any hurry to elaborate and put Chalcey out of her misery.

Chalcey waited.

And waited some more.

And fumed.

And finally lost it. "Will you please tell me what the hell is going on?"

To her shock, Francesca obliged. "Wulf's a Styrian warrior from an alien world. Their priests opened a portal to our world and sent Wulf and his men here to steal women for breeding purposes. An old man with a supernatural affinity for crystals cast a spell to imprison them all in their namesake crystals. That old man became the Guardian of the Crystals, condemned to watch over them all until each warrior finds a woman to redeem him for his crimes. This might come as a surprise to you, but you've been chosen to redeem Wulf."

It was all Chalcey could do to stay in her chair, rather than stagger to her feet and dig out her last bottle of tequila with a view to numbing her shock with alcohol.

Spells and curses? Maybe. Okay, yeah. She'd seen Pieter imprisoning men in crystals—well, a vision of him doing that, but a damned vivid, totally convincing one that was almost impossible to deny. And she'd pretty much convinced herself that Wulf had emerged from the crystal Pieter had given her, too.

But portals to other worlds? Cast by priests? No way. No freaking way.

"Let's put aside the possibility of other worlds even existing for a moment," she said, and hoped that sentiment didn't immediately brand her a nut-job. "Let me get this straight. Wulf and his men came to our world to steal women." Okay, she'd *seen* them do it—kind of—but she wanted confirmation. From a real person.

Francesca didn't bother to mince words. "Yes. It's documented throughout history. Women frequently went missing in those times but of course the disappearances were mostly attributed to misadventure. But there's a discernible pattern to the disappearances if you know what to look for."

Oookay then. Her mother almost sounded like she knew what she was talking about. Almost. "And the reason these warriors needed to steal women in the first place is?"

"All the females native to their own world had died out. Even when the Styrian males mated with *our* women, only male babies were born. They stole women to replenish their population, so their race wouldn't become extinct."

Ah. That part did make sense—not the bit about only male babies being born, because that was weird for sure, but the bit about Wulf's people needing women for their race to survive. "You think this kidnapping of women is still going on to this day? Is that why you're so worried about me? Because you think Wulf is going to force me to go back to his world with him?"

"Not exactly," Francesca said. "I suspect that after the Crystal Guardian imprisoned Wulf and a number of his men, their priests found another world to pillage."

Chalcey had almost reached her limit for suspending belief. She sipped her chocolate and tried not to give into the desire to laugh hysterically. "Boy, I never would have guessed that Pieter was this helluva powerful magician who'd get his jollies by invading my dreams and showing me the past."

From the corner of her eye, she noticed Francesca jerk like she'd been zapped with an electric current. She kept talking, wondering what else her mother might inadvertently reveal. "The old guy really had me fooled with his 'let me show you my pretty crystals' act. I wonder why he chose me? I mean, like I want to relive what he did to Wulf and his men. It's horrible enough to give me nightmares for the rest of my life. I'm not exactly an angel, but I don't think I've done anything bad enough to deserve that."

Francesca wasn't even attempting to hide her shock. She stared at Chalcey, her pupils hugely dilated. "You know the Crystal Guardian's name. A-and you've dreamed of him."

"Yep. Him *and* Wulf. And more than a dream, too. More of an *experience*, if you get what I mean. It was so vivid it was like I was there. Heck, why else do you think I'm sitting here listening to this? It's not because you've helped clean up and made me a mug of chocolate. Normally our conversation would go the same way it always does when you go on about auras and suchlike. I'd tell you it was rubbish. You'd argue with me and try to convince me otherwise. I'd refuse to listen, and you'd flounce off home and I wouldn't hear from you for another six months or so."

The instant the words were out, Chalcey snapped her mouth closed, ashamed by her tirade. She could tell by the sheen of tears in her mother's eyes that she was hurt. Deeply. Francesca was trying to help. She hadn't deserved Chalcey's scorn.

Her gaze slid away from her mother's, and they both retired to their metaphorical corners to lick their not-so-metaphorical wounds. Emotional baggage was a bitch of monumental proportions. "I'm sorry," Chalcey said. "I shouldn't have said that."

Francesca waved away her apology. "You only told the bald truth."

"Yeah. Doesn't make it better though, does it?"

"No. Not really."

Even though it was hard to hold tight to emotional baggage when chocolate and marshmallows were involved, Chalcey could feel a tightness behind her eyes that heralded the onset of a killer stress headache. She needed to wrap this up before it hit her full force and she couldn't think straight. "So tell me what you know about Crystal Guardian. Pieter. Or Pietersite, if we're going to get technical with true-names and such."

Francesca sucked in a deep breath and let it out very slowly—the kind of gesture people made when they had bad news to impart. Chalcey's apprehension increased exponentially.

"You're correct that Pieter's true name is Pietersite," Francesca said. "He's named for a crystal, as I'm sure you're aware. And there's no doubt he is a powerful sorcerer. But not even his affinity with crystals could save him from the backlash of his curse. The spell he wrought bound him to the men he imprisoned. Until each warrior atones for his sins and has a chance to bond with a woman who could redeem him and potentially be his true mate, Pieter is condemned to remain their guardian."

Pieter's spell filled Chalcey's mind and the words spilled from her lips. "Verily the crystal for which thee be named/ Shalt form the prison in which thee be bound /To atone the sins for which thee be blamed/ 'Til thee be blessed and thy true love be found."

Francesca made a choking sound, as though her throat had tightened around words she wanted to speak.

But Chalcey hadn't finished. "Kyanite, Shattuckite, Danburite, Malachite, Okenite—"

"Stop!" The color drained from her mother's face until her blue eyes resembled shining sapphire baubles nestled in sheet-white parchment. "No more, please. Chalcey, do you have any alcohol handy? I-I really could do with a drink."

"Just a minute." There was something she hadn't quite grasped yet. Something too important to allow herself to be distracted by the lure of alcohol. "What do you mean when you say there's a chance that I'm not 'irrevocably bound' to Wulf yet? What exactly does 'irrevocably bound' mean, any-way? And, more importantly, how does it happen?"

Chalcey guessed from the tiny frown between her mother's brows that Francesca was debating whether or not to come clean. She was about to come down hard on her mother and insist, when Francesca spoke. "Since arriving here, Wulf has forged a bond with *you* and only you. He feels physical pain if he's not near you. And each time you are sexually intimate, the bond between you only grows stronger. But for now it can still be broken. It is not yet irrevocable."

"Oookay." That sure explained Wulf's weird comments about hurting if he was away from her. "So how exactly does the irrevocable bit happen?"

"For the bond to be irrevocable and the Testing—" Francesca pronounced "testing" like it deserved a capital T "—to be scheduled, within one month, or twenty-eight days to be precise, you must exchange true names and have sex with him three times. Then, if you both pass the Testing you will be Wulf's life-mate."

Chalcey thought back to when she'd passed out. And to Wulf collapsing on top of her. Uh oh. Seemed more than likely the exchanging true names bit was a done deal. "What's this

*Testing* deal?"

"It differs. I know of one Testing that took the form of a physical test provoked by outside influences. And two that seemed a more internal process, a test of will or depth of feelings, if you like."

Chalcey's jaw sagged. She placed her mug carefully on the table before she dropped it. "You've found three other Crystal Warriors? Who are they? Where are they now?"

"You and Wulf are my main concern at the moment. When you're safe from him, there'll be plenty of time to discuss everything else." Her gaze skittered away. She was hiding something.

Later, then. As Francesca had said, there was plenty of time. But Chalcey still had questions that needed answering. Important questions—life-changing, even. "What's with the whole having sex three times thing? Is three a magic number or something?"

Francesca shrugged, somehow making the weary gesture elegant. "Apparently."

Chalcey blew out a pained breath that did nothing to ease the panicked tightness in her chest. "What happens if I don't do the wild thing two more times with Wulf, or I fail this Testing?"

"If the bond doesn't fully activate for whatever reason, or if you don't pass the Testing, Wulf will be bound to his crystal again. And this time, Pieter will be able to destroy it and Wulf both. Which he will, of course. Why wouldn't he? One less Crystal Warrior for him to guard."

Chalcey gasped for enough breath to fill her lungs. Her mother's words were like a kick in the gut. Francesca was talking about a man's life—*Wulf's* life!—and she'd tossed off the comment like she was discussing the unfortunate demise of a pet goldfish. "You're kidding me," she said. Hoping against hope that her mother was yanking her chain. And suspecting that she wasn't.

Francesca worried at her lower lip with her teeth.

There was something crucial her mother hadn't revealed. The stakes were high—Francesca wouldn't have flown out to see Chalcey on a mere whim. Chalcey instinctively knew if she let on how she really felt about Wulf, how she didn't believe his punishment fit his crime, Francesca would fob her off with platitudes, and she'd be back where she started. Fighting her lust for Wulf. And ignorant of the consequences if she gave in to it.

She decided to put Francesca's mind at rest, play it light and casual. "No worries then. I'm completely safe. The chances of me becoming life-mated to Wulf are zilch."

"Are you sure?" Francesca's gaze raked Chalcey's face, searching for the truth.

"Oh, come on. This is the real world. There's got to be a logical explanation for all this. Binding two people magically through sex? It's like some warped fairy tale!" Please let it be a fairy tale. Please? Because, dammit, Wulf had gotten under her skin. She didn't want him to suffer any more. She definitely didn't want him to die, either. But that didn't mean she wanted to be mated to him and have some spell hanging over her head for the rest of her life.

"You have no idea how much I wish it were a fantasy, Chalcey. But it isn't."

Chalcey clutched at one last hope—that her mother wouldn't be able to prove any of this. Then she could shrug off this entire conversation, delude herself that her weird dreams and encounters with ancient old magicians and alien Crystal Warriors had never taken place. Pretend she'd never met Wulf, never kissed him, never had sex with him. Pretend she could go back to her pathetic little life, unscathed by her encounter with him. "Even you admit that this could all be conjecture. How do you know it's true, Francesca? You, personally, I mean."

Francesca's poise shattered. Before Chalcey's shocked gaze,

Francesca seemed to shrink in upon herself and age a decade. Her face became drawn and etched with suffering, as though reliving some terrible tragedy. Chalcey wanted to look away, give her mother some privacy to get herself together. But she couldn't.

"Because Pieter once chose me to be bound to a Crystal Warrior," Francesca said. "Just like he's chosen you."

Shit. Chalcey hadn't seen that coming, either.

"I sensed you were in danger," Francesca said. "I knew something was wrong. That's why I had to come—to see for myself that you were okay. And when I saw Wulf, I knew I was too late. He'd already beguiled you."

Her mother's words had pinned Chalcey to the spot, as though she'd morphed into some exotic butterfly sacrificed to satisfy a collector's whim. The kitchenette's creamy-toned walls, a color she'd specifically chosen for its light, spacious feel, abruptly closed in on her. This changed everything she believed about her mother, everything she thought she knew. What Francesca had told her…. It freaking well rewrote history.

She struggled with the welter of emotions ebbing and surging through her woefully unprepared mind, and felt compelled to do something. Anything. She scrambled to her feet in a flurry of movement that rocked the table and sent the cheap, lightweight chair skittering across the floorboards.

"Chalcey?" Her mother's voice shook.

Francesca was trying to hold it all in, to hang on to her composure, but she was devastated. Chalcey could see it in her mother's eyes, in the way she held herself—all quivering muscles, as though she would collapse in a boneless heap on the floor if she let go.

Chalcey went to her mother and hugged her, offering comfort she no longer knew quite how to give. Francesca clutched Chalcey like a lifeline. Her body shook. And then she gathered the shreds of her control and went very still.

Her mother's unnatural stillness was a sure sign that she no longer welcomed the embrace but Chalcey couldn't remember the last time she'd willingly hugged her mother. She lingered a moment before disentangling herself. "I'll get that drink you wanted," she said. "God knows, I could do with one myself right now."

She fished out the key to the liquor cupboard from its hiding place inside the empty laxative container. Hey, it made a good hiding place. Not even her roommates from her old apartment had figured it out. Mind you, she'd always believed that if Francesca's husband, Edgar, ever came to stay, she'd be forced to find another hiding place. Edgar always looked constipated.

Brandishing a bottle at Francesca, she said, "This is 80 proof *Casa Noble* Tequila. It's one hundred percent blue agave *Reposado*—my favorite. Well, only because I can't afford the *Añejo*." She plunked the bottle on the table with a calculated flourish.

She'd developed a penchant for tequila while dating a young Mexican guy back in her teens. Like so many middleclass Americans, she'd thought that the only way to drink tequila was the lick, sip, suck method. She was summarily branded an ignorant heathen, and informed only tourists wanting to make spectacles of themselves drink tequila like that. Live and learn.

"And if you're going to partake of a good Reposado, you have to have the correct glassware, a traditional two-ounce glass called a *caballito*. So of course I've bought a set of those, too." Chalcey knew she was rambling, regurgitating all this nonsensical stuff to stave off a huge case of emotional fallout. In this case, rambling was far preferable. But she was fast running out of ramble. Heaving a sigh, she resumed her seat at the table.

Francesca quirked an eyebrow into a perfect arch. "Are you intending to drown your sorrows or mine?"

"Both." Chalcey poured the pale liquor into her mother's glass, filling it almost to the rim.

Francesca took a hesitant sip, swallowed and gasped, fanning her face to catch her breath. "Phwoar! This is really good!"

"You sound surprised. It *is* good. It may not be the best but it's still pricey. And it's my last bottle. I won't be able to splash out on any more for a while."

"And you're sharing it with me? I'm touched, Chalcey."

Chalcey hit her mother straight between the eyes with her suspicions, no warning, no preamble. She needed to know for sure, and she told herself it was the only way. "Thought you might need it—especially since one of those names I recited was *your* Crystal Warrior."

A slow blink. "You're very observant, Chalcedony."

Ah. Back to "Chalcedony". Francesca was distancing herself again. Erecting the barriers that she'd hidden behind ever since Benigno's death.

At least now, Chalcey had some inkling of why.

She took a swig of her drink to bolster her courage. "Dad was the reason you couldn't bond with your Crystal Warrior, wasn't he?"

Francesca's gaze sharpened, whipping out to punish Chalcey for doubting her love for her husband. "Benigno was in the last stages of his cancer. I wouldn't leave him. Not even when Malach begged me to. Not even when Benigno—" Her lips compressed into a thin, bloodless line. She downed the entire contents of her glass and slammed it onto the tabletop, daring Chalcey to join the dots. Daring her to judge.

If Francesca's chosen Crystal Warrior, this *Malach*, had been anything like as insidiously compelling as Wulf, Francesca wouldn't have stood a chance. How on earth could Chalcey judge her?

Tears laced Francesca's lashes. Maybe she'd teared up because of the tequila. Maybe because of—

Epiphany number two. Chalcey's dad had been no fool. He would have figured out Francesca had met someone else. "Dad knew about your Crystal Warrior," she said.

Francesca refilled her glass without bothering to ask permission. "I told him everything. I thought he'd despise me, but your father only wanted what was best for me. He didn't want me to have to sit by and watch him fade away. It hurt his pride that he was in so much pain he could no longer hide it. He pleaded with me to go, to take you and make another life for myself. And God help me, Chalcedony, to my everlasting shame I was tempted.

"But no matter how much I thought I loved Malach, I loved Benigno too. I wouldn't leave him. Malach understood that and he respected my choice, even though it meant he would lose his chance at redemption. Even though it would cost him his life. He was a brave man."

Chalcey's mind whirred up a gear. "Hold up. You knew it would cost him his life. How did you know the stakes were that high?"

"Pieter explained everything after I chose the malachite crystal. I think he believed that full disclosure was necessary due to my... circumstances."

The husband-dying-of-cancer circumstances. Riiight. How thoughtful of Pieter. But boy, had that ever backfired on him. So it kind of made sense the old man had decided to keep Chalcey clueless and leave it to nature—or rather, Chalcey's rampant hormones and too-soft heart that made her a sucker for a sob story. Bet he hadn't counted on Francesca's interference, though.

Her stomach twisted when she thought of what her father had been put through, knowing his wife had fallen in love with another man. And Malach, too. Knowing he'd been so close to a chance at redemption, only to have it ripped away when Francesca chose her dying husband over him.

In Chalcey's dream, Malach had been Wulf's second in

command and—

Wulf. God. How would Wulf react if he knew that Malach had been doomed by a twist of fate that'd chosen the wrong woman for him? Or perhaps the right woman. Just at the very worst time in her life imaginable.

Chalcey considered how she felt about the possibility of condemning Wulf to the crystal a second time. And sending him to his death.

A shudder coursed down her body. She rubbed her arms, wishing everything could go back to the way it was before. But the cat was out of the bag now. She couldn't pretend ignorance.

She sipped more tequila, swirling it in her mouth, watching Francesca carefully over the rim of her glass. When she swallowed it down, the warmth pooling in her belly loosened her tension, and her tongue. "That explains a lot about—" The bitterness twisting her mother's face silenced her.

"About why I was so cruel to you after your father died, Chalcedony? Why I was so emotionally distant? Why I *settled* for Edgar?"

Cripes. All of the above. Francesca had nailed it. "Yes."

"Why don't you tell me, Chalcedony. I'd really like to hear what *you* think my reasons were."

Her mother's voice oozed that particular tone parents cultivate especially for their children. That slightly smug tone always drove Chalcey crazy. She was an adult, too. She'd been through some pretty crappy stuff and survived. She had valid opinions, dammit. So couldn't they have a decent conversation without Francesca inferring that she was too young to know anything about life?

Normally Chalcey would have been stung enough to toss off some smart-assed retort. But the underlying guilt and pain in her mother's voice helped strangle her immediate knee-jerk reaction. No sarcasm, just let her have it straight. Less painful for them both that way.

"You were depressed for months after Dad died because you were mourning him *and* Malach. I know you loved Dad very much. So to have even considered leaving him, you'd have loved Malach deeply, too. I bet you've spent every single day since then, wondering whether you made the right choice by not even trying to save him. I bet you feel guilty as hell knowing you sacrificed him for the sake of spending another few months with Dad."

Francesca rocked back in her chair like she'd been slapped hard. She blinked away tears. But Chalcey wouldn't stop. Couldn't stop. She had to get it all out. "And then you married Edgar—a man you don't love—because you believe you don't deserve to be happy. You're still punishing yourself. God. Dad would be rolling in his grave. You said it yourself: All he ever wanted was for you to be happy. You loved Malach. You should have at least tried to save him. Dad would have understood. And I would have stayed and taken care of him, like he always took care of me."

Her mother's features hardened and her mouth tightened, like she was biting back words better left unsaid. "You were ten years old, for God's sake! And you're wrong. I didn't love Malach like I loved your father. And I would never have left your father for him. Never!" Her voice had risen to a banshee screech.

"Okay okay, I get it."

Francesca pressed a hand to her chest and took a couple of deep breaths, composing herself. "You must understand, Chalcedony. I thought it was all terribly romantic at first. I thought Malach was everything I could desire in a man. I thought I'd been given a second chance at love. I wouldn't have to watch Benigno die a slow, pain-filled death. I could leave your father without feeling guilty because I'd been chosen for higher purpose, to redeem a Crystal Warrior and save his life. But the reality of it soon killed the romance. How could I be so selfish as to leave your father when he needed me? How could I even think about my own happiness at a time like that? In the end the decision was simple because I realized that nothing I felt for Malach was real. He was a fantasy, nothing more."

"So what do I have to do? Where does this leave us?"

"How do you mean?"

Chalcey had a sudden rush of insight that made her stomach churn and her skin crawl with horror. She didn't much appreciate this new, insightful side of herself. The bitch needed a good slapping. "Are you telling me all this because you *want* me to try and save Wulf? Or because you *don't*?"

As Francesca drained her glass, Chalcey watched the alcohol-induced color seeping back into her cheeks. "Malach told me of your Wulf," Francesca said. "He was—*is*—a brutal, pitiless warrior. He never lets anything stand in the way of what he wants. And what he wants is you, Chalcedony. If you hadn't initiated the bond, you might have come through this unscathed but now it's too late. Sleeping with Wulf has set you on a path that will force you to make a painful but wholly necessary decision."

"Meaning?"

"Meaning, if you hadn't let him take advantage of you and initiated the bonding process, he would have just been another man. And when the time was up, he would have returned to his crystal. No harm, no foul. You've brought this on yourself. Now you have to end it."

Recalling her reaction when Wulf had first kissed her, Chalcey doubted with every fiber of her being that Wulf could ever have been "just another man".

She banished thoughts of that kiss from her mind and struggled to fill in the missing pieces. "Okay. I've initiated the bond but if it's not irrevocable yet, can't Wulf bond with someone else?"

"No. Not now. If the bond hadn't been initiated, Wulf might have been given the chance to form another true-bond.

But now—" Francesca exhaled sharply through her nose, a gesture that suggested exasperation, as though Chalcey was being dimwitted. "If you save him, you and he will be bonded forever. You'll always be drawn to him. No other man will make you feel like he makes you feel. And you'll never know if your feelings for him are real."

Despite the liquor in her belly, icy tentacles clutched at Chalcey's heart. "So this... this... *thing* with Wulf and me is going to run its course, regardless. If I choose to finish the bonding process, we could still fail the Testing. And even if I do nothing at all, it's still a death sentence for him. In approximately three and a half weeks, he'll go back to the crystal and Pieter will kill him."

"That's correct."

"Shit."

Francesca reached across the tabletop and clasped Chalcey's hands. "I'm sorry, Chalcedony."

It was only then that Chalcey realized she was shaking. "Me, too," she whispered.

"I know you'll make the right decision."

What the hell was that supposed to mean?

"If it's any consolation," Francesca continued, "Wulf is ignorant. He knows nothing about this. He only knows that he's been released from the crystal and he's drawn to you and no other woman. But I doubt it's even occurred to him what he feels for you could be more than mere lust. He's not a gentle man like Malach was. Wulf has no compassion and no tolerance for weakness. Men like him don't do love."

Yeow. That tone was razor-sharp. Her mother really didn't like Wulf at all.

Francesca snapped her fingers beneath Chalcey's nose. "Pay attention. This is important. If you stay away from him, refuse to have any further physical contact with him, he'll never know your rejection was the catalyst that sent him back to the crystal."

*And to his death.*

The unspoken words echoed throughout the room.

Unspoken or not, they were cruel words. Words with consequences Chalcey would have to live with for the rest of her life. "And Wulf not knowing it was my refusal that condemned him makes it okay?"

"It makes it easier on you. That's all."

Jeez her mother could be cold-hearted. "Did your Malach know all this? Did you tell him?"

"Yes. Yes, I did. I felt I owed him that much."

"And you're sure you made the right decision?"

Her mother blinked. "Yes. Of course. If I'd been in my right mind, I would never have looked at another man. And I would never ever have considered leaving your father."

Yeah, right. Francesca could justify it all she wanted but Chalcey knew her mother had been torn. This fervent declaration was merely her way of coping with her decision. A decision that had condemned a man to death.

The little laugh that escaped Chalcey's lips became more like a sob. She scrubbed her face with her hands. "What if Pieter has screwed up big-time and I'm not Wulf's true mate? What if my rampant hormones have robbed him of a chance to bond with some other woman, and sentenced him to death?"

Francesca toyed with her glass. "How do you feel about Wulf, Chalcedony? What was it like when he touched you for the first time?"

She thought hard about that question.

"I see," Francesca said.

Hang on, she hadn't even answered.

Or had she? She would have given anything for a mirror to see the expression on her face right now.

"And when he seduced you?" Francesca asked.

"You mean, aside from the lamentable fact it was the best sex I'd ever had in my entire life?"

Francesca said nothing, merely stared at her, stony-faced.

Chalcey ducked her head, ashamed of her flippant response. "It felt like I'd found the piece of myself that was missing," she said. "He made me whole."

Francesca heaved a sigh. "That's what I was afraid of. You can't give in, Chalcedony. The feelings these Crystal Warriors inspire in us are insidious and almost impossible to resist. You have to keep telling yourself they're not real. And remember, Wulf will not hesitate to be as ruthless as he deems necessary to get what he wants. You must be ruthless, too." She grabbed Chalcey's mug and glass, and carried them to the sink.

Confronting Wulf would have to wait until tomorrow. Chalcey needed time to think this through, to decide how much to tell him. Besides, it was waaay past midnight, and Francesca was stifling yawns and glancing at her expectantly. So of course Chalcey offered her a bed for the night—her own bed. Which, after some unsubtle prompting on Francesca's part, soon extended to the duration of her stay.

Chalcey mentally kicked herself for being such a wimp. She had the distinct feeling her mother wasn't going anywhere until this thing with Wulf ended. It promised to be a hellishly long, stressful, three-and-a-bit weeks.

Since she had no desire to elevate her stress levels still further by having to share the bed with her mother, Chalcey chose to sleep on the self-inflating camping mat she'd used before she could afford a proper bed. She wedged the mat in the corner of her bedroom. And she twisted and turned for what seemed like endless hours, one moment stifled by her blanket and the next stifled by her thoughts, until finally, she couldn't stand another second of listening to Francesca's calm, even breathing—like her mother didn't have a care in the world. How could she sleep so peacefully when Chalcey's life—and Wulf's, too—was such a god-awful mess?

She tiptoed out into the studio, carrying her makeshift bed, her mind swirling, struggling with everything she'd been told.

Ignorance, in this particular case, would definitely have been bliss. And if she did choose to ignore the possibility her mother had one big-ass agenda, and did choose to believe everything she'd been told, then she had a very difficult choice to make about Wulf.

Then again, why was it so difficult? He was to-die-for good-looking, built, amazing in bed—uh, make that shower. And he seemed to really like her. A lot.

What the freaking hell was her problem?

Well, for starters, he was be-spelled. Crystal-mazed. A man like Wulf—a warrior—didn't fall head over heels for a woman and blindly pursue her. If *she'd* been in his place, imprisoned, and then released into an alien world, the last thing on her mind would have been sex. And it wasn't just because he was a male, genetically designed to have sex on the brain twenty-four-seven. The intensity of his feelings for her was unnatural. There was no other explanation. They simply had to be a product of supernatural influences beyond his control.

Same with the intensity of her feelings for him.

Hah. Even knowing that changed nothing. She knew what she had to do. There was no real choice at all. That was the difference between her mother and herself. Chalcey couldn't turn her back on Wulf and do nothing about the knowledge she'd been given. Wulf was no fantasy. What they *felt* for each other might be a fantasy manufactured by the Crystal Guardian's clever spell, but Wulf was a living, breathing man. He deserved a chance. If she had her way, it'd be a fighting chance, too. She set the bedding on the floor and settled down, closing her eyes and trying to blank her mind.

Something gently caressed her inner thigh.

"Eeep!" She clapped a hand over her mouth, worried about waking Francesca. The caress shifted and warmth cupped her groin. Her inner core moistened and she shuddered, reacting as though a lover was pushing a finger inside her and stroking her most private, intimate places. She knew there was no one in the studio space with her, no one hiding beneath her blanket. She checked anyway. And pinched her arm in case she was fingering herself, and was just too out of it from the tequila to realize.

The sensuous stroking continued. She fought the seduction of invisible fingers and hands moving over her body, gentling away her fears and coaxing her to give herself up to pure sensation. The stroking stopped, the pressure eased and withdrew. Breathy warmth teased her nipples erect. Gentle pressure pushed her back against the thin mattress as phantom lips found hers, kissing away the last vestiges of resistance.

Assured of her acquiescence, those ghostly lips skimmed down her body as knowing fingers sifted through her pubic hair, parted her folds and pushed inside her again.

She could not think beyond the lips caressing her, the warm wetness of the tongue probing her, licking her, the fingers pushing in and out of her. Gasping, she writhed… convulsed…. Came.

Satiated, draped bonelessly across the mattress, her mind drifted. And she saw him. Wulf.

He pressed his fingers to his lips and blew her a kiss. *Now we will sleep.*

Chalcey smiled. Her eyelids began to flutter closed. She yawned and snuggled down beneath the blanket, drifting toward slumber… for all of five wonderful minutes before her brain managed to gather enough energy to perform the equivalent of a huge kick in the pants, jerking her back to wakefulness.

Sleep? After that… that… whatever it had been? Not gonna happen.

She crawled from her cozy nest, and tiptoed into her room to find some clothes. Taking immense care not to disturb her mother, Chalcey managed to snag some jeans and a clean t-shirt from her drawer, and find a pair of sandals. She snuck back into the studio to get dressed, and then, sandals in hand, she headed downstairs.

Wulf's metaphysical lovemaking had been outstanding. But outstanding or not, there was no way she could allow him to have this much influence over her. It was going to stop. Right now. If only she had the remotest clue exactly what "it" was, and how to make him understand why it was a bad thing.

It was going to be hard but she had to be strong.

Oh boy. Bad word-choice. Very bad. "Hard" only brought to mind vivid images of a very hard, very distinctly male portion of Wulf's anatomy.

She groaned, afraid that this was going to take more will-power than she possessed, afraid that she wouldn't be able to resist him if he tried to seduce her again—non-metaphysically, this time. And damned if she wasn't tingling all over with excited anticipation at the prospect.

# CHAPTER ELEVEN

THE WALK TO Sam's inner-city apartment building took about half an hour—enough of a walk that by the time she arrived, Chalcey couldn't think of anything better than crawling into bed. Alone. No surprises after what had gone down this evening.

Add to that, she was pretty darned pissed that she had to walk in the first place. The joys of being too broke to justify a taxi.

The good thing was that whenever she got overly tired and cranky, the *last* thing on her mind was sex. She figured that put her in the perfect state of mind to resist Wulf's considerable charms. This time, no amount of gorgeous male physique or cajolery was going to have an effect on her. Nyuh uh.

She pushed through the revolving door and entered the lobby. It was all very classy. Heaps of marble and dark wood festooned with fancy designer pot plants. In complete contrast to all the studied opulence, Chalcey was aware she resembled something a cat had dragged in. Even if she hadn't been aware, it became patently obvious that she lowered the tone of the place from the way the young guy at the front desk eyed her.

Since he was new and didn't know her, Chalcey half expected to be informed the tradesmen's entrance was at the rear. Lucky for him, he was too well-trained for that. "Samantha Greenwood, please," she said.

"And you would be?"

"Chalcedony Laureano. Ms."

He made a point of glancing at his watch.

"She'll see me. Make the call." Belatedly she added, "Please."

Being an ultra-polite sort himself, his only reaction to her blatant insincerity was a slight flaring of his nostrils. "Just one moment, Ms Laureano." Pause. "Please."

"Touché." Chalcey grinned at him to show she appreciated his sally, and there were no hard feelings. She drummed her fingers on the counter while he consulted his computer screen and keyed in Sam's extension. A brief conversation consisting mainly of "Yes, ma'am" ensued.

"You can go on up, Ms Laureano." He escorted her to the elevator and keyed in the PIN to give her access to the penthouse level.

She wondered how he'd have reacted if she'd leaned over and keyed in the PIN herself. Probably wouldn't have blinked an eye. Unlike the stuffy older guy who had the day shift. He would have thrown a fit, and then gone on and on about security protocols. "Thanks," she said.

"You're welcome, ma'am."

She hid a grimace at the oh-so polite exchange. And the whole security thing. Sam might pretend otherwise but she did secretly enjoy at least some of the privileges that accompanied vast wealth.

The elevator doors smoothed shut while Chalcey brooded over how to apologize to Sam for being such a jealous bitch, and then get Sam out of the way while she had a heart-to-heart with Wulf. She wanted—needed—to talk with him alone. The subject matter was just too delicate to have an audience, even if that audience did happen to be her best friend. Or at least, her hopefully still best friend.

Crap. Maybe high-tailing it over here hadn't been the best idea she'd ever had.

The elevator pinged confirmation that she'd arrived and it

was too late to slink back home. Not when she'd already woken Sam.

She crossed the few steps to the massive double doors and had lifted her hand to punch the doorbell, when someone yanked the door open.

Sam stood in the doorway, swathed in a barely-there silk robe. "It's about time," she hissed from the darkened room. "Did the elevator break down or something? You took long enough!" She grabbed Chalcey's arm and dragged her inside, pushing her toward the nearest guest bedroom. "He's in there," she whispered, heading back to her own master suite.

"Sam, I'm so—"

"What's taking so long, babe?" a muffled male voice demanded.

"Coming!" Sam called.

"Sure wish I was!" the man groused. "Get your ass in here and finish what you started."

*Eeuuuw!* That was so much more than Chalcey needed to know. Sounded like Marcus was still on the outer. She wondered who Sam had waiting in her bed. And how come Sam had broken one of her personal rules by inviting the guy back to her apartment. Cripes. The world sure was changing. And not necessarily in a good way.

"Sam, I'm sorry about the other day. With Wulf. I was a bitch. Forgive me?"

"Nothing to forgive."

Sam enfolded her in a hug that threatened to crack Chalcey's ribs, and vanished into her room, leaving Chalcey standing all on her lonesome in the dark. Huh. Grossness and TMI aside, at least she didn't need to worry about Sam eavesdropping on her little tête-à-tête with Wulf. Sam would be way too busy, uh, finishing what she'd started.

Chalcey eased open the door to the guest bedroom and peeked inside. The super-king-sized bed sported a Wulf-sized lump in the middle. She ventured closer. In the dim light offered by the partially opened blinds, she could see that he lay on his side, facing away from her, with the sheet draped across his hips.

She padded over to the edge of the bed, content to stand motionless until her eyesight adjusted enough that she could drink in the long lines of his heavily muscled back. He stirred as though sensing her regard. She sucked in a startled breath as he rolled onto his back and flung an arm out toward her. Thankfully, he slumbered on, so she grasped the rare opportunity to look all she liked with impunity, without having to resist the lure of his brilliantly blue eyes. Wanting her.

He was beautiful. A superbly fit male in the prime of his life.

She bent toward him, leaning closer to brush a stray lock of his hair back from his face.

His eyelids fluttered and opened. His gaze locked with hers. His lips curved in a gentle smile. "Chalcedony," he murmured. "I hope you are real, and not a fantasy."

A wave of sexual hunger slammed her, stealing her ability to breathe. She backed away as he sat up, and the sheet fell away. He was naked. And obviously pleased to see her. Very pleased indeed.

She ran her tongue over suddenly dry lips, and then quickly closed her mouth. The gesture might be construed as overtly sexual. An invitation.

Wulf's eyes had darkened. His lids lowered slightly, mouth parting to show his perfect white teeth. He ran his tongue over his upper lip.

She didn't know whether he consciously intended to mimic her gesture, or was sizing her up and deciding exactly where to take a bite out of her. Anticipation fluttered in her belly. "That was you in my dream, wasn't it? Making love to me even though you weren't physically there. How'd you do that, Wulf? It was as though you were there with me, touching me. How is it possible for you to mind-fuck me like that?"

"I do not know. I imagined you so clearly that it seemed you were truly here with me. I enjoyed thinking of how best to pleasure you, Chalcedony, and imagining you reacting to my touch." He smiled at her, the feral smile of a predator. He crawled across the mattress toward her, slowly and gracefully, like some big jungle cat.

He was dangerous. If she wanted her heart to stay in one piece, she should run hell for leather. She knew this unequivocally, and yet she wasn't moving. Too late she realized she'd backed herself against the wall.

She squeezed her eyelids shut in an attempt to banish him from her senses so that she could think. This was not what she'd planned. She'd only wanted to talk, to thrash out some of the worries churning in her head, and discover what sort of a man he really was.

His big hands spanned her waist, tugging her far enough from the wall to slide his hands behind her and cup her butt. She sensed him lowering his head, slowly, torturously slowly. His breath caressed her face with warmth and promise. She didn't dare open her eyes but she knew his lips hovered just above hers. She quivered with the effort to hold still, and not close the slight distance between them. And when he possessed her lips, all thought of flight or self-preservation fled and she uttered a ragged whimper.

His kiss was tender, soft. It teased her senses, tantalized, made her want more. It took all the will she could muster not to thrust her tongue into his mouth and take what she wanted.

When his lips finally moved away from her mouth, she opened her eyes. Seeing the desire in his gaze, the desperate hunger written on his features…. Before she could establish any sort of brain function, she had to issue a stern mental reminder about what a hugely bad idea it would be to give in.

"Wulf—"

He nibbled her neck, sending pleasurably shivery frissons skittering over her skin.

"Wulf."

He wedged a knee between her thighs, nudging her legs apart and pressing closer—so close that his erect cock nudged her stomach. She fought to stop herself from thrusting her hips. Someone groaned, a needy, yearning sound. And she realized it was her.

His large hand cupped her breast, squeezing her nipple through her t-shirt. His lips found the wildly beating pulse at her throat. She wanted to abandon herself to the sensations pouring over her, to sheath his cock in her hand and make him groan for her, as *she'd* groaned for him. But if she did that, she would be lost. They needed to talk. Now. Before her will-power completely dissolved.

He insinuated one hand beneath the hem of her t-shirt and spread his palm over her bare stomach. Heat flared beneath his hand. It rippled over her skin, flashing outward, enveloping her in delicious warmth.

"Wulf!" It took all her strength to push him away.

He blinked down at her, surprised. "What is the problem, Chalcedony? Do you not want me to bed you? Your body's responses tell me otherwise."

He leaned toward her again but she flung up her hand. "No. Stay away from me. We need to talk."

"No? You tell me, no?"

"That's right. I'm not one of your willing bed-slaves. I can choose to say no. And when I say no, you don't get to force me into your bed. You don't have the right."

"Force you?" He stepped back from her like he'd discovered she was contagious. "I never *forced* you, Chalcedony. You wanted me—there could be no mistaking that fact. And I wanted you. So I took you."

"That's precisely my point, Wulf. You took me, just as you were about to again. I have some say in this, too, you know. What about what I want?"

He stared at her, a deep frown etched between his brows.

"Did I not give you pleasure in the shower?"

"Yes—lots. To be honest, it was the best sex I've ever had. But that's not the point."

"Then if I gave you pleasure, what is the issue? We have no other partners we are beholden to. We will join again and pleasure each other, as has been the way of men and their women since time immemorial."

She gusted a sigh and scrubbed her fingers through her hair, tugging on the ends, hoping the sharp little pains would help her find the right words. How on earth did she explain this to a man whose entire culture was based around taking women for whatever purposes they desired? "Look, it would take more time than I have right now to explain a sexually emancipated woman to you. So I'm not going to even try. Suffice it to say, things are vastly different between men and women of my world."

The poor guy looked even more confused, if that was at all possible. Confusion didn't sit well on his handsome features. Chalcey got the unsettling impression that Wulf was a man who'd never been confused about anything in his entire life.

*Hah. Sorry babe, you'd best get used to it.*

The sex-starved part of her was saying "Hurry up already! Get naked and let's have fabulously mind-blowing sex with Wulf again." While the other part, the supposedly rational, intelligent part, wanted to insist Wulf put his clothes on right now, so they could talk things to death and kill the passion. It was like having Jekyll and Hyde arguing in her head.

"How about you put some clothes on?"

"I think not. This time, you have invaded my space, Chalcedony. This time, you do not get to dictate the terms."

"Oh. Okay. I guess I can manage." Sure, they had to talk, but they could still talk if he was naked, right? And he looked good naked. So very, very good. Looking was still manageable. So long as she didn't touch, everything would be peachy and she'd remain in control. So long as she didn't reveal how much she wanted to jump him right now....

Steeling herself to put on the act of a lifetime, she edged around him to perch on the edge of the bed. She patted the mattress beside her. "Okay, Wulf. Take a load off and let's talk this out. I've learned some stuff from my mother that I think you should hear about before we— Ah, before anything else happens between us."

He sprawled on the mattress beside her, leaning back on his elbows in a position that made a certain very much awake, and very distracting portion of his anatomy, very obvious. "Very well, Chalcedony. First, we will talk."

For the time being she ignored the implications of that "first", loaded with the promise of what might come *second* though it was. She tore her gaze from his groin, thanked God the dim light hid her flushed face, and got down to business. "Why exactly do you think you're so attracted to me, Wulf? Don't you think it was unusual to feel so strongly about me the first time you saw me? Or is it that you just can't resist big breasts?"

"Why would I not be strongly attracted to a beautiful woman?"

A reluctant smile curled her lips. That was a really superb answer. The silver-tongued devil sure knew how to flatter a girl.

As if he'd read her thoughts, he asked, "Do you not consider yourself beautiful, Chalcedony?"

"Me? Nah. I'm too tall and except for these—" she pointed to her breasts "—I'm not at all curvy in the right places. If I didn't have my double Ds, you wouldn't even give me a second look. Plus my hair is an untamable disaster, and my mouth is too big."

"You are beautiful to me, Chalcedony."

Oooh, he was good. Really good. "It's sweet of you to say so. But I suspect the real reason you're attracted to me is because I've been chosen as your potential life-mate by the

Crystal Guardian. I think neither of us has much of a choice about our attraction to each other because of this curse-thingy. And I don't know about you but—"

He grabbed her forearms and shook her to silence. "Curse? What curse?"

"You know, Pieter's curse. The one that bound you and your men to the crystals."

He stared at her, nostrils flared and lips pressed tightly shut, like she'd suddenly grown two heads. "Repeat this curse to me, Chalcedony."

His terse tone and bruising grip on her arms brooked no denial. She sucked in a shaky breath, determined not to let the fear creeping into her heart prevent her from seeing this through to the end. "Okay. Let's see if I can remember. Um, verily the crystal for which thee be named, er, shalt form the… the… prison in which thee be bound. Yep, that was it."

He shook her again, but more gently this time.

"Hey! Thinking, here! Quit doing that or I'll stuff it up." She closed her eyes against the intensity of his tightly reined fury, and recited the first part silently again. "Okay, got it. Verily the crystal for which thee be named, shalt form the prison in which thee be bound, to atone the sins for which thee be blamed, 'til thee be blessed and thy true love be found. Corny, I know. Whoever made it up was no Shakespeare, but those are the exact words I heard him say in my dream-vision-thingy."

He released her and she rubbed the circulation back into her arms. "So. Do you want to hear what else I know, or would you rather try to seduce me again?" It was meant as sarcasm, a defensive measure against the anger she could sense in him. But it came out as a breathy plea. The plea of a woman who wanted a man in the worst way.

His gaze lingered at her mouth, lowered to her breasts, lingered there again. Desire flared in her heart, in her needy body. She dug her nails into her palms to keep from reaching out to touch him.

"Seducing you is always foremost in my thoughts, Chalcedony. But this once, I think it prudent for me to control my desires—difficult though that may prove for me with you so near."

Ohhh my. He was such a charmer.

"Please, Chalcedony, tell me everything you know."

She scooted across the mattress and wedged a couple of pillows against the headboard before stretching out and making herself comfortable. "Brace yourself. This is gonna blow your mind."

CHALCEY WATCHED THE planes of Wulf's face turn to uncompromising stone, his kissable lips compress into a tight uncompromising line. She no longer feared his reaction to her revelations. Now, uppermost in her mind was dealing with her horror for everything he'd suffered, her empathy for his frustration at having so little control over his fate.

She understood a little of how he must feel. It'd been so much easier when she hadn't known about the spell, when she hadn't understood the stakes. Then it'd only been about him and her. A man and a woman who lusted after each other. Just sex—if it could ever be "just sex" of course—and possibly, *maybe*, some sort of a relationship that would inevitably follow its own course.

Now, everything they felt, or might feel for each other, was tainted, overshadowed by the strong possibility that their attraction was not of their own making, and they were being manipulated by supernatural forces.

If Chalcey chose to complete the bond, it might not be because of any true feelings she might have for him. It might not truly be her choice. She knew it. Wulf knew it, too. She hated that everything she believed she felt for him might be false. Words could not describe how much that knowledge sucked. It was too cruel.

But however bad her own situation appeared, Wulf's was far worse. If they failed the Testing, Pieter would bind him back to his crystal and destroy him.

"How did it feel, Wulf? In the darkness, all alone for centuries—it must have been hellish." She needed to hear the full extent of his suffering. She had to know and understand, so that she could know and understand him. Surely the pity and compassion she felt for all he'd suffered couldn't solely be a result of the bonding spell. Surely those emotions, at least, were true and real.

He stirred and grasped her hand, pulling it into his lap. He turned it palm up and circled his thumb gently over her skin. If she didn't know better, if she didn't know how strong he was, she might have believed he sought comfort.

Silence blanketed the room and for once Chalcey didn't feel the need to keep it at bay with smart-assed comments or senseless chatter.

"'Tis black." His voice sounded empty, devoid of emotion. "No, more than black. An absence of everything, even light. I cannot see any part of my body, not even my hand when I hold it to my face. There is no sound. I hear nothing, not even the screams I know are tearing my throat apart. And I feel nothing, not the touch of my own hands, or the clothes I know I wear on my body. 'Tis endless lack of sensation. I am suspended in a great nothingness with naught but my own thoughts to keep me company.

"Before.... Before I was imprisoned, I did not believe in *Halja*—the place you call Hell. But now I do. Because I have been there. And suffered. And I am glad that Malach's suffering has ended. I would wish death upon him, rather than condemn him to another lifetime of eternal nothingness."

"What—?" Chalcey swallowed to ease to harsh dryness in her throat. "What did you do to deserve that sort of a punishment? Why did Pieter hate you so much?"

His face tightened. "You are so very certain that I committed a crime, Chalcedony." Then he puffed out a sigh. "Who can know what truly lies in a man's heart? Doubtless the old man suffers too, in his way. His spell condemns him to live until we, his victims, find our life-mates. And knowing the warriors of my world, and how they look upon women, that task is an onerous one, indeed. To live on and on in the body of an old man, weary of life, yearning for eternal sleep, but denied? 'Tis a form of torture, too. I believe that my men and I are not the only ones punished by his spell."

He was silent for a while, his jaw clenching and unclench-ing as he sought the right words. Or perhaps relived the events leading to his capture.

"As for our crime against your people? We Styrians did not believe it to be a crime. Our priests commanded us to do what needed to be done to ensure our race survived. Without wom-en, we had no way to procreate. And because our progeny were always male, we needed more women. We stole your world's women, yes, but our race's very survival depended upon them. Even so, no woman was ever forced to lie with a man. 'Tis not our way. I cannot speak for how the Choosing ritual is done now—or indeed, if 'tis still done at all—but in my time we treated all the women well. Their every need was taken care of."

Someone had to play devil's advocate. "But you took them away from their homes, their families and everything they knew, Wulf. Your people took them for breeding stock. And however much your captives might have eventually accepted—even liked—the men who chose them, you took away their choices. That was unforgivable."

"Perhaps. But if the old man is as strong in magic as he ap-pears, why then did he not simply send us home and destroy the gateway from our world to yours? I do not think my men and I deserved the punishment meted out to us."

"Me, neither." Chalcey couldn't do it, couldn't take the easy way out by refusing to complete the bonding. She couldn't condemn Wulf to oblivion and then death. He'd suffered enough.

So what was a soft-hearted girl to do when a hot naked man needed saving?

Well, duh. Jump his bones of course. Besides, she reasoned that she'd found a loophole in this whole living-together-forever-as-life-mates thing. Once Wulf was safely a permanent part of her world and no longer bound by the crystal, he could go his own way if he so chose. And she could get on with her life, too. Without him.

At least, that's what she told herself.

She also figured they should get the whole sex and bonding bit out of the way, so they could move on to the Testing bit of their unorthodox relationship. And as she lay in Wulf's arms after having fabulously mind-blowing sex for the second time that night, the bond proclaimed itself completed.

"Did you hear that, Chalcedony?" Wulf asked.

"If you mean that bell-like chiming in my mind? Yep. I did."

There was nothing more to say. They'd fulfilled the terms of the bonding by exchanging true-names and having sex the requisite three times. It only remained to be seen whether they would pass the Testing or fail.

Wulf woke her in the early hours of the morning. And this time, it was more than sex. This time, it was truly making love, so tender, so achingly poignant, that she wept. And as she arched beneath him and sobbed his name, it was then that she realized the truth. Be-spelled or not, she'd fallen for Wulf. Hard.

The Crystal Guardian sure knew how to pick 'em.

Evil bastard. One day he would get his.

# CHAPTER TWELVE

C HALCEY WANDERED FROM Sam's guest room and nearly bit off her tongue when she spotted Sam's surprise guest lounging full-length on a couch, flicking through TV channels. She'd have been tempted to make her excuses, and grab Wulf and hustle him out the door, if she hadn't been so concerned about Sam. Of all the guys she must have had to choose from last night, did it have to be this one? Was Sam freaking insane? It was enough to give a girl chronic indigestion before a single morsel of food passed her lips.

"Samantha," Wulf said. "May I have a private word with you?"

His tone was so polite and carefully neutral that Chalcey shivered. *Uh oh.* She sank into the nearest seat at the kitchen table. She didn't have to be a rocket scientist to know that Wulf, too, was majorly unimpressed by Sam's choice.

The man of the moment finally seemed to notice Sam had other company. "Well well. If it isn't tits on a stick. Whassup, Chel-sea?" He tossed the remote on the floor, rolled off the couch, and slimed over to the table, choosing to plunk his jerk-off ass into the chair opposite. He tossed Chalcey an ingratiating smile, like he hadn't just insulted her, and expected her to be thrilled to bits he'd remembered her name, even if he didn't pronounce it right. He chose to ignore Wulf. Probably the only smart thing he'd done lately.

Chalcey made a noncommittal noise and closed her eyes to

send a brief prayer for a happy ending to this god-awful farce. She blamed herself. She shouldn't have played down her encounter with Ray. She should have told her best friend exactly what had happened, and how scared she'd been. Surely then Sam would have been a heap more choosy.

Shit. What a mess. It'd be a miracle if this breakfast ended without somebody doing bodily harm to somebody else.

"Samantha," Wulf said, an edge to his tone conveying that he was just the teensiest bit pissed.

Sam wouldn't meet his gaze. "Later, okay, Wulf? I'm a bit tied up at the moment."

Sam's usual practiced nonchalance when it came to casual encounters of the sexual kind was an epic fail. All Chalcey saw spread across Sam's face was guilt and self-loathing. She would give Sam eleven-out-of-ten for her attempt at Happy Home-maker, though. She'd donned a frilly apron over that ass-skimming silk robe from last night, and taken a staggering amount of food from the refrigerator. Now she was frying up bacon, eggs and hash browns, and studiously ignoring the elephant in the room.

Poor Sam. She'd really screwed up this time. Chalcey had half-expected she would try to excise Marcus from her life by using the most convenient hot-looking guy available. She hadn't expected the aforementioned hot-looking guy to be Ray. Worse, Sam didn't look at all thrilled about how her night had gone, either. He must have been a real jerk.

Ray chose that moment to leer at Chalcey. He compound-ed his crimes by glaring at Wulf as though he'd like to spear him with his fork, sneaking supposedly covert glances at Chalcey's cleavage, and ogling Sam's ass.

If Chalcey hadn't been so completely certain that the shit was going to hit the fan, she might have found his antics more amusing. Well, that and the fact she was freaking out at the thought of a knife-wielding scumbag having anything at all to do with her best friend, let alone spending the night. Her throat was so tight, it was all she could do to choke down her orange juice. Please God, Wulf would refrain from doing something drastic. Like hauling a certain waste of oxygen onto the balcony and tossing him over the railing.

Wulf, however, seemed content to let the matter slide— perhaps for Sam's sake. Whatever the reason, Chalcey finally allowed herself to relax. Wulf was more than capable of dealing with whatever Ray dished out.

Sam put the finishing touches to her cholesterol-laden fry-up. She dumped the serving platter onto the table, and instructed them all to tuck in. Ray filled his plate, and then proceeded to fill his face without even acknowledging Sam's efforts.

Wulf scowled at the other man. Evidently it was perfectly fine to sit and watch a woman slave over a hot stove, so long as you thanked her nicely afterward. Humph. He'd be sorely disappointed if he expected Chalcey to buy into that credo. And rather hungry a lot of the time, too.

"Thank you for your efforts, Samantha," Wulf said. "This hearty fare is much welcomed, for I am hungry indeed this morning."

"Thanks, hon," Chalcey said, mindful of her manners. "This is wonderful."

Sam beamed. "No problem, you guys."

Wulf threw Ray a pointed glance, but the dumbass didn't take the hint.

Chalcey decided it might be prudent to clue him in. "Ray?" she said, oh-so-sweetly interrupting his single-minded mastication of his food. "You gonna thank Sam for cooking you breakfast? She's gone to a heap of trouble."

"Huh?" He glanced up from his plate and seemed surprised to find himself the subject of three critical gazes. "What're you all staring at?"

Sam rolled her eyes and fluttered a hand in a gesture of mock-despair. "Forget it, guys. It's not important."

"I disagree," Wulf said. "My people have a saying that has served us well for countless generations: Show gratitude to your woman and you will never know hunger. But show her contempt and her food will nourish you no longer.'"

"What the fuck's that s'posed to mean?" Ray mumbled around a churning, half-chewed mouthful of sausage and egg.

Wow. Classy.

"You did not show Samantha any gratitude for her efforts to feed you," Wulf said. "Ergo, you are an unconscionably rude bastard."

"Is that so?" Ray tossed his fork aside and stood so abruptly that he sent his chair crashing to the floor.

Chalcey noted that his eyes were glassy and slightly unfocussed. Crap. What the hell was he on? She tried to catch Sam's gaze.

"Indeed it is so." Wulf remained seated and began to eat.

"I showed her enough gratitude last night," Ray said. "She had a good time—a real good time." He made a V with two fingers, lifted them to his lips and waggled his tongue between them. All the while, he stared meaningfully at Chalcey, as though he expected her to be envious.

Eeeew.

"It's her should be thanking me after what I did for her. Least she can do is cook me up a good feed. Isn't that right, babe?"

Sam didn't deign to respond. And she still wouldn't look at Chalcey.

"I said, isn't that right, babe?"

"Yes, Ray." Sam spat the words. "You give good head. Happy, now?"

Yikes. Sam was sooo not impressed. She sat rigidly upright in her chair, an angry red flush staining her neck and crawling up her face. Yep, majorly pissed. This could get ugly real fast. Ray had really crumbled his cookies. Good. Hopefully Sam'd kick him out on his ass, and be a heap more careful about who she brought home from now on.

Hopefully. Any time now would be real good.

Radiating smugness, Ray righted his chair and sat down to finish his breakfast. It took mere seconds before he put his foot in his mouth again. "Heard you enjoying yourself last night, Chel-sea. Got a bit rough, huh?" He made a production out of stroking his chin and drawing attention to Chalcey's bruise. "Figured you liked it rough. I told Marcus you were gagging for it. Told him he should go for it. Girl like you'd show him a real good time, wouldn't ya, Chel-sea?"

He looked her up and down in a way that made Chalcey want to rush off and scrub herself clean in the shower. With steel wool. "Yeah," he said. "You look the type to show a guy a good time. Know what I mean?"

"Gee, thank you, Ray. I know exactly what you mean." Charming. This guy was first class pond-scum.

Chalcey dared a sideways glance at Wulf. He'd gone still. Too still. Ray was about to get his comeuppance.

"Wulf," Samantha murmured.

"Samantha."

They stared at each other, communicating in some wordless fashion. In perfect unison, they rose from their seats to take up positions either side of Ray.

What followed was a faultlessly choreographed sequence of events that left Chalcey openmouthed, and impressed as hell. Wulf plucked Ray from his chair, cuffed him 'round the head a few times to make his point, and then dragged him across the room by the scruff of his neck. Completely unhurried, Sam strolled to the door and flung it open a split second before Wulf slung Ray through it, and then she slammed it shut.

Next, she sauntered over to the phone. "Hello, security? This is Samantha Greenwood. I have just ejected a Mr. Ray Walker from my apartment. Would you please send someone up immediately to escort Mr. Walker from the building? Oh, and be careful. He may have a knife on his person. Yes. Yes, please. Absolutely put him on the no-go list. Thank you. And you have a good morning, too."

Wulf and Sam then sat down to finish their breakfast, ignoring the pounding on the door and the ugly imprecations Ray was squawking from the hallway. A short time later, Chalcey heard raised male voices and then ominous silence.

In Sam's place, Chalcey would have called the cops. It was now or never. She had to get this off her chest. "You're my best friend so I hate to say this, Sam, but I'm going to anyway. Ray is a foul-mouthed dick. And I think he's using, too. That makes him even more dangerous."

Sam paused, fork halfway to her mouth. "Yeah. Enough with the lecture, Chalce. I should have listened to you."

"You deserve better—Marcus, for instance. You know he turned up at the party asking after you." *And planted one on your best friend, but let's not go there.*

"Mmmm." Sam lowered her eyes and continued eating.

Chalcey knew better than to press the point. If she began to loudly extol the virtues of a relationship with Marcus, Sam would likely ignore him on principle. Chalcey had said her piece and she wasn't about to harp on about Sam's appalling taste in men. Best friends didn't do that to each other.

Wulf, apparently, agreed, and the three of them finished breakfast in thoughtful silence. Then, to Chalcey's utter astonishment, Wulf cleared the dirty dishes from the table, rinsed them off, and stacked them in the dishwasher. He hummed as he put in the dishwashing tablet, carefully programmed the dishwasher and turned it on.

Sam intercepted Chalcey's slow blink of surprise. "He's fascinated with anything electronic," she whispered. "It's entertaining as hell watching his expression when the TV's on, or he's listening to the stereo. It's like he's enthralled."

Chalcey could well imagine he would be, considering where he'd come from. She envisioned his people as nomadic tribes who lived in tents—sort of like romanticized versions of

the Bedouin. Not exactly prime real estate for housing elec-
tronics or white-ware.

"Coffee?" Wulf inquired from the kitchen.

Chalcey glanced at Sam, who nodded, her green eyes twin-
kling with glee. "Yes, please."

"Chalcedony?"

"Er, yes? Please." Two days and Sam had already managed
to partially domesticate him. Way to go, girlfriend!

Chalcey watched Wulf as he moved about the kitchen. Despite his size, he moved with a cat-like fluidity and the
inherent grace of a born fighter—a man whose body was a
weapon. Even in jeans and an immaculately tailored shirt—no
doubt courtesy of Sam's bottomless purse—he oozed contained power, as though he could explode into violence at a
moment's notice if sufficiently provoked. There was something uncivilized and primitive about him. At least by the
standards of your average modern American man. She had no
doubt whatsoever that Wulf was considered the epitome of the
ideal male in his own world.

He began to grind the beans in an old wooden and brass
hand-grinder fixed on the wall. Chalcey raised inquiring
eyebrows at Sam. "Didn't think that thing worked. Thought it
was a purely decorative antique or something."

Sam shrugged. "Me, too. Mom gave it to me. Didn't even
realize it worked until Wulf started mucking around with it.
According to him it's important to hand-grind coffee beans—
something about releasing more flavor into the brew. That's
why he refuses to use my electric grinder, about the only
electric gadget he hasn't taken to."

They observed him winding the handle of the grinder for a
while longer. "Are you sure he knows what he's doing?"
Chalcey asked.

Sam grinned. "Chill. He knows exactly what he's doing. He
didn't appreciate the way I made the coffee at all. It's almost a
ritual for him, like a Japanese tea ceremony or something. And

I have to say he makes a great French press. Seems our coffee is similar to a brew he drank back in his— Back home."

Chalcey narrowed her eyes at Sam but she was all wide innocent eyes and guileless expression. "What's the big deal about him making coffee, Chalce?" she asked.

"Oh, nothing. I'm just surprised he makes such a production out of it, is all." And here she'd been worrying that Wulf would struggle to fit in to his new life. He was adapting well. Maybe there was hope for him yet in this world. The ability to make a good coffee was an excellent start, anyway.

Sam's voice interrupted Chalcey's little domestic fantasy of Wulf wearing a frilly apron—and nothing else—and wielding a feather duster. Talk about porn for women. "Sorry, what did you say?"

"I said, so when are you going to tell me where he really comes from?"

Chalcey leaned back in her chair, smoothing her features to hide her shock. "What do you mean?"

"I'm not stupid," Sam said. "It's screamingly obvious he's not from this part of the world. I was curious, so I asked him straight. He's told me a bit about his background but there's a lot more to it, isn't there, Chalce? I think he's a time-traveler. So how did he get here?"

Chalcey glanced in Wulf's direction. It was his story, his fate. She had no right to blab it to Sam. "There's really nothing to tell," she began, racking her brains and steeling herself for a furious bout of prevarication.

"Tell her, Chalcedony," Wulf called from the kitchen. "Tell her everything. I give you my permission."

"You sure?" She tried to read his impassive expression.

"I am sure."

"All right. But you'd better make that coffee good and strong. I have a feeling she's gonna need it because what I know is pretty out there."

"Indeed."

To her eternal credit, Sam did not laugh in Chalcey's face and accuse her of being a complete and utter head-case. She could be very grown up when she wanted to be.

She did smirk an awful lot during particular bits of the story, though. Especially after some pointed questioning on her part forced Chalcey to admit they'd already got the making love thrice bit out of the way. Sheesh. Now Chalcey could add "sex-crazed" to her growing list of dubious personal attributes.

"That's some story, Chalce."

"You don't believe me?"

"Oh, it's a fantastic tale but I believe you all right. How else could *you* manage to hook a man like Wulf?"

"Gee. Thanks for the vote of confidence." Chalcey made a rude face at her friend. Even though she'd kind of been thinking the same thing herself.

"Kidding." Sam sipped another cup of Wulf's excellent coffee. "So happens I believe in curses and the like."

Chalcey snorted, and quickly turned it into a cough when Sam's deadly serious expression didn't falter. "You do?"

"Have done ever since I was a little girl and my mother took me to see this spooky old fortune-teller." Sam giggled in a self-conscious fashion. "The woman went on and on about this darkness that she could see hovering about Mom's aura. Claimed some jealous bitch had cursed Mom to eternal unhappiness, so she would be forever seeking a man capable of fulfilling her, and forever failing to find him. I had nightmares for weeks afterward."

Chalcey felt her eyes go huge and round and owl-like. Mrs. Greenwood had been married four times already and was apparently eyeing up a potential fifth candidate.

Sam correctly interpreted her expression. "Exactly. So what are you going to do?"

Chalcey glanced sideways at Wulf, locking gazes with him as he sipped his coffee. "Wait for the Testing, I guess. And hope like hell we pass."

He reached over the table and squeezed her hand. "You will not fail me, Chalcedony. I have faith in you. Do not be fearful. If it is my fate to be destroyed by the old man at this month's end, then so be it."

"I'll be damned if I let that happen!"

"Do not say that—not even in jest, Chalcedony. Having been damned for what seemed like eternity, I assure you that you would not like it overmuch."

Chalcey drained her coffee cup. Her stomach gave one of those twisting lurches and her mind pricked. She'd forgotten something. Something important. Her gaze dropped to her watch. Mickey's hands showed it was just gone ten-thirty. "Shi-it! Teacher's meeting at eleven. I have to fly."

"I will accompany you," Wulf said.

"There's no need. It's just routine stuff. You'd probably be bored witless."

Sam disagreed. "But what about your mother, Chalce? It might be a good idea to have Wulf around to help you defend yourself."

"Defend myself against Francesca? Why? Don't you think that I can handle my own mother?"

"Chalcey, Chalcey, Chalcey." Sam shook her head. "Frankly? No. She's going to take one look at you and know you've, er, fully consummated your relationship with Wulf. If I know Francesca, she's going to have kittens. And you're going to be hip-deep in her crap."

"What do you mean she's going to take one look at me and know I've had sex?"

"What do you reckon, Wulf?" Sam drafted him to her cause and Chalcey had to endure them both gazing intently at her.

Wulf sighed. "You are right, Samantha. Francesca will know immediately. I will have to distract her."

"That's ridiculous!" Chalcey scoffed. "And exactly how are you going to distract my mother, Wulf?"

"You'll be late," Sam interjected. "I'm calling you a taxi. And it's not ridiculous at all." She grabbed the phone.

"God, Sam. How the hell can someone know I've had sex recently simply by looking at me? And hang up that phone because I don't have enough cash for a taxi. We'll just have to run like heck."

"Soon I will have earned enough cash to pay for our transportation," Wulf said. "But in the meantime, Samantha has been generous enough to advance me a loan. I will pay for the taxi."

Chalcey had started for the bathroom, intending to check out what everyone else was able to see. Hang on…. She halted. "Earned it? How?"

"He can tell you in the taxi on the way," Sam said. "And Chalce? Take it from me, your mother will know what you've been up to the moment she lays eyes on you. Mothers are uncanny like that. My mom always knew when I'd had sex. That's why I bought my own place—I got sick and tired of the lectures every morning over breakfast. It ruined my digestion. Trust me, Francesca will know."

Every morning? Chalcey almost felt sorry for Mrs. Greenwood. Almost.

Sam smiled enigmatically. "Taxi's probably here. Good luck with Francesca. You're gonna need it."

Wulf ushered Chalcey out the door. "Bet you're wrong!" she yelled over her shoulder.

"Bet you I'm not," Sam said. The door slammed, cutting off Chalcey's chance to have the final word.

"Do not worry, Chalcedony," Wulf said, as the elevator descended. "I undertake to shield you from the knowing eyes of the local populace and divert their attention from your sorry state."

"My sorry state?" She glared up at him. Damn man was grinning from ear to ear. "Oh, you!" She punched him on the arm, and then shook her abused knuckles. Yeow.

All the same, she didn't look at the front desk clerk as she passed. And she avoided looking the doorman in the eye as he opened the door to the taxi, too. If she did have "I had sex last night. Whoopee!" indelibly scrawled across her forehead, it was better to be safe than sorry. She would play it cool. Her mother would never know.

CHALCEY WAS STILL reeling from learning that Wulf had scored a gig as a bouncer at one of Sam's favorite clubs when she pushed open the door to the studio. "Hey guys!" she greeted Jai, Paulo and Leah. "Sorry if I kept you waiting."

Francesca hurried from the bedroom. "There you are, darling. I've been worried sick—" The words died on her lips. "Chalcedony!" Her hand fluttered at her throat like she'd morphed into some retro movie heroine. "How could you?"

Everyone turned to stare at Chalcey. Their gazes fastened on her face, then did a full head-to-toe sweep. She smoothed her hair. "What?"

Jai recovered first. Hands on hips, he chortled with a vast degree of unholy delight. "Go, Chalce!" He threw back his head and howled in a credible imitation of a wolf, and then he slapped Wulf on the back. "You the man!"

Paulo's grin nearly split his face in half. "Had a goood night, huh, Chalce?" He dropped a wink. "It's about time you cut loose, sweetie."

Oh. My. Freaking. God. Chalcey covered her face with her hands. She was so done-for.

When no further comments were forthcoming, she risked a glance at Wulf from between her fingers. He had pride-filled male written all over his face. In fact, all three guys were grinning like idiots. Men.

And Leah? She was looking Wulf up and down, mouth still agape with what Chalcey presumed to be incredulous awe.

Leah blinked, and her gaze cut to Chalcey. "Yum," she drawled. "You go, girl."

Sheesh. No help there.

Chalcey finally plucked up enough courage to check what her mother thought. Francesca, of course, was the only one present who didn't appear to believe that Chalcey having sex was at all amusing or awe-inspiring. Her eyes were cold as little steel ball-bearings. "I need to talk to you, Chalcedony. Right this minute."

Chalcey opened her mouth to state the obvious, that she was about to begin a staff meeting and Francesca would have to wait, when Wulf cut in. "I would like to talk to you first, Francesca."

Francesca glared at him, looking very much like she had a hankering to carve out his liver with whatever blunt instrument was handy. Finally she nodded. "Very well. We will talk."

Wulf cupped her elbow in his hand and led her toward the bedroom. Chalcey caught a glimpse of her mother's face before Wulf closed the sliding door carefully behind them. All Francesca's fury had vanished. Now her expression conveyed anguish, as though physical contact with Wulf brought terrible memories to the fore.

Poor Francesca.

And poor Wulf. Chalcey didn't envy either of them the coming conversation. But at least her own confrontation with Francesca had been averted. For now, anyway. Francesca was unlikely to let it rest.

"That was tense," Leah finally said, breaking the awkward silence. "Your mom's pretty protective of you, huh?"

Chalcey would have loved to retire somewhere private, where she could gaze deeply into a mirror and try to spot what everyone else had so easily read in her face. Instead, she acted like a professional and got down to business. "Yeah. She's a worrier. Let's get started. We've got a lot to cover."

As she went over class lists, timetables, lesson plans, codes of conduct and the myriad other tasks she hoped would contribute toward running a successful dance studio, Chalcey's mind kept wandering to Wulf and Francesca. She would kill to know what they were discussing.

She racked her brains for anything Francesca could conceivably say or do to ruin things with Wulf. She couldn't think of a damn thing but that didn't mean she was home-free. She knew her mother, knew what Francesca was capable of. Francesca had self-justification down to a fine art—she wouldn't have had the stomach to condemn Malach otherwise.

Chalcey was committed to Wulf now but she didn't trust her mother to respect her wishes. When it came to Wulf, she didn't trust her mother at all.


FRANCESCA SUFFERED HIM to escort her to the tiny kitchen before she rounded on him. "Get your hands off me."

Wulf pulled out a chair and applied firm pressure to her shoulder. "Sit."

She obeyed him. Not that she had a choice in the matter. And she knew it. She eyed him like he was a rabid dog, crouched and ready to rip out her throat if she made a wrong move.

He puffed out a breath through his nostrils. He would get nothing useful from her in this state. "Would you like coffee?"

"Tea," she said.

"Tea." Of course it would be tea. Nothing would be easy for him where Francesca were concerned. He filled the electric kettle, plugged it into the wall socket, and flicked the switch. This appliance differed from Samantha's but the on-switch was obvious enough. He depressed it. After a few seconds, the rumble the appliance made told him he'd not forgotten a step.

Pride warmed his belly. Such a small accomplishment, but significant all the same. He could adapt to this world he'd believed magical. In time, even the wonders of electricity and heated water on tap would seem prosaic and unremarkable.

He rummaged through the canisters on the countertop, and found nothing resembling tea leaves. One contained little

bags of what looked like tea leaves. Rather than face Francesca's scorn if they proved to be something other, he held the
canister out to her. "I do not know how to make tea without
leaves and a pot. If you wish a drinkable brew, then best you
instruct me."

She blinked at him. A tiny frown creased her brows. "You
would accept instructions from a woman?"

"Of course."

"I can't say I'm enthralled by the prospect of teabags but
they are convenient. Pop one in the cup, pour over boiling
water, and let it steep. I'll help myself to cream and sugar."

"Be my guest." Wulf knew full well the implication that he
was at home in Chalcedony's private rooms, while Francesca
was merely a guest, would irk her.

When she had resettled herself in her chair, he sat opposite
and allowed her to drink her tea. The silence grew as he observed his opponent—for that was how he thought of her. She
was dangerous, this woman who'd been chosen for Malach,
only to spurn him and condemn him to death.

Certainly, Wulf considered Malach's death a blessing to a
second incarceration in his malachite prison, but he could not
like Francesca for her choice. Her dying husband had begged
her to seek happiness with the other man in her life—even
given his blessing. Yet what had she done? Chosen a dying
man over one who could have lived.

He could perhaps have forgiven her for Malach's death if
she'd failed the Testing. What he could not forgive, was that
she'd not tried at all. She'd cast Malach off, left him to his fate.
And worse, to Wulf's mind, she'd told Malach exactly what
she'd learned from the old sorcerer.

Malach had known the full implications of her choice, and
faced his fate with dignity befitting a warrior of his strength
and caliber. But to be so close to redemption, only to be condemned by a woman who refused to give him a chance? Pure
torment. Enough to drive a man to insanity. Wulf could only

pray to his gods that Malach had not languished overly long in his crystal prison a second time. And that when the sorcerer had destroyed his crystal, Malach's death had been swift and clean.

"Why am I here?" Francesca said, shattering Wulf's reverie. She shrank back in her chair when he fixed his full attention on her. A little of what he'd been contemplating must have been etched on his face.

"Chalcedony has told me of your past with Malach," he said. "She came to me last night, and told me everything. And afterward, we completed the bond."

"Idiot girl!" The last remains of Francesca's contrived poise dissolved, and her hatred lashed out like a whip. "I told her everything to protect her, so that she'd make the right decision. And what does she do? Run straight into your arms and—"

"Give me a chance at redemption. She is a courageous woman, your daughter." He cocked his head to one side, examining her features, comparing. "I think she must take after her father."

Francesca reared up from her chair, and leaned over the table. He knew what she was about to do. He allowed it, and did not attempt to block her blow.

She stared at his cheek, her expression a mixture of fierce satisfaction and horror. And when he did nothing, she collapsed back into her chair, limp, all the fight and fury drained from her. She cradled her wrist in her lap. Her mouth worked, but she could not summon the words.

"I will get you ice for that." He half expected her to flee the instant he turned his back to pull a tray of ice-cubes from the small freezer section of the refrigerator. He could not tell whether she'd decided to brave his company, or whether she was too drained to move. Regardless, she'd saved him the effort of restraining her before he'd said his piece.

He handed her a dishtowel filled with ice. "Some advice,

Francesca. It would behoove you to learn to punch. A punch has far more chance of inflicting damage than a slap."

He noticed that her hand shook when she took the ice-pack from him. "And one last thing," he said. Though her gaze never wavered, she stiffened, expecting the worst. A smart woman, Francesca.

"Do not interfere with Chalcedony's choice."

"Or?" Her question was the merest whisper. If he'd not been watching her intently, he might have missed it.

"Or you risk losing that which you hold dear."

Francesca gasped and recoiled. Her complexion paled to a color akin to bones bleached in the desert sun. "Are you threatening to murder my husband?"

Wulf blew out an exasperated breath. "You are so very willing to believe the worst of me. No, you foolish creature. I am not threatening your husband. I am cautioning you to accept that Chalcedony is a woman grown, and must make her own decisions. You have disclosed everything you know and now 'tis up to her. If you continue to meddle, you risk losing your daughter. Do not force her to choose."

He did not linger to see whether she accepted his words. Chalcedony had chosen to bond with him, knowing full well the ramifications. Francesca would be a fool to alienate her daughter to such an extent that Chalcedony would excise her mother completely from her life.

Francesca did not strike him as a fool.

Wulf put the woman from his mind as he strode from the kitchen. His focus from hereon in would be Chalcedony. If his life were to be measured in weeks, he would live every day as though it were his last.

And, by the gods, if he could spend each night until the Testing in Chalcedony's arms, he would die with a smile on his face.

# CHAPTER THIRTEEN

I T HAD BEEN no surprise to Chalcey when Francesca voluntarily took up residence at the Four Seasons, a fancy hotel not far from Sam's apartment. Her mother had finally accepted it was too late, that Chalcey couldn't leave Wulf now. It would hurt too much. It would tear her apart.

Her relief at the prospect of her mother leaving couldn't have gone unnoticed, for Francesca hadn't deigned to so much as check in via phone. Chalcey couldn't find it in her to worry about her mother's state of mind. She had enough on her plate without having to pussyfoot 'round Francesca and constantly justify her choices. Like fretting over Sam and Marcus, running a business, and worrying about her students. And angsting over this upcoming Testing crap.

It wasn't like she could study for it. There was no Cliff's Notes version on how to pass a test set by a devious old Crystal Guardian with a big-ass grudge and a heap of magical woo-woo at his command. Or how to cope with the knowledge that failure would cost a man's life.

Businesswise, at least, everything was falling into place. Student numbers were still on the up and up, forcing Chalcey to schedule more and more classes until she was stretched so thin that Jai put his foot down. "Quit being a chicken, and just commit already!" were the exact words he'd used. By that, he meant taking on Paulo and Leah as teachers once they'd worked out the required notice at their current studio.

Jai was right, of course. So she'd done it—committed to taking on more staff. And immediately after making the call, she'd felt so ill she had to rush off to the ladies' bathroom. Wulf had been there for her, as he'd been there for her ever since he'd moved in. He'd held her hair back from her face as she retched over the toilet bowl, and he'd rubbed the aching muscles in her back. When she'd finished rinsing her mouth and brushing her teeth, he scooped her up and took her to bed, where he held her until she stopped shaking. No sexual overtures, just the comfort of his solidly muscled body enveloping hers, keeping her warm and safe until she was in charge of her emotions again.

In truth, with an über-sexy alpha male like Wulf around, Chalcey was kidding herself if she believed she was in charge of anything. Like the side of the bed she preferred, for example. *Her* favorite side was now his side.

And speaking of beds—specifically the things men and women tended to do in them—he was beyond amazing. When they made love, he savored every inch of her body, playing her until she was taut as a bowstring, whimpering with need. Only then would he give her what she wanted and enter her, filling the cold, empty place where her fear of losing him lurked.

He'd also repeated the shower incident with more than interest. And he'd seduced her atop her small kitchen table, which now had a distinct wobble and would never be the same again. Not to mention the stairwell, and a few other places she would never have thought of trying.

Chalcey had morphed from a woman more than capable of justifying her lack of opportunities to have sex—and happy to ignore the lack—to insatiable. She couldn't get enough of him. Didn't matter what time he got home from his bouncer gig, she would awake the instant he stepped foot in her bedroom. And damned if she wouldn't be ready for him. In the deepest darkest recesses of her soul, she knew it wasn't real, it wasn't her. She wasn't a rampant sex fiend. She was terrified of failing him, losing him, and the sex was her way of indelibly etching him onto her heart. She knew all this and she didn't care.

As Wulf had done with her body, he even made the name "Chalcey" his own. No one else said it quite like him. No one else could imbue that particular combination of letters with such incredible intimacy and lush promises of bare skin, entwined limbs and drawn-out pleasure. There was definitely something to be said for a guy with an accent. Not to mention a guy who insisted that her full name, Chalcedony, fitted her perfectly in every way.

According to Wulf it was a unique name, a name as beautiful and sensual as the crystal itself. Chalcey, stubborn to the last, disputed this quite vehemently.

As soon as she'd been old enough to understand how weird a name she'd been stuck with, Chalcey had demanded that her mother show her a piece of chalcedony. And she'd been majorly disappointed—so disappointed, in fact, that she'd burst into tears and begged her mother to change her name. There'd been nothing beautiful or sensual about the dirty-white geode her mother had produced. And not even the polished crystal Francesca had ordered in an attempt at appeasement had impressed Chalcey. Was she supposed to be pleased that while other girls' mothers named them things like Emily and Laurel and Susan, she'd been named after a creamy white egg-shaped stone marred with veins of freaky-looking lava-orange?

Wulf had soon banished her long held childhood dismay by describing chalcedony as he knew it. *Blue* chalcedony. A crystal that, once tumbled and polished, glowed with an unearthly beauty that had stolen his breath. The online image he'd shown her had finally smothered any belief that he'd been exaggerating. And for the first time in her life, Chalcey found herself liking the full version of her name.

About the only fly in the ointment were the relentless prank calls. Her answering machine was so inundated with them that weeding out the genuine calls had become a mission in frustration. If her studio wasn't so new, and she hadn't already invested in advertising and business cards, she'd have considered changing her number. She didn't believe Ray was the culprit—not even he could be so stupid. He had to know he'd be the prime suspect. Call her paranoid, but she was considering taking Jai with her to bank the class takings. No point taking unnecessary risks if there was some weirdo out there who looked on a dance studio as an easy target.

Chalcey perched on the edge of the desk in her tiny office to leaf through a bundle of mail. She examined the envelope from her accountant more closely. Funny. It didn't look like his usual bi-monthly newsletter that she usually tossed unread.

She ripped open the envelope and read through the letter. "Shit. Shit. Shit! It's not fucking fair!"

"What is wrong, Chalcey?" Wulf asked.

She tossed the letter aside and then slumped, hugging her middle. "Seems my accountant's screwed up my tax returns— only like, ever since I took him on. And with back taxes, the IRS says I owe six grand. Six frickin' grand! He apologizes for the mistake. Mistake? God! I am so firing his ass!"

She chewed her nails as she reviewed her woefully limited options, barely noticing when Wulf gently removed her fingers from her mouth. "I've got enough put away to cover upcoming expenses and the lease payment due in a couple of weeks," she said, "but not enough to cover this, as well. My bank manager and the finance company I approached have already turned me down. I am so screwed. Fuck."

Wulf cupped her hand around a mug of freshly plunged coffee and sprawled on her two-seater couch to drink his own. "Explain this *finance company* to me please, Chalcey. Is it akin to a moneylender?"

She took a bracing sip of coffee. "Exactly right. Except in this case, 'money-lending' is a misnomer because the miserly bastards aren't damned well lending me any. Both said basically the same thing. The area's not that flash and I won't attract the student numbers I need. Income from a dance studio is erratic, and I'm too inexperienced at running a business to be a good credit risk. I don't have any collateral so if I default on my payments they have nothing to sell up to recoup their losses. Yadda yadda."

"Are they in any way correct, or do they merely breathe wind through the holes in their arses?"

She inhaled her mouthful of coffee and managed to splutter, "Good one!" before a coughing fit got the better of her. "Gahhh…. Ahem! That's better. Well for a start, yes, the income from a dance studio can be erratic, but I'm hardly a profligate spender and I'm smart enough to squirrel away money from the boom times to offset a sharp decrease in class numbers. And as for my experience? They want experience, I can give them fricking experience. I've been ballroom dancing since the ripe old age of five and I've been a dance teacher at other studios since I was fifteen. I've always been able to attract new students to my classes—and keep them. On top of all that, I'm a damn good teacher and there're at least a half dozen studios that'd offer me a job tomorrow. But I don't want that. I want my own studio. All I need is a chance. I can make this work. I know I can."

He launched himself from his prone position on the couch to tug her away from her perch on the table. Chalcey didn't protest when he settled her in his lap and kneaded the frustration and panic from her shoulders with strong, capable fingers. "I believe in you, Chalcey. And so do Jai, Paulo and Leah. When I watch you dance, I see passion and joy and pure love of the dance. Others see it too, and that is why they want you to teach them to dance—so they may experience for themselves just a tiny bit of what they see in your face."

Tears burned her eyes. Aside from her dad, no man had ever praised her like that before. Or shown such implicit faith in her. As soon as she'd hit puberty and her breasts had ballooned to their current overly generous proportions, any male over the age of about thirteen had been more interested in her chest than what made her tick. It had taken a displaced warrior from another world and a time centuries past, to look deep into her soul and know the joy that consumed her when she danced.

The prospect of being hounded by the IRS brought her plummeting back to earth. "Thanks, Wulf. You're wonderful, you know that?" She reached up to urge his face closer so she could reward him with a kiss. And oh, it was all she could do not to deepen that kiss and take it to the next level. It was damned near impossible to tear herself away from him. His gaze told her he knew how she felt. And understood why she felt the need to distance herself.

"But the truth is, Wulf, no matter how much faith you have in me, I have to come up with a very large amount of money. And I have no idea how."

"I am given to understand that Francesca is wealthy by way of her second union. Perhaps you could ask her to help you."

"No way." She shook her head. "I borrowed money from her and Edgar once, and I swore I would never do it again. Edgar charged me as much interest as a bank would charge. And then he poked his ferrety nose into every little part of my life, confiscated my credit card and insisted on approving every single expenditure until I'd off paid the loan. It was a fricking nightmare—like having my own private IRS auditor bugging me on a daily basis."

"What about Samantha?"

"She would loan me the money like that." Chalcey clicked her fingers. "But I have to do this on my own, Wulf. I have to prove to everybody—and myself—that I can do this. If I borrow from Sam this time, what happens if I can't make the next payment? I won't use her as a cash cow. Besides, haven't you heard the old adage that you should never borrow from friends? It's a surefire way to ensure they don't remain your friends for long."

He rested his chin atop of her head and hugged her close to his chest. "You will think of a way. Why do you not talk to Sam, anyway? She may have some ideas. She is very clever. I believe she works hard to hide her intelligence, believing it not appealing to the men she pursues."

"Mmmm. Might just do that."

"Do not fret, Chalcedony. This will all work out, you will see."

She heard Jai yodel at her from the studio—a not-so-subtle hint about the time. "Uh oh, duty calls. Time to go get ready for the class."

Wulf released her and she stood, smoothing her skirt over her thighs. "Sure you don't want to join in, Wulf? You must get awfully bored just sitting there watching. I'm sure there'd be no problems rustling you up a willing partner."

"No thank you, Chalcey. I am happy to watch you. I do not find it at all boring."

Apprehension scuttled tiny centipede-like feet over her skin. Would he be content to sit around and watch her after the Testing? Would he be this besotted with her after his curse was lifted and he was stuck with her for life?

Crap. She wasn't gonna go there at the moment, not with the specter of a hefty tax bill hanging over her. She pasted a bright smile on her face. "Better get a shirt on then, or all the ladies in the class will be watching you instead of me."

More often than not Wulf didn't bother with a shirt. In the studio it was either bare chest rippling with muscles and washboard abs, or his leather vest. Right now it was bare chest. Like she was ever going to complain.

During his stints as a bouncer, he compromised by wearing the clothes he'd arrived in, along with the outrageously expensive full-length leather duster that Sam had bought him as a gift to celebrate his new job. In the unorthodox garb, he somehow managed to contrive to look both sexy and menacing at the same time. It was a truly hot look. But for Chalcey, the bare chested look was even hotter. She burned to get him alone, run her palms over his body, and have her wicked, wicked way with him.

"Sure you don't want to join in?" she asked, hyper-aware that she sounded husky with want and need.

"I am a warrior, not a dancer. I am sure."

"Okay," she said. "But don't let watching the class stop you from catching some shut-eye. You haven't been getting much sleep lately."

He quirked an eyebrow. "How can I sleep when you are so enticing, Chalcey? 'Tis your fault I get no rest. You are insatiable."

"Humph!" She turned on her heel and walked out before he spotted her blushing.

Wulf followed her into the studio to greet Jai, before disappearing into the bedroom. Her gaze followed him. Her breath sighed out, signaling her longing. And her sigh was echoed by both Jai and a new female student who'd arrived early to enroll.

"Whoa, mama!" Jai fanned himself with his hands. "The temperature's rising, it isn't surprising that he—"

"Certainly can can-can!" The newcomer finished off the song lyric with a throaty laugh. She stuck out her hand. "Hi, I'm Esmeralda. You must be Chalcey. And he must be... yours?"

Chalcey shook her proffered hand. "Who? Jai? Not hardly. Sorry, Jai. No offence."

"None taken, doll."

"I mean Mr. Bare-chested Warrior King," Esmeralda said.

"Ohhh. Him. Yes, Wulf's definitely mine." She couldn't help her terribly smug smile.

"Pity!" Both Jai and Esmeralda chorused.

Covertly, Chalcey checked Esmeralda out. She had long-lashed eyes of a blue so deep that it was almost purple, a café au lait complexion that even a certain actress cum Revlon model would envy, and a tall, leggy figure à la a famous Australian lingerie model. Complete with expertly applied cosmetics, figure-hugging dress, and high-heeled sandals, she was an exquisite package. With a big secret.

"To answer your question, yes," Esmeralda said.

"Sorry. Didn't mean to be rude."

Esmeralda's practiced smile didn't reach her eyes. "Am I likely to be a problem for you?"

"Not me personally, but it sort of depends on what exactly you're looking to get out of the class, Esmeralda. If you're looking for dating material, then so long as no one gets upset during class-time, it's none of my business. However, anyone acting inappropriately or obviously sleeping their way through my students will be subjected to a personal dressing down from *moi*, and a referral to a dating agency. Is that likely to be a problem for you?"

"Not a bit, Chalcey. I'm here to have fun and learn to dance."

It was Chalcey's turn to smile. Genuinely. "It doesn't mean you can't flirt and have lots of fun. And shit, girl, the way you're put together, I reckon you'll be having heaps of fun."

Esmeralda beamed. "When I rang, Jai said you'd be cool with it."

"Oh, I'm cool with it. In fact, from my lofty pedestal of hindsight, I'm looking forward to watching two certain men in the next class pant after you."

Jai's eyes lit up and what could only be described as an evil smile flit across his handsome face. "You mean the unlovely Patrick and his partner in slime, Cliff?"

"Correctamundo," Chalcey said. "Gold star for you."

"Oooh, yes!" Jai rubbed his hands together and performed a little dance of mock glee. "They need to learn a lesson about keeping their hands to themselves and you're sooo their type, Esmeralda. I'll give you the nod when our boys arrive and then you can unleash your charms on them."

"I do appreciate the opportunity to hone my flirting techniques," Esmeralda purred, fluttering her eyelashes at Chalcey and thrusting out her chest. "Wouldn't do to lose my touch."

"You go, girl," Jai said.

"Play nice, you two," Chalcey said. "I don't want any trouble."

"You mean any *more* trouble, Ms I-Had-Two-Men-Fighting-Over-Me Laureano."

"Gee, thanks so much for reminding me of that particular episode, Jai."

People began to filter in to the studio and mill around by the payment desk. "That's my cue to go extort some money," Chalcey said. "And Esmeralda?"

"Yes?"

Chalcey patted her arm. "I really hope you do find a nice, understanding man."

"Thanks." Pain creased her smooth features for a moment. And then Jai engaged her in a whispered conversation and pointed out a man who'd just walked in, and was arrogantly surveying the room like it was his own little empire.

Esmeralda and Jai giggled like highschoolers.

Chalcey bit her lip to hide her smirk. Let the games begin.

The class she was teaching for this particular timeslot was beginners' *Ceroc*, also known as French Rock Jive. Ceroc is a fun, upbeat partner dance, done to any sort of music with a decent beat, perfect for those who are uncomfortable with the flamboyant nature of Salsa, or being mashed up against a stranger's groin as per the Lambada.

Because many brave souls like Esmeralda dared front-up to a class solo, there were usually uneven numbers of males and females, which suited Chalcey fine. She preferred to organize the class into pairs and work a rotation scheme. So if, say, there were two extra women, after the first move had been walked through, she asked the guys to stay put, and all the women to "move down two guys" and dance with a new man, leaving two new women to stand out for a rotation. Many people who came with partners were rather disconcerted to find themselves split up for most of the class but Chalcey firmly insisted they would learn the moves more quickly if they danced with other people. Most students quickly became comfortable with the concept. As an added bonus for the dance teacher, there was less likely to be sniping between permanent couples because "he isn't leading properly" or "she keeps trying to lead".

This evening's class had three too many women, including Esmeralda, so all the women on the dance floor would have to move down three men. Chalcey started the class, and once the melee of moving down was sorted, everyone relaxed and became absorbed in the lesson.

"Right everyone," Chalcey said, raising her voice to be heard over the chatter. "Now you've got the aptly titled First Move down pat, let's move on. The next move is the Comb. It's a move used by the male lead to change hands in preparation for a right-hand move coming up next. Jai's gonna demonstrate it for you."

Esmeralda caught on really quickly and was soon flashing her sexy smile at her various partners. Chalcey noticed that she upped the wattage to devastating effect whenever she paired up with Patrick or Cliff.

Both men seemed smitten. Chalcey wondered what Esmeralda would do if any man in this class made a serious play for her. Date him, and hope he'd be understanding when she revealed her true self? Be upfront right from the start and risk scaring him off? Esmeralda was a big girl and Chalcey had no doubt she could handle herself, but it had to be rough. Real rough.

"All right, move down three guys. Cool. So now we'll walk you through the First Move, followed by the Comb, and add on the Shoulder-pull."

She generally taught beginners between six and eight

moves, which all joined together in a mini-routine. In the half-hour changeover period before the next class started, she and Jai would keep the music going to encourage groups to stay on and try out what they'd learned. Chalcey loved watching the students who felt confident enough to ask someone other than the partner they'd come with to dance. After a few weeks, if all went well, a core group would start meeting up to go clubbing and show off their new moves, which was good for business. Word of mouth beat formal advertising hands down.

The hour-and-a-half-long class was about three quarters through when Wulf took up his customary seat on one of the stools by the water cooler. Thank goodness he'd put on a shirt, meaning she might actually be able to concentrate on what she was supposed to be doing.

"Okay, ladies and gents, let's put these moves to the music." She winked at him as she bent to select a track of appropriate dance music for beginners. "Hiya."

"Hello, Chalcey."

The way he said her name, all sensuous syllables and soft promises. The way he looked at her—like he wanted to throw her over his shoulder and cart her off to the bedroom. Her pulse raced and heat rushed straight to her sweet spot. Her nipples tightened as though he'd run his fingertips over her breasts, even though he hadn't even moved from his seat. And from the slight smile playing on his lips, he knew exactly the effect he had on her. He was pure seduction, all-consuming and addictive. She didn't stand a chance.

She sucked in a deep, calming breath. She'd already pressed Play on her iPod when the fine hairs on the back of her neck stood to attention. Turning to face her class again, she found every single gaze focused intently on her and Wulf. It seemed as though their private desires had suddenly become tangible, ensnaring her students, provoking them to respond in kind. Their glazed, hooded eyes and parted lips reflected Chalcey's own lust. The studio oozed sexual desire.

Jai stared at Wulf, his gaze glittering with hunger. He ran his tongue over his lower lip and his mouth curved in a sultry smile.

"Jesus, Jai!" Chalcey grabbed her dance partner's hand and dug her nails into his palm. "Snap out of it."

He blinked, and shook his head. "Shit, girl, I feel like I've just popped a handful of Viagra. The heat you two generate is dan-ger-ous!"

"Sorry. I don't know what just happened but—"

He glanced down at his groin and grimaced. "Don't worry 'bout it. More action than I've had in a while. Let's get this class going again before we have an orgy on our hands."

Chalcey spared a glance at Wulf, but he appeared just as confused as she was right now. She had no choice but to put this bizarre incident behind her. "Right, everyone!" She clapped her hands sharply to get the class's attention, and started in with the instructions. "Starting with guy's left hand holding lady's right, beginning with the First Move then Comb. Ready? Listen for that beat. And one, and two, and three, four! Step out, together, and swivel and back—"

As she yelled the familiar instructions over the music, she swept an anxious glance over her students. The spell she and Wulf had inadvertently cast had dissipated, thank God. Their eyes had lost that burning longing. Everything was back to normal. Well, as normal as her life could be right now.

From the corner of her eye, she spotted Sam heading for Wulf.

Cool! She'd been nagging Sam for ages to come and watch a class. Or even better, join in. She wondered who Sam had brought along to partner her, or whether she'd come solo.

Then she saw Ray enter through the stairwell door. He glanced around and sauntered over to the rear of the studio, where he lounged against the wall to watch the class.

*God. Why me? Please don't do this to me.*

It would be damn hard to act professional and suck up her

animosity if Ray wanted to sign up for a class. Presuming that's what he was hanging around for. Presuming he wasn't waiting for Sam. He had some nerve. What the hell was he playing at?

Screw being professional. As soon as class was over, she was going to ask him to leave. Chalcey wasn't the type to pick and choose her students, but there had to be some benefits of owning her own studio.

Sam jerked and then stiffened. She'd obviously spotted Ray but was pretending to ignore him. Smart girl. If Ray became a problem, Chalcey would sic Wulf on him and—

A noise that sounded suspiciously like a growl rumbled from the stool where Wulf was sitting. Oh crap. Sam, Wulf *and* Ray in the same room?

Disaster potential: one hundred percent. Couldn't get any worse—

Duh. Of course it fricking well could. Marcus strolled through the doorway and made a beeline toward Sam. He greeted Wulf with a handshake, and then bent to kiss Sam's cheek.

Chalcey's heart fluttered with gooey relief. Sam had rung him and was gonna give him another chance. Woohoo! Go Marcus. Now if he could just hold himself in check and play it casual so as not to scare Sam off again, they might make it.

Sam whispered something to Marcus. Marcus's chin jerked around. He appeared less than thrilled when he caught sight of Ray.

"Move down three guys!" Chalcey yelled, her gaze riveted on the drama unfolding while the female students all found a new dance partner.

Ray sneered at Marcus. Marcus glowered back. The ambience in the room cooled until it began to feel like Chalcey had been caught buck naked during a hoar frost. Chilly didn't even begin to describe it.

Oh joy. With an inward groan, she focused on her students. *Please remind me again why on earth I ever wanted to be a dance teacher and have to deal with real, live people on a daily basis?*

"Everything okay, doll?" Jai said. "You seem distracted."

"Tell you later." Unless Ray or Marcus or Wulf—or even Sam—did something stupid. In which case she'd fill him in immediately. For now, all she could do was pray everyone would hold their tempers.

AS THE CLASS—thankfully—ended, Chalcey glimpsed Sam speaking earnestly to Marcus and placing a cautionary hand on his arm. He shook her off and headed straight for Ray. Sam turned a stricken face to Wulf, and he seemed to be trying to comfort her. Chalcey didn't need to be a rocket scientist to know a potentially disastrous testosterone-fueled confrontation was headed her way. Again.

"Er, Jai?" She yanked his sleeve to get his attention. "See that sleazy looking blond guy? Well, his name is Ray, and he's not too popular with either Wulf or Marcus, that scowling dark-haired guy with the Van Dyke beard."

"Oh?" Jai, scenting gossip, inevitably asked, "Why's that?"

"Long story. Tell you all about it later."

"You'd better, if you know what's good for you." He practiced his most menacing frown and cracked his knuckles so loudly that Chalcey winced in sympathy. "Want me to tell this Ray guy to vamoose?"

While Chalcey was weighing up her limited options, Ray solved the problem by slinking off toward the door, and she lost sight of him in the crowd of people who'd arrived early to get in some freestyle before the next class.

Wulf had gone over to talk to Marcus and both men appeared relaxed. Chalcey heaved a relieved sigh. "Crisis averted, Jai. Target has removed himself from imminent peril by pissing off out of here."

"You know, Chalce, that faux military-speak's sooo hawt!

Suppose you and Wulf get off on playing with his stiff little soldier, huh?"

She whacked him on the arm. "God, Jai. You are so disgusting!"

Jai preened. "I try babe, I try. Uh oh. Scanners reading a male of unknown origin performing an illegal maneuver, resulting in injury to his partner's toes. Target acquired. Moving in to rectify situation before permanent damage is done."

She groaned at his attempt at a computerized voice. "Oh, do go away and leave me in peace."

He saluted as he marched off.

Chalcey had just decided to grab a stool and put her feet up before the next class began, when he rematerialized at her side. "Some of the newbies want to see some real Ceroc, Chalce. Feel up for a demo?"

She groaned. "Do I have to?"

"Yes."

"But—"

"C'mon, Chalce. Beginners are our bread and butter, and we need them to want to move up to Intermediate and Advanced. I know we both enjoy teaching beginners but it's not exactly stretching our skills, so let's show them a bit of freestyle to give them something to aim for. It's good for business."

"I know, I know. Preaching to the converted. All right, choose some music and please, don't try any of those new Advanced moves we've been practicing, okay? The last thing I need right now is to land on my ass in front of a load of beginners. That definitely wouldn't be good for business."

"Darling, I promise that even if you do end up on your ass, I'll make you look sensational. After all, as my old ballroom teacher used to say: The woman is the picture and the man is the frame."

She mimed sticking her fingers down her throat.

Jai flicked through her iPod playlist and sniggered. "Jimmy

Sommerville's *Comment Te Dire Adieu*? Talk about blast from the past."

"Yeah, all right. Guilty as charged but it's a solid one-hundred-thirty beats per minute for when my beginners are ready for a bit of a challenge. And as I'm not made of money, and don't have the time to be fanatically up with the latest music like you are, Paulo very kindly ripped all my CDs onto my old laptop and loaded them onto my iPod. If Jimmy doesn't do it for you, how 'bout some Corona—*Rhythm of the Night*?"

He made a face. "It'll have to do, I suppose."

"Music snob."

"Music tight-ass. With, like, *the* most appalling taste in music evah." He pressed Play and grabbed her hand.

It felt good to be challenged for a change. Demos were choreographed to the nth degree, whereas freestyle had that element of surprise about it. Chalcey had to watch and feel her partner's lead, be relaxed enough to be led by him, but vigilant enough to anticipate his next move. And if she got caught out, so long as she improvised and *did* something, rather than standing there like a ditz, no one watching would even realize she'd stuffed up.

Jai was nothing if not inventive with the way he put moves together, so Chalcey was having loads of fun. Until she spotted Ray again. He was like a bad smell that wouldn't go away. He grabbed Esmeralda's arm and yanked her toward him to whisper in her ear.

"C'mon, you intermediate level dancers, don't be shy!" Jai encouraged some of the more advanced students to take the dance floor.

When Chalcey next caught a glimpse of Ray and Esmeralda, surprisingly, they were dancing. But Esmeralda had taken on the role of male lead. What stood out for Chalcey in that brief moment was the misery distorting Esmeralda's lovely face.

Jai set Chalcey up for a Drop Kick, supporting her under the armpits as she shifted her weight to her left leg, and pulling her backward into his arms. He bent down so far her backside almost touched the floor as she kicked her right leg high in the air. When he brought her back upright, Chalcey's gaze honed in on Ray just in time to see him grope Esmeralda's breasts. Chalcey expected the über-confident Esmeralda to immediately assert herself and slap Ray's face, and readied herself to stop the demo and back Esmeralda up. Instead, she was shocked to see Esmeralda swipe at her eyes with the back of a hand.

"Wind it up, Jai. We've got trouble."

"Sure thing, babe. Is it the same guy you mentioned before? I spotted him sneaking back in."

"Mmm hmm. He's pawing Esmeralda."

"Asshole."

Jai finished with a Killer Pretzel, an Unravel/Ravel/Seducer combo, then stepped away from Chalcey and bowed. Amidst applause from the onlookers, they both advanced upon Ray.

Chalcey was beyond angry at his behavior. How dare he treat a woman like that! And in *her* dance studio. He was gonna be out that door so fast he wouldn't know what had hit his nasty ass.

Before she could get to him, Marcus intervened. He dragged Ray away from Esmeralda and crowded him back against the wall. Chalcey heard Marcus snarl at Ray, who of course took umbrage and swung wildly at him. Marcus ducked, and stiff-armed Ray across the neck, pinning him against the wall.

"Break it up, you two!" Jai barked.

Chalcey had opened her mouth to support Jai when from behind her, Wulf's voice rumbled, "Or you will be forced to deal with me."

Marcus released Ray, and the two antagonists stared at Chalcey for a moment, as if trying to figure out how the heck that voice, so heavy with menace, could possibly have issued from her mouth.

Recognition dawned on Ray's face. His gaze darted about, searching for an escape route.

Sam and Esmeralda stepped out from behind Wulf. Perfect timing. Nothing like solidarity in the face of an asshole.

Sam slipped an arm around Esmeralda's shoulders. "Don't, Wulf," Sam said. "He's so not worth the effort. And if he pressed charges, you'd lose your job."

"Wha'sa matter, Sam?" Ray sneered, refusing to be cowed. "Men not enough for you anymore? You hooked up with *that*—" he pointed to Esmeralda "—now, huh? Even for you, that's a real lowering of standards."

Good one. He sure had some mouth on him. And a short life-expectancy, if Sam and Esmeralda's narrow-eyed, furious faces were anything to go by.

Both women lunged forward but were grabbed before they could inflict any serious bodily harm. Marcus took charge of Sam. Jai had his hands full with Esmeralda. Chalcey supposed she should have been grateful to both men for preventing a scene but secretly, she was disappointed. She would have quite enjoyed the spectacle of Sam and Esmeralda pounding Ray to a pulp. Sometimes it was a real bummer being a responsible adult.

Revenge, however, was very sweet. "Ray," she cooed. "I have some wonderful news for you. You're no longer welcome at my studio and you're banned until further notice—like when hell freezes over. Now you're obliged to vacate the premises. But because I'm basically a decent person, you get to choose how you do that. You can either slime out of here under your own steam, or Wulf will kick you down the stairwell and turf you out on your sorry ass while we all cheer him on. Your choice."

Ray sneered some more. "That right?"

Dick-for-brains. Couldn't he see he was outnumbered bigtime?

"That is right." Wulf stepped forward and cracked his knuckles. "It has been a while since I have been afforded the pleasure of a one-on-one fight with a worthy opponent. Unfortunately, I do not believe you to be particularly worthy, but one must take one's pleasures where one is able." He directed his next comment toward Chalcey. "I do hope his blood doesn't stain this shirt. 'Tis a favorite of mine."

She swallowed an inappropriate giggle as Ray visibly gulped and turned an interesting shade of green.

"Are you ready to fight me, Ray?" Wulf bent his knees, dropping down into a fighting stance. He projected lethal power, his entire body coiled and awaiting the opportunity to inflict some major pain.

Ray was obviously thinking along similar lines, for he straightened his clothing and opted to leave. His eyes glittered with impotent fury. Or drugs. Chalcey was ninety-nine-point-nine percent certain he was on something. He cast her a filthy look that promised retribution as he exited the studio.

"I will follow to make sure he leaves," Wulf said, striding toward the door.

"Good idea. Be careful."

"Sorry about that, folks," Jai said, for the benefit of those who'd witnessed the altercation. "He's just some scumbag who thinks he can come in here to feel up women, and make a nuisance of himself. But we don't put up with that crap. Ever. Anyone got any problems with the way they're being treated by another student, they come and see me or Chalcey, okay?"

Chalcey noticed Patrick and Cliff, who were both walking the line with their antics so far as she was concerned, looking decidedly less confident. Good. At least there'd been a silver lining to this crap.

"Glad that's over," Jai said, vast relief coloring his tone. "That Ray guy's a real lowlife. Can't think why any self-respecting woman would want anything to do with him."

"Yes, well." Sam had the grace to blush as she shot an apologetic glance at Esmeralda.

"I'm fine, sweetie," Esmeralda assured her.

"So what are you and Marcus doing here?" Chalcey asked, taking Esmeralda's pleading expression as her cue to change the subject.

"Marcus tracked me down and invited me along to watch a class," she confessed. "We thought we might try the beginners Ceroc class."

"You'll love it!" Chalcey said, beaming. "The intermediate class starts in about ten minutes." She wiggled her eyebrows and mouthed, "Tell me all about him later!" behind Marcus's back.

An eager female student dragged Jai away to show her a move, and some semblance of normality descended.

Wulf reappeared, and Esmeralda thanked him and Marcus for sticking up for her. Although she seemed calm enough, her voice shook a little.

Chalcey's brain kicked into gear and suggested a brilliant way to help Esmeralda forget all the unpleasantness. "Esmeralda, I've got to cash up and get ready for the next class. Why don't you do me a huge favor and show Wulf some moves? I'm dying to get him to join in a class."

They both eyed her doubtfully.

"Go on. You've got the routine we learned tonight pretty much down, Esmeralda. You should have no trouble talking him through it." Chalcey walked off and left them to it before either could raise any protests.

While she cashed up and got ready for the next class, she snuck glances at them. Once Wulf loosened up, he wasn't a half bad dancer. He certainly had rhythm, and the two of them danced quite well for absolute beginners. Her attention was diverted by a couple of brand new students but when she next spotted them, Esmeralda had a smile on her face that could have lit the room. "See you next week!" she trilled as she departed with a bunch of other students.

Wulf waited until Chalcey finished signing in the newbies before he approached. His brows were scrunched, eyes narrowed, lips downturned—a man who'd been thinking real hard about something, was still puzzled, and was about to tip over into frustrated as heck if he didn't get some answers.

"What's up?" she asked. "Surely it wasn't *that* bad. I thought you both looked great out there."

"She— Esmeralda. She is woman who is not truly a woman."

"That's right. She's a man who dresses like a woman."

"But if she is a man, then how can she have real breasts?"

Ah. This wasn't gonna be easy to explain. "My guess is that she takes female hormones and has had a breast augmentation—that's when doctors uh, operate to give a man like Esmeralda breasts, or a woman bigger breasts. So, Esmeralda looks like a woman on the outside, but unless she's had a complete sex change, she's still a man from the waist down. If that makes sense."

It took him a while but he eventually got it. And, inevitably, had more questions.

"This sex *change*. Your world has methods of making a man fully into a woman?"

"Yep."

"How?"

Now it was Chalcey's turn to blush. "Um… it's not something we should discuss in public, okay? Uncomfortably graphic and all that. Just take my word for it. Surgeons—you know what a surgeon is?"

He nodded. "I watched ER with Samantha."

"Right. Of course you did." Sam had a secret that no one else knew. She liked to chill out on a Sunday morning and watch DVD episodes of ER. And Grey's Anatomy. She even liked Nip/Tuck.

"These days," Chalcey said, "surgeons can operate on men to change them into women so you'd never know to look at them."

Horror flitted briefly across his face, then acceptance and finally, wonder. He shook his head. "'Tis an amazing world you live in, Chalcey. Amazing indeed. Full of wonders I could never possibly have imagined."

"And that's a good thing, I hope?"

"Indeed."

"I take it you'd be quite happy to stay on then, if everything works out for us?"

His answering smile melted her heart. "My life would not be worth a single grain of sand without you, Chalcey."

She smiled back. "That's the nicest thing anyone's ever said to me in my whole life. C'mere." He bent so she could kiss him on the cheek.

"Chalcey," he murmured, his voice making her shiver with want. "Samantha tells me she has devised some plans to alleviate your lack of funds."

She puffed out a sigh. Back to reality. Money troubles would do it every time. "I just bet she has. And they're all probably completely outrageous, if I know her. I don't even want to think about that little problem right now, 'coz I've got to get this next class underway."

He kissed her. Lingeringly. With tongue. "Then I ask that you think of me until I return from my work, Chalcey."

"Oh, I will," she promised, resisting the urge to fan the heat from her face. "I certainly will."

He slanted her a toe-curling, wholly masculine look, that told her he knew exactly what kind of naughty thoughts she'd been thinking. She watched him until the door closed behind him, releasing her from his spell.

She glanced at Mickey and heaved a sigh. Roll on the hours. She turned her mind back to her upcoming class and tried not to be distracted by thoughts of the things she and Wulf would get up to as soon as he returned from his shift. Rippling muscles and bare, sun-darkened skin. His thick, dark hair tickling across her flesh as he kissed his way down her body....

Hoh boy. She sure had it bad. If their sexes were reversed and *she* had the misfortune to possess a penis, it would be permanently upstanding. When Wulf was with her, she was sexually aroused. And when he wasn't with her, she was thinking of him and aroused. He did things for her libido she never thought possible.

Her life was just about perfect. Well, except for her cash-flow issues. And the big-ass specter of the Testing hanging over her.

The Testing....

Shit. Chalcey had never been very good at taking tests. As a kid, her mind tended to go into full-on panic mode and present her with a big fat blank, no matter how much prep she'd done.

If she flunked this one, she'd never forgive herself.

# CHAPTER FOURTEEN

"HELLO?" Chalcey heard the faint shout over the water running in the shower.

Rats. The time must have gotten away on her. Cleaning bathrooms—her favorite thing in the world. *Not.* She'd been hoping to get them all done before Jai turned up to go through the new intermediate level routines. "Won't be a sec, Jai!" she yelled.

She gave the cubicle one last swipe with her cloth, ditched her spray-bottle, and headed into the studio. Where she did a classic double-take. Sooo not Jai.

"Sorry for the delay," she told the visitor. "And before I ask how I can help you, how the heck did you get in downstairs? Because this time, I definitely remember locking the street door." And she'd even used the security latch… once or twice.

He dangled a set of keys before her face. Huh. Like *that* explained everything. She couldn't help noticing his wristwatch. It probably cost more money than she would ever make in her entire life. Not that she'd swap her beloved Mickey Mouse watch for his in a million years, but that didn't stop her from breathing an envious little sigh.

He pocketed his keys and stuck out his hand. "William Sparling."

Chalcey made a move to shake his hand, and then realized she was still wearing pink rubber gloves. Ack. How embarrassing. She yanked them off and tucked them into the waistband of her shorts. "What can I do for you, William?"

He cocked his head to one side, eyebrows raised. "You don't remember me, do you?"

He was a corporate lawyer type, clean shaven, with prep-school haircut and handsome "of course you can trust me" features. His beautifully tailored suit screamed designer, as did his terribly shiny shoes. And given that he had a key to access her building, Chalcey figured she definitely should remember him. But she drew a big fat embarrassing blank.

She screwed up her nose and decided to get it over with. "Sorry. Have we met before?"

"I own the building."

"Shit!" She clapped a hand over her mouth. Ooops. Too late. "Jeez, sorry, Mr. Sparling. I have so many students coming and going, sometimes faces and names get to be a bit of a blur."

He appraised her, taking in her bare feet, disreputable t-shirt splotched with damp patches from the shower spray, and tatty shorts. His face split into a grin. "Call me Will. Have I caught you at a bad time?"

"Hey, anybody who gives me a valid excuse to quit scrubbing shower cubicles is more than welcome to interrupt. Can I get you a coffee?"

"No thanks. Can't stay long." He swiveled on his heel, doing a full three-sixty, his gaze darting about the studio. "I was seriously considering selling the building and cutting my losses before you showed an interest. You've done a great job with the space."

"Yeah. I like to think so."

His gaze lingered on the partially open sliding door leading to her private rooms. "I gather you've made use of the storage rooms and that ridiculously tiny kitchenette, too."

Uh oh. She made a noncommittal noise. If he was going to object to her living on the premises, she could be in trouble.

"Could I take a look at the bathrooms you put in?"

It was an innocuous enough request. She couldn't think of any reason to refuse. His affable manner didn't prevent her from wondering what was up, though. She led him through to the men's bathroom and stood back while he peered into the cubicles.

"Nice job," he said. "Must have cost a bit."

"Yep."

"Glad the studio's doing okay."

"Yep." If you didn't count the money that she owed the IRS because of her dumbass accountant, everything was peachy. "So what's the real reason for your visit, Will?" She watched his face carefully.

He noted her scrutiny but merely chuckled. "Ms Laureano, I—"

"Call me Chalcey."

"Chalcey. I saw your studio's ad and wanted to come over and talk to you in person. Or rather, my wife wanted me to."

She relaxed and exhaled a breath she hadn't realized she'd been holding. "Lemme guess. She wants to start dance classes." She squinted at him, gauging his expression, then took a punt. "And she wants to drag you along, too."

He chuckled. "You're good."

"And I'm betting you're not entirely keen."

"You got that right." His face creased in a mock scowl. "I've got the whole two-left-feet thing going on."

This, she could handle. "Have either of you done any dance classes before?"

He shook his head and added mournfully, "I think she's keen on Salsa."

"Could be worse." Chalcey smirked and waggled her eyebrows. "Could be Lambada."

"Lambada?"

She thrust forward her hips and treated him to a quick butt-wiggling demo. Poor guy gulped and turned quite pasty beneath his tan. "Tell you what, Will, how 'bout I give you and your wife a couple of trial Ceroc classes. No charge. Ceroc's the easiest class for absolute beginners. It's similar to Salsa in that it's still a partner dance, but it's a little more versatile 'coz it's done to any music with a decent beat. Means you can easily dance it at parties and clubs and such. Plus it's much easier to learn than Salsa. If you hate it, no harm done. But I'm picking your wife will love it and she'll probably keep coming on her own. And since she doesn't need to bring a partner, she'll have a perfectly good time without you."

His turn to raise his eyebrows while he contemplated the ramifications of that last statement. "Okay. Thanks."

Chalcey was also betting he'd keep fronting up, if for no other reason than to make sure his wife didn't get hit on by other guys in the class. Sneaky but hey, business was business.

She snagged a timetable from the Perspex holder screwed to the wall by the staircase and handed it to him, pointing out the days and times for the beginners' classes. "Give me a ring before you front up, so I can make sure whoever's at the desk knows not to charge you."

He folded the timetable and stuck it in his jacket pocket. "There was one other thing."

"Oh?" She chewed her lower lip, hoping it wasn't anything dire. Such as wanting to up the cost of her lease. Or, horrors, shorten the term.

"No need to panic, Chalcey. Having you here has been a boon, believe me. There's been far less vandalism since you moved in. No, it's about the empty downstairs office. I've been unable to lease it so I've decided to help out a friend of my wife's by letting his company use the area for overflow storage—just files and suchlike." He shrugged, palms out, like he was apologizing. "I've given a key to his PA. And once everything's moved in, there'll likely be an office junior or two hefting archive boxes in and out. I wanted you to know so you don't panic if you see people hanging 'round."

"Appreciate that. Thanks. I'll remember not to use the security chain during the day." Shouldn't be hard, considering.

They shook hands and she escorted him downstairs.

"Chalcey, forgive me for lecturing, but you might want to consider locking the stairwell door to your studio when you're in here alone. If someone does break in downstairs, they could waltz straight on up and surprise you in here." *Like I did....*

He didn't need to say it aloud. She threw him a sheepish look. "Yeah. You're right. Guess I am pretty lax about security sometimes. Now I know you've handed out a key, I'll be more careful, I promise."

"Good. The downstairs office space is alarmed. I could organize one for you, too, if you like. A woman like you, on her own in an area like this—you can't be too careful these days."

Chalcey wondered whether Will would be half as concerned for her safety if he got an eyeful of the warrior-turned-bouncer who was currently sleeping off his shift in her bedroom.

Jai let himself in with his key just as they reached the bottom of the stairs. "Hiya, doll-face." He gave Will a once-over that had the poor man flushing to the roots of his hair. "And who might this be?"

"Will, this is Jai, my dance partner and co-teacher."

Jai struck a pose designed to display what had been poured into his butt-hugging jeans and muscle-tee to the best advantage. "Well, hiii, Will."

"Don't even go there," Chalcey told him. "Will's the owner of this building. *And* he's married."

Will's blush flamed an even brighter shade of crimson.

"Dang. The good ones are always taken." Jai took pity on Will and turned his attention to Chalcey. "Did you know some asshole's tagged the front of the building?"

Will smacked his forehead with his palm. "And that was the other thing I meant to mention. You'd better take a look, Chalcey."

She blanched, feeling sick to her stomach. "Shit. They better not have tagged my sign." She elbowed her way past the two men to rush outside.

Her studio sign was still pristine but the rest of it wasn't pretty. The brickwork had been defaced with swathes of black spray-paint. But that wasn't the worst of it. The tagger had scrawled, *FOR A GOOD TIME PH 1800 COCK-TEASE.*

She frowned. A certain scene at a certain nightclub pricked her memory....

She knew exactly who'd done this. And if he was dumb enough to pull something like this, odds on, he was responsible for the nuisance calls, too. She felt the unnatural warmth of an angry flush paint her face. "That little prick!"

"You know who did this?" Will asked.

"Oh, I know all right. He accused me of being, uh, *that* at a nightclub when I got POed with him trying to feel me up. Then he followed me home, and didn't take too kindly to being shown the error of his ways by my, uh, boyfriend." She'd been going to say "friend" but Wulf was far more than a mere friend.

Jai narrowed his eyes as he put two and two together. He clicked his fingers. "The same asshole you threw out of the opening night party."

"Yeah. He's got a bit of a chip on his shoulder." To put it mildly. And considering her relationship with Wulf, the man who'd recently chucked Ray out of Sam's apartment, Ray was probably choking on a huge case of the vengefuls. Not that she wanted to go into all that with the building's owner. He didn't need to know.

"What was that guy's name again?" Jai asked.

"Never mind that," Chalcey said, and directed her attention to Will. "I'm really sorry about this. I'll get this cleaned off right away and—"

Will held up a hand to halt her apologies. "I'll deal with it. Tagging is an issue with a couple of other buildings I lease out, so I keep a company on retainer. And if you give me this guy's name, I'll have one of my buddies pay him a visit."

She opened her mouth but before she could protest he elaborated, his eyes dancing with amusement. "He's a cop, not a personal hit man. I may be a filthy rich bastard, but I don't consider myself above the law."

He stared at her expectantly, awaiting her response to his offer. Which she was pretty sure he figured was a foregone conclusion. Another alpha male. Great. Just great.

Jai joined in the whole "let's stare at Chalcey until she caves" thing. And raised the stakes. "If you don't give Will a name, I'll tell Wulf," he said. "And if I know our friend Wulf, he'll quite likely deal to the guy more permanently next time around."

Chalcey resisted gnashing her teeth. Barely. "You're both as bad as Wulf. What is it that makes you men think we need you to solve all our problems? Is it genetic, or something?"

"Chalce," Jai said, his tone warning.

Her gaze cut to Will, who grinned unrepentantly. "I'll find out one way or another," he said. "The hard way, if I have to."

She believed him. "All right, all right! You two are worse than my freaking mother. His name's Ray. And other than a description, that's all I've got. I can't recall his surname but Sam—"

Jai had already managed to extricate his mobile from the pocket of his skintight jeans and tapped in Sam's number. "Hey, babelicious, it's Jai. Listen, Chalcey's had another little run-in with that asshole Ray. Nah, it's nothing serious—a lovely personal message spray-painted on the side of her studio. Nah, our lovely new friend Will's gonna handle it. Just need Ray's surname, doll. And anything else you can give us on him."

Will pulled a small leather-bound notebook from the inside breast pocket of his jacket and held a silver pen poised to take notes.

"Raymond Walker," Jai said, for Will's benefit. "Lives in an apartment on Taylor Street. 2B. Drives an old muscle car. Maybe a Camaro. Got it. Thanks, babe. See you and Marcus at class, okay? Kiss, kiss!"

Will stopped scribbling, snapped his notebook shut, and stowed it back in his pocket. "I'll pass this on to my cop buddy. He'll have chat with your Mr. Walker, and keep an eye on him. Maybe do a few drive-bys in case Walker feels the desire to shift from nuisance pranks to something a little more serious."

Chalcey debated mentioning Ray's liking for sharp objects. And her suspicions about his drug use. Aw, hell. Cop or not, she couldn't in all conscience let Will's friend confront Ray unprepared. "Tell your friend to watch himself. The first time I encountered Ray, he pulled a knife on my boyfriend. And I'm pretty sure he was high." Hmmm. *Boyfriend*. It had a nice ring to it. Real nice.

"Duly noted. Thanks for the heads up."

"God. Sorry about the drama. My life's usually watching-paint-dry boring."

"No drama. Leave it with me. And I'll send my guys around to deal with that—" he waved a hand at the graffiti "—this afternoon."

"Thanks. For everything."

Will shrugged. "No problem. It's part and parcel of being a landlord. And I'll see you at the studio. Sooner, rather than later, if my wife has anything to do with it."

Chalcey managed a smile. "Oh, go on. You'll like it once you get into it, I promise."

"Hope you're right." He pressed a card into her hand. "Call me if you want an alarm installed, or if any of the comings and goings downstairs cause you any hassles." He strode off down the pavement, heading for a shiny black SUV.

She caught Jai eyeing Will's butt. "Quit drooling. He's married, remember?"

"Yeah. So you said. A man can dream, though, huh?"

"Yeah. A man can dream." She slung an arm about his

shoulders. "C'mon, *babelicious*. I've got a bathroom to finish up and we've got routines to work on."

Unfortunately for Chalcey, the instant Wulf wandered from the bedroom into the studio, Jai decided to fill him in on Ray's tagging efforts. Jai then compounded his multitudinous sins by dragging Wulf downstairs to show him Ray's tag firsthand.

"Did you have to tell him?" Chalcey grumped at Jai when he sauntered back into the studio.

"Yep. Dude needs his ass whupped. And your kick-ass Wulf-man is just the guy to oblige him."

"Thanks for nothing." She dared a glance at Wulf. His features were a blank, but his eyes…. They spat ice-blue fury. Jai had obviously explained the meaning behind the graffiti, too. In detail.

"Hey." She laid a hand on his forearm and squeezed gently. "Ray's just being a dickhead. He imagines he has a thing for me and he's pissed I'm not interested. There's nothing to worry about."

"Do not be so sure, Chalcedony. This man appears a little obsessed by you."

"Shit, Jai." Hands on hips, Chalcey glared at her dance partner. "What exactly did you say to him?"

Jai didn't appear at all repentant. "I only told him what he needed to know."

Great. Guaranteed, what *she* thought Wulf needed to know, and what Jai thought Wulf needed to know, were at opposite ends of the spectrum. "Wulf. Listen to me. This is Ray, we're talking about. And the phone calls, the tagging—it's pranks. Kids' stuff."

"Phone calls?" Jai just had to ask.

Wulf held Chalcey out at arms' length. "There have been phone calls from Ray?"

She scrunched up her face, searching for the best way to defuse this. "Uh, just a few hang-ups. Nothing drastic."

"Hang ups?"

"Somebody rings, you answer and there's silence, or heavy breathing, and then they disconnect. No biggie. Besides, I don't even know for sure it's him."

Jai shook his head and clucked his tongue. "I'm glad the lovely Will is getting one of his cop buddies to keep an eye on this dude. Ray's got issues with you, doll."

"Yes, well. I have issues with him, too. But because he's hardly going to be allowed back in my studio, or Sam's apartment, I'm unlikely to run into him again, am I?"

"Guess not."

Wulf surprised her by gathering her into his arms and holding her so tightly that she squeaked. He buried his face in her neck, and the attraction between them flared, skimming Chalcey's skin with the promise of pleasure.

"If anything were to happen to you, Chalcedony…."

She fought the insidious desire to melt into his arms, to let him take care of her and solve all her problems. "Nothing's gonna happen to me. Ray's a coward and he'll soon get sick and tired of bugging me and find another girl to bother. Now, can we get back to our practice?" Her tone was clipped and short, signaling to anyone with half a brain that this topic was like, sooo over.

Wulf only released her when Jai hit Play on her iPod. The music started up and Jai grabbed her hand to swing her into the first move of the routine.

Wulf backed off to give her and Jai room. He watched for a few minutes, arms crossed over his chest, face impassive. Then he swiveled on his heel and stalked off. "I am making coffee," he called over his shoulder.

"Yes, please!" Chalcey called after him.

"And if that scum touches one hair on your head, I will kill him."

She missed a beat and almost stumbled. "What did you say?"

"Nothing."

Jai swept her up into a Seducer and as she arched back, she turned her head to stare at Wulf's retreating back. Nothing? Yeah. Riiight. God help Ray if Wulf ever got hold of a sword.

THE RAGE POOLED in his gut. His fists clenched and un-clenched. Clenched again. He recognized the signs of a berserker-style fury. And in his own world, back in his own time, he would have embraced it. If any man had threatened one of his household, or encroached upon his property, he would have been well within his rights to challenge the man to a duel. And kill him, if he deemed the insult a serious enough matter.

Much as he'd dearly love to seek Ray out and cut the cow-ardly dog to shreds, he had neither sword nor dagger. And he was no longer ill-informed enough to believe that those who upheld the law in this land would turn a blind eye if he slit the man's throat.

Nor would Chalcedony look kindly upon him killing the man, no matter how much Ray insulted her honor and invad-ed her privacy. Upholding a person's honor and the right to exact retribution, were not concepts that were properly under-stood here, in Chalcedony's world. A pity. Many of the criminals featuring on a "crime show" he'd watched one night at Samantha's apartment would benefit from harsher punish-ments for their crimes.

Denied the simple pleasure of punishing Ray until he begged for mercy and promised on his life to leave Chalcedony be, Wulf punished the coffee beans.

Chalcedony had not owned a coffee grinder—she'd bought already ground coffee in bricks. Wulf had bought her a bag of coffee beans and a grinder with his first paycheck. Now, how-ever, he chose to attack the beans with a mortar and pestle. It was either that or smash something, and earn Chalcedony's wrath.

Pulverizing beans was a poor substitute for the real thing.

She should have confided in him about Ray. She should have trusted him to make this right. She should have—

Wulf shook his head. There were many things he would be far more comfortable if Chalcedony would do. But she did not fit into the mold of the women Wulf had known. He could not make her act as one of them, could not make her fit into his antiquated worldview of women. And nor would he want her to. She was an outspoken, resourceful, fiercely independent woman. She did not need a man to take care of her and coddle her and protect her. If she had concluded Ray's antics were not worth dwelling upon, then he had to respect her decision.

He didn't like it, but he would respect it, and allow her to handle it. He would also be primed and ready to step in and deal with Ray if the situation escalated.

His anger and frustration had abated somewhat but his body craved a physical workout. If Jai and Chalcedony hadn't already been using the studio he would have taken the large space for himself. The precise movements of the many battle-forms designed to strengthen both body and mind would have helped him work off his frustrations.

Of course, he could always wait until they'd finished their session, and challenge Jai to a mock-duel. He did not believe any workout he got with Jai would be as thorough as he liked, but the man was fit and strong. He might surprise Wulf. Not that Jai would win the challenge, but he might acquit himself reasonably well.

Wulf scooped out the powdered beans and measured the correct number of spoonfuls into the old plunger that he preferred over Chalcedony's automatic coffee machine. When the water had boiled, he added it to the plunger, and waited for the coffee to steep. He placed three mugs, sugar and cream on the tray along with the plunger, and then he carried the tray into the studio.

Jai and Chalcedony had finished working through their

routine. Jai's eyes lit when he spotted the third mug. "You made me coffee? I owe you big-time, Wulf-man. Been looking forward to a cup for the past hour."

Jai helped himself to cream, and eyed Chalcedony, who had added a teaspoon of sugar to her own mug. "No sugar for me," he said. "Gotta watch the figure, you know."

She stuck out her tongue at him. "I need the energy."

Wulf grinned at Jai. "If you owe me, as you say, then there is a boon I would claim."

Jai blinked at him. "Sure thing. Name it."

"I need a physical workout and I would spar with you."

"Me?" Jai choked on his mouthful of coffee. "You mean, like, wrestling?"

"He means, like, hand-to-hand combat," Chalcedony said, obviously enjoying Jai's discomfort.

"Ah. Well. I'm not really into that sort of thing. And these wooden floorboards? Not exactly designed to break a fall, if you know what I mean."

"You could always take Wulf down to the Y," Chalcedony said. "I'm sure they have an area with mats that you could use to beat the crap out of each other."

"Shut up, Chalcey. Not helping."

She laughed at Jai's horrified expression and then turned to Wulf. "So you want a workout, huh?"

"I do. What do you have in mind?"

She put down her mug and gave him a saucy look that had him easing the fit of his trousers.

He watched her saunter into the bedroom. "Jai," he said, his gaze still glued to the doorway Chalcedony had disappeared through as he placed his mug on the tray. "I regret that we must arrange to spar some other time."

"I'll lock up," Jai called after him as he headed for the bedroom. "Don't let her get too rough with you!"

"And don't let the door hit your ass on the way out, Jai!" Chalcedony yelled.

Wulf heard Jai's chuckle but he only had eyes for the woman lying atop the bed.

"Come here," she said. "And I'll give you a workout you won't forget."

He slid the door shut behind him. "I look forward to it."

# CHAPTER FIFTEEN

C LASSES WERE OFFICIALLY over for the evening, and the remaining students were getting in a bit of freestyle practice while Chalcey and Sam brainstormed how Chalcey was going to come up with six grand plus change before the IRS started knocking on her door. Of course Sam had immediately offered to give her the money. Or loan her the money. Even charge her interest on said loan if she couldn't stomach it any other way.

Chalcey refused each offer. But she was wavering. Boy, was she ever. Especially since none of Sam's other ideas had been very practical so far. Like the modeling one. No way was Chalcey going to "do some modeling on the side" when she hated being in front of a camera. And, in the unlikely event that she did get on the books of some agency, where the heck was she supposed to find the time? Sometimes she wondered whether Sam lived in the real world.

Esmeralda slinked up to perch on the edge of the registration desk. "Couldn't help overhearing. You know, I dated an accountant for a while. Didn't last. Was fine until he realized I was serious about the whole sex change thing. Then he called it quits. Wanted it both ways, you see. Tits *and* dick. Greedy bastard."

Her statement had completely floored Sam, who stood there gaping, unable to think of a single thing to say.

Classic frame it and hang it on the wall for posterity moment. Chalcey's laughter bubbled up and spilled out. "God, Esmeralda, is there anything you won't say?"

She shrugged. "When you've been through the sort of things I've been through, nothing embarrasses you anymore."

"I can only imagine."

Esmeralda hitched up her dress and crossed her shapely legs.

"What I wouldn't give to have your legs," Sam said.

Esmeralda stuck her legs straight out and contemplated them critically. "Yeah, they're not bad. Hair removal's a bitch though. It's so time-consuming being female."

"I wax," Sam said.

"I have to shave," Esmeralda said. "Hairs come in too dark to get away with leaving them long enough to wax. What about you, Chalcey?"

"Same. Hair removal's one of the only times that I sincerely wish I took after my mother rather than my dad."

"Fine body hair's the only good thing I inherited from my mother," Sam said.

Chalcey patted Esmeralda's bared thigh. "Better put those away, sweetie. They're attracting attention."

Esmeralda peeked at Chalcey from beneath her lashes, hope flaring in her eyes. "Oooh! Who?"

"Over there, by the sound system." Chalcey jerked her chin at a guy holding up the wall, his gaze glued to Esmeralda's legs.

"Oh. Him. He's sweet," she said, a flush of color painting her to-die-for cheekbones. "A little too sweet. Don't know he'd have the stomach for the truth."

"It's tough, huh? Not knowing how they'll react?"

"You have no idea, Chalcey." Esmeralda heaved a gusty sigh. Her bustier seemed about ready to pop its hooks and eyes, and her admirer's eyes widened still more.

"The perfect guy's out there, Esmeralda. One day he'll find you."

"Hope so." She visibly shook herself. "Anyway, I didn't

come over here to talk about me. I have an idea how you could raise the money you need."

Chalcey leaned back in her chair, tapping her chin with the rolled up sign-in sheet. "Oh? Do tell."

"You could hold an auction." Esmeralda threw up a hand to prevent the automatic response that was about to spill from Chalcey's lips. "An auction of men. *Dates* with men, to be precise. A whole bunch of us—" her emphasis on the word "us" made it clear she meant transgenders like herself "—auctioned ourselves off a few years ago to raise money for a friend with HIV. We held a charity gala. Raised a heap of cash for his treatments." Her gaze went all dreamy and unfocused. "I had the best night. The guy who won me said I was worth every single dollar."

Sam's gaze lit with unabashed admiration. "Omigod. That's a fan-freaking-tastic idea!"

"Sorry to pour cold water on a hot suggestion," Chalcey said, "but where the fricking heck am I gonna find a whole bunch of young, fabulously good-looking men, willing to auction themselves off for my good cause?"

Sam's green eyes sparkled with glee. "You're speaking to the girl whose stepfather number two owns a modeling agency, remember?"

"How could I forget? That male model you set me up with—" Chalcey shuddered, making it a totally theatrical gesture to emphasize her point. "God. Had to fend the girls off with a stick every time we went out. Damned near impossible to have some alone time. Look, Sam, even if you do manage to rope in a heap of gorgeous himbos, there's still the whole charity tax write-off minefield to wade through. I've already been red-flagged by the IRS. Last thing I need is some anal-retentive IRS dude sniffing 'round and discovering I'm not registered as a charity or whatever."

Sam clicked her fingers. "Easy. We'll just pitch you as a worthy cause to my mother and her do-gooder charity committee. Let them do all the paperwork while you reap the benefit." She high-fived Esmeralda. "You," she said, "are a girl after my own heart."

Esmeralda grinned. "You're very welcome, Samantha. Provided I get an invite. Otherwise you're in for one helluva bitch-slapping."

Chalcey covered her face with her hands and slumped forward on the desk. For good measure, she mimed banging her head on the desk, too. "Oh, no. What have I done?"

THE INAUGURAL "MALE SALE" was nearly a wrap. Combine the ticket sales with the money each auctionee had fetched so far, and it looked set to be a raging success.

Chalcey still wasn't convinced that auctioning off men was kosher, but it was too damn late to be doing anything about it now. Besides, any lingering doubts she harbored about this auction paled into insignificance when compared to her worries about the Crystal Guardian's Testing.

Six days left. A lifetime. And no time at all.

Her fears gnawed at her until she pressed a fist to her stomach and banished them. For now.

Officially, the proceeds of this event were to benefit various needy, female-oriented organizations. Sam had presented Chalcey's case to her mother's charity committee, and argued that not only did Laureano's Dance Studio promote fitness and a healthy lifestyle, but that Chalcey's humble studio was single-handedly responsible for increasing the self-esteem of the neighborhood's young women. Not to mention keeping them off the streets and out of trouble.

When the committee had the temerity to demur, Sam pointed out they sponsored many events to raise money for young women's sports teams, but girls who weren't into popular sports were neglected. Dance traditionally showcased refinement and elegance, something today's teens were sadly lacking. Dance shouldn't be a poor relation to athletic sports.

It deserved equal consideration from the charity committee, yadda yadda.

The committee bought it. Or perhaps they merely agreed to get Sam off their case so they could get on with their fancy catered lunch in peace and quiet. Regardless, Laureano's Dance Studio had forthwith been deemed an auction beneficiary.

Chalcey had been thrilled, of course. Except when she'd contemplated the horror of Mrs. Greenwood and her cronies copping an eyeful of a Lambada class. Scantily dressed women shaking their groove thangs and flashing their panties... not a heckuva lot of refinement or elegance to be found *there*.

After enduring a "Don't let me down" lecture from her mother, Sam had thrown herself into organizing this event with a vengeance. God only knew how she'd pulled it together so quickly. She'd sent out invitations, had the studio professionally decorated for the evening, and hired waiters to serve drinks and hors d'oeuvres. A stage had even been laboriously carted up the stairs in pieces before being assembled in the studio. This piece of essential equipment was for the auctionees to parade up and down upon to better display their, uh, *wares*.

Right now there were an awful lot of said wares on display, and not just on the stage. The studio was packed with exquisitely dressed women who practically oozed money and slightly frantic bonhomie. Their male partners, if they'd dared bring them, appeared slightly less enthused, but seemed content to watch their womenfolk drool so long as the food and drink kept coming.

Interspersed amongst the guests were a number of gorgeous young men dressed in all manner of revealing costumes, from Roman gladiator to Tarzan. Even a dashing Fred Astaire in black tie and tails but missing a shirt. Somehow, Sam had convinced these mouthwatering paragons of male perfection to donate their services. Chalcey's best guess was they were all wannabe models, and Sam had promised to put in a good word for them with stepfather number two.

Not a one of those handsome himbos rocked Chalcey's world. They were all too smooth and sculpted to be real.

Esmeralda sashayed past in a painted on sequined sheath, arm in arm with the guy who'd been ogling her at the studio. She winked at Chalcey, and then puckered up and blew a kiss.

"Good luck!" Chalcey mouthed, hoping that for Esmeralda's sake, her date wouldn't be put off and morph into a total bastard when Esmeralda revealed all.

She hitched up the bodice of her gown. Recycled, of course. Black, went without saying. Vintage—she'd splashed out. She'd even ditched her Mickey Mouse watch.

"You look beautiful," Wulf had told her before he kissed off her lipstick. She'd believed him—at least until her guests began arriving, all wearing stunning designer gowns and dripping with bling. For the first half hour, she'd felt like a drab little peahen amongst all the peacocks. Now, she was so jaded by all the fake smiles and air-kisses, that yet another ostentatious waving of a hand to better display one's latest umpteen carat diamond only made her want to yawn.

She spotted Will's wife, Anna, chatting with a bunch of women over by the bar. Anna looked stunning. She projected the same air of cool elegance as Chalcey's mother. But unlike Francesca, Anna had a wicked sense of humor. She gave Chalcey a wave, and as one of the males who'd recently been "for sale" strutted past with his "date", mimed panting like a dog with her tongue hanging out.

Anna and Will had duly turned up for their first freebie Ceroc class, and Anna had such a wow of a time that Will had to practically drag her off the dance floor. She'd even bought a yearly pass, which would let her do as many classes as she liked, whether it be Ceroc, Salsa, Lambada, Latin, or whatever. Will hadn't displayed quite the same degree of enthusiasm but he'd pasted on a smile and bought a pass, too. Much to Anna's delight.

And Chalcey's. She liked Anna very much. And Will, too. They made a great couple, gave her hope that marriages *could* work, that people could fall in love and stay in love. Case in point, Anna hadn't seriously bid for anyone tonight. Why would she, when she already had a guy she loved, a guy who loved her back and would do anything to make her happy?

In complete contrast, Mrs. Greenwood's cronies had dived right in, enthusiastically bidding and tossing money around like paper. Four of them had topped the bids on their chosen man and were smugly parading around arm-in-arm with their prizes, taking every opportunity to show them off. If the intent faces and covert glances of those women who'd not yet won a date were anything to go by, there'd be some fierce bidding for the final man.

Oh. My. God. The final man.

Chalcey knew she should have been thrilled they were raking in the money for those worthy causes, not to mention her own worthy cause. She'd even managed to smile at all the right times, and say all the right things. She hadn't put a foot wrong—yet. But how she was supposed to get through the coming ordeal without making an idiot of herself, she had no idea. If Sam hadn't insisted on her presence, she'd have hidden away in her bedroom and pulled the comforter over her head.

Champagne flute in hand, Sam shimmied over, beaming from ear to ear. "It's going great, don't you think, Chalce?"

"Sure seems that way," she said.

"Oh don't be like that! *He* suggested it, not me."

"Are you sure you didn't encourage him to do this, Sam?"

"I didn't. Cross my heart and hope to die."

"If I find out you're lying, you'll hope to die all right. Slowly and very, very painfully."

Sam grinned. "He insisted on helping with the fundraising. What was I supposed to do? Tell him he couldn't?"

"That would have been an excellent start," Chalcey said.

The music kicked in, and Sam had to lean in close to be heard. "Don't worry about it, Chalce. He'll be okay, I promise. You'll see."

Chalcey glared at her. "And how, exactly, can you promise that? You haven't rigged it, have you?"

"Of course not!" Sam appeared so genuinely shocked that Chalcey was inclined to believe her.

Until a truly nasty thought intruded. "And don't think that *you're* going to bid for him, either, Samantha Greenwood. If I see that arm of yours even twitch in an upward direction, so help me, I'll rip it off with my bare hands."

Sam rolled her eyes. "I know, I know. Besides, Marcus might not be impressed if I bid for Wulf, tempting though the thought may be."

"It's going okay then, you and Marcus?" Not that Chalcey was probing or anything. Merely insatiably curious.

"Better than okay. I think we have a real chance to make it work. He's great, really great. And he genuinely seems to care about me—despite my dubious past."

Chalcey hugged her. Carefully, so as not to transfer the ruby-red glittery stuff adorning Sam's dress onto her own. "No reason why he shouldn't. After all, he's the one who's benefiting from all your, er, past *experience*. The guy should be more than grateful."

"Oh, he is. Believe me."

"I'm really happy for you, Sam."

"Me, too. Oooh! Jai's about to start the bidding." Sam turned her head to focus on the spotlight.

Jai, resplendent in a gorgeous tailored tux, made a huge production of his bow and took the mic. "And now, ladies and gents. Last, but by no means least, we have a special treat for you. Our final man for sale tonight hails from a foreign land so, uh, *mysterious*, I'm not even sure exactly where it is. I give you Wulf, the Warrior King!"

Sam craned her neck and stood on tiptoe. "Do you see him

yet?"

Of course Chalcey saw him. With his Herculean physique, Wulf was hard to miss at any time. On stage, wearing his original leather garb, he was incredible. He'd gotten hold of a sword, and he swung it, performing a complicated set of moves with consummate ease. He looked every inch the warrior lord he professed to be. Chalcey could well imagine that if he proclaimed his true origins to everyone in the room right at this moment, not a soul would doubt him.

Her breath caught as she watched the man who'd once stood captives on a block and displayed them like livestock for sale, now displaying himself for sale to the highest bidder. Doubtless Wulf had considered that when he offered himself up to this spectacle. Perhaps in some small way he was atoning for those past deeds.

Chalcey glanced around the studio, gauging reactions. All eyes were on Wulf. Raw envy raked the faces of those women who had already successfully bid. Guess it wouldn't be seemly for them to bid for another man. She almost felt sorry for those eleven women who'd already won, to her mind at least, vastly inferior men.

Almost.

But Wulf was hers. She couldn't stomach the thought of any other woman going on a date with him. Not even a platonic one. For a good cause. *Her* good cause.

The room erupted in a flurry of loud, enthusiastic bids. Chalcey interlocked the fingers of both hands to stop herself from joining in the bidding. That wouldn't go down at all well, given she was one of the charity cases benefiting from this auction.

Jai held up a hand. "Now hold on, ladies. I know you're eager but Wulf is just warming up!"

*Oh, no. Don't you dare. Don't you dare encourage them any further, for God's sake!* Chalcey gave Jai dagger-eyes and made a slicing motion across her throat. But Jai's attention was fixed on Wulf, and he didn't spot her frantic gestures.

Wulf sheathed his sword and strode to the front of the stage. But instead of the provocative, strip-show-like routines the other men had performed, he stood legs apart, arms at his sides. His gaze scanned the room.

He spotted Chalcey. And locked gazes with her. His sun-burnished skin was sweat-glossed from his exertions. His superbly muscled arms and eight-pack glistened. His stillness was so complete that he might have been a statue. Except for his eyes. No sculptor yet born would have been able to capture the reality of those burning blue eyes.

Jai closed his gaping mouth and turned to the crowd. "What do you think, ladies? Does the Wulf-man do it for you?"

"Hell, yes!" someone called out. "He can warm my bed for me any time!"

*Bitch. There'd better not be any bed-warming.*

"Do I hear two thousand?"

"Two thousand one!"

"Two."

"Three."

"Two thousand five."

The other eleven auctionees had all topped out around the four-grand mark, with one Adonis-like young male even going for five-and-a-half. Within five minutes, bidding for Wulf had gone above six thousand dollars and showed no sign of taper-ing off. Obviously a seriously fabulous chest, and some equally serious abs, provoked a *serious* desire to impulse shop.

As bidding neared the seven thousand mark, it soon be-came apparent that two ladies were engaged in a furious bidding war for an evening with the man Chalcey loved.

Her veins buzzed with horror. Coward that she was, she shut her eyes, severing the link Wulf had forged with her. Leaving him on his own.

"Seven thousand!" a horribly familiar voice called.

Chalcey's eyelids popped open and her gaze darted around the room.

"Seven and a half!"

Well, that was a bit of a surprise. The screech had come from Sam's mother, Mrs. Greenwood.

Chalcey craned her neck until she finally caught a glimpse of the other bidder. Hell's teeth! What was she playing at?

"Sam!" she hissed. "What on God's green earth possessed you to invite my mother to this auction?"

Sam's face had paled to chalk-white beneath her makeup. She looked exactly how Chalcey felt—appalled beyond measure. She clutched Chalcey's arm, digging in her fingertips hard enough to leave bruises.

"Ow!" Chalcey pried Sam loose and rubbed her arm.

"God, Chalce, this is terrible! What are we going to do?"

"Relax. I'm sure she'll have a good explanation for this debacle. She'd better, anyway."

"But Mom seems totally set on having him. Check out the expression on her face. It's… it's… embarrassing!" Sam wrung her hands. "My own mother's got the hots for your boyfriend. I didn't think she was even interested in sex anymore!"

"Yeah, well. Wulf could kick-start a woman's libido even if she was at death's door." It seemed to have escaped Sam that Chalcey was just as appalled by the spectacle of *her* mother bidding for Wulf.

"Not helping, Chalce," Sam said.

"Sorry."

"Eight thousand dollars!" Francesca called out.

"Eight and half."

"Nine thousand!"

Sam and Chalcey glanced at each other, then their gazes swiveled back to their mothers. Mrs. Greenwood's mouth was set in a grim, determined line. Francesca looked cool, calm and collected as per usual, but Chalcey recognized that determined glint in her eyes.

"Uh oh, this could get messy," they said in unison and held their collective breaths.

"Ten thousand even!" Mrs. Greenwood screeched, her face triumphant with the certainty that she'd outbid her opponent.

But she didn't know Francesca Laureano-Owens.

The crowded studio was suddenly so silent and still that Chalcey could have heard a droplet of champagne trickling down someone's gullet.

"Twenty thousand dollars," Francesca said.

This announcement was greeted with a multitude of gasps, quickly smothered. Gazes darted back to Mrs. Greenwood— who inclined her head and graciously withdrew from the bidding.

Sam let out the breath she had been holding with a *whoosh*. "Thank God for that," she whispered in Chalcey's ear. "I was having frigging kittens at the thought of her winning him."

"Warrior King going once," Jai announced into the stunned silence. "Going twice. Sold to the gorgeous blonde in the stunning cerise gown, for twenty thousand dollars!"

Francesca raised her glass to Jai, acknowledging his compliment.

Jai rested his hand on one cocked hip as he gazed at Francesca's prize. "And I would have to say, cheap at twice the price."

There were shouts of agreement as Chalcey's mother threaded her way through the throng to climb up on to the stage next to Wulf. "May I?" She held out a hand to claim the mic from Jai.

Chalcey didn't quite know what she expected—perhaps that Francesca would sign a check and let Wulf go on his merry way. Or perhaps "donate" her prize to her daughter. No strings attached, of course. After all, Wulf belonged to Chalcey. Francesca knew how she felt about him.

"I'm honored to contribute to such worthy causes tonight." Francesca paused to smile prettily and milk her generosity for all it was worth. "And I'm looking forward to taking full advantage of my prize—tonight as it so happens. My partner and I have a reservation at Adagio."

Chalcey should have remembered that where Francesca was concerned, things never did go to plan.

Impressed oohs and aahs echoed throughout the room. Reservations at Adagio were as scarce as hen's teeth. Francesca would have had to pull serious strings to get a table.

The truth smacked Chalcey like a stinky wet fish. Francesca had planned this. She hadn't bid on anyone but Wulf. She'd planned to win him—must have been prepared to pay whatever it took. And now she planned to wine him and dine him and dazzle him. Amazing what an obscene amount of money could buy. Anything, it seemed. Even a night with the man your daughter loved. Paid for with your doting husband's money.

Chalcey pushed her way to the stage. She didn't dare glance at Wulf as she stalked up the stairs. She couldn't face him right now. She dragged her mother off to one side for a not-so-private chat. "What the hell do you think you're doing, Francesca?" she hissed.

"Whatever do you mean, Chalcedony?"

"I mean this farce with Wulf. What the hell else would I be meaning? Look, if you're thinking about using this dinner date to try to split Wulf and me up, it's not going to work."

"Very well."

"So you'll withdraw your bid."

"Oh, I couldn't possibly do that, darling. Not when I've already pledged my donation—it wouldn't be right."

She sounded far too reasonable. Chalcey searched her face for clues. "I'm sure Edgar will be very interested to hear about—"

"Relax, darling, it's only a little dinner date. Edgar is hardly going to object to that, especially since he already knows this auction is for such a worthy cause. Wulf and I are merely going to share a nice meal and chat a bit. What possible harm can there be?" She sashayed to the front of the stage again and bestowed a serene smile upon the curious crowd.

"Chalcey?" Jai's concerned eyes sought hers, silently pleading that she not make any more of a scene. "Will you be so kind as to come and present the prize to, er, Mrs. Owens?"

"Please, call me Francesca," Francesca said.

"Think I'll leave presenting the prize up to you, Jai," Chalcey said, and it took every ounce of control she could summon to keep her voice steady. "You'll do a far better job of it than I ever could. I'd only make a fool of myself." *And strangle my mother.*

Francesca used Jai's back as a support while she wrote out her check for twenty thousand bucks—an amount that would have made Chalcey break into a cold sweat. It was mere pin money for the Owenses, though.

Francesca basked in the applause, looking so damn smug as she presented the check to Jai, that Chalcey clenched her fists at her side so she didn't give in to the temptation to bitch-slap her mother. She couldn't take it anymore. Couldn't stand here, locking her knees so she wouldn't shake, pretending that she was fine with this. She stepped down from the stage.

Risking a glance at Wulf over her shoulder, Chalcey saw his brows knit in a perplexed frown. The tentative smile she managed for his benefit slid from her face when Francesca caught her gaze, looked directly into her eyes, and smiled.

It was a triumphant smile and it chilled Chalcey's heart.

She wasn't being paranoid. She was right to worry. Francesca's acceptance of her relationship with Wulf had been a sham. She'd only been biding her time. Now that she had alone time with Wulf, she would do her utmost to sabotage his relationship with Chalcey. And Francesca, of all people, had the best chance of convincing Wulf to sacrifice himself and give Chalcey up. Just like she'd convinced Malach to give *her* up.

Chalcey was sure that Francesca had suffered terribly by being forced to choose her dying husband over her own Crystal Warrior. And perhaps she wanted to save Chalcey from a similar pain if she and Wulf didn't make it through the Testing. Whatever Francesca's motives, it was too late. Chalcey was already in too deep. She loved Wulf. Francesca couldn't change that.

Nothing could change that.

She held onto that thought like a lifeline while her heart pounded in her ears and her stomach twisted into knots.

"Are you alright, Chalce?" Sam asked. "You're shaking. Have you eaten anything at all tonight?"

"I'm fine," she lied.

"At least Wulf going out for dinner with your mother won't be so bad. If it was Marcus up there, I'd rather have *my* mother wining and dining him than some other sex-starved harpy. Francesca's happily married and you know exactly what she's like."

"Yes, I know exactly what she's like." And that was precisely why Chalcey was so afraid.

Chalcey watched Jai accept her mother's check on behalf of Mrs. Greenwood's charity committee. She listened to everyone cheering as he announced the total that had been raised, and listed the organizations that would benefit. She wished she had the guts to race up to Jai and demand her mother's check. She wished she had the guts to rip it up and throw it back in her mother's face... and the balls to insist that Francesca leave without Wulf, and never show her face again.

The spacious studio closed in on her. Her chest was so tight that she struggled to breathe. It ripped her heart to shreds seeing her mother arm-in-arm with Wulf, parading him about like a prize stallion.

Worse by far would be sticking around until Francesca led him away for their cozy little chat at that fancy restaurant. Even more heartbreaking would be imagining just what they might be discussing. And wondering whether Wulf would give credence to her arguments, and be convinced to give Chalcey up.

"Sam, something's come up. I've got to get out of here. Hold the fort for me, will you? Jai can lock up." Before Sam could protest, Chalcey slipped away from her and headed out the door.

The ball was now in Wulf's court.

# CHAPTER SIXTEEN

C HALCEY CHOSE A local watering hole. She ordered a couple of tequila shots and watched the minute hand on the clock behind the bar tick inexorably onward. Two choices. Go home and trust that Wulf would show up, none the worse for his little chat with Francesca. Or show up at Adagio and drag his ass home. Maybe drown her sorrows and *then* show up at Adagio. Yeah. That'd work. She'd be immune to embarrassment and humiliation and her mother's barbs after she'd downed a few more shots and got loosened up and ready for a fight.

*Francesca's doing you a favor.*

*If he doesn't love you, better you find out now—before the Testing.*

*Put him out of your mind. Forget him.*

*He's not worth it. You can do better.*

All lies.

She couldn't do better. And love had little to do with anything—not when their true feelings were complicated by Pieter's spell. Spells and curses be damned, she wanted Wulf in her life. She wanted him any way she could have him. Period. End of story. She tossed the first shot down her throat and waited for the false heat to warm her belly.

"Fancy meeting you here." His voice slimed down her spine.

Without bothering to turn around, she downed her second

shot and clicked her fingers at the barman to hit her with another couple. "Not interested. Go away."

He leaned on the bar and ordered a beer. Sheesh. This guy couldn't take a hint.

"I see you haven't changed a bit," he said. "Still the same old Chalcey."

She shot him a sideways glance from beneath her lashes, and nearly fell off her stool. The long hair he used to slick with gel and tie back with a leather thong was currently a shaggy, unkempt mess, but it was definitely him. Terry—or Terrence, as he'd insisted on being called.

Her old dance partner. The one she'd dumped because he'd been incapable of comprehending that the intimacy necessary between dance partners on the contest circuit was fake. Just because she gazed into his eyes and did the sultry thing when they danced, didn't mean she'd sleep with him. Nor that he had any right to be jealous when she so much as glanced at another man.

Great. Just great. She'd rather deal with Ray than with Terrence right now. And considering how much she despised Ray, that was really saying something.

"Terry." She raised her shot glass to him and tossed it down her throat.

"So. Haven't seen you 'round the competition circuit."

"Nope."

"You're still dancing with Jai."

"Yep."

"Pity."

"You're entitled to your opinion." Jeez. How rude did she have to be before he got the message?

"Where's the brick shithouse?"

"Huh?"

"Your *boyfriend*," he said.

This time she swiveled on her stool to confront him directly. "How the hell do you know I've got a boyfriend?"

He swigged his beer, wiping his mouth with the back of his hand. "Checked out your opening night party at your studio. Couldn't resist. Nice space. You might even make a go of it if you get yourself a decent partner to help out."

Meow. Terrence had never liked Jai—always had some snide little remark at the ready. He couldn't stand that Jai was by far the better dancer. He'd never understood that Jai would always be the better dancer, because for Jai, dancing wasn't about technical perfection. Jai danced from the heart, and it showed.

"I didn't see you there," she said.

"I know."

He seemed very pleased with himself. Oh God. He'd probably witnessed the whole nasty encounter between Marcus and Wulf. And doubtless he'd had a fun time spreading equally nasty rumors about her studio around the dance community. He hadn't taken it at all well when she'd dumped him and asked Jai to partner her.

"Where is he?" Terrence asked.

Persistent, much? "Why do you want to know about Wulf?"

"So that's his name."

"What's it to you, anyway, Terry?

"Just curious. So where is he?"

"He's busy tonight."

"Oh, yeah? Good for him. How's about we go somewhere private—just you and me—and catch up on old times? You never did thank me properly for buying you that costume."

Wow. Loaded statement. She speared him with a ball-shriveling glare. "How's about we *don't*, Terry. How's about you get it through your thick head that I'm not interested, okay? How's about that?"

"For fuck's sake, Chalcey. It was only a suggestion. No need to get your panties in a wad."

"Go away, Terry." She couldn't deal with this right now.

She waved to snag the bartender's attention and downed her shot, thumping the empty glass down on the bar with enough force that she wobbled atop the barstool.

Terrence grabbed her upper arm, his fingers pressing into her skin hard enough to bruise. She gave him her best evils. "Get your hand off me. Now. Or you'll lose it."

He ignored her request. "Don't be like that, Chalcey. You and me. We were good together, right?"

The bartender materialized with the shots. "This guy bugging you?" he asked, searching Chalcey's face.

Terrence released her with a scowl and chugged his beer.

"Yep." She rubbed her arm. "He's bugging me. I seriously wish he'd piss off and leave me alone."

The bartender gave Terrence the fish-eye. "You heard the lady. Piss off."

Terence bristled. He'd never appreciated being told what to do. Even the slightest hint that his footwork or arm positioning wasn't up to scratch would set him off. "You work here, right? You got no right to interfere with a private conversation." He curled his lip at the bartender, eyeing him like he was inferior for working the bar.

The bartender polished a glass with his towel and shot Terrence a "don't mess with me if you know what's good for you" glare. "It's my place, bud. I can do what the fuck I like. You wanna make something of it?"

The testosterone levels skyrocketed. God. Couldn't she even have a quiet drink without drama? Chalcey downed both shots in quick succession.

Another guy eased on up and clamped a hand on Terrence's shoulder. "Reckon it's time you hit the road, buddy."

"Yeah?" Terrence shrugged off the hand and rounded on the newcomer. "Says who?"

The guy flashed an ID of some sort and merely stood there, rock-solid, letting his ID speak for itself.

Terrence held up both hands and backed away, all belligerence and cocky arrogance punctured. He tried a smile on for size, but it only looked sickly. "Didn't mean no harm." He jerked his chin at Chalcey. "She's a looker, right? Can't blame a man for trying, right?" He turned on his heel and fled the bar, barreling through the door so fast, he nearly assed over.

"Buhbye, Terry. Be seeing you…. Not." Chalcey turned her attention back to her shot glasses.

"Ms Laureano, I think it's time you went home."

She blinked at the newcomer. "How d'you know my name?"

"We have a mutual friend."

She closed one eye and squinted at him, searching her memory. "We do?"

"Will Sparling."

"Ohhh. Will. Sure. Any friend of Will's is a friend of mine." She toasted him with an empty shot glass. "Shit. It's empty." She didn't remember drinking it. She pointed to the glass and waggled her eyebrows at the bartender.

"I think she'll pass on that," Will's friend said, and to Chalcey's chagrin, the bartender nodded, obviously agreeing with him.

"How about I take you home, Ms Laureano?"

"But I want another drink. And then I have somewhere I need to go. Or maybe not. I haven't decided yet."

"Reckon you've had enough, love," the bartender said. "Dude here is a cop. Do me a favor and let him see you home before you attract any more attention from scumbags hoping to take advantage."

She fixed her gaze on Will's friend. He was about an inch shorter than her, but stocky, and certainly no lightweight. His gray-peppered hair had been shaved so darn close to his skull it made her wince. His jeans had seen better days, but his t-shirt was bright white. Her gaze drifted to his left-hand ring finger. Yep. Married. It had to be that or a very attentive girlfriend.

He grinned in such a boyish fashion that it was difficult to figure why he'd spooked Terrence so thoroughly. "I'm not gonna hit on you, Ms Laureano. Cop's honor." He placed a hand over his heart.

"Okay, Will's friend. I guess I'm ready to go home now."

"That's my girl."

Chalcey settled her tab with her emergency credit card and tucked it back into the teeny tiny evening bag Sam had loaned her.

Will's friend assisted her to climb down from the barstool with a hand beneath her elbow. She was rather grateful for the courtesy. A full-length, dry-clean-only cocktail dress and killer heels wasn't ideal attire for perching atop high barstools.

As it turned out, nor was it the most comfortable of outfits to totter home in. She got a few feet down the pavement before she halted to step out of her slip-on pumps and shove them beneath her armpit. The crisp night air cut straight through the fabric of her dress. Damn the cost. She didn't fancy walking home barefoot. And, lucky her, she was about to come into some money so she could afford to use her emergency credit card again.

"You can walk me to the nearest cab rack if you like, Will's friend."

"I'd give you my jacket. If I was wearing one."

"Awww. That's sweet. Appreciate the thought, Will's friend."

"Call me Rick."

"Call me Chalcey. It's less of a mouthful than Chalcedony."

"You can say that again."

"Blame my mother." Yeah. Blame her for a lot of things. "So how come you happened by my bar, Rick? And don't try and tell me it was just a happy coincidence. I may be half drunk but I'm not all stupid."

"Will mentioned your auction, so I made it my mission to cruise past your studio a couple of times. When I spotted this guy lurking, at first I thought it might be your other admirer, Mr. Walker. Figured I'd stick around for a bit, see what he was up to. Sure enough, what do I see? You rushing out the door, and him following you."

Chalcey's stomach gave a lurch. She suspected the sick feeling wasn't caused by a little too much tequila, either. "Terrence followed me to the bar?"

Rick nodded. "Who is he?"

"Ex dance partner."

"With a grudge?"

"If dumping him a few weeks out from a competition counts, then yeah. I guess so." She summoned a laugh, and winced when it sounded off.

"Look, Chalcey, if you're really worried about this guy, you could come down to the precinct and take out a restraining order on him."

She chewed that over. Tempting. But— "Nah. Terrence always was a bit of a creep but I don't think he'll bother me anymore. You frightened him off big-time. I bet he's peeing his pants right about now."

"Perhaps. But I'm seeing you home, just in case." He collared a cab and ushered her into the backseat before giving the cabbie the studio's address.

"But what about your car? Didn't you leave it parked somewhere near the bar?"

He waved a hand, dismissing her concerns.

"Thanks," she said.

"You're welcome." He grinned again. "Any friend of Will's is a friend of mine."

"I see a free dance class in your future, Rick."

He slanted her such a startled glance that she giggled. "Haven't heard that line before, huh? Will and Anna are doing classes. You should bring your wife or sister or whoever to a class, too. Bet you'd both enjoy it. "

"Nice sales pitch," he said.

She shrugged. "What can I say? I'm a nice person."

"So, why's a nice girl like you getting trashed in a bar?" He tapped his cheek, and narrowed his gaze. "Lemme guess. Boyfriend troubles?"

"You're good. Yeah. Boyfriend troubles."

"Tell me about it," he invited.

He was a cop, and a friend of Will's. So she explained about the auction. And her mother's part in it. Of course, she still had enough sense left to avoid mentioning all the supernatural woo-woo. No point in giving Rick the impression that she was certifiable.

"Not a good look, your mother bidding for your boyfriend. She sounds like a real piece of work."

"Gold star for you," she said.

He awkwardly patted her arm. "It's just a dinner date. It'll be okay. You'll see."

The cab pulled up out front of her studio, and Rick instructed the driver to wait while he walked her to the door. He hung around while she fumbled for her key. And told her that he wasn't leaving until he heard her deadlock the door from the inside.

Will's friend Rick was a thorough man.

Chalcey dragged herself up the stairs and through the doorway into the dimly lit studio. Sam's plethora of eager flunkies had cleaned up all the mess. The place was spotless— so immaculate that, except for the temporary stage, no one would ever have guessed there'd been a function earlier.

She cocked her head to one side, blinking rapidly when her vision blurred as she contemplated said stage. Maybe she could keep it, use it for classes. Teachers could dance on it. Sure would make it easier for people to see them. She pictured a class in her head. Maybe not. Being elevated above students would be just asking guys to peer up skirts. And if by some chance Leah didn't mind, well *she* certainly did.

She whacked a hand in the general direction of the light

switches, hit them to off more by accident than design, and wobbled through to her bedroom. It crossed her mind that she would probably regret not removing her makeup—foundation and mascara smeared all over the pillowcase, goopy panda-eyes and such—but tonight, all that cleansing, toning and hyped-up palaver would only delay her from what she craved. Oblivion. Her only concession to comfort was stripping off her dress and hanging it up before she tumbled into bed.

The trouble with not drinking enough to actually pass out was that even though she was tired and sick, each time she lay back and closed her eyes the world spun and she wanted to throw up. She'd pry open her eyelids, sit up until the nausea receded, lay down again, and the whole damn cycle would start over.

After a half hour, she seriously contemplated crawling into the bathroom and sticking her fingers down her throat. But she was a wuss. So she suffered. Until thankfully, at some stage she drifted off to sleep. Probably with her eyes open, because she didn't remember closing them. And when she awoke, they were grainy and swollen and sore as hell, like someone had tossed a handful of grit in her face.

She rolled out of bed and lurched to her feet. The world tilted, and so did her abused stomach. Clapping a hand over her mouth, she broke into a shambling run.

When she'd finished throwing up a bucketful of tequila shots, had washed her face and bathed her eyes, she vowed she was never going to overindulge in alcohol again. No matter what the provocation. In fact, she felt so damned wretched that she vowed to give up alcohol entirely.

Well, except for the tequila she bought as a special treat. Because that was really, really good tequila. And expensive, so she wouldn't be able to afford it very often.

She finally pulled her crap together enough to wander into the kitchenette and make some coffee to wash down the aspirin. It was then that she realized she was missing something even more important than her morning caffeine fix. Ice-cold fear smashed her like a ton of bricks. She sprinted back to her bedroom, ignoring her thudding head.

Wulf was not asleep in her bed. Nor was he anywhere else in the studio. She knew this for sure, because she raced around and checked everywhere he could possibly be. The kitchenette where she'd just been, behind the stage in the studio, the bathrooms, each shower and toilet cubicle…. Then, desperation making her stupid, she checked places he couldn't possibly be unless he'd become a contortionist.

No Wulf.

She dragged her sorry butt back to the bedroom, all the while lecturing herself that there was no need to panic. He must have returned while she was out cold, woken up before she had, and headed out again. Yeah. That was it.

She focused on the bed, noting its one obviously slept-upon pillow. Rumpled bedding on the left side. A perfectly made-up, smooth right side—*his* side. She couldn't hide from the truth any longer. Wulf hadn't come home last night.

The bedroom closed in on her. She needed space, air. She staggered out into the main studio and stood, head hanging, sucking in deep shuddering breaths. Enough. She had to do something, had to know for sure.

She perched on the edge of the registration desk to use the phone. Her hand shook as she dialed Sam's number. She swung her foot in time to the phone's rings.

Finally, Marcus answered. "Is Wulf there?" she asked, too anxious to bother with pleasantries.

"That you, Chalcey?"

"Yes. Is he there?"

"No. Is something—?"

She hung up and dialed the club where Wulf worked, just in case he'd gone straight there after his dinner date. Not that he had any reason to, since he'd taken the night off. But he might have gone in if someone had called in sick, right? No answer. Not surprising since it was now past eight and the club would be closed.

She even dialed Adagio, only to hang up when the restaurant's message service kicked in. What could she say? "Excuse me, but did you happen to notice a really large man dressed in leather pants and a vest asleep under a table when you closed up for the evening?" Huh. She'd sound like a crazy woman.

She gnawed her thumbnail while she dredged up the courage to make the next call. Pacing the floor did nothing for her state of mind. Dammit. If she didn't do it now, she'd never summon the courage to do it later.

Hotel reception dialed her mother's room. The call took an eternity to connect.

"Hello?"

His husky, sleep-filled voice kicked her right in the gut. She doubled over, gasping, on the verge of puking up her guts again. Betrayal hammered her soul.

"W-Wulf?" she finally managed to gasp. There would be a logical explanation for him answering the phone in her mother's suite. There had to be.

"What is it that you want, Chalcedony?"

She clutched the receiver, her knuckles turning white. What the hell kind of a question was that? "You. I want you." She squeezed her eyelids shut. If she said aloud what she was thinking, she might make it true. She couldn't bear it to be true. But not knowing was killing her. "I don't care where you spent the night. Or who you spent it with."

His pause seemed to go on forever, while her heart tripped in her chest and her skin went hot-cold-hot. And then his voice lashed out at her. "After what we have gone through together, how can you think so little of me? Do you truly believe that I would seek solace in the arms of another?"

She nearly dropped the phone. "But my mother. She—"

"Enough. I will discuss this no further."

His voice sounded flat and so desperately tired that

Chalcey's heart ached. "I'm sorry! I didn't mean it. Of course I didn't think that you and she— You have to come home. Please, Wulf. I-I *need* you. When are you coming home?"

"I am not coming home, Chalcedony. Francesca was correct. We are not meant for each other. I know that now. And I accept my fate."

Dread squeezed her heart. "No! You can't. Whatever she said to you— It doesn't matter. You belong here, with me. Come home, Wulf. Please?"

"I cannot. For your sake, I cannot."

"No!" She screamed into the disconnected phone. "No."

The truth hit her, and there was no escaping it. She'd been using Pieter's spell as an excuse to hold a tiny part of herself back from Wulf. But what she felt for him was crystal clear. It was something that she'd never felt for any other man and no spell could replicate those feelings. At night, wrapped in his arms, listening to his even breathing as he slipped into sleep, she felt warm and safe and loved. She loved him. Real, gut-wrenching, want to be with him forever, love.

She found herself lying on the floor, staring at the ceiling, with no memory of toppling from her seat on the edge of the registration desk. Tears welled, dripped silently down her cheeks.

She loved Wulf. And instead of telling him that, she'd blathered on about *wanting* him, *needing* him, everything but telling him the truth.

And God, how she wished that she'd told him, made him listen, forced him to believe her, because maybe, just maybe, it might have made a difference. But now it was too late.

# CHAPTER SEVENTEEN

THE STAIRWELL STEPS creaked, slicing through her misery. It could only be Wulf's footsteps that she heard. He'd forgiven her for thinking the worst of him, forgiven her for being a jealous fool and a coward. He'd come back to her. She wiped her eyes with the heels of her hands, swiped at her runny nose and hauled herself to her knees.

She experienced a brief moment of burgeoning hope before some primitive part of her brain analyzed the footsteps and dashed her hopes. Even before the door opened and they entered the room, Chalccy had slumped back to the floor and given herself up to heaving sobs that wracked her body.

"Christ!" Marcus's shocked voice echoed though the studio. "What the fuck happened, Chalce? Are you hurt?"

Heels clacked on the floorboards. Sam gripped her arms and tried to turn her over but Chalcey had curled up into a fetal position, hugging the floor as though her life depended on it. At that moment, she believed that it did. Facing reality was going to kill something deep inside her.

Sam took charge. "Hang up that phone and help me get her into the bedroom, Marcus. Let's see if we can get some sense out of her."

With Sam's help, Marcus maneuvered Chalcey into his arms. "Jesus, she's ice-cold! What the hell is going on?"

"Of course she's ice-cold, dumbass. She's only wearing

panties and she's probably been lying here for at least an hour, thanks to you. If you'd woken me when she called, we'd have gotten here before she ended up in this state."

"How the fuck was I to know? And why is she like this anyway?"

"Duh! Because obviously Wulf hasn't come home from his big night out with Francesca. Let's get her in to bed and warm her up."

They bickered like an old married couple, a fact that should have made Chalcey grin like a loon. She hadn't even realized that she was half-naked, and that should have embarrassed the heck out of her. But everything seemed to be happening through a grayed out, misery-infused haze. She felt detached from the world, cocooned, incapable of feeling anything but pain and anguish.

And guilt. So much guilt.

Sam and Marcus put her to bed, tucking her beneath the covers like parents would settle a small child. They argued over what to do about her, too, their muted whispers hissing back and forth in the darkness of her mind.

Sam placed her warm palm on Chalcey's forehead. "Open your eyes, Chalce. Talk to me. Tell me what happened or Marcus is threatening to call a doctor."

Prying open her eyelids was a mammoth chore. Chalcey gazed up at the concerned face of her best friend. She tried to speak but could only manage a croak.

Sam clicked her fingers. "Glass of water."

Marcus left the room in a rush.

"It's Wulf, isn't it, Chalce? And it's more than him not coming home last night." She brushed the hair back from Chalcey's face. "Have you two split up?"

Chalcey nodded, staring up at Sam through a blur of tears.

"But I thought you'd decided to see it all the way through to the Testing?"

"I had."

"And?"

"He… he doesn't… want to."

"Shit." Sam swiveled as Marcus returned, took whatever he handed to her and examined it minutely. "Good idea. Thanks, hon. Chalce, I want you to sit up a bit and swallow these." She pressed a couple of pills into Chalcey's hand. "They'll help you to sleep."

"Sleep. That's good. I want to sleep." Chalcey washed the pills down with gulps of water from the glass Sam pressed to her lips.

"So where's Wulf now, do you know?" Sam asked.

"With Francesca. At her hotel."

Sam growled deep in her throat like a mama cat protecting her kittens. "Should have known that uptight bitch would have something to do with it."

"Francesca?" Marcus asked.

"Chalcey's mother. She bought him at the auction."

"Oh," he said. Then, "Ohhh!"

So Chalcey wasn't the only one who'd thought the worst. But that was no solace. Not now. She started to cry again, great gulping sobs of despair. "It's… it's over, Sam. I've failed. F-failed the Testing. P-Pieter's going to… to… destroy Wulf. K-kill him. It's… it's over!"

"Shhh, Chalce." Sam gathered Chalcey into her arms to rock her while Marcus rubbed her back. "It'll be all right," Sam crooned. "I promise."

The real world receded as the drugs took effect, wrapping Chalcey in comforting cotton wool. Sam gently but firmly pushed her back against the mattress.

Chalcey stared at the ceiling. It was all fuzzy-looking, like someone had blurred its edges. Sam was fuzzy around the edges, too. And Marcus. Chalcey, though, was buoyant, floating above the black abyss of her pain. Maybe later she would let it claim her. For now, all she wanted to do was sleep.

But Marcus wouldn't stop asking questions.

"What's she talking about, Sam? Who's going to kill Wulf? And what the fuck's this *testing* she's going on about?"

"Erm, it's nothing, hon," Sam said. "She's upset and she's not making much sense. Because of the drugs."

"Bullshit. You know exactly what she's talking about. Tell me."

"I can't."

"Why not? Don't you trust me to keep my mouth shut? Maybe I can help."

Even through her drug-induced fog, Chalcey recognized his hurt. He thought that Sam didn't trust him enough to include him. This, at least, she could fix. "Tell him, Sam," she whispered. "Don't let him think you don't trust him. Tell him everything. It doesn't matter anymore. It's over. I've failed and Wulf's left me. Soon it'll be too late, anyway. He'll be gone forever."

*He's gone. It's over.* We're *over.* Her mind shut down and she embraced unconsciousness.

She dreamed that Wulf was trapped in his crystal again. He whispered her name, over and over, clinging to it like a lifeline. But Chalcey didn't answer him. She didn't call his name or try to establish a link with him through the bond they shared. She didn't confront the Crystal Guardian and attempt to rescue Wulf from his crystalline hell. She turned her back on him, repudiated him. And the fragile bond between them snapped.

Wulf sensed the breaking. He fought like a demon. He gouged his wrists and throat with his nails, trying to rip through skin and muscle so he would bleed out. He screamed, great howls of despair tearing over and over from his throat until he was hoarse and could scream no more. Finally, he fell silent. And even though she knew he suffered, she did nothing.

She woke with a pounding jack-hammer of a headache, and a massive case of the dry-horrors from the sedatives. She clung to one thought. Wulf had only relinquished her to protect her, because if they failed the Testing, he didn't want her to suffer.

God help them both, he was being noble. Stupid bastard.

She had to fight for him. There was still time. The twenty-eight days decreed by the Crystal Guardian's spell wasn't yet up. Chalcey had to make this right, do her utmost to strengthen their bond in the hope that if—when—the crystal took him, she would be able to call him back. She had to at least try to make him listen to her, try to make it clear how she truly felt. Or she'd never, ever forgive herself.

She rolled out of bed onto her hands and knees, and stayed there awhile with her head hanging until the room stopped spinning. Then she crawled to her feet, lurched over to the chest of drawers, and yanked out some fresh clothes.

All she could say about the shower she took was that it was wet and hot, and it did the job. Despite using the ladies' bathroom, which was a slightly different configuration to the men's, despite the pale peach shower curtain instead of green, the cubicle was so filled with memories of Wulf, and the first time they'd made love, Chalcey had to grit her teeth to get through even the short time it took to wash.

She shoved herself into her clothes, dragged a comb through her tangles, and headed downstairs.

Too much to hope for a clean escape. Halfway down she encountered Sam, loaded down with croissants and bagels, freshly squeezed OJ, and a couple of coffees.

"Damn." Sam grimaced. "Thought I'd be back before you woke up. So where the heck d'you think you're going?"

"Four Seasons hotel. I have to talk to Wulf."

Sam nodded slowly, her green eyes flashing with satisfaction in the gloomy stairwell. "You're going to fight for him. Good. Saves me from having to roust you out of your funk and kick your ass. Want me to come with?"

Chalcey considered the offer. Tempting, so very tempting to have Sam for back up to prod her if she faltered. Not to mention bitch-slap her mother if Francesca interfered. "No.

Thanks, but I have to do this on my own."

"I hear you. But you're not going anywhere without food." Sam shoved a bagel bag at Chalcey. "Coffee or OJ?"

"OJ." She needed the vitamin C kick more than the caffeine.

Sam handed over a juice. "The rest will be waiting for you when you get back. Except for the coffee, of course. I'll have to drink that for you. Go sock it to him, Chalce. Don't take 'no' for an answer, you hear me? Good luck."

Chalcey hugged Sam around the coffees and juice and bags, and then continued on down the stairs.

"Call me if you're not up to walking back," Sam yelled.

"I will."

"Promise?"

"I promise."

As she finished the last bite of her bagel, Chalcey reasoned that if she asked hotel reception to ring ahead, neither Wulf nor Francesca would permit their room number to be given out. And as luck would have it, there were two guys on the reception desk. She hung back until the youngest guy manning the desk was free, then strolled over to coax the room number from him.

"Hi, I'm Chalcedony Laureano. I'm having breakfast with my mother, Francesca Laureano-Owens? But I can't for the life of me remember what her room number is. I'm hopeless before I've had my first coffee of the morning." She leaned on the desk, crossing her arms beneath her breasts and rocking forward to afford him a prime view down her cleavage. For good measure, she gave a breathy giggle. "Gosh, I'm such an airhead. I wrote it down somewhere, too, but I can't remember where I put the note."

He was talented young man. He managed to call up Francesca's details on the reservations computer with one eye on the screen and the other on Chalcey's best assets.

"I'm treating her to breakfast," she said, batting her eyelashes like an oversized Kewpie doll. "Can you recommend somewhere nice? Not too expensive, though. I'm a bit broke at the moment."

"The café just down the corner from here does a great budget breakfast," he said. "Their pancakes are the best."

"Hey, thanks!" she cooed, laying it on real thick. "You're a real sweetheart." She sucked in a deep breath. And held it.

His gaze was glued to her cleavage when he said, "Room 616. Go right on up."

Score. Chalcey headed on up. She rapped on the door of 616. She heard footsteps inside the room. Coming closer….

WULF OPENED THE door. Chalcedony breezed past him before he could even voice the words he'd rehearsed to deny her admittance.

"You're supposed to check before you open the door," she said. "I could have been anyone."

He'd been expecting something like this. Francesca didn't know her daughter as well as she believed. Chalcedony wouldn't give him up without a fight. "Why did you come here, Chalcedony?"

She sank gracefully onto the couch and draped her arms over its plush back. "Nice suite. She sure doesn't stint when it comes to creature comforts. And speaking of Francesca, where is my mother, anyway?"

Her gaze cut to the one and only bedroom. He shouldn't blame her for thinking the worst of him. Except that in his secret heart of hearts he did. Until he'd disabused her of the notion she had believed that he'd betrayed her, and that knowledge cast a pall over his soul.

"Don't tell me she's still snoozing. Why don't you go wake her up, Wulf? I'd appreciate the chance to tell her face-to-face what I think of her."

Her gaze raked him, lingering. He wore only light cotton sleep pants. It took every bit of willpower he possessed to dampen his desires and not physically react to her hungry gaze. He lost the battle and turned on his heel, heading toward the kitchen area.

"She is not here," he said, when both he and his hard, eager cock were safely out of sight behind the counter. "She traveled back to her husband last night."

"Oh?" Momentary surprise and then a nod of understanding. "She set this up so I'd think the worst and show my true colors. Clever—I've got to hand it to her. So who's paying for the room? You?"

He scrubbed his hands through his hair. "No. The next few days have been paid for by your mother. I may stay here until I am—"

"Sucked back into those unlovely hunks of wulfenite crystal?"

"Yes."

"Gee. How generous of her. Still, it's the least she could fucking well do for you, considering."

"Why are you here, Chalcedony? Is it to torment me? To remind me of what I am giving up?"

She launched from her seat and didn't halt until she stood directly behind him. "Yes," she agreed, inching forward until her breasts brushed his back. "And I'm going to continue to torment you until you stop being so fucking noble and come back home."

She rose up on tiptoe, brushing her lips against his earlobe. "To me. Where you belong."

He couldn't help himself. He allowed her to turn him to face her. A grave error, for she pressed her lips to his in a fleeting, butterfly caress that left him wanting to unclench his fists from his sides and reach for her, hold her still and devour her.

His muscles strained with the effort to remain still but his torment was only beginning. She speared her fingers through his hair to cup her palms about his skull. And, gods help him, she kissed him, long and deep. It was as though she was willing him to open to her, to surrender, to accept that he was hers. It was as though she was pouring her heart and soul into that kiss.

And although it devastated him to hurt her, he did not yield. He reached up to manacle her wrists. Gently but inexorably, he disentangled her fingers from his hair and set her away from him. For her own good. "Why are you here, Chalcedony?"

"Because I love you."

Longing and yearning shone in her eyes but it wasn't enough. It would never be enough. He wished he could reveal the truth because this was not a game. This was not a courtship ritual, where one half of a couple hinted and teased, testing the waters before moving on to the next stage. This was Chalcedony. She was his life, the only woman he'd ever loved. And she deserved his honesty. But if he told her the truth, she would never willingly leave him.

Last evening had been a special hell but he'd made peace with his decision. Now, with Chalcedony before him, with the scent of her luring him, her touch seducing him, his resolve threatened to weaken.

He had listened to Francesca state her case in defense of her daughter and agreed that if the Crystal Guardian came for him, Chalcedony would suffer—as Francesca had suffered when Malach was taken. He had countered that if they passed the Testing and he was released from the curse, Chalcedony would suffer not at all, for he loved her and would cherish her until the end of his days.

"Ah," Francesca had said, her expression not triumphant, as he'd expected, but immeasurably sad. "And have you considered that Chalcedony's love for you is fake? That everything she professes to feel for you is nothing more than a cruel joke to give the Crystal Guardian the last laugh once the curse is broken?"

"Then I will suffer the loss of her, true. And she will forget me and move on, as all lovers who've parted ways eventually do." He'd shrugged and taken another bite of his steak, trying to make light of the very thing he'd come to fear most while the expensive food turned to ashes in his mouth.

"I carry the guilt of Malach's death to this day," she'd said. "The pain never eases. It's as fresh as the day I walked into our motel room and found it empty except for those two pieces of malachite. And then Pieter took even those from me, so I had nothing left of Malach but my memories. I've never gotten over him. Never. He haunts me."

Wulf had known that for the stark truth. And he waited for the sword to fall.

She'd sipped her wine, and slain his last defense with the one question he could not refute. "Are you willing to risk Chalcedony's future happiness?"

He was not. Above all else, he would not have Chalcedony suffer as her mother had done—and still did. He could not take the chance that they would fail the Testing. Best he break faith with her now. And rather than gloating over her success, Francesca had told him how best to achieve that break. He'd thought it an excellent plan, one that could not fail, until now.

Still Chalcedony waited—waited for him to crush her to him and kiss her and make everything right again. He could see the expectation in her eyes, in the way she held her body poised, tensed with anticipation.

He slashed her hopes and uttered the words that would make her hate him. "I do not believe you love me, Chalcedony."

Her legs gave out on her. He almost reached for her. But the gods were on his side, for before he could move, she locked her knees and backed away from him, her disbelief clawing a great gaping hole in his heart.

"It's true," she told him, her voice shrill. "It's true! I love you! Why won't you believe me?" She hit the couch and collapsed into it, grief etched into every line of her beloved face.

"I believe that you *think* you love me, Chalcedony. But what you feel for me is not real. 'Tis Pieter's spell. Nothing more."

"And you? Do you truly believe that your feelings for me are fake? All this time we were together, every time we were intimate, every time you touched me, is that what you truly felt?"

"I loved you."

She reeled as though she'd been slapped, and he knew she understood.

*Loved.* Past tense.

She swallowed, as though choking down a lump in her throat. But she wouldn't give in. Not yet. "What's changed?"

"Everything."

Denial bubbled on her lips, but she couldn't speak, couldn't get the words out. For that small favor, at least, Wulf would be eternally grateful.

He steeled himself to the cold implacable resoluteness of a warrior incapable of gentleness, or loving gestures, or feather-light caresses across a woman's bare skin. "I will not allow you to sacrifice your chance at love for me, Chalcedony. I refute our bond and set you free."

"If… if this is because my mother—"

"Do not blame Francesca for my decision. She merely clarified what I have long suspected."

"And that is?"

"We do not belong together. 'Tis but another form of slavery to be-spell a woman and bond her to a man not of her own choosing."

"And if it is my choice? If I willingly choose you after the Testing?"

"Ah, but there is the crux of the matter. For we will never truly know if you are willing, or merely influenced by the bond we share. Pieter's spell is a cruel one. And I will not allow you to become the victim of such cruelty."

She gazed into his eyes, scrutinizing him for a sign that he was lying.

He gave her nothing. He gave her nothing when she'd given him everything, when she'd ripped out her heart and laid it at his feet.

"And is that your last word?"

He could not trust himself to speak so he nodded.

She jerked to her feet like a child's puppet. "Well that's it, then. No point in telling you it doesn't matter whether this is a spell, because I love you now and now is all that matters. No point in telling you I'll willingly undergo the Testing and life-bond with you. Not point in telling you I'll do anything, sacrifice everything, to save you from that goddamned crystal. Because I love you."

He didn't recall her moving but suddenly she was there, right up in his face. "Once this was all over, you could have gone your own way if you didn't love me enough to stay. I would have understood and let you go. Goddamn you, I would have understood!"

Still, he gave her nothing. Until finally she broke, lashing out at him, hitting and scratching, kicking and screaming like a madwoman.

He didn't defend himself. He stood and took it all, never flinching, never making a move to stop her, not even when she scored his face with her nails. And when she'd exhausted herself, when she was drained and limp and hoarse from yelling, he turned on his heel and opened the door. "It is time for you to leave, Chalcedony."

"Goddamn you to hell, you stubborn bastard," she whispered.

And as she stumbled out the door, he said, "You will thank me for this, one day."

She didn't look back at him. Not once. But he clearly heard her reply. "No. I'll hate you, Wulf. I'll hate you for not even giving me a chance to try and save you."

He stood in the corridor, by the hotel suite door, and watched her walk to the elevator and smack the Down button. He watched her walk inside. And even though she'd disappeared from his view, he watched until the doors closed with a shattering finality that pierced his soul.

# CHAPTER EIGHTEEN

WHEN CHALCEY WANDERED into the kitchen, Sam and Marcus glanced up and then quickly down, concentrating far too intently on their breakfasts.

"Morning," she said, ignoring the undercurrents swirling around the room.

"Coffee's on." Sam waved a casual hand toward the counter. "Marc made a fresh press a couple of minutes ago."

Chalcey poured a coffee and leaned against the counter, cradling the cup in her palms. Despite their efforts to be covert she spotted both Sam and Marcus shooting glances at her. Great. Obviously they knew exactly what today was. There went her chances of trying to pretend nothing was different, that it was merely a day like any other.

She took a sip of coffee and tried not to grimace at the bitterness. It was not a patch on Wulf's brew. He had a magical touch when it came to coffee.

Crap. Now that she'd thought about him, her composure was totally screwed. Tears burned her eyes. She'd never realized that tears really could burn. They were only mildly saline weren't they? How could they burn? But these did. As had the tears that she'd cried for Wulf each night since she'd lost him.

She stiffened her spine before facing Sam and Marcus again. "It's okay, you two. You don't need to walk softly around me. I'm not made of glass. I know you know what today is, so just say it, all right? Then we can get back to being normal."

Sam's gaze oozed such compassion that Chalcey yearned to turn tail and flee. Either that or fall to her knees and lay her head in Sam's lap so Sam could comfort her while she blubbered like a baby.

"It's exactly twenty-eight days since you first met Wulf, isn't it, Chalcey?" Marcus finally said.

"Yep."

"So?" Sam prompted.

"So, I'm going to work. I've got a private lesson with Esmeralda coming up—she wants to move up to Intermediate level. Plus I need to work through a lesson plan. I'll see you tonight, guys. Still okay for me to stay on until the weekend? I'm not getting in your way or cramping your style?"

"No," they both chorused.

"Yeah, right. Look, you've both been wonderful but I need to go home sometime. I can't hide out here forever."

"Why not?" Sam asked, her brows creasing in a frown. "Don't you like my place, or something?"

"Like it? I love it. It's completely fabulous, you nitwit. But I didn't convert the storage area of my studio into a living space so I could freeload off my rich best friend for the rest of my life. Besides, I think it'd be good to have some time to myself. Figure out where I'm at, so to speak." She managed a credible smile, a genuine smile, which rather surprised her. But then, watching Sam and Marcus working things out was worth a smile or two. They were perfect for each other. "You two young lovers need some space. You don't need a freeloading guest right now."

Sam glanced pointedly around the spacious apartment and snorted. "Plenty of space from what I can see. I've even been considering getting a dog."

Since Sam had always insisted that *she* was the only bitch allowed in her apartment, Chalcey chose to ignore that incredible statement. She would believe Sam's yen for canine companionship when she laid eyes on the puppy. "What if you two have a burning desire to jump each other's bones some place other than the bedroom, huh? Would hate to think I'm depriving you of the chance to be truly depraved. And you and I both know I couldn't afford the cost of a visit to your shrink to get over the trauma I'd suffer if I walked in on you two *in flagrante delicto*."

Vivid images of making love to Wulf in some pretty interesting places flooded her mind. Her grin faded.

"So, are you going to try and talk to him again?"

Sam wasn't going to let her off easily. So much for Chalcey's pathetic attempts to distract her.

Chalcey took another sip of coffee. Her stomach rebelled. She whirled toward the sink and poured the rest of the coffee down the drain. Toast. She'd make toast. Wulf had never made her toast so perhaps she would be able to stomach that.

"Well? Are you?"

"No, I'm not. He made his choice and now he has to live with the consequences. If he prefers death over a life with me, then who am I to convince him otherwise?"

"That sucks, Chalce," Marcus spoke up. "If you really love him, you should give it another shot."

"Good try, Marcus." She stared him down until he got the hint to drop the subject.

Sam pinned her with a thoughtful gaze.

Uh oh. Wait for it….

"When I ditched Marc, I made the biggest mistake of my life by screwing Ray. But Marc gave me another chance. And when he tried it on with you, I gave him another chance, too."

Marcus choked on his coffee. "You know about that?"

Sam smiled.

"Crap!" He glanced at Chalcey.

"Don't look at me," she said. "You're on your own with this one."

He gulped. "Sam. Sweetheart. I only kissed Chalcey because—"

"Aha! So you did kiss her. Babe, you are so busted."

His jaw hung open as the realization that he'd been thoroughly played dawned.

"She's evil, Marcus," Chalcey said. "Just thought you should know."

Sam huffed on her fingernails and buffed them on her robe. "Chill, Marc. I forgive you for kissing my best friend because we were on a break."

He recovered enough to growl deep in his throat. "Considering who *you* hooked up with when we were on that break, you'd damned well better!"

She walked her fingers up his chest. "I'll forgive you—so long as you make it up to me." Her voice was a purr. They exchanged significant glances that had Chalcey squirming and planning on being elsewhere tonight.

Sam dragged her besotted gaze away from her equally besotted boyfriend's. "So?"

Rats. So much for dodging that bullet. "So, what?" Chalcey asked.

"Are you going to give him another chance?"

Chalcey might have reiterated that Wulf had already said all he needed to say, that he'd made his choice, and she'd made hers. But she would have been lying.

Dammit. Guess she was going to have to suck it up and give him one last shot. She picked up the phone and dialed his hotel. When he picked up the extension in his room, she said, "Meet me at the studio. You still have a key?"

"Yes."

"I'm leaving now."

"Very well. I am taking a taxi. I will meet you there."

She rang off and turned to meet two hopeful gazes. "Don't say another word," she said. "And if you know what's good for you, you won't get your hopes up. He's determined, and I can't see me changing his mind."

"If you want to wait five minutes, I can give you a lift on my way to work," Marcus offered.

"Thanks, but the walk will help clear my head." She rinsed her cup and plate in the sink, and then snagged the duffel full of her dance gear and headed out the door. Once she'd exited Sam's building, she walked as slowly as she could, planning what she was going to say. Not even splurging on a halfway decent takeout coffee helped her organize her thoughts. This was going have to be ad-libbed from the heart.

All too soon she rounded the corner and stood outside her studio. The street door was ajar. Huh. Wasn't like Wulf to be so careless. He'd taken Will's advice about security to heart, and had been vigilant about locking the street door. Perhaps he wasn't as calm and sure about his choices as he'd sounded.

Chalcey left the door ajar so Esmeralda wouldn't have to phone up when she arrived for her lesson, then dragged herself up the stairs. Her mind whirled with all the things she wanted to say. Did she need to say them for her own benefit, to help alleviate her own guilt and pain, or might they be better left unsaid? But if she didn't say them, for the rest of her life she would always wonder.

The rest of her life. A life without Wulf.

With each step, she died a little more inside.

At the internal door to the studio she paused. She could head back to Sam's. Call Esmeralda and reschedule. Then she wouldn't have to face Wulf—face having her heart ripped out all over again.

*Don't be a fucking coward, Chalcey*. She squared her shoulders and pushed open the door.

THE STUDIO DOOR opened. Wulf dared not move too quickly for fear that he would topple over. He refused to give the rabid bastard that satisfaction. With agonizing slowness, he slid his gaze sideways.

Dread sliced through him. Chalcedony stood at the threshold. Her mouth gaped as she took in the smears of blood where he had dragged himself across the floor. Shock turned to horror as she turned her gaze on him.

Wulf snarled a silent curse. He'd hoped…. He'd hoped she wouldn't come, prayed to every god he knew that she would change her mind about meeting him here, and leave him to his fate.

He sucked in a deep breath, filling his lungs, ignoring the agony that ripped through his abdomen and the flood of wetness that soaked the material of the shirt beneath his fingers.

"Run!" His hoarse shout throbbed through the room.

The madman aimed his weapon at Wulf. "I'm warning you. Shut the fuck up or—"

"Terry?" Chalcedony's voice was tight and strained. "What the hell have you done?"

"My name is Terrence—not fucking Terry!"

"Okay, okay. Calm down. What's going on, Terrence? Why are you here?"

Chalcedony's stricken features blurred to a hazy outline. A hazy outline that seemed to be coming closer. Wulf blinked and she came back into focus. Damn her. Did she have no sense of self-preservation? He could only watch, profound fear for her safety compounding the lightheadedness of blood loss, as she approached the man—Terrence—her hands held palm up at chest height, proclaiming that she was no threat.

If the bastard hurt her, harmed a hair on her head, Wulf would strangle the man with his bare hands. It mattered not how many more of the things Terrence had called *bullets* pierced his body. He would not leave the woman he loved to the mercy of a madman.

"Just showing your boyfriend who's boss, Chalcey," Terrence said, his high-pitched voice suggesting that he was not as in control of the situation as he would have Wulf believe. His words tumbled out in a rush. "I came here looking for you so's

I could get that dance costume back. It cost me a mint, yanno. And it's not like you're ever gonna wear it—you made that real clear. Thought I'd stick it on eBay or something. Recoup my losses. But he wouldn't let me into your room. He was gonna chuck me out. Me! He wouldn't listen, even when I threatened him with the gun. Dumbass didn't even know what one was. Can you believe that? What is he, retarded? Had to shoot him when he went for me. Self-defense. You understand, don't you, Chalcey?"

"Yes. Of course I understand." Now Chalcedony's tone sounded pleasant and calm with only the merest tremor.

Wulf was proud of her strength, her courage. Even so, he wished with all his heart that she'd run. Stubborn, stubborn woman.

"Wulf is a very scary-looking guy when he's pissed off," she said. "No one could possibly blame you for shooting him, Terrence. It was an unfortunate accident. I'll ring for the EMTs. They'll get him all fixed up and everything will be peachy."

Wulf couldn't suppress the hitch in his breathing as she headed straight for the phone.

Terrence's gaze darted to him, and then slid back to Chalcedony. The blunt nose of the weapon wavered.

Wulf tensed, willing the man to keep the weapon aimed at him. He released a little of the pain he'd been holding inside with a long, drawn out groan, and shifted slightly, hoping to command the man's attention.

Chalcedony grabbed the phone. "Hello? Ambulance, please."

"Chalcey?" Terrence frowned, indecision flitting across his features. His weapon was still pointed at Wulf, but his gaze, his focus, was now on Chalcedony.

"You should put the gun away, Terrence," she said. "We wouldn't want another accident, would we?"

"You shouldn't have done that," Terrence said.

"Done what?"

"You didn't cover the phone's mouthpiece, you stupid bitch. You shouldn't have done that!"

Wulf didn't hesitate. He slumped to the floor and rolled onto his side. From somewhere, he found the strength to get his feet beneath him. He launched himself at Terrence, shouldering him to the ground. Even as they fell, Wulf was reaching for the man's weapon, hoping to knock it from his hand. He missed.

Cursing, he grabbed the man's wrist and twisted, feeling the bones grinding beneath his grip.

Terrence punched him in the stomach. It was akin to being kicked by a warhorse, and as the pain ripped through him, Wulf blacked out.

From a great distance, he heard Chalcedony scream.

He forced his eyelids open. Terrence had looped one arm around her neck in a chokehold.

He'd failed. An insane madman had the woman he loved. But Wulf could thank the gods for one small mercy: The gun was aimed at him, not Chalcedony.

"Keep that up and I'll shoot him again," Terrence said.

"Bastard." Chalcey's voice was a pained rasp. "I'll. Kill. You. Myself."

Even now, when the situation was hopeless, she struggled.

Blood loss grayed Wulf's vision. He knew he was about to pass out again. And this time, he did not believe he would awaken. But before he bled out and passed from this world he had one last message for her.

"I love you, Chalcedony!"

Wulf's shout chased Terrence as he dragged Chalcedony through the door into the stairwell.

The door clanged shut. "I loved you from the moment I laid eyes on you but I didn't understand what I was feeling." Darkness shrouded him. *I didn't know. I... didn't... know.*

# CHAPTER NINETEEN

CHALCEY AWOKE TO hell. The air was thick. When she gasped a breath it scorched her throat. Her head throbbed. She was disoriented, struggling to process the information her senses were conveying to her brain. Her vision filled with an expanse of shiny black. Her nose bumped a surface that was bone-hard, overlaid with satin smoothness. And then she realized that she was being carried over someone's shoulder.

She pummeled his back with her fists. "Bastard!" The word tore from her throat, leaving it raw. She coughed, gasped another breath, forced out the words. "Put me down!"

"Easy, Chalcey. I got you."

That voice, familiar despite being husky from the acrid smoke. Not Terrence. Smoke…. Why was there so much smoke?

Her rescuer coughed and spat. "Almost out. Hang in there."

"E-Esmeralda?"

"Yep." Esmeralda negotiated the last couple of steps and then she was pushing through the street door, out into the blessedly fresh air.

Chalcey gasped for breath and choked. She coughed. Her head threatened to explode. She couldn't stop coughing, couldn't get enough air. Black spots cavorted in her headspace, and the next thing she became aware of was an eerie wail in the distance.

Funny, she didn't remember Esmeralda putting her down. She must have blacked out for a moment. She lay on the ground, staring up at a blue-on-blue sky, its perfection marred by a plume of ashy-black.

The screech of sirens scoured her skull. The pain in her head escalated. It hurt to think but there was something important she needed to remember. Someone important.

She rolled to her hands and knees, crawled to her feet. And stood, paralyzed with horror, staring at her studio. Flames wreathed the lower half of the building, reaching hungrily for the upper story, reaching hungrily for....

OhGodohGod. "Wulf!"

Hands steadied her beneath her elbows. "Easy, ma'am. You should sit down. Fire department and paramedics are on their way."

She stared, uncomprehending, at the grim-faced cop who was trying to ease her back down to the ground. "No," she said to him, clutching his forearms and locking her knees. "Can't. Wulf's in there."

The cop turned aside to speak to someone, his tone urgent.

Then Esmeralda was peering into Chalcey's face, her eyes huge with shock. "You sure, Chalcey? You sure Wulf's in there?"

"Yes. He—" Another coughing fit stole her words.

"Oh, God." Tears overflowed Esmeralda's eyes, tracking shiny little trails of cleanness down her smudged cheeks. "I found you out cold about halfway up the stairwell, Chalcey. Looked like you'd slipped on the stairs trying to get out. The smoke.... My only thought was getting you the hell out of there. I didn't think to look for anyone else. Fuck. Fuck!"

The cop wasn't having any of it. "You got her out, sweetheart," he said to Esmeralda. "You probably saved her life. There's nothing more you could have done."

The sirens cut off. There was a moment of peaceful throbbing silence, and then voices, shouting orders. In the melee of organized chaos, Chalcey walked away from the cop.

"Chalcey!"

Esmeralda's voice, high and uncertain. And then a stream of words that Chalcey couldn't make out, didn't want to understand because she didn't want to hear them. She broke into a run, hurtling toward the burning building, heart pounding in her chest, lungs laboring for breath.

Someone—the cop—grabbed her by the arm, swinging her around to a halt. "You can't go in there, ma'am!"

She clawed at his hands, desperately trying to free herself. "Have to. Have to save him. Wulf!"

"Chalcey!" Another man helped the cop restrain her. "Chalcey, it's me, Rick." He grasped her arms, shaking her gently when she stared at him, uncomprehending. "Will's cop friend, remember? Calm down, sweetheart. Everything's gonna be okay."

"You're wrong." She collapsed against Rick's chest. There was no point in fighting any more. It was too late. "Wulf." The cough built in her throat. She swallowed it down. "Wulf."

"Medic!" someone yelled.

"Chalcey?" Rick's voice. "Tell me about Wulf."

"There was a man." *Don't cough.* "The one from the bar. Terrence Cabot." *Swallow. Don't cough. You have to get it out, have to tell Rick.* "He had a gun. Shot Wulf. Grabbed me. Threatened to shoot Wulf again if I— If I didn't— Oh, God. Wulf. I— Should never have left him."

Rick's arms tightened around her. He spoke over her head to someone. "I'll take it from here. You stick with the other woman—"

"Esmeralda," Chalcey whispered.

"Follow Esmeralda to the hospital and get her statement."

"On to it," the cop said.

"Wulf?"

Rick knew what Chalcey was asking. "The stairwell caved

in before the firefighters could get up to the studio. They're still searching but it's not looking good. I'm sorry, Chalcey."

"I'm sure they did all they could." Her voice sounded mechanical, as though all humanity had been stripped away, leaving an automaton who mouthed the polite phrases but didn't—*couldn't*—feel them. She closed her eyes.

Rick took charge. He stuck with her as the medics chivvied her onto a gurney. He was there when they loaded her into the ambulance and drove her away from the remains of a life she'd worked so hard to build, away from the remains of the love she hadn't been brave enough to hold on to.

This couldn't be real, had to be a nightmare. Wulf couldn't be dead. She'd have felt it when—*if*—he'd died. She would have known the moment his soul left his body and was consigned to the hell of the crystal. They were linked, bonded. She would have known, felt it.

A peculiar wailing sound filled her head. She could see the medic bending over her, see his lips moving, but she couldn't hear anything except the wailing. It sounded like a lost soul departing this plane of existence. And perhaps it was. Perhaps it was Wulf's soul.

Rick held tightly to her hand and stared down at her, the corners of his eyes crinkled with concern. She wondered if he could hear the wailing, too. And then she realized that *she* was making the sound.

A sharp prick in her arm. Coolness flooding her veins. Then nothing.

SHE HATED HOSPITALS, the smell of disinfectant and desperation. She hated the poking and the prodding, the endless questions from the doctors and nurses. She wanted to go home… until she remembered she had no home. Until she remembered what she'd lost.

The hospital staff insisted on keeping her overnight for observation. Tomorrow, she was told by a too-cheerful doctor, if there were no complications from smoke inhalation, she might be discharged. She would worry about it then.

Rick's visit was in his official capacity. "We found Terrence Cabot. He admitted to everything. You got that huge bump on the back of your head because you fought him when he grabbed you, and both of you took a tumble downstairs. You were knocked out and he broke his arm. Pity it wasn't his neck. Would have saved us a heap of paperwork."

A smile ghosted across her lips at the sourness in his voice. Rick obviously wasn't a fan of paperwork.

"He left me there."

"Yep. Scarpered. Bastard didn't even bother to check how bad you were injured."

"Did he set the fire, too?"

"About the fire. Still waiting on the final report but preliminary findings say it started in the vacant downstairs offices being used for storage."

"Oh." She hadn't even considered how the fire might have started until now. Everything had happened so fast that it was still mostly a blur. She'd been too busy coping with the devastating aftermath to dwell on the details. "Thanks for letting me know."

"Does Cabot smoke?"

"Not to my knowledge. Why?"

"Just curious. Turns out Cabot's been fixated on you for a while, Chalcey. He thinks losing you is the reason his life's turned to shit. He convinced himself if he got back together with you, and you were his dance partner again, everything would be peachy-keen. He's been stalking you for weeks. He's the one responsible for all the hang-up calls."

She was too numb to feel shock. "Wow."

"That surprises you?"

"He used to get cranky if I looked at anyone else but…. Yeah, it surprises me. I had no idea. I was only his dance partner, Rick. We never dated. And I never slept with him."

She reached for her water glass, and took a sip. Her throat still felt raw, and it hurt to talk. "I thought Ray was the only creep I had to worry about."

Rick shrugged. "Walker looked good for it. When we called him in, he confessed to the graffiti. And, with a bit of encouragement, a few other things. Such as sexually harassing you and your friend Esmeralda. She's not pressing charges. You?"

Chalcey shook her head. "No. Wulf—" God. She squeezed her eyelids shut until the agony eased enough that she could say his name. "Wulf dealt to Ray. I figure he already got most of what he deserves."

"Yeah. Walker told us. In more detail than we could ever possibly want."

"Somehow that *doesn't* surprise me."

"So. We need a statement. I figured it'd be better if you talked to someone you know. Feel up to telling me what went down?"

"Yes." *No.* She did it anyway, carefully skirting the stuff about magical crystals and curses and Wulf's origins. She didn't want to spend the night in a psych ward.

The next bunch of visitors were more difficult to cope with. Sam and Marcus showed up first. As soon as Chalcey was discharged they would take her home—to Sam's apartment. And she'd stay there as long as she liked. No argument. And once that was all settled to Sam's satisfaction, it was awkward and stilted. Sam kept starting to speak and then clamming up. Marcus would squeeze her hand and she'd lean into him.

Watching the two of them.... Chalcey's heart broke. She was happy for them, but it was hard—so gut-wrenchingly hard—to see them together like this, in love, when she had lost the man she loved.

Jai and Esmeralda stopped by—Esmeralda clad in a hospital gown a shade of green that she insisted was hell on her complexion. Chalcey summoned a smile and played the game because she was damned if she would contribute to the guilt

Esmeralda was trying so desperately to hide. She wanted to say something to Esmeralda that would make it all okay, but she was afraid the words that would spill from her mouth would be cruel, hurtful words. Words that would devastate Esmeralda. Words like, "You should have left me there to burn. I'd rather be dead than have to live on without him." Esmeralda didn't deserve that, so Chalcey kept everything locked up tight inside her. So tight that her hand shook, and when she reached for her water glass, she spilled it all down her front.

Jai rang for a nurse. He threw Chalcey a knowing glance, and ushered Esmeralda from the room.

Will and Anna visited, too. They hovered anxiously around her bed, offering glasses of water, and expressions of sympathy, and promises to help her find another studio to lease. Like she gave a shit about her studio anymore. But she thanked them anyway, and pretended gratitude. Maybe later—much, much later—she would attempt to rebuild her life. For now, she just wanted to get through the next hour, the next day.

And when everyone had finally said what they had to say and left her in peace, she turned off the light, and stared at the ceiling until sleep took her.

She dreamed of Wulf.

In her dream he was without substance, a shadowy indistinct form tumbling in a seemingly endless void. He was fading, falling, spinning helplessly, unable to save himself. And she knew when he did finally hit the bottom, his life-force would disperse and be consumed by the ever-hungry blackness.

This was no dream. This was real.

She called his name but he didn't hear her—couldn't hear her—because her voice was swallowed by the roiling darkness that engulfed him.

She shouted his name again, his full name this time, and her voice morphed into something more than mere sound. It became a tangible living presence spun from desire and want and raw aching need.

"Wulfeniiiiite!" Over and over she screamed his name, imbuing the echoes with her love for him, and sending them hurtling down into the void to find him, wherever he might be. She drained herself to the point of exhaustion but she refused to give in. And somehow, some where or when, she found him.

The skeins of her love wrapped around Wulf's body, infinitesimally slowing his descent. With each scream that tore through her, Wulf became more substantial and his hazy form more delineated, until she could discern his features... and the spark of awareness that shone in his eyes.

She gathered herself for one final effort, knowing in her soul that if she failed, she had no more strength left to give. She couldn't fail him again. She wouldn't.

She honed her life-energy itself into a psychic arrow and launched it at Wulf. It pierced his heart. He screamed soundlessly. His body convulsed, and for a brief, heart-stopping moment she believed that her instincts had been wrong, that she'd destroyed him. Then the mystical link she'd forged between her plane of existence and his, flared and strengthened.

"Wulfenite!"

A sighing breath and then, "Chalcedony."

Fully formed now, and self-aware, Wulf hung suspended in nothingness. And as Chalcey watched, a tiny mote of light winked into existence, illuminating the darkness. It radiated hope and trust and forgiveness, but most significant of all, undying love.

She saw him smile. A pulsating warmth bloomed in her chest, directly over her heart. She knew her love had saved him from his fate. At least for a little while.

*This* was the true Testing, this dream that was not a dream. Only she had the power to save Wulf. And she knew what she had to do.

# CHAPTER TWENTY

C HALCEY JERKED AWAKE, her ears echoing with an unfamiliar sound. Her heart thudded until she identified the trill of Sam's mobile phone. Sam had insisted on leaving it with Chalcey in case she needed it. Not that she did. The only person she'd be likely to ring would be Sam. And speaking of Sam, this was probably her, calling to find out what time to pick Chalcey up from the hospital.

She answered the call, but before she could speak a voice said, "Sam? It's Will."

"Hi, Will," she croaked. "It's me, Chalcey."

He paused. "Shit. Isn't this Sam's number?"

"It is. She left me her phone."

"Right. Sorry it's so early. Hope I didn't wake you."

He sounded weird. Strained. "Do you want me to give you Sam's landline?"

"Ah, no. I was only passing on a message for you, anyway."

"Okay."

Pause.

"What's up, Will?"

"God. This is so fucking hard that I'm just gonna come right out and say it. My cop buddy, Rick, tells me that they haven't found any human remains."

"Oh." The chill pierced her bones and her stomach plummeted to her toes. Then relief, washing through her, banishing the chill. Of course there wouldn't be any remains. There wouldn't be any because Wulf had already been taken by his crystal.

"Plus the fire department's preliminary findings point to the fire being accidentally lit. Most likely a cigarette in a trash can. Christ." He laughed, and it was a savagely unhappy sound, full of guilt and remorse. "How fucking trite is that?"

"An accident? But I don't smoke. My studio is non-smoking, and none of my friends—"

"The fire started downstairs in the rooms being used for storage."

"Yeah. Rick mentioned that already."

"Appears more than one person has been smoking in there. And some dumbass chucked a cigarette butt in a trash can full of shredded files."

"Oh." She stared at the wall of her hospital room and tried to think of something to say that would ease the terrible guilt she could hear in Will's voice.

"The arson specialist—or whatever the hell he's called— said that in his professional opinion, the fire might have been contained with minimal damage except it wasn't only files being stored in the area. It was toner and inks and art supplies and a whole heap of highly flammable crap. God! I should've checked before I let them use it for storage. I should've—"

"It's not your fault, Will. It was just an accident." Or… perhaps the Crystal Guardian's final petty revenge—spiteful magic that had prevented her from saving Wulf, and con-sumed everything she'd worked so hard for.

Yes. That fit. It was a far more palatable explanation than losing her last chance to save the man she'd loved because of a careless smoker.

"I'm sorry, Chalcey. Look, if your insurance company gives you any trouble about your contents, I'll pick up the tab. And if there's anything I can do for—"

"Thanks, Will. I appreciate you calling. But I've gotta go." She disconnected before he could say anything more. She knew guilt was eating him alive—yet another person who felt responsible for Wulf's death. But not Will, not Esmeralda, not even Terrence were to blame for what had happened to Wulf. Chalcey was the only one to blame. She was the only one who could bring him back to life.

Chalcey crawled from the bed and shoved herself into the clothes Sam had brought over in a smart designer overnight bag. A quick splash of water at her face, and a scrunchie to tie back her mess of hair, and she was presentable. Mostly. If no one looked too closely.

Discharging herself was easy. She waited until the harassed admin staff were busy with enquiries, and sauntered on past. She'd sort out the paperwork later. Or Sam would, on her behalf. Sam was good like that.

Facing the world outside was surreal. People and vehicles buzzed past, intent on getting wherever they were going, oblivious that a man's life was at stake. The long walk zipped by, and it seemed only a blink in time before Chalcey stood before the charred, skeletal remnants of her studio.

Her breath caught. She had to remind herself to breathe. She could never have foreseen that confronting the wreckage of her life could be so goddamned painful. But it wasn't her studio—the dream she'd worked so hard to attain—that she mourned. Losing Wulf…. Losing him hurt so bad that she wanted to sink to her knees and howl her pain to the world.

"Huh. Bet that sucks."

The words were like a slap in the face, yanking her from the misery that had threatened to drown her. She whirled. And puffed out a sigh. She so didn't have time for this crap. "Ray. What are you doing here?"

He detached himself from the shadows of a neighboring building and slouched over to her. "Just keeping an eye on ya, babe. Yanno, in case you need some consoling."

He giggled. His gaze wandered over her, hot and wanting, lingering at her breasts.

His pupils were hugely dilated. Illegal substances for breakfast. Nice. "I don't need anything from a loser like you," she said.

"Awww, c'mon. No need to get nasty."

She counted to ten. Very slowly. "Look, Ray. You're a good-looking guy and I'll bet there're heaps of girls who'd drop their panties for you the instant you crooked your little finger. But I'm not one of those girls. Now go away. I'm busy."

He threw her a sly grin. "Yeah? Doing what?"

She deliberately rounded her eyes and stared over his shoulder. "Is that a cop car?" She waved. "Hi, Rick!"

As Ray started to turn, Chalcey drew back her fist and clocked him right on the bridge of his nose.

He howled, clapping both hands over his face. She followed up by kicking him in the groin.

He doubled over, gagging and clutching his groin, his face beet-red, eyes bulging. "Last warning, Ray," she said. "Don't come near me again."

"You hear that, Mr. Walker?" the real Rick said, from directly behind her. "Don't bother Ms Laureano again."

Ah crap. Busted. She swiveled slowly to face Rick. And Will. The grapevine sure moved fast in this town. "Guess I'm up for assault, huh?"

"I didn't see a thing," Rick said. "Did you?" he asked Will.

"Not a thing."

They sauntered over to Ray and each took an arm.

"Seems to me Mr. Walker might be returning to the scene of the crime," Will said. "Can't think of any other reason he'd be hanging 'round my building. Can you, Rick?"

"Maybe the fire was no accident, after all. What d'you say to that, Mr. Walker?"

Ray's answer was a strangled gargle.

"I think it's time you and I had another little chat, Mr. Walker," Rick said to him. "If you can't speak, just nod."

"He's high," Chalcey said. "You might luck out and find

he's got something stashed on him."

"And wouldn't that make my week," Rick said.

"You going to be all right, Chalcey?" Will asked, his face all screwed up with concern and guilt and worry.

"Yep. I just need a moment. Please. I won't do anything stupid, I promise."

"You better not." Rick scowled at her. "You know how I hate paperwork."

"Call you later, okay, Will?"

"See that you do," he said. "Or Anna will be on my case. Worse, she'll be on yours. And believe me, Chalcey, you'll get no damn peace if that happens."

"I promise."

She didn't bother to ask who had called them when her empty hospital bed had been discovered, or how they'd known to look for her here. She wasn't interested. Just as she wasn't interested enough to watch them drag Ray away. She didn't care what happened to him.

She turned back to her studio.

What remained of the building's entrance had been cordoned off with warning tape. Chalcey ducked under it and clambered atop a pile of rubble, looking for… something. She didn't know what, exactly.

Panic seeped into her pores as she stood there, overwhelmed. What the hell had she been expecting? A miracle? Wulf to magically appear?

She braved a step and a hunk of rubble shifted beneath her feet. She fell to her hands and knees and that was when she felt it, a solid, rough hunk of something that didn't belong there beneath her fingers. She unearthed it from its blackened nest and rubbed it on her t-shirt, hardly daring to hope. Oh. My. God. She'd found one half of the wulfenite crystal.

She scrabbled in the muck, uncaring of the desperate picture she presented to anyone who happened to pass by. The other half had to be somewhere near. *Please don't make me search through all the rubble. Please!*

Some instinct prompted her to close her eyes and she squeezed her eyelids so tightly shut that she saw stars. She skimmed her palm over the debris, and randomly grabbed the first thing that came to hand. Her heartbeat echoed in her ears. She forced herself to open her eyes, to verify what she already knew. The chunk of debris in her hand was the second piece of Wulf's crystal.

She cleaned both pieces of crystal as best she could, spitting on them and rubbing them with the bottom of her t-shirt. She examined them, noting the jagged edges of the breaks, mentally calculating how they'd fit together. A moment of breath-stealing doubt hit her like a punch in the stomach. She shrugged it off. This would work. It had to.

Holding half of the crystal in each hand, she slowly brought them together, fitting them to each other so that the halves made a whole.

There. Done. She held her breath, expecting… well… shit! A fucking great clanging sound at the very least. This was mind-boggling, supernatural woo-woo at work here. Shouldn't something impressive happen?

But nothing did.

She climbed awkwardly over the pile of debris until she reached the pavement and stood rooted to the spot, staring at the crystal cradled in her hands. It was an unprepossessing thing. Dirty-brown, jagged and uneven, not particularly pretty. Certainly not a talisman capable of containing the life-force of a vibrant, passionate man like Wulf in its depths. But it had. And it had been her only hope.

Soul-weary and miserable, she was about to dash the crystal to the ground when the truth smacked her between the eyes. The two halves had fused together into one whole. She held a whole wulfenite crystal in her hands.

This wasn't over.

Chalcey clutched the crystal to her chest like it was the

most precious thing in the entire world, and strode from the wreckage of what had once been the most important thing in her life. She left that part of her life behind without a backward glance or a single regret. She was focused on one thing and one thing only: Finding the Crystal Guardian. And when she found him, he would give her back the man she loved or she'd make him eternally sorry he'd been born.

She half expected to be put through some major hoops before she was "allowed" to find the little store selling crystals again. She walked to the same café where she'd met Mr. Chapel, the tight-ass finance broker, and when she slid her gaze to the neighboring store, there was Pieter's store. In the same place, exactly as she remembered.

Huh. Pieter must have decided that she'd suffered enough for the moment. Whoop-de-fucking-do. She'd marvel over that some other time.

She charged through the doorway, her eyes tearing as her vision fought to adjust to the too-bright light.

He was there behind the counter, just as he'd been twenty-nine days ago, when this all began. This time, he was polishing crystals with his handkerchief. "Chalcedony," he said gravely.

"Pieter, I presume. Also known as The Crystal Guardian."

He inclined his head. "You presume correctly. How may I help you, Chalcedony?"

How could he help her? Chalcey's hand twitched. It took every ounce of will she could summon not to smash him in the face with Wulf's crystal. "Don't fuck with me, old man. You destroyed everything I've worked for and you nearly killed me in the process. And—"

"What makes you think I set fire to your building?"

"Oh, come on. You'd have me believe it was an accident? Please."

"It could simply have been your delightful Mr. Ray Walker, seeking to punish you for rejecting him so thoroughly."

"If you know about that, then you'll also know Sam both

rejected *and* ejected him, too. Why punish me, and not her? I'm not buying it."

He quirked an eyebrow at her. "Fate moves in mysterious ways."

"Spare me the bullshit. Fate is a vindictive old man who gets off on making me suffer, and making my friends feel guilty for things they had no control over."

"I can give you back everything you hold so dear, Chalcedony. All you have to do is ask."

"I don't care about my dance studio. I don't want *everything*. I only want Wulf."

"I see."

She clenched her fingers around the crystal. "No, you don't see. You don't have a fucking clue. So I'll spell it out to you in plain simple words that even a warped, centuries old bastard with a shriveled heart can understand. You took Wulf from me. I love him and I want him back. Now."

"Wulf is not mine to give."

The old guy was a tough cookie, she'd give him that. "All right, Pieter. I'll play your little game. What do I have to do to get Wulf back? Anything at all. Name it and I'll do it."

He smiled at her then, a smile filled with eons of regret and sadness. "Be sure of what you want, Chalcedony. Be absolutely sure."

"I'm sure. Name your price." The words were barely out of her mouth before she was transported to another place. Another world.

Wulf's world.

She was ten years old. She'd cuddled her favorite doll each night until she'd been taken by the Stone Warriors. Her doll had been left behind, along with her ma and her da, and everything else she loved.

Terrified and terrorized, she stood before hundreds of greedy-eyed men, shivering despite the unrelenting heat. When she wouldn't move, couldn't move, a man yanked her this way and that. His rank sweat crawled over her, clogging her nose, making it even more difficult to breathe.

Someone yelled from the crowd, demanding a proper look at the merchandise. The man grabbed the neckline of her chemise and ripped it from neck to hem. The crowd roared with raucous laughter. She sobbed but she knew better than to try to cover her body with her hands. That would only provoke a humiliating punishment. She locked her knees, willed herself to remain upright.

They called this place the Choosing Block. Her, and the others like her who'd been stolen, called it Hell's Rock. The slab of stone felt rough and hard beneath her bare feet, grounding her, forcing her to realize that this was reality and not the nightmare she'd prayed long and hard for it to be.

Harsh voices called out, vying to bid for the prize…. Her.

She whimpered and dared rub the still-painful brand on her upper arm. Her eyes stung with tears. She burned with shame as the bidding continued and her face, her body—everything about her—was publicly discussed.

She'd been told numerous times that she was pretty. She'd been proud of her blonde hair and dimples, the way she could run and jump and keep up with her older brothers. Now she wished she was ugly. Deformed. Unwanted.

After it was over, her new master came to claim her. He yanked her up over his shoulder, then descended from the Block. His fellow warriors congratulated him. They slapped her rump as he pushed his way through the crowd.

She knew that she would never see her home or family again. This was her life now. She'd heard enough talk to know her fate. Raped by her master. Forced to bear child after child until her womb dried up.

She prayed that God would take her soon….

CHALCEY SLAMMED BACK into her own body with a lurch. Her skin was sweat-slicked, mind tormented and sickened by what she had experienced.

"Do you still want him, Chalcedony?" the old man asked.

She closed her eyes and visions of the girl-child raced through her mind. Chalcey felt the girl's terror again, so real and so strong that it threatened to overwhelm her. She sent the girl's spirit a silent prayer, and then forced it from her mind.

Wulf had told her about his world and his customs. His people auctioned women of childbearing age only. The women sold were never forced to lie with their buyers—that was each woman's personal choice to make. Always. And there were harsh punishments and hefty fines levied upon any man who dared believe that he had the right to force himself upon a woman he'd won on the Choosing Block.

A woman could choose to leave the man who'd won her at auction after six moons if she so wished—no questions asked—and the auction brokers would pay her half her auction price. Many chose to stay with the men who'd chosen them, and raise the sons they bore. Others chose the Choosing Block again, eager to accumulate enough wealth to purchase permanent living quarters and servants of their own. And some women petitioned to set themselves up in a trade. Given the rigorous training demands of a warrior culture, there were plenty of opportunities for women to set up shop, or cook and clean, mend clothing and the like.

Wulf claimed that a woman's choices were respected, as were the women themselves. And Chalcey had believed him.

But the brand the girl had on her arm—the painful brand Chalcey remembered rubbing—was no "ceremonial mark of acceptance into the fief" such as Wulf had described.

He had also told her that any young girls taken were cared for by a group of older women until such time as they came of age. So why was a ten-year-old girl—a child—standing on the Choosing Block shivering in fear?

Which version was true, Wulf's or Pieter's?

Chalcey shuddered, fighting the chill in her soul, desperately not wanting to believe what she'd just experienced, but so afraid that it was true. It had felt so very real.

She peeled open her eyelids. "Is it true? Is what I just saw true?"

The old man stared at her, his expression closed, refusing to give anything away.

"Goddamn you, Pieter. Is it true?"

"If it were true, knowing what he is, would you still want him, Chalcedony?"

She glared at him through tear-filled eyes. "Yes! Yes I want him. I'm a horrible, pathetic excuse for a human being, all right? I know he stole women for breeding stock. I know what he's done and I still want him. I can't help it. I know why he did it and I forgive him, okay? He's suffered enough. But more than anything else, I love him. Warts and all. I'm sorry, but that's the way it is. What more can I say?" She heaved a shaky breath and fought for composure. Ranting at the old man would not help her case. "I believe what Wulf told me, not what you showed me. I believe Wulf, not you."

Pieter gazed deep into her eyes, probing her soul. Whatever he saw there made him sigh and shake his head. "Very well. On your head be it. Give me his crystal, Chalcedony."

"What?"

"The crystal, please." He held out an imperious hand.

She hid the crystal behind her back, prepared to protect it with her life if need be. "Why do you want it?"

"You must learn to trust people, Chalcedony."

"I do trust people. A few anyway. But not you, old man."

His lips quirked. "Your honesty is refreshing. The crystal please, Chalcedony. I give you my word that I harbor no ill-feeling toward your Wulf."

Still she hesitated.

From beneath the counter, Pieter took a sturdy wooden board. He placed it atop the counter and stood back. "Place it here, please."

She opened her mouth to protest.

"Place it here so that your Wulf may be returned to you. 'Tis the only way."

She shut up and did as he instructed. She wasn't happy about it, but what else could she do? She had to take the risk. "What are you going to do?"

"Stand back."

He spoke with such authority that she automatically backed away. And before she could react, he'd plucked a silver hammer from thin air and smashed the crystal to smithereens.

"Noooooooo!" She lunged at Pieter. If she'd gotten hold of him in that instant, she'd have strangled him with her bare hands. Instead, she found herself standing on the pavement outside what was now a fancy boutique. The little store had vanished.

"Damn you to hell, Pieter!" Her outburst provoked startled expressions and full-body cringes from passersby. She covered her face with her hands.

"Have faith." Pieter's disembodied voice echoed in her ear.

She sensed someone behind her. She whirled.

He stood not a yard away, waiting.

"Wulf!" She launched herself at him.

He caught her and lifted her into his arms. She wrapped her legs around his waist and smothered his face with kisses while he laughed with such pure delight that her heart clenched. Leaning back slightly, she stared into his blue, blue eyes.

"Do you love me?" she asked. No, demanded. "Really love me? Really, really, really, love me?"

"I will love you for the rest of my life."

"Not only because of the curse?"

His gaze held hers. "Nay. 'Twas no curse that compelled me to grapple with a madman when I believed you endangered. But I knew long before then that my love for you was the most important, precious thing in my life. I merely lacked the courage to admit it to myself, let alone to you."

She had to ask. She had to know. "What happened to you in the studio, Wulf?"

"Do not fret over what you cannot change, Chalcedony. The Guardian did not allow me to suffer overlong before the crystal took me."

"Like being trapped in that damn crystal wasn't worse than being shot and slowly bleeding out, or dying in a fire."

She buried her face in his neck and he held her tight, soothing away nightmarish memories with the warmth of his body and the careful strength of his big hands.

"Shhhhh. I had faith that you would come for me. And you did."

"Are you real, Wulf? Or just a dream?"

"Chalcedony."

His voice caressed her like liquid silk, sparking an instant reaction—waves of heat melting her limbs, a throbbing yearning and a desire to take him right now, in public, where everyone could see. He kissed her, teasing her lips lightly with his tongue until she parted them for him. She moaned and he let her slide a little way down his body, pressing her closer to him. Intimately close.

"Oh yeah." She sobbed and laughed at the same time. "Definitely real."

# Epilogue

S HE CALLED AGAIN while you were at class," Wulf said. "You know she will not give up. Why do you not simply talk to her and have done with it?"

Chalcey heaved a sigh. "Look, Wulf. You might have forgiven her but I sure as hell haven't. In case it's slipped your mind, you nearly died. Remember?"

"But I did not."

"But you could have." Chalcey understood Francesca's reasons for trying to break them up, but it would be a while yet before she had it in her to forgive her mother and let Francesca back into her life.

For the first time since her dad's death, Chalcey was truly happy. All it had taken was finding a man who loved her for more than her bra-size. A man who would give her the world if he could. A man who loved her to bits and beyond, who showed her how he felt with intimate caresses that got her all hot and bothered, and whispered words that made her insides go all soft and marshmallowy.

Wulf made her heart sing. He believed implicitly in her. So much so that he stood over her, arms crossed over his delectable pectorals, until she shucked her stupid pride, untied her tongue, and asked Sam to be her guarantor for a loan.

"Thank God!" Sam said. "It's about frickin' time you let me help you." And she immediately made an appointment with her fund manager.

Chalcey puffed out a sharp breath that almost, but not quite, sounded like a raspberry. There went her dream again, reduced to operating statements and profit projections. This time, though, Sam's fund manager proved far more appreciative of Chalcey's ability to run a successful dance studio than fastidious Mr. Chapel. Or Chalcey's soon-to-be-ex jerk of a bank manager.

Rick and his cop buddies weren't quite so accommodating. It was a good thing Wulf got on so well with Sam that she treated him like a slightly naïve younger brother. And it was a real good thing Sam had a rather talented ex-lover who was happy to rustle up a passport and some pretty convincing fake history for Wulf in return for an amount of cash that made Chalcey feel faint. But it was Will who finally convinced Rick and his cop buddies to quit plaguing Wulf with questions about how he'd escaped the blaze, and where he'd disappeared to before he turned up miraculously unscathed.

Chalcey proved incapable of thinking up a coherent lie. "Isn't it obvious that because he's alive, standing right here in front of you, he must have escaped? So what if he doesn't remember how?" was all she could come up with.

"What she said." Wulf made a noise that sounded like a growl.

Chalcey cast a sideways glance at him and bit her lip so she didn't smile and ruin the moment.

Rick shook his head in mock-despair. "Not good enough. I need something concrete to put in my report. My boss is a details freak. He likes everything tied up in a nice neat bow."

"For chrissakes, give it rest, Rick," Will said. "I'll talk to Mac Butcher and get him to put this to bed."

"Yeah?" Rick didn't appear convinced by Will's blasé attitude. "How you gonna do that?"

Will grinned. "I'm sure a rather large donation to the force will ease the way."

"And I'll match it," Sam piped up. "But I want to meet with

Mr. Butcher and tell him personally how much I'm going to be donating. Me and Will can meet him together, okay? I'm sure we can make him see reason."

Rick cast a jaded eye over Sam's ass-skimming red dress, and matching red wedge-heeled sandals. She pouted for him, pursing her glossy red lips. Give her a dainty set of horns peeking out from those auburn curls, and a forked tail, and she'd personify the devil sent to tempt a man.

"Poor bastard won't know what's hit him. I'll set it up. I'll be in touch."

"Thanks for being such a sport, Rick," Sam cooed.

He shook his head. But he did loosen his tie, flick open his top button, and let Sam ply him with coffee while Marcus looked on, smiling indulgently. "Rich chicks," Marcus said to Rick. "They won't take no for an answer."

"Yeah. I kinda got that."

When Rick had gone, Chalcey attempted to explain the whole truth and nothing but the truth to Will. She and Wulf had agreed he deserved an explanation. But she only got as far as Wulf emerging from the crystal to rescue her from Ray before Will halted her. "I'm a hard-nosed businessman, Chalcey. I don't believe in magic and miracles. I'm simply happy for you both that Wulf's alive and in one piece. Now, I have a potential studio for you to check out. I reckon this might be the one."

"Is it the defunct fitness club you mentioned over the phone?" Sam asked.

"Yep."

"Oooh, Chalcey!" Sam's eyes shone with excitement. "I checked it out online and it's perfect! You're gonna love this one."

The very next day, Chalcey signed the lease to a building in a much nicer part of town. She suspected Will had manipulated things behind the scenes. Finding a building that had until recently been a fitness club and needed only minimal renovations, at a very reasonable price, wasn't something you happened upon by happy coincidence. But she was beyond caring what strings he'd pulled. Will was a friend, and that's what friends did: Help each other out.

Just like Chalcey helped soothe Sam when Marcus spooked her again with hints it was time they made their relationship more permanent. Chalcey swore he only did it to wind Sam up. Marcus knew Sam well enough to understand how big of a deal it was for her to let him move into her apartment. That was tantamount to a lifelong promise of commitment for Sam.

The new and improved Laureano's Dance Studio was soon up and running, and business boomed. So much so, that Paulo and Leah complained about being overworked. Chalcey decided she would have to bring another teacher or two on board. Gosh. Wasn't that a shame?

And Wulf, too, thrived. Chalcey knew he wouldn't be content to be a nightclub bouncer forever, but for now, he was happy. Between the two of them, they'd almost managed to scrape together enough to put a down payment on their own apartment so they wouldn't have to impose on Sam and Marcus any longer. Perfect timing. And Chalcey knew Wulf would be happier still when she told him the news.

She glanced at the pregnancy test again, just to be sure she wasn't imagining things. Nope. A positive result. She hugged the knowledge to herself for a moment more, the joy stinging her eyes. The only thing she could wish for right now would be that her dad was alive. He'd be so damned proud of her. And he would have approved of Wulf, too. She was sure of it.

That night, Chalcey cuddled up to the man she loved, and he stroked her stomach and marveled at the tiny miracle growing inside her. Her mind wandered. She and Wulf had often discussed the other Crystal Warriors and wondered what had become of them. Francesca had intimated that a few had passed the Testing with their chosen mates. They could still be alive. Or perhaps they'd already lived and died in times long past.

But what of those who'd either not completed their bonds, or failed their Testing? Had they truly been destroyed by the Crystal Guardian? Somehow, the old man didn't strike Chalcey as a murderer. Pieter had the opportunity to destroy Wulf when he'd been taken by the crystal for the second time, but he hadn't.

Wulf believed that Pieter was inextricably linked to his captives. "Perhaps even the omnipotent Crystal Guardian has a lesson to learn before he can finally find peace," he said.

"Or perhaps your gods have found a way to punish him for what he did to you and your men," Chalcey said.

"Perhaps."

One day—soon—Chalcey would have to talk to her mother and compare notes. Francesca could have been wrong about a lot of things. Maybe *her* Crystal Warrior, Malach, was still alive, suffering endlessly. Maybe all the unbonded warriors were still alive, imprisoned in Pieter's crystals until the right women were chosen for them. Women like Chalcey, who would forgive them their past sins and love them enough to set them free.

~*~

# About the Author

MAREE ANDERSON WRITES paranormal romance, speculative fiction romance, fantasy, and young adult books. She lives in beautiful New Zealand, home of hobbits, elves, and kiwis—both the fruit and the two-legged flightless variety. Her first novel for young adults, the multi-award-winning Freaks of Greenfield High, was optioned for TV by Cream Drama, Inc., Canada. She recently released the fourth book in her Crystal Warriors series, and is currently working on a third book in the Freaks series.

For more information about Maree's books, please visit her website at: http://www.mareeanderson.com

# Acknowledgements

I'D BEEN WRITING for a couple of years when the first draft of this manuscript (then titled *Chalcedony's Wulf*) won the Romance Writers of New Zealand Clendon Award for full-length romance manuscript. Five published stories later (and a whole lot wiser about crafting stories!) I happened to open up my unpublished manuscripts file and this one jumped out and smacked me upside the head. I've always loved this story—it's the book of my heart. I read through it again, and decided that Wulf was far too interesting and complex a man for the reader to only get to know him through Chalcedony's eyes. He needed his own voice. *The Crystal Warrior* is the result.

And now there are some people I need to thank:

*My Red Sage editor, Judith*: Without your mentorship, I wouldn't have had the guts or the knowledge to tackle a major rewrite like this. I loved working with you, and I hope we get the opportunity to work together again in the future. You're the best!

*Barbara and Peter Clendon*: I'll always remember my very first RWNZ Auckland chapter meeting, when you told us to, "Write the book of your heart." You've always encouraged and supported me, and told it like it is. Finally, here's the book of my heart. Thank you both.

*The Clendon Award first-round reader judges*: Thank you all for loving this story and the next two Crystal Warrior books so much that all three become Clendon Award finalists... which finally led me to conclude that I didn't actually suck too bad at this writing thing. I hope you love this story as much as you did the original, and that Wulf still has to power to make you weak at the knees in the best way.

*The members of Romance Writers of New Zealand* (especially my fellow Auckland chapter members): I feel blessed to have found such a supportive bunch of people who have been so willing to share all their industry knowledge and experience. You guys rock!

*My wonderful husband and our truly awesome kids*: You've been with me right from the start of this journey. Couldn't have done it without you. Love you!

M.A.

Other books in The Crystal Warriors Series

RUBY'S DREAM
(Kyan & Ruby's story)

JADE'S CHOICE
(Malach & Jade's story)

OPAL'S WISH
(Danbur & Opal's story)

~*~